I0818324

THE GRAY STOPGAP

Look for other DL Tolleson titles
from The Lighthouse Press, LLC
www.TheLighthousePress.com

For more about the author and his
literature please visit the web site
www.DLTolleson.com

THE GRAY STOPGAP

DL Tolleson

The Lighthouse Press, LLC
Mobile Alabama

The Lighthouse Press, LLC
Publishing books since 1998

The Lighthouse, "L," icon is a registered trademark of The Lighthouse Press Limited Liability Corporation, formerly, The Lighthouse Press, Incorporated.

The Lighthouse Press, LLC is an independent publisher, previously out of Lighthouse Point Florida (after which the corporate name is derived) that has re-located to Alabama. We publish titles in fiction and nonfiction across all genres and represent established as well as debut, authors. Our titles are available at or through local bookstores and on the World Wide Web. Please visit our web site for more information.

www.TheLighthousePress.com
P.O. Box 9612, Mobile, AL 36609

Tolleson, DL
The Gray Stopgap: a novel / DL Tolleson
[Subjects: 1. Artificial intelligence—Experiments—Fiction.
2. Artificial intelligence—Biological applications—Fiction.]
Genre: Spy stories. Adventure fiction.

ISBN (13): 978-1-932211-23-8
ISBN (10): 1-932211-23-3

Printed in the United States of America

PUBLICATION/EDITION HISTORY
Arrangement with author / October 1999
Arrangement with author / December 2000
The Lighthouse Press, Inc. / December 2001
The Lighthouse Press, LLC. / March 2016

3 4 5 6 7 8 9 10 • 20 19 18 17 16

For Mom and Dad.
My real-life heroes.

And of course, for Amaila.

Author's Introduction

For what it is worth, this is the fourth edition of *The Gray Stopgap*. It is designed, laid-out, corrected and illustrated as was originally envisioned.

Corrections and aesthetics aside, this is an unconventional, genre-crossing novel, punctuated by instances of immoral evil. It represents what *Washington Times* newspaper film critic and essayist Richard Grenier characterized when summarizing another author's worldview: "As George Orwell pointed out, people sleep peacefully in their beds at night only because rough men stand ready to do violence on their behalf."

But this novel did not always faithfully reflect those aspects of society. This *Introduction* explains how that changed and why it is important to you.

The twenty-year, eight-draft and four-title gestation of *The Gray Stopgap*, involved a complex growth similar to the person for whom it was written. He was the proxy for you and other potential readers. His name is unimportant. However, his story—*who he was, how he became that person and what happened to him*—is fundamental to this novel.

He admired his adopted parents, the father in particularly. The man had married into the responsibility of a wife with two children from a previous marriage, all before the adoption. A hard-working, caring man, he became a father to three children not biologically his own, thus radically altering the course of what had been the boy's hopeless existence. This new father was a touchstone by which the boy compared all men.

The boy modeled his morality after that of his new parents. And when measured by the changing values of the 60s, 70s and 80s, this made the boy an enigmatic anachronism. In terms of propriety, he may have seemed like something right out of the old family television shows of the 1960s.

For this person I sanitized fictional reality. Evil came across as little more than a metaphorical traffic stop while en route to Sunday church services. That's a morally just and wholesome segment of society, but it is not the reality that I was trying, and failing, to portray.

It was a New York literary agent who, while declining representation of my novel—and me as a client, critiqued and advised me on what I had written. His guidance showed me that only through an honest exposé of characters will a fictional experience transcend as an accurate perception of reality, be it good, bad or somewhere in-between.

Poet Samuel Taylor Coleridge called this, "That willing suspension of disbelief." It is the inclination of a reader to freely accept a fiction as reality. It depends upon the portrayal of *people* as characters, *life* as plots and *true-to-life* conversations as dialogue: or at the very least, a consistently believable reality, à la J.R.R Tolkien's concept of a sub-creation.

My dilemma had been in modeling morality—or lack of morality—exhibited by characters of dubious origins. For many readers, the reality of the moment is lost when an unsavory character sputters, "darn it," in lieu of a more realistic (profane) expletive the character would utter, given his or her background and socialization. Likewise, the reality is to expect an adulterer to contemplate an illicit rendezvous with internalized carnal frankness and not the restraint of the timid.

In short, I had failed to simulate reality by imposing a morality with which my reader was comfortable, but which was in no way indicative of someone cut from the cloth of my characters. In coming to terms with this, I realized that alienating my reader by the creation of an objectionable fictional "reality" depended upon that reader.

And of all the people who might have served as your proxy, the one I had chosen—the one for whom I had originally written the book—had a history of which I was not fully aware. He had, I began to learn, more than just a passing exposure to evil.

He was born into poverty, presumably the youngest of at least six children locked in a house. His first year-and-a-half mostly consisted of a hot, darkened room I would not presume to describe and a diet of condensed milk. Two of his older brothers eventually broke through a window and made a run for it. The younger of these two, a four-year-old, escaped. This put into motion the State's eventual involvement, culminating in three adoptions by three families. Another of his siblings was, perhaps, taken in by a relative. Two of his older siblings remained.

Adopted at two-years-of-age, he suffered from malnutrition, rotting teeth, asthma, seeing ocular distortions of light at night and a host of maladies requiring medical care for six years. Blood vessels bursting in his eyes, staph infections and fevers necessitating ice baths were a few of the issues stemming from the conditions during his first two years of life.

When his parents thought him ready, he learned more: one of his childhood friends was actually his older brother (the four-year-old who had escaped and since harbored a guilt that his escape had not been sooner or sufficient to the task of saving everyone). He also learned of the adopted sister, with whom he would be attending school. Hell for her had been merely a change of address. Her ongoing, years-long endurance of unspeakable criminal abuse manifested itself in a rebellion that, to outsiders, seemed inexplicable. And then there were the two siblings who had not been adopted: left behind, they were mentally handicapped by the environment from which the others had been freed.

Memories now haunt them all, save one. Maybe it is a defense mechanism of which he was unaware or unable to control. But whatever it is, it has banished the good with the bad, leaving him with only a dozen or so images of an idyllic childhood. And something else was left. It is always there, brooding, and just beyond the reach of his conscious grasp.

So, do you really know your neighbor? Can we fathom a victim's mind without knowing the reprehensible depravity causing the damage? Can we realistically ponder these questions without the unspeakable sight of whatever Medusa gives rise to our asking? And if not in fiction, how else are we to comprehend the unholy reality we choose to ignore?

You need neither ask nor answer these questions. But they *are* a part of the reality from which this novel breathes life. If this weighs heavily upon you, if you are a survivor of our darkest injustices or if you desire to avoid such things, be forewarned. While the judgment of eternity is a certainty, the slivers of injustice that slip through our hands are those I chose to expose and balance—if only in the pages of this novel.

—DL Tolleson
Dallas/Fort Worth, Texas
March 2016

THE GRAY STOPGAP

For wrath kills a foolish man,
and envy slays a simple one...

—Job 5:2
NJK

PROLOGUE

THE EXPERIMENT

August 1, 1977
Yosemite National Park, California

1

Karns Gray regained Consciousness.

"I called the Chancellor," said a distant feminine voice. "Help's coming."

He felt a towel smooth across his brow. He saw it taken away—soaked with blood.

His vision blurred. She floated at the edges of perception, visible for seconds at a time—mixed with waves of dizziness. She lowered her head while looking at him, the silk-like strands of long black hair against his chest.

She looks like Gail, he thought, *except her eyes are brown*.

Those brown eyes were wide with—was it fear? Confusion? It really didn't matter. She was a soft face resembling Gail—a soft voice trying to speak over the high-pitched noise in his head.

He tried to move.

"Please be still," she said, placing her cheek against his face. "You're hurt too much to move."

"How many?" he rasped.

"Just one," she answered.

"My driver?"

"He's dead. Now hush."

He tried to move again.

"Please," she begged, running a gentle hand through his blood-soaked hair, cradling him to her warm face.

"I'm here," she whispered. "You're safe now."

He relaxed, on the verge of shock—between life and death.

"I'm here," she whispered with tears. "You're safe now." She hoped he was in shock, beyond feeling pain.

"I'm here," she repeated, sensing his comfort. "You're safe now."

The flames died to mere flickers. Darkness returned. The ground was moist, the dirt dark and earthy smelling. It wasn't a dry dirty scent, but one promising new life. He heard a faraway sound. It was like—

"Run!" he gasped, reaching up and grabbing her blood-soaked blouse. His sudden outburst frightened her back to reality.

"Run!" he repeated, his voice fading. "Don't be...seen."

For a moment she stared. She heard the helicopter in the distance.

"Run..." he mumbled, his eyes fluttering. "Run..."

She eased him down and stood to signal the helicopter. She looked skyward, then down. Her eyes darted about.

She's worried about the killer, he thought. *He could be near—somewhere.*

She bit her bottom lip, glancing around frantically.

The helicopter blades beat the air. She gave a startled glance toward a movement in the trees.

The truck fire leaped, awash in a downdraft of wind. She fell to her knees, carefully cradling him. She wanted to run—he could see it—had seen it in 'Nam.

"I'm here," she said to him. "You're safe now."

The blades continued to beat the air.

"I'm here—"

The blades.

"You're—"

The flames.

"—safe—"

The dark.

"—now."

The killer.

"Debbie!"

She looked up, Gray's blood streaking her face.

A man in a black trench coat moved toward them. His white hair, failing to reach the top of his head, disappeared into the trench coat's upturned collar. Two sea-green eyes reflected the flames from behind a prominently streamlined nose. Recognizing the Chancellor, she visibly relaxed.

"It's okay, Debbie," he said.

A second man wearing a dark jumpsuit appeared.

"We'll take care of him now," the Chancellor was saying. "Get in the chopper."

There was a rush of people milling about and Debbie watched a stretcher being laid beside Gray. She accepted the second man's extended hand but pulled back. Glazed with tears, her eyes focused on the second man.

"It's okay," said the Chancellor, "he's our copilot."

She yielded, allowing the copilot to help her.

"He tried to kill him," she feebly explained.

"Did you see him?" the Chancellor asked.

"It was awful," she mumbled. "He just pushed Mr. Gray off the road."

"Did you see the other man?"

Debbie shook her head *no*, looking down at her shaking hands.

"You did fine," the copilot assured her.

She barely nodded, continuing to stare at her blood-stained hands.

"It's all right, you did fine," the copilot repeated.

"Did I?"

"I'm not sure, Mr. Chancellor," said the copilot, "but I think she's in shock."

"Debbie," the Chancellor said, nodding in agreement to the copilot, "you saved his life, okay? I'm proud of you."

She nodded with a vague smile.

"Hellava first field assignment for a seventeen-year-old girl," the copilot said, taking the dazed girl by the elbow.

"Yeah," the Chancellor agreed. "Get her in the chopper."

"Yes, Sir," the copilot replied, leading her away.

Gray realized he was being carried to the helicopter. A voice said something about lashing the stretcher to the chopper's skid.

"I don't dare try moving him to a sitting position in the helicopter," the voice added, "he might have internal—"

"No need to explain, Doc," the Chancellor interrupted, leaning over to Gray's face.

"Karns..."

Gray moved his eyes slightly.

"Karns..."

Gray focused on the Chancellor.

"I'll get you fixed up, Pal."

"Robert?"

"Yeah?"

A vague smile flickered across Gray's face. "See Debbie?"

"Yeah, Karns."

"She looks like... Gail."

The Chancellor unnecessarily glanced to the wide-eyed girl.

"Yes, she does."

Gray smiled again, fighting the wispy fringes of black in his vision. "Pretty..."

The Chancellor climbed into the crowded chopper. "Go!"

The helicopter rose into the night, banking into a turn.

Gray caught sight of the two vehicles flickering in the flames below. The dancing firelight merged—looking like a giant burning sun in the dark forest. He suddenly remembered a cool day during a hot August.

The summer had been unsparingly intense—August had seemed like a sultry steam bath. As the month wore on, the heat gave a last reprisal and then offered an unexpected reprieve.

The last day of August closed its evening with billowing cotton clouds highlighted with watercolor orange. His mind elsewhere, it might as well have been thundering and lightning as far as he was concerned.

He wheeled off the highway and onto the campus exit, his thoughts rushing ahead. He turned into the parking lot and found an empty slot at the far end.

The college, as well as the surrounding parking lots, was constructed with no apparent logic. Many of the students with whom he had spoken felt a prize of cheese should be awarded upon the discovery of their classrooms.

He unconsciously cut short his walk to the academic buildings by crossing the posted, *Do Not Walk On Grass*, area. Standing at the entrance to the inner courtyard, which the academic buildings surrounded, was a dark-tanned woman in blue jean shorts. It was Gail James, an attractive classmate in his literature class.

She waved.

“Fancy meeting you here,” he called out, smiling.

She laughed, pushing back a wisp of her waist-length hair.

“Today’s the day,” he added, walking into speaking range.

“And you’re sure of your grade, right?” she said with a grin.

“A, ‘D,’ or below,” he confirmed.

“For my sake,” she came back with a laugh, “I hope not.”

They made their way into the courtyard and through the maze of classrooms. Once in class they settled back for an hour of waiting. With the end of class came their graded papers.

“Well?” Gail asked, trying to peer over Gray’s shoulder.

“Well what?” he questioned, suppressing a smile.

“Come on, Jack, what’d ya’ make?” She didn’t know his real name.

He held up the stapled report so she could see a large red, ‘C.’ He could have easily scored an, ‘A,’ but he was trying to blend-in, not standout.

“According to our deal,” she said with laughter, “a, ‘C,’ or better and you have to take me out.”

He returned her grin. “Heck of a chancy way to get a date, huh?”

They both broke into laughter...

The vibrating of a helicopter came back and Gray’s eyes focused on a white, moonlit landscape. The classroom was gone, replaced by zooming shapes appearing through a low ceiling of thin clouds. The fires were gone. He wasn’t even sure how long he had been lost in the past.

He looked up to see a dull reflection on the side of the chopper.

“You always think of Vietnam when you see a helicopter?” Gail asked.

He dropped his hand from shading his eyes and looked over to the young woman rising from the passenger side of his car. The slit in her dress briefly revealed a shapely, tanned thigh.

“Sorry,” he apologized, closing the door and checking that it was locked. “I’ll not do it again.”

She eyed him curiously. “My father’s friend used to do the same thing.”

“And?” he questioned with an innocent smile.

“And he had been there. So how old are you really?”

“Old enough,” he answered.

They were moving across an empty street, the evening sun flashing the purple shadows of her flowing dress. A half step behind, he listened to her heels on the cement, admiring her swaying walk. In the immediate foreground, skyscrapers reflected the lingering embers of evening yellows and reds.

She looked over her shoulder, catching Gray’s intense gaze.

“What?” she asked, a playfully knowing smile about her lips.

“I can’t get over how beautiful you look,” he answered honestly.

She pushed back her flying hair. “Well you’re no slob in that black suit, Mister.”

They reached a large, bubble-shaped building and he retrieved a set of tickets from the admission window.

Once inside, they were seated in an upper balcony.

“I hope you like stage plays,” he whispered.

“I said I did, didn’t I?”

He nodded.

She gave another dazzling smile, revealing a minutely chipped tooth; an enticing flaw. She touched his arm with a gentle squeeze.

The house lights dimmed and the show began. Several minutes into the presentation, she crossed her legs and the dress parted. Gray casually looked from the smooth legs to her profile. He looked to the stage once more, failing to notice her smile. Somewhere below, a singer concluded a song and applause reverberated like the sound of a helicopter...

He looked up, expecting to see the nearly invisible sweep of chopper blades in the night sky. Instead, there was a luminous ceiling. No Gail. No helicopter.

Where the hell am I?

“His eyes are open,” a voice said.

“Specifically,” said a calm and soothing second voice, “he is conscious.”

"Karns?" said the first voice and a man leaned into his field of vision, blocking the light above. He had salt-and-pepper colored hair and a closely trimmed beard that was mostly obscured by a surgical mask. Gray judged him to be prematurely graying and somewhere in his late thirties.

"It's Dr. Farrell," the man continued.

"He is only able to communicate through me," said the calm voice.

"Can he blink once for no and twice for yes?"

"He is unable to voluntarily control blinking. He hears, but his voluntary responses are dysfunctional."

"Why?" Farrell asked.

"Unknown."

"Hmm," Farrell thought aloud, then to Gray: "Do you remember me?"

Yeah, but where am I—what's happened?

"He remembers you, wants to know where he is and what has happened," the calm voice reported.

Who the hell is this guy?

"And I quote," the voice added, "'Who the hell' am I?"

Farrell straightened, focusing his attention on a large hemispherical bubble sitting atop a cylindrical base at Gray's head. The bubble, five feet in diameter, encased a luminous gray mass. Separating the luminous mass into smaller subsections, a spider web of fiber optics pulsated with light. Attached to the bubble via a maze of electrodes, was a Plexiglas "helmet" worn by Gray. The surface of the helmet device was smothered with what appeared to be thousands of needles, each illuminated with a pinpoint of glowing white light. In reality, the "needles" housed near microscopic sensors. Mounted on gyros the sensors were capable of tracking the electrical impulses of the brain.

Five people in lab coats surrounded the bubble, all intent on portable computers attached to Gray, the bubble or both. Debbie Allinder was one of them. The room was round and nearly empty. Thick tinted observation windows broke the monotony of gray metal walls.

Farrell looked back to Gray. "You're in a specially designed lab—it's like a hospital. You were in an accident. Do you remember the accident?"

Gray thought a moment, remembering the helicopter that flew over him and Gail when they were downtown on their first date.

"He is remembering," related the soothing voice, "a Saturday afternoon three years ago. The memory is of his first date with a young woman. They attended a stage production in Fort Worth, Texas."

"Three years ago?" Farrell quizzed.

"It is a process of association," the voice explained. "He was replacing his post-accident helicopter flight with the memory of a helicopter he saw while enjoying himself in the past. He has been in this state for the eight hours of unconsciousness. The most recent recollection of a helicopter in his unconsciousness is a neurological link to helicopters remembered from his military tour of duty in Vietnam."

"The man has a thing about helicopters," someone joked.

Ha–ha, Gray thought.

"He is now expressing criticism of the humor—"

Christ, Gray thought, *what's happening?*

"—and is still wondering what is happening."

"Your thoughts," Farrell said, turning his attention to Gray, "are being related by an artificial intelligence called FORBS. Do you remember the experiment?"

Experiment...? This is Project Hacksaw—the Einstein experiment?

"He remembers," the seemingly disembodied voice of FORBS said.

"Then you recall the accident," Farrell asked.

Accident?

"Yes," FORBS said.

Wait! What accident?

"There is still time to back-out," Farrell said.

Wait!

"He is ready to proceed."

"Listen," Debbie interrupted, moving into his field of vision. Only her eyes were visible above a white surgical mask. "You agreed to this experiment after a tremendous emotional setback. The car accident has further complicated things. We've patched you up okay, but you've been unconscious."

Stop the experiment, FORBS, Gray thought frantically. *Something's wrong!*

"He understands," FORBS said, "but wishes to proceed."

Oh shit, Gray thought.

"We believe FORBS can still complete the synaptic mapping," Farrell cut-in. "But the 60 percent chance of success we anticipated is out the window. We are not only unable to communicate directly with you, but also uncertain of the biofeedback. In other words, if there's signal interference from FORBS, it could affect your bio signals. We may not know what feels wrong to you. I think this very unlikely, but considering all these variables I'd certainly understand your desiring to delay."

Damn it, Gray thought—

"The possibility of damage—or possibly pain—could be greater than we originally discussed," Debbie added. "You've received a trauma to the head and the normal bio-signals are—well they're kind of scrambled. With all due respect to E.H., I don't recommend doing this now."

Gray thought; *tell them—*

"He is aware of the consequences," FORBS calmly said.

Oh, shit! I can't believe this shit!

Farrell sighed and looked over at Debbie: "Find Austiff. Tell him Mr. Gray is conscious and willing to proceed."

The Director? Gray thought. *I've got to tell him what's happening.*

"Yes, Sir. I'll get the back-up monitor while I'm at it," Debbie was saying to Farrell.

"Something else wrong?" Farrell quizzed, his voice tired.

"It's probably nothing, but FORBS' pattern is intermittent."

"FORBS? That's odd."

"Yeah," she nodded, "I'd expect the same of Mr. Gray, but his is very steady."

"Maybe it's not the monitor."

She shrugged, then turned to another of the staff and whispered instructions.

Jim Austiff, Gray thought, *If I could just tell him—*

"It's almost as if the patterns are the same," a voice was saying.

"That's my main concern," Debbie whispered back. "But that's really not possible—it has to be the monitor. Just keep an eye on these synaptic activities, okay?"

"Is Mr. Gray still with us?" Farrell asked.

"Yes, Dr. Farrell," FORBS responded. "He is still listening."

Farrell looked at Gray. "I realize everything we've told you sounds very risky—"

No duh!

"—but I really don't expect any difficulty. These are just things we were concerned about but really haven't any hard facts to point to—per se. FORBS is an exceptional piece of engineering—biologically and synthetically, and you really should be just fine."

At least you've convinced yourself.

"He compliments you for designing me," FORBS spoke.

A conceited, lying computer, Gray thought. *I can't believe this. It's like—*

"Thank you, Mr. Gray," Farrell smiled back. "I'm rather proud of FORBS."

I can see that.

"He notes that is apparent," FORBS said.

Farrell smiled with a nod of acquiescence.

You know FORBS, I've only seen one other like you, Gray thought, remembering a previous discussion with Debbie.

There was silence while several of the people performed what Gray figured were preliminaries to whatever was yet to come. Listening to Debbie give her final instructions, he again recalled how much she resembled Gail—which was why he was in this incredibly stupid situation. He brought his mind back to the present and the plan from which he had just drifted away.

Only one other like you FORBS, Gray thought again.

"Dr. Farrell," FORBS said quietly.

The Doctor turned. "What is it, FORBS?"

"Is there another synthetic intelligence like myself?"

"No," the doctor replied. "You're the only one."

What an idiot, Gray thought. *The other one's even capable of space travel. I bet ol' FORBS can't handle that!*

"Are you certain?" questioned FORBS.

"Ready when you are, Doctor," said a man.

Farrell nodded but turned a stare upon the bubble.

Tell ol' FORBS the truth, Gray thought. *That he's a second-rate copy.*

"Are you ready, FORBS?" Farrell asked after a concerned pause.

"Yes."

"Mr. Gray, are you ready?"

The other one, Gray thought, *is better. Smarter.*

"He is," FORBS answered, then to Gray said: *What is the other one?*

It was odd, hearing a strange voice in his head—like having a stray thought in a completely different voice. Even that struck him strange. He had never considered the possibility that thoughts had a "voice." After all, you never hear them with your ears.

You're nothing compared to the other one, Gray thought.

A hum filled the room as the only door slid open to allow Debbie into an interconnecting chamber leading to an outer room.

Once in the chamber, Debbie pressed the close button and the door began to seal.

"Dr. Farrell," FORBS was saying. "Where is the other synthetic intelligence?"

"There isn't one," Farrell said, a hint of concern in his voice.

Yes, there is.

"Karns Gray believes there is," FORBS said.

Debbie focused her attention on the puzzling conversation.

"Really now?" Farrell said. "And what is it called?"

Hal

"Hal," FORBS repeated quickly.

"Never heard of it, FORBS."

Created by Arthur C. Clarke.

"Created by Arthur C. Clarke," FORBS echoed aloud.

"The transmissions are starting," said a voice, "and something is wrong with this brain scan."

The door sealed, separating Debbie from the room.

"Arthur C. Clarke," Debbie mumbled.

The outer door opened and Debbie saw Austiff returning with a large steaming cup of coffee. His red hair was messed about from lack of sleep, and he certainly didn't look like the Director of one of the most effective intelligence agencies in the world. But he was.

"I think something's wrong, Jim," she said, moving to one of the observation windows.

"Why?"

"Mr. Gray was thinking of Hal just before the experiment started."

"Who?"

"The computer in the movie *2001: A Space Odyssey*. We were kidding about it during the initial test for this experiment."

"You mean the one where the computer..."

They looked into the room to see the lights flickering.

"Took over," Debbie finished, "and killed everyone."

In the sealed room, Karns Gray violently shook as though electricity was coursing through his body. The lights blinked out.

Gray felt as if his head was about to explode. While he couldn't see or move, he sensed something was wrong. His head felt as though it was spinning. A surge of pain lodged behind his eyes and it was all he could do to remain alert. He was certain he had blacked out. When and for how long he didn't know.

"My God," he heard Debbie saying. He tried to mentally shake the cobwebs from his mind. His eyes wouldn't open or maybe they were open and everything was dark.

"They're dead," Debbie was now saying. She seemed far away. He then realized another sound was present—something sounding similar to a scuba diving regulator.

"They're stone-cold," said another voice: it was Austiff. "That's impossible. They just—"

"The whole room is this way," Debbie interrupted.

Gray felt a gloved hand touch his chest, followed by Austiff saying; "Gray's still alive."

"We've got to get him out of here," Debbie said urgently.

"What's happened?"

"I'm not sure exactly," she answered, her voice moving closer, yet still sounding as if it were at the bottom of a well. "But we've got to get him away from this thing."

"You think he was really trying to tell us something?"

"If he wasn't," she replied solemnly, "he should have. Come on, help me get these electrodes off."

Gray heard a shuffle of feet.

"My flashlight's going dead."

"Hurry," she ordered, "these environmental suits won't protect us long. We haven't got much time."

"What the hell is happening, Debbie?"

"It's FORBS; it's draining every drop of energy it can get."

"What do you mean—"

"Hurry, damn it, or all three of us will be dead!"

Feeling the electrodes jerked away, Gray was suddenly falling into a dark pit. Overhead he thought he saw several lights slowly brightening.

2

As the house lights returned, there was a standing ovation.

After a meditative pause, Gail joined in and her lustrous dress cascaded downward, whispering in the cool shadows near the floor.

They melted into the crowd as it sifted into the halls, spilled down the stairs and onto the tiled vestibule. The claustrophobic voices acoustically echoed empty against temple-like ceilings.

Gray opened a glass door and they escaped into a dark breeze more refreshing than the cool, manufactured air of the building.

"It's a wonderful night," Gail said cheerily, "and it was a wonderful show."

"Wonderful," Gray joked, watching people fade into the surrounding parking areas. He was caught by her vibrancy—her youth. He nearly expected her to fling her arms out to take flight.

Instead, she inhaled the night air and threw a dazzling smile.

They found the car and drove to her apartment. He escorted her to the door and she thanked him for a, "wonderful," evening. She slid her key into the lock.

"You know," she commented, turning to study his dark blue eyes, "I've never met anyone like you."

He gave her the questioning look that usually follows such trite expressions.

"No, I'm serious," she said, noticing the look. "You can't be as innocent as you seem—I know that."

"Sounds deep for a country girl," he responded.

"And you're acting shallow for a city boy."

They smiled simultaneously.

"You look young, but you're too... Too mature."

He shrugged.

"But," she added, "you've got a handsome smile."

He accepted the compliment with another vague shrug, and then, "I'll see you in class tomorrow, right?"

"Of course."

"Well, good night," he said, moving away.

"Good night," she replied, watching him move down the sidewalk.

"Jack!" she called.

He stopped.

"I really had a nice time."

He smiled. "So did I."

She evaporated into the shadows as though she had never existed.

The drive to his apartment slipped by as a haze. He barely remembered to pick up an early edition of the newspaper. Turning into the parking lot of his apartment complex, he shut-off the headlights and coasted into an empty space.

The apartment wasn't decorated. It never would be. The one bedroom flat was void of pictures and personality. His assignment required the barest of cover. No one would attempt to learn he wasn't a genuine student and no facade was created outside the college environment. As a result, a rented sofa, love seat, chair, table and bed were the only furnishings.

Kicking his shoes off, he loosened his tie and pulled the classified ads from the paper. A brief scan assured his assignment remained the same and he tossed the paper aside. He lay back to think about Gail. He realized he was foolish; he was becoming involved with a civilian while undercover. Making it harder was the possibility this case could easily last another year. For the first time in his life, he was falling in love.

Being an introvert he had dated only a few times while in high school and college. He had never understood all the emotions involved when dealing with people. "Your aloofness is a natural gift of youth," his father had once said. "Enjoy it while it lasts."

That aloofness was tested in Vietnam. In looking back, it seemed to him that this was his salvation during combat and his tormentor ever since. The doctors had called it, "Post Traumatic Stress Syndrome," and while he never feared the flashbacks, they were horrific images he would rather avoid.

And for a time—after meeting Gail—the flashbacks vanished. Perhaps she had taken their place—he didn't know. He did know, however, that she was an extreme contrast—someone so utterly dissimilar that he was inexplicably drawn to her. She was simple—refreshingly simple. Ideas or cloudy concepts did not drive her. She lived from day to day, hoping to make a niche in life. She embraced the challenge.

And her beauty... Her beauty...

He fell asleep thinking about her long silky hair and green eyes.

The next day dissolved into a pool of weeks drifting along like his drive home from the first date. The impromptu luncheons and brief encounters became frequent and important.

He learned her father had died earlier in the year and she lived with her mother while pursuing a degree in childcare. She had married at seventeen and divorced at eighteen—a month prior to her father's death.

He was at a loss to understand why he grew to love her so fast and thoroughly. Then again, this was probably a lie. It was true he had loved other women—in the physical sense. But he had never earnestly loved another woman. It reminded him of Jay Casper, a young man who had died in Vietnam. But the enemy didn't kill Jay. Jay died at the hands of a, "Dear John," letter. Gray couldn't believe anyone could love so deeply.

But, here was Gail. She almost seemed to represent everything he thought a woman should. She was thirteen years his junior, but seemed more mature than he. That he had mistaken experience for maturity would not occur to him until many years later.

For a young girl never straying far from home, she mysteriously embodied an inescapable allure. She was so strikingly mystical, he felt unable to really get inside her head. He never knew what she thought. She was alien. A beautiful and completely mysterious alien.

They nearly first made love in a car on a dead-end street under construction. She later said she thought he was a virgin—he had been so gentle and in awe.

They quickly amassed favorite songs, eateries and places. There was a torrent of dinners, movies, plays and lake trips. A typical day would unwind from morning until late evening in a secluded cove at the lake.

A leisurely returning drive to the city and dinner in the Berry Street Keg would lead to an intimate night. When he finally revealed the truth about his identity, she only smiled and asked a few trivial questions. Concerned that she was hiding her feelings, he assured her everything he felt was real—that he had not lied about his feelings or love. Unimpressed, she said his assurances were unnecessary.

"I knew there was more to you than you let on," she said. "You're not as good a liar as I am."

"I just wanted you to know you can trust me."

"What makes you think I can be trusted," she questioned.

He didn't have an answer and felt like an idiot for having blown his cover.

"Karns," she said, almost to herself. "Not as strong sounding as 'Jack.'"

He felt a pang of anger. She was trivializing the admission he had just made. There had been assignments in his past when people were killed just for knowing his name. Granted, that was another time—another place. But nonetheless, his identity was a closely guarded secret. A very select few had ever known his name...

"I realize what you've confided in me," she said, putting her hand on his arm. "I love you, too."

And just that quickly, his anger dissipated. He chastised himself for harboring even the faintest of animosity toward her. It was things like this that made her seem physically close and emotionally involving, but just out of reach. He felt as though he was a part of her family and yet always on the outside looking in—like an odd end table everyone accepted but knew didn't match the furniture.

Then came the doubts. Not about her unspoken pledge of silence—he never doubted that. She loved her wine and dancing. She loved the wild side. More than once he suspected she chose others. Why she mutually was a part of his life was a mystery he could not unravel. It was as if she were uncomfortable with the security of the relationship—perhaps any relationship. Or maybe he was too sedate, he had thought. Whatever the reason, he often felt a tingling in the pit of his stomach—as if he were strapped in for the most terrifying roller coaster ride of his life. That, he decided, was what she was about.

But it didn't matter.

He loved her.

It was obsession but felt no less than love.

In the guise of love, it was tested—she enjoyed freedom.

As obsession, it was strengthened—such resolve is beyond testing.

A hastily scribbled note left on his car would dissipate the tension like a hot knife through butter.

One note read:

Darling,
I know you're angry. But making-up
is the best part. Please come by.
Love,
Gail

He was angry. He did go by. Making up was the best part.

She never said, "I'm sorry," and she knew to withhold the truth was not a lie. And so she never lied.

One card read:

Of all the places in the world I like...
I like being in your arms the best.

She had scrawled across the inside cover:

No matter when, no matter where!
All my love,
Gail

It was a tempestuous storybook romance for which they were too intelligent. The summers were long, and they had all the time in the world—for the moment.

A year after meeting, they were engaged. It was just the next moment in a chain of moments. The following moment was an overcast November. Her phone call instructed him to drive to her mother's house, and not to expect good news. The drive usually took about 30 minutes. After exiting the main highway, he drove the last ten minutes' distance in 20 minutes. He knew what was coming.

Gail answered the door chime by opening the door and blankly looking into his eyes.

"You look awful," she said, sounding indifferent. "What's wrong with your eyes?"

"Sinuses, I guess," he lied.

She unnecessarily tightened the sash of her dark blue velour robe and started down the hall.

He followed, noticing the red belt of her robe didn't match—or maybe it was suppose to be a different color. He consciously stopped his mind from rambling, which was a new experience. He realized it was apprehension—like a child's rambling narrative in the face of certain punishment.

When they were in her room, she abruptly turned to face him. He was struck by how she resembled someone recovering from illness. She wasn't wearing makeup and her eyes, he noticed, were red—not unlike his own.

"I'm pregnant," she said calmly.

He didn't respond, bracing himself for more.

"It isn't yours."

"So?" Even as he spoke the word, he knew the gesture was in vain. Perhaps that's why the word almost stuck in his throat and tasted dry in his mouth. He felt lightheaded.

She walked toward him, removing the engagement ring from her pocket. She nearly shoved it out at arm's length. "Here's your ring."

"I don't want it," he came back, his voice almost a whisper. "You keep it."

"No," she said, clenching the hand of her limp arm into a fist. "I don't deserve it, and you deserve someone better than me."

"It doesn't matter, we can still marry. I can raise it as if it were mine." He knew his voice was hardly above the silence of the room. It was as if something were sucking the very breath from him. It was all pointless—so utterly forlorn.

"No... It isn't fair to you," she came back. Shoving the ring into his hand, she noticed his eyes starting to glass over. "And don't cry."

"I'm not," he came back, his voice choked. He had never felt this. He was physically aching from a constriction in his chest. He started to say he needed a glass of water, but the excuse was so damned obvious he merely disappeared into the bathroom.

The tears came. He couldn't stop them and didn't try. After a few minutes, he composed himself. He felt empty—as if his soul had rotted away, leaving only the jagged splinters of decomposing deadwood. But the tears were under control—something else he had never needed to control before. He walked back into her room.

He stood silent a moment, looking at her sitting on the bed. She seemed absorbed in staring out the window.

"I love you," he managed to say in a tone not his own—his heart heavy as if it were a thing of lead—yet mangled as if bleeding.

"I'm sorry," she came back. No remorse appeared in her voice. It was matter of fact. "I've been wanting to tell you—I've known three weeks. I just didn't know how to tell you... I wasn't sure." She left it hanging.

"Gail..."

She gave him a cold look.

He moved to the bedroom door.

"Bye," he said. He wanted to say something else, but that was the only thing that came out, absurd though it sounded.

The tears came again. He made it to the living room before his legs seemed to lose their strength. He sat down, partly because he couldn't see, partly because he felt frail and partly hoping she would change her mind.

A couple of minutes later he left the house.

On the drive back, he prayed she felt pain. Not for vengeance, but out of love. He knew she was hurt—he knew because he was. He knew because his heart relentlessly rammed against his ribs—aching his chest and blinding his eyes. He knew because of the pain—heart-wrenching pain so intense it was frightening.

He prayed, but was so immersed in pain he wouldn't listen for an answer.

He hoped for death and turned to drinking. When he continued living, he started taking aspirin for constant headaches. He graduated to sleeping pills and then...

And then he couldn't remember. The nights and days blurred. His job blurred. Life blurred. Like the proverbial time bomb, it was only a matter of time.

At last, he understood why Jay Casper killed himself.

PART ONE

SKYLAB

July 9, 1979
Washington, DC

3

Washington, DC—the land of big government and hyped glory. A large booming city where no lot is vacant and no stone left unturned when planning for the future. The ice-cubed buildings and two-story offices dot her skyline in bold pride. The financial education capitol, with its late moonlit high-society dinner parties and silk-dressed ladies whispering about that new cute boss—or the bow-tied men boasting about how they really got the best out of that last business transaction, even if they did forget her name. More often than not, "transaction" ambiguously translated into, "sack-action."

DC. The District of Comfort—the richest metropolitan area in the United States of America, with profiles of the top 100 markets. They could all be found here; presidents past, present and future; statesmen, congressmen, lawyers, doctors, clerks, construction workers, wide-eyed sex symbols, pimps, prostitutes, bums and slums. In short, Washington, DC has it all.

Below the crust, the free-flowing money and the clean-swept office buildings could be found the core of world power. Unnoticed by casual visitors, agencies like the Federal Bureau of Investigations, the Central Intelligence Agency and the Office of Central Strategic and Tactical Operations worked around the clock at keeping peacetime and wars in order. Agencies such as OCSTO were the organizations handling the things people take for granted—from national world affairs (in and out of bedrooms) to presidential assassination freaks.

It was agencies such as OCSTO that required the leadership of men like James F. Austiff. His life's ambition could be summed up in the word, "need." Unlike most men of his status, he was given to unexplainable courses of action—always when he saw the need justifying the means.

As was his daily habit for the last year, Austiff arrived at the professional building at nine o'clock and proceeded directly to the elevator. The lift deposited him on the fourth and top-most floor, and he continued to his office while straightening his tie. Lettered in a gold avant-garde font across the glass entry door was:

400
LAW OFFICE

The reception area was furnished with a bleached blonde secretary, desk and a variety of chairs banked with magazine-covered end tables. The light tan carpet covered 15 feet in all directions and disappeared down a hall to the left.

Austiff walked into the office, pausing to gather several folders from the bleached blonde goddess rising from behind the name plate, "Laura Phinor."

She pulled a number of files from her desk drawer and slipped them into Austiff's hands with a fluid ease.

"Dr. Baker has called three times this morning," she said in an airy whisper, pushing her pink glasses back up the bridge of her nose.

"Oh?" Austiff said. Baker was never the early riser. "Put him through if he calls again."

"Yes, Sir."

"Thank you, Laura," Austiff said with his usual brisk tone, and moved into the hall. A few feet later he glanced to his left to see the assorted tables in the second waiting area.

He moved further down the hall and into a room roughly 3500 square foot in size. Scattered about the room were numerous people at computers and books. Acoustical panels separated the desks in an attempt to provide some measure of privacy for the staff. To the far left were attorney offices, a document processing room, a small cafeteria and a meeting room.

Moving along the wall Austiff passed a glass door marked:

407
Kate Kegley
Attorney at Law

His own office door identified him as **408, James F. Austiff, Attorney at Law**. The hall picked up on the other side of the room and ended at a heavy wood door labeled:

1109

The number had been, "409," but a certain Blake Clines had replaced the, "4" with an, "11" of a different font and size. It was both an inside joke and a tradition among the Chancellor field agents, many of whom Austiff knew from having previously worked with the Chancellor.

Austiff entered his private office. The room from which Austiff scrutinized the agency reflected a uniform and studious taste—if not just a bit singular. In a business-like, "oppression," the dark paneled walls were offset by the building's beige carpet and Austiff's selection of dark brown drapes.

To the décor, Austiff had contributed an allotment of nautical oddities as well as paintings of tall ships. These were his only vices other than his daughter Tammy, cigarettes, rum, a wife and peanuts.

Peanuts... Now there was a subject.

Dry roasted and salted.

The, "bitch," as he thought of his wife, suggested he eat them, so as to curb his drinking. Along with using water as a thirst quenching chaser, the peanut method was just one more in a long list of her suggestions.

Personally, he saw no problem with his drinking—considering it moderate. He dealt with all of the problems and pressures without touching a drop. All, that is, but one: her. She had been a beauty contestant winner in her youth, but never especially bright. She seemed the most radiant whenever she was browbeating him.

Peanuts were rapidly becoming one less vice.

He laid the folders on a desktop already orderly arranged to near capacity with papers and files. Pawning a palm-sized device from his pocket and switching it on, he slowly walked around the room, performing his ritual debugging routine.

Completing the circle, he pocketed the device and moved to the wet-bar for a glass of rum. The glass filled, he sat at the desk poring over the files and a stack of yesterday's transactions.

The phone buzzed and he hit the intercom button.

"Yes?"

"It's Dr. Baker," Laura announced in her airy voice, "line one."

"Thanks," Austiff said, switching the phone to intercom and continuing with his mail: "Hey, Doc."

"It's coming down," Dr. Paul Baker's voice came back.

"Huh?"

"According to NASA, *Skylab* is slated to come down in about two weeks."

"They've been saying that for days now," Austiff said. "It's just a ploy to drum up public interest."

"Not this time," Baker came back, "I understand they intend to force it down."

"When?"

"I'm doing good to know this much, Jim."

"Hang on," Austiff ordered, hitting another button. "Laura?"

"Yes, Sir?" came Laura's voice.

"Get Carl at NASA on the phone and find Blake and Kate. Tell 'em to get their asses up here PDQ."

"Yes, Sir," she managed to slip in before he clicked her off.

"Paul," Austiff said into the still open intercom.

"Debbie and I are on our way up," Baker cut in, anticipating the Director's thoughts. The intercom clicked-off, followed by buzzing again.

Austiff hit the switch. "Yes?"

"Carl Douglas at NASA on three," announced Laura's whisper.

He switched off the intercom, lifted the phone, and pressed the lighted button.

"Carl, this is Austiff—"

He paused a moment, listening to the voice on the other end and swirling his chair around to view the Washington skyline though the partly opened drapes of his office window.

"That's what I'm calling about," he said at last. "So what's the deal? You know that thing has a national security seal on it..."

OCSTO Projects Director David Blake Clines was a stocky man with short-cropped blond hair and a lop-sided grin that struck sympathy in the hearts of women. But he wasn't, "a lady's man," and never claimed to be. Nevertheless, women always wanted to mother him. His current girlfriend called it, "the teddy bear factor." But whatever the attraction, Clines was too job-devoted to exploit his charm.

Surrounded by machines blinking, beeping, flashing and coughing, Clines was a child in a candy store. His job description was simple; research, locate, find and/or develop anything of value to mankind. And although that was his simplification of his duties, everyone agreed it was the best description.

The project of the moment involved observing an experimental Vertical Take-Off and Landing model. Peering into a maze of gauges and data displays, Clines mumbled something to himself and looked at the model sitting on the floor in the middle of the testing room.

The room itself was several hundred cubic feet and occupied a large portion of the third floor of the Professional Building. The simple frosted glass door leading into the test facility was marked by the words:

308

ENGINEERING INC.

The experimental VTOL model holding Clines' attention was the fifth prototype of what was to become the Mini-Ground to Air Saucer (MGAS). Its roots reached back to 1955 when the Air Force announced it was building a saucer-like aircraft through a Canadian company. It was supposed to have been a one-man fighter, capable of speeds as high as 1,500 mph. Using the vertical take-off principle, it was to operate from short runways or no runways at all. Once airborne, it was to fly like any other jet.

At the time of its flight test by Hiller Helicopters, it was the aviation world's strangest flying machine. A small, wingless platform, built for the Office of Naval Research, it received its lift from two propellers rotating in opposite directions, which sucked air through the holes in the platform and blew it downward. For directional control, the pilot simply leaned in the desired direction.

Failing to meet expectations and foundering with improvements, the saucer was abandoned to one of the many warehouses of declassified government projects. Clines stumbled across it while looking for salvageable ideas among the hundreds of declassified experiments.

"Blake," a soft voice intruded.

Clines turned and looked up into the soft blue eyes of Laura Phinor.

"Hey, Laura," he beamed, "look at this." He directed her attention to a small remote control. He pressed a button and the MGAS moaned to life, slowly floating into the air. From the loud hissing noise, she knew it was using more than a fan for lift.

"This is an exact replica of the prototype we're building."

"That's nice, but—"

"The prototype will use modified fuel injection to assist each turbo in boosting the output of the mini-jets. The intake air vents are on the outside, thus we can pressurize the cockpit. It'll have missiles, guns—"

"Blake," Laura interrupted, trying to invest her whispering voice with a commanding tone.

Startled, Clines looked at her. She suppressed the urge to laugh. Standing in his khaki cargo shorts and flower-print, short-sleeve shirt, he looked like a little boy just scolded for talking in church.

"It's really something," she conceded, "but Mr. Austiff needs you in his office."

"What about?"

She shrugged. "All I got was, 'PDQ.'"

Clines reduced the power to the floating model and smiled. "I'll race ya'."

Laura grinned, feeling something akin to motherly pride.

ooooo

When Clines reached Austiff's office, Paul Baker, Debbie Allinder and Kate Kegley were arriving from their offices. Kegley was the Deputy Director and the second most powerful person in the Agency.

Like Austiff, the term, "Attorney," as it applied to her was a shadow of the truth. While they each held law degrees, it had been years since they had entertained any sort of legal-related idea. This was not common knowledge and the stream of, "clients," through their offices insured it remained that way.

Dr. Paul Baker on the other hand, was a practicing physician who concentrated on a very particular clientele. He was also the owner of a medical facility on the second floor. Like Austiff and Kegley, Dr. Baker shared his office space with other professionals who did not have a clue regarding certain aspects of his work. The Office of Central Strategic and Tactical Operations maintained an excellent cover.

The four filed into the office.

"Uh-huh," came the Director's voice from the office chair. His back still turned to the door, only the phone line and one protruding elbow were visible.

"I see," Austiff mumbled. "No—no. Just curious."

A pause drifted by.

"Right," Austiff said with a hollow laugh Clines recognized as the Director's brush-off tone. "I'll do that. And same to you, Carl. Thanks."

"Damn," the Director swore, banging the phone down. He looked up at the four, his having spun the chair and doused the phone in one motion.

"Project Hacksaw is going down."

"Going down?" Clines echoed.

"*Skylab's* orbit has deteriorated. NASA is going to force it down. They're looking at about a week to a week-and-a-half before they get all their ducks in a row."

The room was silent a moment. Kegley spoke; "It is just a deteriorating orbit, right?"

Austiff nodded. "It looks that way."

"What if it isn't?" Clines asked.

"It's coming down no matter what anyone wants," Austiff said. "NASA will control the reentry so as to drop it in the ocean."

"That much weight—over a ton..." Kegley trailed off.

"It won't all burn up," Clines finished.

They all looked at Debbie.

"What?" she said.

"It might be Dr. Farrell's handiwork up there, but it's your research," Austiff said, "so to speak."

"Are you asking if FORBS is making this happen?" She questioned.

"Yes, that's what I want to know. Could this be more than just a deteriorating orbit? And could—could—it survive?"

She shrugged. "It has been sealed from any power source—it shouldn't be responsible."

"'Shouldn't?'" Austiff quoted questioningly.

"For the sake of argument, let's say FORBS did somehow activate *Skylab* and force it down," Debbie came back. "It'll burn-up coming down, right? I mean, it doesn't have a heat shield, right?"

"*Skylab's* not a plane, not a shuttle," Clines cut in. "When it comes down, it won't be able to pick a glide path and it'll drop like a burning stone."

"Exactly," Debbie agreed.

Austiff said something about the speed at which it would be traveling and Clines added that it was only a question of how much would burn-up during the re-entry.

Baker remembered when FORBS was put into the orbiting space station—some damned fool idea about utilizing the technology in the future, when they learned to control it. Even though the Power Converter—the device that transmitted the boot-up codes to FORBS—was also sealed in *Skylab*, he had been concerned about FORBS' ability to use almost any ample energy source off which to, "live." *What if,* Austiff had said two years ago, *FORBS no longer needs to be booted-up? What if the damned thing is just in hibernation?*

And so it was Baker and Debbie who designed the vacuum-sealed container that FORBS and the Power Converter were now inside. The container and the vacuum of space surrounding *Skylab* were the ultimate safety measures. These measures insured FORBS would remain powerless if it ever were freed from the vacuum-sealed sphere in which it had been placed. Even then, Baker mused, Austiff's paranoia included having Security keep tabs on Steve Andrews. It didn't matter if Andrews —the lab assistant who had helped design the Power Converter—had resigned before the project was even halfway finished. Austiff was certain the secret would leak and Andrews would be kidnapped for information he didn't even have.

"My God," Baker whispered, suddenly struck with all the possible loose ends. "The vacuum container..."

They all looked at him.

"Are we certain that thing can't survive re-entry?" Baker asked. "The container we built for that thing is pretty darned resilient, but you know what it did in the lab. With all that heat energy available during re-entry..."

They were silent a moment. None of them had thought about this possibility.

"We'll have a hell of a spill to clean up if it survives," Baker commented in a low voice.

"No," Clines corrected. "It could clean us up. Just how sturdy is that container?"

Baker shrugged his shoulders. "Hard to say."

Clines looked at Debbie.

"It can't stand up to that much heat," she said.

"I don't see any problems," Austiff said. "It should burn-up. But I want you to stay close to NASA, Blake. And you Kate, I want next to the Defense Command."

"Okay," Kegley said.

Austiff looked at Baker and Debbie. "Does it or does it not have a connection with Karns?"

"That's been a very wild theory," Baker came back. "I've never bought it. But I can't prove it one way or the other."

Austiff nodded and looked at Debbie. "What do you think?"

"I can't prove it," she answered, "but they probably are connected."

Austiff didn't understand and it reflected in his face.

"You remember when we were in the chamber, pulling the connections off of Mr. Gray?"

He nodded *yes*.

"FORBS didn't kill him for a reason. What about the EKG and the brain scan? We weren't having monitor problems like we thought—"

"That's open to interpretation, don't you think?" Baker came back.

"No," Debbie answered firmly. "Some of our ball-less eggheads may think so, but they're wrong. What we saw was the same pattern in FORBS as Gray. My guess is they were so closely joined when the power was lost, FORBS was forced to shut down. That forced Karns Gray into the coma. Call it what you will, but they were practically one mind at the time circuits to the room were blown. Are they both now connected in some way? That's a tougher one. We just don't know what the brain is capable of. And as you know, Mr. Gray had absolutely amazing abilities before this happened."

Austiff leaned back, looking at them.

"Don't look at me," Baker said. "She's the Cerebellomedullary Specialist."

Austiff smiled at that. Debbie Allinder had always been one of the brighter stars in the medical heavens, and the area of her expertise hadn't even been created—or rather, she was inventing it. He said: "You be at that hospital when they bring that thing down—just in case."

"I was going to, anyway," She came back.

"Then that'll be it, people," Austiff said.

The four agents left the office.

4

The deep blue curvature of Earth was a revered sight at the alarming height of soundless existence. The planet Earth silently rested—waiting in the void night of space, peacefully revolving on her imaginary axis. Moving—continually moving, ever so slowly, and all the time waiting. Waiting for those minutes, those painstaking seconds when her warm atmosphere would alight with the falling of *Skylab*.

Seventy-seven point five tons of iron and alloy: a glory of engineering. A machine which saw 32,981 orbits of Earth. A space craft with six years of weightless orbiting behind it. On this fateful day, however, *Skylab* would reach a cruel destination: the cold waters of the Atlantic Ocean.

Skylab trackers predicted the station's death between 11:01 p.m. Central Daylight Time (CDT) and 11:53 p.m. CDT. It was to spread its inner workings into a 3,700-mile area of water, somewhere off the coast of Southern Africa.

Controllers set *Skylab* into a tumbling orbit over North America. The tumbling reduced *Skylab's* atmospheric drag, lengthened its life expectancy and insured a marginally safe clearance of the continent.

At 92 miles from the Earth, *Skylab* received another signal. Transmitted at 2:47 a.m. CDT, it briefly ignited a nitrogen gas thruster. This led to a rolling and wobbling motion.

Skylab lived on. After clearing the Madrid tracking station, *Skylab* entered the, "blindside," of its descent. Like a car losing a radio broadcast to static in a valley, the world temporarily lost contact with *Skylab*. Near the edge of the blindside, it sliced into the first of gravity and atmosphere. Sheets of armor-like plating were ripped from its sides and the solar panels burned away. The increasing heat began searing the man-made skin—slowly melting away the shell.

Trackers monitoring *Skylab's* emergence from the blindside, recorded large amounts of debris falling into the ocean. What fell was, they reported, superfluous to represent the death of *Skylab*.

Everyone relaxed.

Skylab was down in ashes.

Abruptly, his heart pounding, Karns Gray opened his eyes.

White.

He moved his head to see more white. The room measured 20 x 15 feet. He knew it. He felt a control box by his right hand and he rubbed his fingers over the small raised letters on each of the buttons. He pressed the button, *Head Up*.

The bed hummed to a sitting position, offering a better view of the room. He looked down to the *Head Up* button, surprised at identifying the words by a mere touch. He was able to, "read," the other buttons by smoothing his fingers over the words. He smiled inwardly, turning his attention to the room.

To the right was a computer screen displaying his heart rate and temperature. An IV drip was suspended over his left shoulder. The remainder of the room was bare—as though built as a canvas for the stark white paint.

Expecting his dreams had lasted only moments, he glanced around for the men he heard before losing consciousness. He was alone.

Suddenly aware of thin wires at the edges of his peripheral vision, he reached to find small electrodes taped to his temples. He pulled them away, tossing them to the floor. The computer screen jumbled then displayed a steady line. He pulled the IV needle from his left arm and tossed it too.

Deciding to look around, he eased his feet to the white tiled floor and slowly applied his weight. His arms and legs were weak to the point he knew they wouldn't hold him. It was a lot like having a bad case of the flu.

He shook off the thought and concentrated on his situation. Try as he may, he couldn't come up with a plausible explanation. The fact was he couldn't stand—and though it was a little late, he doubted the strength to even pull back onto the bed.

He lifted his arm. Although muscular by ordinary standards, his biceps lacked the usual tone. He discounted non-use since that would cause atrophy. There had to be a reason...

Footsteps sounded from the only door to the room, and he watched it open to admit a stunningly attractive woman. Her shinning black hair snaked downward, threatening to obscure her waist. She had large, captivating eyes of rich brown. Her snug fitting sundress drew attention to her cleavage.

He started to speak, but his voice wasn't there. In fact, he felt as if cotton was in his mouth.

"Are you okay?" she asked.

He swallowed for the second time, finally finding his voice.

"Who are you?" he croaked in an unusually deep tone. "Where am I?"

"My name's Debbie Allinder," she said, smiling a row of perfect teeth. "I suppose you're brewing with questions."

She helped him into a comfortable sitting position on the bed.

"It's rather complicated to explain—not that I ever expected to have an opportunity."

A nurse appeared at the door.

"Dr. Allinder," she was saying as she walked in, "is something wrong with...his...mon...itor..." Her voice trailed-off, replaced with a look of astonishment.

"He's awake," Debbie said softly—almost proudly.

"Oh," the nurse mumbled.

He looked from one to the other, dozens of questions vying for first place.

"Let's get him checked over, and be sure the transport is ready."

The nurse nodded and disappeared.

Gray swallowed again. "How long...?"

"Have you been here?" Debbie asked.

He nodded.

"It has been a little while," she answered. "Look, I can't really explain anything right now. After we confirm everything is ticking, we'll move you to another facility."

She placed her hand on his shoulder. "I'll answer everything when we get back to the Office and we're in the Sound Room."

"The what?" he croaked.

At that moment a slew of doctors and nurses appeared and any possible answer was drowned in a whirlwind of confusion.

5

The Sound Room was an area measuring 600 square feet at its center and occupying two thirds of the Professional Building's fourth floor. The walls were made of a sound absorbing substance that performed the task of contradicting what the room's name implied. In reality, it was a soundless room.

Finding the room's center was accomplished only by those familiar with doing so. Dozens of soundless passages created complex mazes in which one could be lost for hours. And in this place, no matter how grandiose the voice, a call for help would be heard only a few feet.

Drumming his fingers on the tabletop in the center of the room, Karns Gray patiently sat in a wheelchair. He had not seen much in the last two hours. There was a brief glance of cars before being wheeled into an ambulance without windows. Twenty minutes later he was rushed through an underground parking garage and into an elevator. He spent an hour in a medical facility on the third floor, where he ate and dressed in his own shirt and trousers. What little he had seen was slightly askew—not quite right. Things like cars he hadn't heard of and clothes that weren't exactly, "in style." The differences were subtle, but they were there.

He took a nearby cup and pushed it under the coffee urn's spout. After filling the cup he leaned back and looked at Debbie Allinder. She sat across the table sipping from her own cup. He guessed her to be in her early twenties, exactly 5'11" tall and about 130 lbs. How he knew her precise height eluded him—but he knew.

"I realize you're disoriented," she said, looking up at him. "Just relax."

He didn't.

"I'm here to help you."

"Where am I?"

She smiled, pushing a long strand of hair behind her ear: "You're in the Sound Room. The walls are coated with stuff that absorbs sound."

"I know," he said, again unsure how he knew, "but where is, 'here.'" To emphasize he pointed to the floor.

"Washington, DC," she answered.

The confusion on his face was masked, yet obvious. She realized the last place he probably remembered was California.

She took a quick drink of coffee. "Mr. Gray—may I call you 'Karns?'"

He nodded consent.

"Well Karns, I'm not an expert at this sort of thing. Perhaps the best way to go about it is to see what you remember—your last clear memories."

"Oh, I don't know," Gray said, again masking his apprehension. "We could just cut to the chase."

"Excuse me?"

"You probably know everything about me, don't you?"

She started to respond, and then thought better of it.

"Right?" he pressed.

"Mostly, but—"

"You're a doctor, right?"

"Yeah, but—"

"Not of the, 'treating physician,' sort though, correct?"

She raised an eyebrow, then: "Is it safe to assume you remember me?"

"No, Dr. Allinder, it isn't."

"Then how do you know—"

"The nurse at the hospital called you a, 'doctor,' but you didn't perform any of the exams. Now that it's just you and me, I figure you're some sort of head doctor—a shrink or something."

"I see," Debbie said with a smile breaking into a brief grin. "Not too bad. I'm a head doctor alright, but not the kind you're thinking of."

He gave a hand gesture for her to continue.

"Technically, I'm what you might call a Cerebellar Synaptologist."

"Oh," he replied flippantly, "one of those. Why didn't you just say so in the first place?"

She laughed. "Well, my medical degree says I'm a Neurobiologist, but I'm a specialist in clinical research on the synaptic functions of the brain. That's sort of it, in a nutshell."

Gray only nodded.

"Look," Debbie said, trying to grasp some sort of control, "I'm not here to crawl around in your head—"

"You're not?" he cut in, his tone somewhere between surprise and sarcasm.

"Well not exactly," she added with a smile.

He didn't smile.

"Tell ya' what," Debbie said, a slight hint of a southern accent in her enunciation. "I'll do most of the talking and you just jump in whenever you remember something I'm talking about. How's that?"

"Okay."

"Alright," she said, opening a folder on the table. "Let's start by getting the classified stuff out of the way."

She looked up, sensing he was suddenly tense.

"I can see this is going to be kind of touchy." She closed the folder, rubbing her forehead with her right hand while deciding the best route to take. "Karns... I work at Biochemical Laboratories, the medical facility in this building. My paycheck is signed by one of the doctors leasing space at BioChem—he runs his practice out of BioChem, just like the other doctors there. Perhaps you'd recognize his name—Dr. Paul Baker? He's your personal physician—the doctor you list on all important papers—right?"

He nodded *yes*.

"We both, Dr. Baker and I, work for the Office. By that I mean OCSTO—the Office of Central Strategic and Tactical Operations. Several of the businesses in this building, all of them legitimate, are owned and operated by people who also offer services to the Office."

"Really?" Gray said. The Office had never physically existed and its director, Jim Austiff, had run a network of agents out of his law office in the outskirts of Washington, DC. As for Dr. Baker, he was in private practice in Seattle, Washington—completely on the other side of the country. Even if he had been unconscious for a month, Gray reasoned, things wouldn't have changed that much. He wanted to trust Dr. Allinder—something about her made it difficult not to—but the holes in her story were large enough to drive trucks through. The fact of the matter was, the Office was to the United States, what the Ninja were to Japan. You might find a few people willing to admit it existed, but you'd never find anyone who claimed to personally know anything about it.

"I realize all this sounds ridiculous to you," Debbie admitted, as if reading his mind. "But there's been a few changes of which you are unaware. And I know you wouldn't normally sit down and start rattling off whatever you know about the Office or your history."

He didn't respond.

"Look," she said, indicating the folders on the table. "I've got it all right here. Everything from the Tai' Chi' Master who trained you to your command in the forces. I know about the prisoner of war and killed in action shams that were pulled on your behalf, too."

"That was just part of the war—public record."

"Not the fake death, Karns. The Chancellor doesn't fake killed in action reports for just anyone."

He focused on her without speaking. Few people knew about the Office. Fewer still about the Director. The number knowing of the Chancellor was the smallest number of all.

She smiled: "He said you wouldn't want to talk."

"Who?"

"The Chancellor."

His mind was starting to race. "Just what do you know about the Chancellor?"

"Quite a lot, actually."

He looked at her hard. She seemed relaxed and in control. He asked: "Where is he?"

"Probably out chasing bad guys."

"I want to see 'em."

"You will."

"Now," he said firmly.

"You can't. Surely you must know my information could only have come from the Chancellor himself."

"After it was tortured out of him?" Gray suggested.

"You see the enemy everywhere, don't you?"

He shrugged.

"This isn't Vietnam."

"Vietnam never goes away. Hell, you could be KGB and everything here an illusion."

She smiled. "That's the least of any possibility."

He smiled back, "Well, I'll admit that's reaching a bit."

She smiled outwardly, but inwardly she wondered how he would react if he realized how much she desired him. She said: "Is this the, 'make her feel at ease,' routine?"

"I didn't know you were easy," he came back.

Her smile faded somewhat. She toyed with the idea of telling him she had been fascinated with him from the day they had first met in Dr. Farrell's lab. She abandoned the idea as quickly as it had developed. She certainly didn't care to look like a fool.

"The Chancellor said you'd be difficult—that you'd sidetrack me."

Gray shrugged.

"He also told me there were only two words that would shake you up enough to make you realize I'm on the level."

He watched her carefully.

"The Chancellor said to tell you, that while I'm not, '1109,' you can trust me just as if I were. And he also said that he's glad to have his, 'Stopgap,' back."

He leaned back. Eleven-oh-nine was the Chancellor's office number in downtown Seattle, Washington. Chancellor agents had began using the number as a verification of anything originating from there. Everyone had a code name known only to the Chancellor. Gray was, "the Stopgap."

At least it was *known only to the Chancellor,* he thought.

"Do you believe me, now," Debbie was asking.

"I'd like to. But some of the things you said don't make sense. Everything is so damned disorienting."

"After what you've been through that's to be expected. Everything will make sense, but you have to help me first. Okay?"

"Okay."

"I need to know how much of your memory is intact."

"Okay," he said with a nod. "Let's just steer clear of classified topics and we'll do fine."

"Don't you think that'll be a bit difficult?"

"Surely not."

"Your entire history is classified, Karns. It's your personal history we've got to talk about."

"My assignments were classified," he clarified. "That doesn't mean I'm classified."

She looked at him with concern and then: "Yeah, of course. So let's talk about your childhood."

"Okay," he said, his dark blue eyes almost pulling her in.

Now that he seemed cooperative, the fact he had forgotten that *he* was a classified resource of the National government was something she decided to not reveal.

Hiding her distraction, she glanced at the folders on the table. When she looked up, he was still staring.

"What would you like to know?" he asked.

"Where were you born? What's your first memory?"

He stared blankly, searching his memory.

"Well?"

For a moment he seemed to hear something distant—like the sound of the ocean.

"Karns?" she asked.

"I don't know," he mumbled, lost in thought. He remembered hearing a voice...

Karns...

It was strained, as if calling through the wailing of wind and rain—as though trying to be heard over crashing waves.

Karns...

He recalled opening his eyes to see a gray room. It was cool. Impersonal. Conservative. Gray.

He liked the color.

The color of whales.

The great oceans and vast depth must give the whales the cool feeling of that color.

Karns...

He recognized the gray room as his earliest memory—except for that voice and the vague awareness of the ocean engulfing and comforting him.

Karns...

He remembered the cool room as part of a hospital, a new concept to him when those in charge explained what it was. They—the doctors—thought he had amnesia.

Karns...

Simple memory loss, they explained. Probably from the shock of a boating accident and being washed ashore they surmised.

Karns...

They asked him his name.

Karns, the voice echoed.

"Karns," he told them.

"Karns what?" they asked, as if, *"Karns,"* wasn't enough and there should be more.

So he gave them more: *"Karns Gray."*

"What do you remember?" Debbie asked in almost a whisper.

Gray blinked, realizing he wasn't in the gray hospital—that he had been lost in thought.

"I was supposedly washed ashore in Virginia in 1941," he said, recalling how alien everything had seemed—like now. "I was later adopted."

"Tell me about your adopted parents."

"Not much to tell. His name is Samuel and hers—" he paused to smile. "She had a beautiful name: Paige Alexandra."

He paused again, remembering. "When I was a teenager, we moved to Corpus Christi in Texas," Gray said.

"What was your father's occupation?"

He looked at her thoughtfully, then said: "He's a Shipwright."

"A Shipwright?" she asked, curious.

"Builds ships—boats."

"How about after you moved away. What do you remember?"

"I ended-up in Vietnam."

"And?"

"And what?"

"What happened?"

"I fought."

Debbie picked up a folder and glanced in it. "I understand you are an accomplished fighter."

"I do okay in a pinch."

"You don't care much for talking about the war, do you?"

"I'd rather not," he admitted. "I remember it very well, if that'll help any."

She smiled. "Okay. Let's move on. Do you remember Gail James."

He looked at her—astonishment on his face.

"I'm sorry," Debbie said, "I didn't mean—"

"I don't want to talk about her," he said quietly.

"I understand," she said.

He remained silent—withdrawn.

"I don't want to dig up ghosts," she said, nearly whispering again. She reached across the table, touching his hand. "I just want to help."

He looked at her.

"Please..."

He nodded okay.

"She's part of the reason you're here," Debbie went on, more slowly this time.

He listened.

"Do you remember the experiment? We jokingly called it, 'the Einstein Experiment?'"

It sounded familiar. His forehead wrinkled as he searched his memory.

"It was described as a long shot with about a 60 percent chance of it working."

He still looked blank, then: "I remember someone saying the 60 percent chance was, 'out the window.'"

"Dr. Farrell said that," she replied looking at him.

"Who?"

"Dr. E.H. Farrell."

"I remember him," Gray said slowly, recalling the salt and pepper beard.

"The Chancellor said you were at the end of your rope—do you remember that?"

"Just tell me what all this has to do with what's wrong with me," Gray came back.

"Excuse me?" she questioned, having lost her train of thought.

"I'm sorry," he said, rubbing his forehead. "It's just..."

"I know, you're very disoriented, confused—"

"It's not just that."

"What then?"

"Well, when you touched me, I knew your body temperature," he answered.

"I see."

"No, you don't," he came back, a strange expression on his face. "I even know your heart rate. I know that the open area of this room is 600 square feet. The table is three feet by five feet. Sound carries into the passageway in here only zero-zero point four beyond 20 feet. The room temp..." He stopped.

"Do you realize what I'm saying?" he then asked her. "Do you have any idea what I can feel, smell, hear and sense?"

"I know," she said in a soothing voice.

"What's happened to me?" he questioned, extending his hands out as if seeing them for the first time.

"You really don't know, do you?"

He shook his head slowly. "Know what?"

"Karns... You've always been that way."

"What?" he snapped.

"Everything you described is in your file. You've been able to do those things since you were first found. You even have photographic memory. It's normal for you."

"Are you crazy?" he questioned, leaning forward. "No one can do this—"

She gave him a smirking look, as if to say, *but you're doing it.*

"Well," he clarified, "no one is *supposed* to be able to do this."

She smiled, amused by his discovery and happy he hadn't realized it was the reason *he* was a classified government secret. She felt they were making progress and didn't want him clamming up now. She said: "You can."

"Yeah," he mumbled.

"Just a few more questions, okay?"

He shrugged.

"What's the last thing you remember—before waking up this morning?"

"Except for some strange dreams..." His voice trailed off as he stared without really seeing her. He looked down, concentrating on the accident. The seconds passed into a minute.

"I was in a burning car," he said at last. "Someone—a girl, pulled me out."

She nodded, almost impatiently: "Describe her."

"Young—19 or 20. Long hair like yours. Eyes like..." His voice faded as the realization dawned on him. He looked up at her.

"I pulled you out," she answered his eyes.

"I was on an assignment," he said. "What were you doing there?"

"You had been taken off an assignment," she corrected. "And it was my first field assignment."

"Just give it to me straight."

"I'm suppose to make you remember this."

"Well I'm a little foggy, so help me out."

"You were the best agent the Chancellor had until you took an assignment to catch a weapons and drug smuggler that you had been after during the war. Unfortunately, you got involved with a civilian named Gail James."

He only looked at her, reliving the memory.

"You kind of went into a tailspin. You were more dangerous to yourself than the bad guys."

He nodded.

"Since you were the agent with the best brains turning to mush, the Chancellor offered you an experiment in which to participate. Something that could've killed you. You took it. Your, "accident," was a case of someone trying to kill you—but we never found out who."

"Go on."

"You were suppose to meet me and we were coming here—to Bio-Chem labs. After the accident, you were flown to the nearest hospital for emergency surgery, and then moved here to undergo the experiment. I recommended against it, but it went ahead anyway."

He listened, watching her with intense eyes.

She took a sip of coffee. "Its classified name was FORBS, an acronym for Farrell's Oral Response Bio-computer Source."

"Whew," Gray breathed.

Debbie smiled. "It is a mouth-full. It was built just a little over two-and-a-half years ago. The idea was to create a self-aware computer: an artificial intelligence that could think and carry on conversation—not just process information like any run-of-the-mill desktop computer. It was a remarkable step in the right direction."

"Computers," Gray said, "can already carry on conversations."

"But they can't think," she explained. "FORBS could think. It could actually *learn*. It wasn't just *artificial* intelligence. It was *synthetic* intelligence."

"The difference being...?"

She thought for a moment, composing an answer: "Artificial intelligence duplicates the thinking process. An artificial intelligent computer appears to think because it extrapolates. But even though the results are inferred or conjectural, they are still arrived at by a deductive or inductive method. Synthetic intelligence isn't restricted to deductive or inductive thought. It isn't a duplication of the thinking process, but rather the result of a duplicated brain—"

"Wait," he cut in, "you're saying this thing was a—*a brain?*"

"Exactly." She leaned forward. "It was *designed* to be self-aware, to develop values and personality. It could actually, literally *think*. Just like a person, it could even respond to inspiration."

"I have to admit I've never even heard of synthetic intelligence."

"It's not exactly a Webster-defined term," she responded. "Dr. Farrell said it had to be better than artificial, that it had to replicate not just human thought, but the processes that led to human thought. He said that only a synthetic computer could make the leap from tangible database to intangible mentality. Or as he put it: 'It's a computer that dreams.'"

Gray looked properly impressed. "What was your role in all this?"

"I had written a thesis on the possibility of creating an artificial brain. The Chancellor showed it to Dr. Farrell, who was working on that very concept. The next thing I knew, I was on the Office payroll and looking at a very crude working model. My job was to perform experiments on animals to determine if the data in their brains was transferable to the working model."

"I see. Did it work?"

"Yes and no."

He waited for the explanation.

"The working model, essentially a synthetic or artificial brain, appeared to duplicate whatever data was in the animals. But since we didn't understand what the animals were saying, we didn't know if the synthetic brain was just replaying gibberish or what. It was like we had the software, but not the right hardware in which to play it.

"So we decided to build a human-based model."

"How could you *build* something like that? I mean, what sort of materials did you use?"

"It's an extremely complicated task, requiring a microscopic merging of animal tissues with computerized components."

"What sort of animal tissues?"

"In the beginning, the cerebral tissues of monkeys. When we graduated to the human-based model, we used human cerebral tissue that had been donated for scientific research."

"I see."

"And that's where the Einstein Experiment came in."

"The what?"

She flickered a smile. "It was officially called Project Hacksaw—a randomly generated name. We started calling it the Einstein Experiment —a joke—of sorts. Anyway, you were linked to FORBS in an effort to map the synaptic pathways. We had several goals, but we specifically wanted to see if FORBS could retain what it copied from you, and if in the process it would form new neurological pathways."

She could see the questions on his face.

"In other words," she said, "FORBS was to copy the data—the actual bioelectrical and biochemical activity of your brain. Basically, when the electrical signal gets to the point of the cleft..."

She stopped, realizing the technical aspects were getting in the way.

"Don't let this dumb look stop you," Gray commented dryly.

She smiled, then tried a different approach: "Have you ever rubbed your shoes on the carpet and shocked someone?"

"Uh, yeah," he stuttered, caught off-guard by the question.

"Well that's what happens when a thought or a sensation—neurons, if you will—are transmitted in your body. The thought or the sensation actually jumps from one cell to another like a spark. And that is what FORBS was suppose to copy from you."

Gray nodded, grasping—if not the idea—at least the concept.

"We called it, 'synaptic mapping,' or, 'brain mapping.' But it seems, that what we wanted wasn't what FORBS wanted."

"If this thing—FORBS—was already a success, what was the problem?"

"The problem was that it had developed much more than we realized. I believe that it wanted more than just mere existence. It wanted to *live*—so to speak The only thing that saved our asses was FORBS' power configuration."

"What do you mean?"

"FORBS was initially activated by a device called a Power Converter. By entering the coordinates of the Converter and FORBS, the Converter initiated a siphoning program that allowed it to draw in power from a nuclear source, then transmit the access code—"

"Hold on and slow down," Gray cut in. "Why coordinates and an access code?"

"It was self-sufficient and that made it potentially dangerous. Since no one knows what a self-aware computer thinks about, a failsafe system was designed so that we could shut it down—just in case."

"I see. And the nuclear power? What's that about?"

"Once a satellite link-up between the Converter and FORBS was established, the Converter *converted* nuclear power into a transmission that literally powered up the computer. The access code I mentioned, was then transmitted and that activated the synaptic unit."

"Jeez! Why so complicated?"

"What you don't realize, is that the access code was a sort of format signal. Being almost a human brain/computer hybrid, FORBS could turn around and use that access code to connect to any computer anywhere, through satellite link-up or directly. Theoretically, it might even have been able to read minds."

Gray looked shocked. "How's that possible?"

"We're talking about a direct connection of energy like shooting a broadcast signal into a TV set."

He shrugged, indicating he didn't understand.

"Essentially, that's all thought processes are. Data in the form of neurons. If FORBS could access any computer, why couldn't it access any brain? It was all just data to FORBS."

"And you guys hooked me up to this thing?"

"You volunteered, Karns. After we had explained all of this to you and pointed out the very real dangers involved, you were like, 'where do I sign?' You were really screwed-up."

It was vague to him, but even as she was speaking, bits and pieces were coming back.

"Throughout all the tests, I kept telling you not to risk it. But I guess you were just too hell-bent on killing yourself without pulling a trigger."

He nodded slowly. "So what happened? How did it all go wrong?"

She took another drink of coffee. "It happened so fast, we never even got the chance to use the shutdown command. The moment the experiment began, FORBS made his move."

"How?"

"The nearest we can figure, FORBS attempted to transfer to you."

"'Transfer?'" he echoed.

She nodded, *yes*. "Don't let this go to your head, but you have what I consider a very high degree of synaptic activity. The speed of the neurons across your synapses is measurably faster than any I've documented—which is what made you an ideal candidate. Theoretically, your brain can handle neuron transfers at higher volume and a higher speed than most people. If a computer wanted a human brain, yours would be its first choice."

She paused, sipping her coffee. Then: "I believe FORBS short circuited your neurological functions. I also believe you fought it and that's why it killed five men in the process."

"Killed five..." His voice trailed off for a moment. "How?"

"The same way it theoretically could read minds," she answered solemnly, "only in reverse. They were drained of life, Karns. Their molecular structure was realigned in such a way that the bioelectrical and thermal properties of their bodies were siphoned right out of them. They were stone-cold within minutes—Dr. Farrell one of them. Their body core temperatures were those of people who had been dead for days. Even the ambient room temperature dropped. And, unbelievable as it sounds, FORBS was able to extract power from the oxygen molecules of the room. We had to suit-up in environmental gear just to get you out."

"Why didn't I suffocate, then?"

"Well, when we got you out of there, your heart rate was around five beats per minute and your respiration rate was—"

"Five beats a minute?" he exclaimed.

"You survived because you didn't need the oxygen. Whatever

changes were going on inside your body—or your brain—had already begun. As for FORBS... The only reason it didn't drain the entire building was because of the way in which the chamber was designed. The walls were thick alloys—nothing could be transmitted in or out. Anyway, the sudden overload of power to the chamber blew the breakers to the room and prevented FORBS from obtaining additional power."

Gray was shocked and it showed on his face.

"You were the only one left alive inside the experiment chamber," she went on. "After removing you, the Office sealed FORBS into a container and placed it into an orbital space station."

"It's still around?" he asked, trying to believe what she had said.

"No. *Skylab's* orbit deteriorated and NASA forced it to burn-up in the atmosphere this morning. I believe you came out of the coma because FORBS was destroyed. No one really understands the hows and whys. The answers probably died with Dr. Farrell."

"Coma? I didn't think a person could come out of a coma."

"Some do," she answered, "but not as many when the coma last for a long time. In your case, I believe that somehow you were, 'shut down,'" she added emphasis by quotation marks in the air with her hands, "—or put into a coma by FORBS. When it was destroyed, the link was severed, hence no more coma."

"Wait a second, how long was I in a coma?"

"You've been given an amazing gift," she said, avoiding the question. "While you were in the coma, the physical therapist working on you exercised your limbs only two or three times. After that they just touched you and your muscles contracted, moving through their whole range of motion—it was like your brain was on autopilot or something. Nothing like that has ever happened before. I mean you were in a coma, but on some unconscious level—some level we couldn't monitor—your brain told your body to automatically go through the range of motion exercises that the physical therapist performed on you. That's—that's miraculous."

"How long?" he asked, ignoring her attempted sidestep.

"Two years."

"Two years?" he questioned, a scared smile masking his features.

"Almost to the day."

"You mean I'm... I'm 36?"

She nodded *yes,* watching him rub his temple. She said: "There's something else."

"What?"

"Well..." She moistened her lips, unsure how to phrase it. "I really don't know how to explain it—"

"Try."

"Well, no one knows for sure why we age. It's a combination of many things, including wear and tear, certain DNA sequences play a really important part, proper vitamin and mineral balances—I could on and on. The fact is, no one knows. Whatever it is, it's not happening in you. We have 2-year old blood samples from you that... Well, the cells haven't expired in two years—and it makes no difference what we subject them to. It's a side effect no one expected."

She looked away. "Somehow your cells are not dying—or they're able to regenerate, slowing the aging process."

"What are you saying?"

"You went comatose two years ago," she said, looking at him firmly, "and even though you're 36..."

His eyes held with hers.

"...we don't know if your aging has simply slowed down, or if you've stopped aging altogether." She paused and then added, almost sadly: "You might be sort of...immortal..."

6

"We don't know why you're alive," Baker had admitted. "You should have died in the car crash two years ago, or the experiment should've killed you. And it's miraculous you came out of the coma.

"As for immortality—what we do know is this: the telomeres have stopped breaking off and we believe that an unusually high level of chemical activity in your brain, an enzyme most likely, is what's causing those puppies to hang on."

"Say what?" Gray came back.

Baker grabbed a notepad from his desk, flipped it open, quickly scribbled a few lines and held up the sketch:

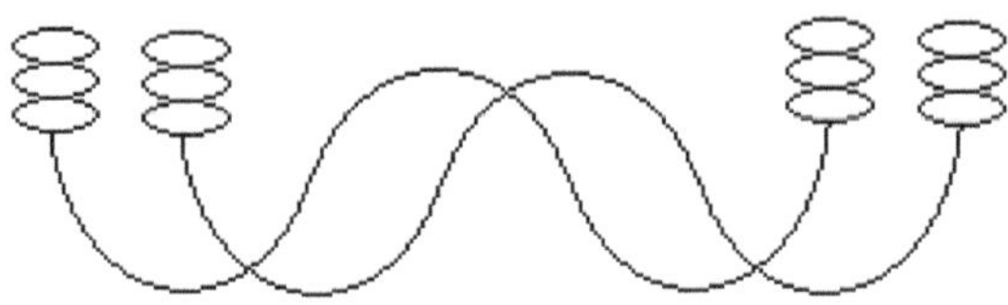

"These two squiggly lines," Baker explained, "are microscopic strands of DNA that all cells have inside their nucleus. They're the chromosomes. On the ends of these chromosome strands are tiny bits of material—bits of DNA sequences—called telomeres, okay?"

"Yeah?"

"Well," Baker went on, tearing the page out and handing it to Gray, "as cells divide or become damaged, those telomeres break off. Not too long ago the medical community discovered those rascals played a pretty important role in aging and in cancer cells. The fewer you have, the older and less mobile you are."

"So you're saying these things on the end here, aren't breaking off?"

"That, and yours are pretty adamant about not being pulled off, either."

"You don't say," Gray mumbled, looking at the picture.

"I do," Baker came back, re-pocketing his pen. "You also have an unusually high level of chemical activity in your brain."

"The enzyme you mentioned?"

"It shows up on your MRI," Baker added with a nod of confirmation, referring to Magnetic Resonance Imaging—a diagnostic scan that rendered anatomical pictures as easily and more clearly than an x-ray revealed bones. "We've speculated your brain is producing a fairly concentrated amount which is helping those telomeres hang on for dear life."

"Hmm."

"Researchers all over the world are going bonkers trying to figure out how to stop aging and it appears you've done it. Now aside from everything we do know, the simple fact is, we don't understand why, how or what all is involved. Frankly, we just flat don't know..."

Karns Gray stared at the mirror over the sink, recalling the two-day old meeting with Baker. Like just about everything else, it had left him feeling a little off balance. But then what was to be expected? The last conscious memory he had was two years old. And the two years leading up to that was something he wished he could forget.

Four years... Gail broke the engagement, and he botched the Ŝulok assignment—it all seemed as if it had only been two years. But including a coma he couldn't remember it had been four years ago.

Four years.

Gray shook his head and sighed.

He moved from the bathroom. It was a Saturday, so only a scant four or five people were working in the facility. The examining rooms and offices were empty. He walked down a hall and into the plush waiting area.

Debbie Allinder was sitting in a chair reading a magazine. She had made it very clear that she preferred, *Debbie*, to the title, *Doctor.*

"I'm ready," Gray announced.

She looked up to see him as she remembered first seeing him two years ago. A gray suit, chiseled good looks, and penetrating dark blue eyes.

"You look *fine*," she said, emphasizing the last word.

"'Fine?'" he echoed.

"Extra fine."

He smiled slightly, not used to such a forward compliment.

She stood. "Well, let's go."

"I'm still a little wary of this surprise."

She moved to him, interlocking arms. "Come on."

Once in her car—a flashy red MGB—Debbie drove through the security gate and out of the underground parking. She pointed the car south through the city. While she made small talk, Gray looked at her—as if really seeing her for the first time. Although Debbie differed from Gail in numerous ways, he couldn't help but compare them. Debbie was taller by two inches. She wasn't as distant. And there wasn't an ounce of, "country," in her. The thought made him smile inwardly, and his eyes moved to her well-shaped legs. He doubted she realized using the clutch worked her mini skirt up as it had. He certainly didn't intend to tell her.

Her figure was fuller, and everything she wore bordered somewhere between professional and sensual.

"Karns...?"

He looked up, realizing he had been staring. She was smiling and, he realized, very beautiful.

"Not that I mind," she softly said, "but you haven't heard a word I've said, have you?"

"Uh, sure," he stumbled. "You were saying you really like Europe."

She didn't stop smiling and downshifted to take a corner. "Yeah, I was. Three blocks back."

"I'm sorry," he said, "I was—distracted."

They looked at each other, trying to read the other's thoughts.

"So what's the surprise?" Gray asked.

"Don't change the subject," she said directly.

"I wasn't aware—"

"So, what do you think?" she interrupted.

"About what?"

"About me."

"That kind of puts me on the spot."

"Paul says you're not comfortable with emotions—actually he said you're introverted. I just want to know what you really think—without all the bullshit."

"That's pretty direct."

"So was staring."

He smiled sheepishly. "Sorry."

"Don't be," she said flatly, taking another corner sharply. "If I didn't want to be noticed, I'd dress like a schoolmarm."

"You always this way?"

"You mean honest?

"I mean blunt."

She glanced at him. "You think I'm too blunt?"

"I think so," he answered with a nod and then; "How old are you, anyway?"

"You're supposed to have the brains—you tell me."

"Suddenly, you're not so blunt," he observed.

"I'm 19."

"I'm a bit old for you, aren't I?" It was more of a statement than a question.

She swerved the car to a sudden stop by a curb and killed the engine. Tucking her knee beneath her, she shifted in the seat. It was a provocative pose, he thought, and she didn't even know it.

"Can I be frank with you?" she asked plainly.

Her manner caught him off guard. He searched her face for an indication of what was coming. All he saw, however, were the large brown eyes and moist pouting lips. It was as if he were discovering her beauty every time he looked at her.

"I thought you were," he said.

She ignored the remark and plunged ahead: "Everyone's been treating you with kid gloves. They tell me you're unstable. According to your file—and you didn't hear this from me—you're emotionally underdeveloped."

He remained silent.

"Your—your—" she struggled for words; "fixation with Gail James is tantamount to a crush—a first love. Your experiences—Vietnam and the like—also according to your file—have only reinforced what you've become."

He looked off a moment and then back at her. "Why are you telling me all this?"

"Karns, I've read your file so many times, I know it by memory. But it's all speculation as far as I'm concerned."

"So?"

She pushed her hair back. "Everything indicates you don't understand people—that you're cold. That's bullshit. You might have been born a pretty cool customer, but at one time you loved a woman to the point of self-destruction. Maybe it hurt so bad you just don't want to expose yourself any more."

He didn't respond.

"Look, maybe I'm more in the dark than the eggheads. All I want to know is where I stand."

He slowly inhaled.

"I mean, this Gail stuff—it's four years old. The woman left you. I want to know if you're ready to start the future."

He started to speak, then held back. He looked off once again, then back at her. She sat silent: expectant.

"I can't answer that," he said at last.

"Why not?"

"I just—"

"What are you going to do, Karns? Chase after her? Start drinking again?"

His expression hardened.

"You never touched a drop until she dumped you. Are you going to do that again?"

"I don't think you know me well enough to discuss this," he said.

She smirked: "Then tell me where I'm wrong."

"I'll tell 'ya," he said in a subdued voice, staring out the windshield. "I did everything short of kill myself—I've never felt anything like that pain. Even all the killing in Vietnam was nothing compared to Gail's stab in the back. Yeah, I still have flashbacks of 'Nam—nothing could have been as horrendous as what happened in that place—but at least I knew there was an enemy."

He looked at her, but she knew he was looking through her and into the past.

"I expected the Einstein Experiment to fail—that was my out: no more gory flashbacks; no more emotional loathing. Do you understand what I'm saying?"

"No," she said flatly.

"I never expected to be here—didn't want to be here. I went into it thinking, 'I'm outta' here.' I wasn't going to have to deal with feeling again. I didn't want to. I can't help the fact I'm here now. I can't alter the fact I feel exactly like I did two years ago. It's like being a damned light bulb. The switch was turned off for two years, then bam, the switch is on, and I'm just a few seconds older. I didn't want this and now you're asking me to just—just forget about it."

"A light bulb doesn't think," she said.

"And it doesn't feel," he added.

A moment of silence passed.

"Debbie," he said, breaking the stillness.

She looked at him.

"I don't want to live in the past. But the past is all I have. You're asking a lot of me. You're young yet—"

"So the fuck are you," she snapped.

He started to speak, but shrugged it off.

She touched his arm: "I'm not angry because you don't want me. I'm mad because you won't let go of something you haven't got." *And I'm something you can have*, she didn't add.

He looked at her a long moment, weighing her words. "What would you have me say?"

She stared at him a moment, then: “Nothing.”

She started the car, all the while coolly staring at him. She shifted the gear and they were out of the city within minutes.

7

At a dock on the Potomac River, several miles south of Washington, Debbie pulled off the road and parked.

They walked across the road and down a set of white painted steps. A row of boats quietly bobbed in their slips. Floating at the end of the dock, a large, old yacht drew their attention. It was a flawless work of sailing art fashioned by Elco Cruisers in New York. Its 50 year old stern was emblazoned with the italicized name, *Paige Alexandra*.

With three separate staterooms, quarters for a crew of two and divans in the deckhouse, the 48-foot Elco slept six passengers. In an age of modern fiberglass, the, "Fairlined," Elco 48 was a timeless example of excellent shipbuilding. Karns Gray stood motionless. He was home.

"Come on," Debbie urged, moving him toward the yacht.

Approaching the *Paige Alexandra* they could see a banner strung along the length of the deck railing. It read: WELCOME HOME GIZMO & GRAY. Jazz music seductively streamed from the forward cabin. Beneath a canopy added onto the rear sundeck, two women were dumping ice into a large chest.

Grinning, Gray carefully made his way across the gangplank—his legs only now regaining strength.

"Blake, you flake," Gray called, "where are you?"

"It's about time," boomed Blake Clines' voice.

The barrel form of Clines came swaggering down the side of the deck. A thin tanned woman followed him. The two women at the ice chest followed after them.

Clines and Gray greeted with handshakes and hugs. Laughing, the men traded insults faster than Debbie or the other women could follow.

"Gentlemen," Debbie finally interrupted, "and I use the term loosely—"

"Where?" the men said in unison, looking off onto the dock.

"All I want to know," Debbie said laughing, "is who the hell is Gizmo?"

"You mean you didn't tell her?" Clines beamed.

"Uh, no," Gray admitted. "They already think I'm crazy."

"It's his little voice," Clines boomed, as if it were obvious.

"His what?" one of the women said. She was wearing worn-out cutoffs and a half-shirt.

"You know," Clines explained, "that little voice that says, 'don't get on the plane,' or, 'if you kiss her, the boyfriend will go ballistic.'"

The shapely, 5' 5" woman behind Clines, poked his side with her elbow.

"Ouch," Clines yelped—not the least bit hurt. To Gray he said, "Allow me to introduce my harem."

He put his arm around the petite woman who had followed and poked him. She had a light brown complexion and shoulder-length brown hair. Wearing a one-piece swimsuit with a wrap-around sarong, she could have just stepped out of a summer fashion advertisement.

"This is my personal squeeze, Sharon Robbins."

Gray shook her hand: "You don't really date this cornball, do you?"

"I think of it as saving other women," she replied smartly.

"You sound sane enough," Gray said with a grin.

"Ahem," Clines cut in, moving Gray to the other women. "These two foxes are Emily and Stephanie Thebbs."

"Ladies," Gray said to them.

"You have them to thank for your yacht," Clines explained.

"Oh?"

"Oh, yes," he came back. "Your father personally picked them to take care of your boat a year ago. They are Shipwrights Extraordinaries."

The one wearing torn-up cutoffs flipped her flowing hair back and smiled. "Hi, I'm Emily." She had a pleasant southern accent.

Gray nodded.

"Actually," Emily added, "we can't hold a candle to Mr. Alexandra. But lucky for us we didn't have to build the yacht—only dry dock it and keep it clean."

"We hope you like it," Stephanie said in a less pronounced accent.

Admiring her French bikini, Gray politely smiled. "It looks great."

"Yeah," Clines joined in, "and the yacht don't look half-bad, either."

The sisters laughed and moved-up the deck toward the cabin.

"So where have you been?" Gray said to Clines.

Clines, moving to the ice chest, said: "Still Projects Director and still globe-trotting—although not near as much. I actually have my very own Engineering Company now."

"Nah?" Gray said with unrestrained admiration.

"Yep," Clines beamed. "It's called Engineering Inc. We specialize in R&D."

"How'd you swing your own Research and Development Company—and more importantly, are you still with 1109?"

Clines leaned closer. "The Chancellor floated me a huge business loan and I did the rest. So, for cost plus a ten percent markup I handle all the R&D for both the Office and the Chancellor—or whatever guise of the week they pay me under."

"But it's your company?"

"Lock, stock and barrel," Clines came back with a grin. "Paid the Chancellor off after the first year."

"You always were the frugal Mr. Fix-it," Gray commented.

Clines reached into the ice-chest to retrieve a bottle. "You wouldn't believe the stuff we come up with. I'm telling you, in 20 years computers and artificial intelligence will be the thing."

Gray almost shuddered. "I've heard all I want about artificial intelligence."

"Yeah, after all you've been through, I guess you would have. Hey, we've got a lot of stuff on the drawing board we owe to you and Debbie."

"Really now?"

"That girl is a kid genius—she hasn't told you squat, has she?"

Gray looked over at Debbie. She was leaning against the railing, watching him.

"She's tight-lipped with everything but her opinion," Gray answered.

"I know," Clines came back, grinning. "We've been working on a few projects together. About the only thing she really goes on about is my best friend."

Gray put his hand on Clines' shoulder. "Your best friend is a bit old for her."

"You're a real stick-in-the mud," Clines retorted, finally popping the top off the bottle. He retrieved a glass from a nearby bag and handed it to Gray. He then pulled another bottle from the ice-chest.

"Non-alcoholic," Clines explained as he uncorked it and poured some into Gray's glass. "I understand you're on the wagon."

Gray just nodded with a content smile. He was incredibly happy just to be looking at Clines.

"All hands on deck," Clines called out.

The Thebbs sisters reappeared. Debbie and Sharon poured everyone a glass of champagne.

Clines then held his drink up in salute: "To Karns Gray. My friend by choice. My brother by soul."

"Amen," Gray said.

They toasted and downed the drinks.

Clines moved over to Gray and clasped him on the shoulder.

"I can't tell ya' how glad I am you're back," he said, gripping Gray tightly.

Gray returned with a clap on the shorter man's shoulder. "I'm happy to be back, Dave."

While Sharon moved into the cabin to turn up the music, Debbie positioned herself next to the two men.

"You know," Debbie said, "if I could get this much admiration from either of you, I'd get a sex change right now."

Clines smiled and looked over to her. "No need, Deb, you've got balls enough as it is."

"Pizza man," a voice called from the dock.

They looked to see a man hidden behind a stack of pizza boxes.

"Well it's about time," Clines said, then turned to Gray "I thought I'd have to talk to you all day on an empty stomach."

"The Lord forbid," Gray commented dryly.

Gray watched the group surround the pizza deliverer.

8

It was 2:00 a.m.

Clines and Gray were seated in deck chairs beneath the canopy—their feet propped on the railing. Two boat slips over, Emily Thebbs was swaying to unheard music on the deck of her boat. Clines and Gray watched in amusement as she stripped off her top and continued dancing.

"That girl is wasted," Clines commented.

Gray nodded, watching Stephanie Thebbs appear and herd her sister inside.

"Good night," Stephanie called, her voice echoing across the water.

"Night," the men said in unison.

"She wanted you," Clines mumbled.

"Which one?"

"All of 'em—'cept Sharon, of course."

Gray was silent a moment. "That's odd."

"What?"

"I thought Sharon was the only one that wanted me."

Clines cast his friend a sideways glance: "Now that you mention it..."

Gray snickered, reaching into the ice cooler sitting between them. He tossed Clines a bottle of beer and withdrew a ginger ale for himself.

Clines popped the top with an opener, took a drink and started shaking his head in amused disbelief before even swallowing.

"You're really goin' to do it," he finally said, catching a breath of air.

"What?"

"Not a drop of alcohol all night," Clines replied.

Gray took a long drink. "It's time to face life."

Clines nodded in agreement. "So, does that mean Debbie has a chance?"

"Don't even start on that."

Clines chuckled and they sat in silence again, each enjoying the moment.

"Remember Yen, the old fart," Clines finally said.

"Master Yen Hwúi?"

"Yeah, what was it he said—'Be.'" Clines had finished the sentence with an oriental accent.

Gray smiled at his friend's quote. "He said that a lot. It boiled down to, 'One of life's greatest challenges, and secrets, is being.'"

"Well," Clines drawled, "you took that stuff more to heart than I did."

Gray's smile held for a moment, then faded. "Obviously I didn't take it to heart enough."

"Yeah, well..."

"Is he still alive?" Gray asked.

"Oh, yeah," Clines came back. "Your father thinks Yen will be alive to see the Second Coming—no matter how many centuries it takes."

"How's he look?"

Still like about 60—damned good for 90."

Gray smiled again.

"He asked about you."

"Oh?"

Clines leaned forward, his eyes squinting. His voice came in a graveled accent: "'So Big Stump, is the Slow One not yet learned to be?' He expected you to come out of the coma long before anyone thought you would."

Gray took a few more swallows of soda. He remembered the old Master like all the ghosts of Vietnam. Like the flashbacks, Master Hwúi seemed to appear at will. The flashbacks were a constant reminder he hadn't achieved, "being."

Be, Hwúi had said. *Just be*.

"Why the hell did he call you the Slow One, anyway," Clines suddenly said.

"Because I'm slow," Gray answered.

"I'm not going to say, 'Oh, yeah, right,' this time," Clines came back. "You're the damned fastest person that old man ever taught."

Gray sighed. “I had practiced perfectly one day. Then at the end of the movements old Hwúi said to me, ‘You have performed poorly, Slow One.’”

“Huh?” Clines grunted.

“That’s what I said. I’ll never forget what he said. He said, ‘Be as Big Stump, it is excellence when so.’”

“What?” Clines questioned. “I was average to good at best.”

Gray smiled. “No, my friend, you are excellent.”

“Which is why you kicked my butt every time?”

“Hwúi measured success in the mind and heart, not the brain and body.”

Clines furrowed his forehead, thinking. “I don’t think you’ve answered my question.”

“I thought the old bird was crazy, too,” Gray said smiling. “And every time he said I was performing poorly, he would tell me to be like you.”

Gray paused to take a drink and shift his weight in the chair, “One day I happened to see you two sparring. No disrespect, Davo, but you were fair—not real good, but not real bad. When I walked up, Hwúi said—”

“‘Ask Big Stump if he thinks of whales,’” Clines cut in, smiling. “I remember.”

“Remember your answer?” Gray questioned, starting to grin.

Clines laughed: “Yeah.”

“You said, ‘Hell no, asshole,’” Gray quoted with a laugh, “‘I’m trying to keep this slant-eyed Chinese bastard from knocking my damned head off.’”

They laughed until near tears.

After a few moments, Gray said: “That’s when I understood. Every time he said I performed poorly, I had been in a dream world thinking about whales or something. To, ‘be,’ means to center on the now—to enjoy the now. To just *be*.”

“Hmm,” Clines thought out loud.

“He told me that it would take me a long time to learn what came natural to you.”

This time, Clines was silent.

"You know," Gray added, "he didn't call you, 'Big Stump,' just because you reminded him of a sawed-off tree."

"Oh, so now you're telling me he thought I was dumb as a stump, too."

Gray laughed. "No, you buffoon. He thought you were well-grounded and connected. 'Like a mighty tree stump,' were his exact words."

"He told me it was because I was a wide, short ugly American."

"Well, there was that, too," Gray came back grinning.

Clines laughed.

"For the record," Gray added, "Hwúi thought you were one of his best accomplishments."

"Really?"

Gray nodded *yes*.

Clines stood, stretching his legs and taking another drink.

"So seriously," Clines said, "how are you doing?"

Gray thought about it a moment, looking out over the water: "I haven't learned to just *be*, yet."

Clines rested his weight on the railing. "What's on your mind? Gail? Ŝulok? What?"

"All of it's pretty fresh," Gray answered, looking at Clines. "Your two year old memories are my memories of a month or so ago."

"Gail's a fairly big chunk, I guess."

Gray nodded *yes*.

"Listen," Clines said drawing Gray's wandering gaze, "I don't pretend to understand what happened any more than you. No matter what she did, or why she did it—I believe she was always yours."

Gray barely nodded. "Yeah, well I was stupid enough to believe that, once."

"Of course it sounds stupid," Clines agreed. "But we were there. You were there. You know what you each felt."

Gray stood, moving over near Clines by the railing. "So what are you saying?"

Clines' sky blue eyes met his friend's hard dark eyes. "I'm saying living means maturing. I wouldn't knock Gail any more than you, but you know as well as I, her life was a series of conflicts and bad choices. She loved you, brother, but she never changed."

"I know this," Gray said, a little agitated.

"I know you know," Clines came back, equally direct. "I just think it's important for you to think it over."

Gray nodded in agreement. "You're right, Dave, you're right. I just wish my feelings would fall in line with what I'm supposed to be thinking."

"Well, there's one other thing you should know, too."

"Yeah?"

"She thinks you're dead."

Gray's eyes, having strayed out over the water, snapped around.

"I figured they didn't tell ya'. 'Man Dies in Crash.' It was only a local story in California, but she saw it—she called me and extended her sympathy."

"Burial service?" Gray asked.

Clines shook his head *yes*.

They looked at each other for several seconds.

"Don't look," Clines finally said, tossing his bottle into a wastebasket. "She stayed away two years and she's thought you were dead for two more."

Clines moved over and clasped his left hand on Gray's shoulder.

"Just relax?" Gray questioned. "Just... Just be?"

Clines' response was a shrug and then in a solemn voice he said: "After all the shit we've waded through, you know what I feared most?"

Gray waited.

"I feared I'd never have the chance to tell you what you mean to me."

"It's okay, Blake."

Clines shook his head, as if to say, *no, I need to tell you*. "When we were stuck in that pit with Hollander—remember that?"

The bloody picture flashed through Gray's mind. He saw the blood, the spikes, and the vomit—all of it. It was a flashback that he had never escaped. He nodded.

"I think about it now and then," Clines went on. "I have these flashbacks—it's like I'm there all over again—right there! If you hadn't been there, man, I—I—"

"It's okay," Gray reassured him.

Clines nodded, loosening his grip on Gray's shoulder. "All the books, documentaries, movies—and I swear I've seen 'em all—none of 'em are close enough."

"It always seemed it was us against the world," Gray commented.

"It was," Clines agreed, thinking of the numerous missions for which they had teamed-up. "Have you given any thought to work?"

Gray glanced down river. "Not much. I thought I might drop in on 1109, see if there's any field work that doesn't involve shooting people."

Clines smiled. "Well, Engineering Inc. has an opening for a partner. If you want it, it's yours on a silver platter."

Gray looked at Clines.

"I'd be honored," Clines answered the look. "Think it over for as long as you like."

"I'll chew on it for a while."

"Good." Clines picked up a cold slice of pizza. "I'm headed home."

"Take it easy."

"Yeah," Clines said. "How about lunch tomorrow?"

"Sure."

"Great. My office? Noon?"

"Done," Gray agreed.

Clines waved a tired hand and headed across the gangplank.

Gray watched him move across the dark dock. A few minutes later he saw the flash of a shiny car as Clines drove away.

Immersed in memories, Gray leaned on the boat's railing.

In the silence, in the dark, he wasn't alone.

9

Debbie's car came to a quiet stop. She looked at her watch for about the fifth time: it was 3:45 a.m. She wondered how she was going to explain this sudden urge. Shaking her head, she opened the door and stood. A moment of dizziness swept over her. After it passed she shut the door and moved across the road.

In the clear starlight the bobbing boats seemed to gleam. Occasional dock lamps illuminated spots down the length of the pier, creating day-glow patches of white paint in broken, dotted lines. She nervously smoothed her wrinkled blouse and made her way down the steps leading to the yacht.

Quietly looming in the night, the *Page Alexandra* gently rode the lazy lapping of the river. Debbie stood alongside the Elco Yacht, telling herself to turn back. To stop chasing. To quit believing.

She walked across the gangplank and onto the deserted deck. Under the canopy she saw a couple of empty chairs, a deserted ice cooler and the empty bottles of the past few hours. She sighed.

"Up early or late?" came a voice.

She whirled around, frightened.

"Shit," she gasped, seeing Gray in a housecoat. He had been standing on the other side of the deckhouse—next to the forward cabin. "You scared me."

He shrugged and turned. She followed him down the deck and into the cabin.

"I'm uh, up late," she answered at last.

"Oh."

She followed him into the galley area. He removed a small pistol from his pocket, sliding it into the breast pocket of a suit coat hanging over a chair. A larger gun and shoulder holster were draped over another chair.

"Were you going to shoot me?" she asked, trying to lighten what she felt was an awkward moment.

"Old habit," he said.

"I guess you're wondering why I'm here," she said. "I was in the neighborhood and—"

She halfway laughed, rubbing her hand over her tired face. "I'm making a fool of myself here."

He agreed with a nod, and moved past her. She followed him out of the deckhouse, up two steps and onto the open deck of the bow.

"I was with Sharon until Blake came back," she prattled on.

"They live together?"

"She stays over at his place a lot." She laid her purse on a small deck table. "I guess you guys had a lot to talk about, huh?"

He shrugged, leaning against the railing.

"Karns..."

He looked around.

"I... Shit, you know why I'm here."

He nodded, watching her move beside him.

"I know, I'm moving too fast, right?"

"Debbie..."

This time she waited.

He shook his head, dismissing the thought.

"What?" she finally asked.

"Yes," he said with resignation. "I'm not ready."

She looked into his face; the dark blue eyes were an unfathomable void. "What is it?"

"We went through this earlier. What would you like to hear?"

"I just want you to talk to me—to be open to possibilities..."

He looked at her, admiring the high cheekbones and pouting lips.

"I can't help what I'm feeling," she said. "And yeah, I'm throwing myself at you. Just talk to me—don't shut me out."

He didn't respond.

"Four years is a long time, Karns."

He looked out over the water.

“How much longer?”

He continued staring across the river. “Sometimes I forget she ever happened... I was looking at some pictures of her here on the yacht... She almost seems a stranger.”

Debbie moved closer. “What is it about her?” She realized frustration was creeping into her tone.

“I don’t know,” he answered.

“Don’t give me that shit,” she said quickly—too quickly.

He ignored her.

“Damn it, Karns—”

He glared at her. He didn’t know why Gail was so important. She wasn’t the first woman with whom he had been. He wanted to blame it on youth, but couldn’t—he had been in his thirties.

He snapped: “*What?*”

She saw the fury in his eyes now. It consumed her. Nothing she felt approached his controlled anger. She was uncertain how to respond.

He could see she was backing off—losing confidence.

“Karns—” she whispered, almost pleading.

He turned to go inside.

“Karns!” she said more firmly. “I’m not attacking you, I—”

He swept around suddenly—so suddenly, her wrists were in a vice-like grip before she realized he had moved. He yanked her down the steps and into the cabin.

As if by magic, the German automatic and sinister .38 semi-automatic pistols were brought out of nowhere. He pointed them away.

“See these?” he growled.

She nodded, shocked and cautious. She remembered Clines’ warning as she was leaving his apartment: *Be his friend first and you won’t have to be careful.*

“Every day I cleaned and loaded these guns,” Gray was saying. “Then I’d put one to my head. Well, I cleaned ‘em tonight and I still wanted to blow my brains out. That’s what I feel. I fought a damned war for a country that doesn’t give a shit. I have flashbacks that are as real as being there. I went through fucking hell—and Gail—shit, Gail...”

He paused, his eyes glaring. When he spoke, his voice was strangely subdued: "I still don't know why she was so important. I was young, maybe—but hell, I wasn't exactly a snot-nosed kid, was I?"

The guns were still there—his dark eyes were boring into her.

"Put away the guns," she said carefully.

They were inches apart, his eyes wandering. She could see he was searching for words, fighting the only enemy he was unequipped to handle—emotions.

"You're hurting," she said in a whisper. "You're angry. You're confused. You're lonely."

He dropped the pistols to his side.

They stood in silence for a moment. He took a breath then returned the guns to their holsters. She could see he had managed to repel the enemy once more.

"The best thing you can do," he said, his voice now tired, "is get as far away from me as you can...while you can."

He left her standing, knowing she wouldn't leave. He knew because she was too much like him.

Debbie watched him disappear down a dark passageway.

A sudden clap of thunder burst the air with such a tremendous force, Gray was thrust into reality with a painful rushing sensation. It was as though he were strapped to a locomotive streaking through a tunnel. His abrupt return to reality left him sweating in the bed.

He dropped his feet to the deck. Although he knew the time, he glanced to his watch. The Rolex hands glowed back 4:50.

He donned his robe from the nearby chair and mopped his forehead. Slipping into the robe he moved from the cabin and toward the small galley. Debbie was curled up on a divan in the deckhouse. She had tossed and turned until nearly losing the sheet covering her. One nude leg and hip glowed amid the shadows created by a dock lamp filtering through a pane of glass. Sleeping on her left side, her right arm was draped across her breasts and dangled in the shadows near the floor. He stared at her a few moments: she was incredibly beautiful.

He moved on and started for the refrigerator when a flash of lightning glinted off the .38 pistol hanging from the chair. He glanced through a nearby portal to see a mist of rain falling. The lightning flickered again, drawing his attention back to the .38. He moved over and sat down, pulling out the pistol and squeezing the weapon in his hand.

The cold silver-plated steel felt good.

"Yeah, it feels real good," said a voice.

Gray looked over to the other man—Jay Casper—sitting in the pit. Blake Clines and Thomas Hollander were crowded in with him. In the middle was the body of Mick Rand—wooden stakes piercing his body. Gray had already forced Rand's eyes closed.

"Jay?" Gray said. "You okay?"

"Fine," Casper said, staring at his own pistol: he had the silencer attached.

A flash of lightning highlighted their camouflage uniforms and the wadded sheet of paper Casper held.

"Bonnie's letter," Casper whispered, noticing Gray's look.

Gray's eyes went back to the pistol.

"It ought to say, 'Dear John,' instead of, 'Jay,'" Casper said.

"Take it easy, Jay," Gray whispered back.

"Ain't much point any more," Casper added while toying with the pistol. "We ain't gettin' out of here alive and even so, Bonnie don't care."

"Jay..."

Sitting at the table, Gray lifted the pistol to his head—but in the muddy pit it was Jay raising the gun to pull the trigger. A muffled thud followed and Casper's blood was everywhere.

Lightning flashed again and Gray had lowered the gun to stare at it. He was relieved to still be in the yacht's galley.

"Damn," he sighed. He wiped the sweat from his forehead and stood with the gun in his hand. Opening the refrigerator, he stared at the near empty shelves. He had long feared that he might—one day—flashback to those grim memories and never return to reality. The flashbacks came at will, day and night. One moment he was in the here and now, and then the next moment he was up to his nose in blood and gore. Dismissing the thoughts, he closed the refrigerator door and headed back to bed.

He stopped in the deckhouse again, looking at Debbie. With a sigh he changed his mind and sat in a rocking chair positioned by her head. He quietly rocked, firmly gripping the gun in his lap.

A blue haze of dim light fell into the deckhouse as another flash of lightning seeped out of the thunder above the yacht. Gray flickered his eyes to the portholes, a brief picture of Jay Casper in his mind. He looked back at Debbie.

Listening to the rain pelting the deck above, he reached out to feel the silky texture of her hair. After a moment, he leaned back in the chair, his grip on the gun loosening.

The dim light streaming through the deckhouse had seemed to take on a cool hue. The blue melancholy light played across the bulkhead; growing accustomed to the cabin—as though it was part of the cabin. Drawn back to Debbie, he thought she looked sad in her sleep and he wondered if she were dreaming. Even so—or perhaps, because so—her pouting lips were all the more enticing. Even in unguarded sleep, with hair gently draping over her shoulder, she was beautiful.

He sighed again, his eyes growing weary.

He remembered Debbie's words when she pulled him from the twisted car—her assurance everything would be safe. His eyes began to flutter shut. He relaxed his loose grip of the gun and his hand fell away.

He drifted into a peaceful sleep, never realizing the pistol was unloaded.

Barely discernible in the shadowy light, the bullets from his guns had spilled from Debbie's hand and to the carpet by the divan.

Part Two

THE EXPORT

June 30, The Present
Chicago, Illinois

10

Archer Commons was dead twice before the Foreign Intelligence Service realized he had slipped through their fingers.

He owed his escape, in part, to being nondescript. At 5' 10", 165 lbs., he traveled just about wherever he liked without attracting the least bit of attention. While his muscular physique required some effort to disguise in clothing, his mediocre gray eyes projected none of the captivating qualities possessed by his fictitious contemporaries. His sculpted build aside, he could usually pass for the run-of-the-mill average looking man. True to his name, he appeared absolutely common.

It was a blending of skills and effortless facades of Russian, Spanish, Italian —a virtual repertoire of nationalities—that gave him the edge he commanded in his occupation. Archer Commons was a spy—and not the ordinary, Johnny-come-lately type, either.

As one of the best green berets produced by the Armed Forces, Commons went to sleep under a hostile Nicaraguan night sky during the revolution in the 80s and awoke the next morning in a field hospital. He hadn't been injured; he wasn't sick. But he was one of the best, the "doctor" told him. The "doctor" also wanted to hire him for a particularly difficult mission in which the Central Intelligence Agency was interested. In exchange, Commons would be paid handsomely and have his choice of an honorable discharge or an increase in rank with all the pay and privileges thereto. Commons agreed, completed the mission and went home. But life at home had changed. Work for a man trained in the Special Forces—foreign intelligence and infiltration, among other talents—was scarce. Commons wasn't college educated—he was what they called a natural.

Then, out of the blue appeared the "doctor." From that day forward, the Chancellor steadily employed Commons. The pay was great, and the risk varied with each assignment.

His escape from the Commonwealth of Independent States, was the result of a postcard in an envelope he had received one week earlier. The postcard read:

> Have a nice trip and see the curio shops.
> Don't break the imports.
>
> —Chauncey

The envelope also included a photograph and an airline ticket to the Republic of Armenia, a never-ending political hotbed within spitting distance of Turkey and Iran.

The assignment was plain enough.

The remainder of the day Commons spent identifying the man in the photograph. Three days later, having learned the man was a CIA agent named Alister Marow, he settled into surveillance as he boarded a plane for Armenia.

While Commons wasn't one to split hairs over semantics, the presence of the Foreign Intelligence Branch—the KGB's replacement—in Armenia was a surprise. Proclaiming independence from the former Soviet Union during the August 1991 coup, Armenia was like the mythological god, Janus. Its one face was of a country following the example of Georgia and Moldovia, which drove toward democracy after the '91 coup. However Armenia's other face was of a country only paying lip service to democracy. Run by former conservative Communist Party leaders hiding from the pro-democratic changes in the central government of Moscow, Armenia fought the political separatism within its own body. Commons was most concerned about this second political face; the Foreign Intelligence Service, was another two-headed creature. It was supposed to have little resemblance to the KGB, and it had no business being in Armenia. Commons doubted the former and worried about the latter.

The political inconsistencies had no effect on Marow. A boorish man of Russian extraction, he was fluent in the native languages and wound up killing four Foreign Intelligence Service agents, bumping around several government weapons installations, and getting well sauced on vodka. He accomplished all of this in the span of a week. After having killed the first two agents, Marow returned to his rented room to find his luggage being ransacked by the woman he had previously picked up. Whatever her excuse, Marow found it wanting. He took her to bed, had his kicks and killed her. She turned out to be the third agent Marow finished off.

Promptly fading into the woodwork, Marow strangled the fourth and final agent and disappeared from sight—to everyone but Commons.

Marow spent four days on his assignment—whatever it was. The last two days he trekked across Turkey. In a small harbor town on the Mediterranean Sea, Marow boarded a boat waiting in the night. Commons watched the two men receive Marow by slaps on the back and warm handshakes. The boat cast off, and Commons turned to leave the dock. It was at that point, Commons discovered he had picked up his own tail. Forced to kill the man, he planted false papers on him in hopes of buying some time to leave the country.

With this in mind, he boarded a northbound train into Georgia, and from there he boarded a second train into Russia. One hundred miles down the rails, he killed yet another Foreign Intelligence Service agent—or at least that was what he seemed—and left a second set of false papers. Jumping from the train, he struck out on foot.

Five miles later he stumbled across a farmhouse and an old crop duster. Paying the farmer, he was flown some fifty miles further east from where he walked into a town and shelled out bus fare for a trip back west.

Once again arriving by foot at the farmer's house, he lay in the cropless field, waiting for the inevitable Foreign Intelligence Service to show up and question the old Russian. It was nearly an hour later when two black sedans came speeding along the road. They skidded to a stop in front of the house and two dark-suited men pounded at the door while two others loitered outside. Commons was surprised it had taken them this long. He had seen several similar cars around the countryside all day. He wondered if the officials had attempted to reduce the area of investigation by using the telephone. Not that it would have helped them in this case—the farmer must have spent all his money on gas and plane repairs; there were no phone lines running to the worn down house.

Within minutes they were rushing from the house. The two cars spun around and thundered down the dirt road. Commons could see the dust thrown up for a half-mile as the cars sped eastward, their shapes fading into the darkening landscape.

Sneaking across the field, Commons slipped into the old barn where the decrepit plane was kept. He lodged the last of his Russian money in the warped barn doors—more money than the farmer/aviator would see in his whole life—and pushed the plane out.

Moments later Commons turned the plane northward and settled back for a night flight within spitting distance of the ground. He had no idea how extensive the search for him was, or if it included air support. That being the case, he figured it was safer to avoid possible radar contact.

By morning light he flew over the Bering Sea and sighted an American oil freighter, complete with helicopter. Buzzing the ship several times assured their attention. He cut the plane engine and ditched the old bird in the chilling water.

Once hauled aboard, he flashed CIA identification and ordered two things: a flight to the nearest U.S. naval ship and a dry set of clothes.

On the evening of the same day, Commons was flown to a position some 300 miles southeast of Iceland where he landed on a U.S. naval aircraft carrier.

Producing Naval Intelligence identification, he was flown to a remote airfield in Greenland from where he was whisked to Canada. The following morning saw him on a commercial airline flight bound for Chicago.

When a thoroughly worn out Archer Commons arrived at his hotel, a message was waiting with instructions to be executed that evening. So after showering, shaving, and using a, “make-up kit,” for just such occasions, he took a taxi to a nearby shopping mall. He walked into one of the larger department stores and to a sunglasses display. And there, before God and country, shoplifted a pair of sunshades.

Two policemen, handcuffs, a reciting of his rights and a trip to the city jail later, Commons was booked, given a phone call and locked in a cell.

11

Commons had been sitting an hour when he heard footfalls and the guard appeared.

"Your lawyer," the guard announced, unlocking the door to admit a woman sharply dressed in a suit. Her shoulder-length brown hair was held back by an ivory hairpin.

"Call when you're ready," the officer said and locked the door. He vanished down the hall.

"Do you have anything to say?" the woman said in a soft voice.

He smiled. "It's perfectly safe. No video or audio."

She sat to his side: "How are you, Arch?"

"If it wasn't for these strange meeting places, I'd be fine."

"I have only a few questions," she said steadily, opening her briefcase "First, was Mr. Marow followed before breaking into the Armenian installations?"

While Commons had yet to report one syllable of his mission, he had long ago stopped being amazed at how the Chancellor was "all knowing." Commons suspected that more than one Chancellor agent worked some of his assignments.

"No one followed him until after he had broken into the third complex," Commons answered the woman. She was an assistant to the Chancellor. "And that was actually in Georgia. That's when he picked up a foxy whore—Foreign Intelligence. Of course, I'm sure you guys already know that."

"No, we didn't," she corrected, pursing her soft lips. "Are you saying the Foreign Intelligence Branch had agents in Armenia and Georgia?"

"Yeah, and they were acting like the old KGB."

"Perhaps they were actually members of whatever agency Armenia is currently using."

"Nope," Commons came back. "Every one of these guys had false ID, but they were Foreign Intel officers, alright. Everything from how they operated to the threads they wore verified it."

"I see."

"I make it a point to check on who I'm forced to kill. And between Marow and myself, there are six dead Foreign Intel agents."

"You weren't to harm anyone," she said firmly.

"Excuse me all to hell," Commons raised his voice. "I'm so damned sorry I didn't let the little imports kill me first!"

"What happened?" she asked, ignoring his outburst.

"I don't know, exactly. I've not seen that sort of thing since the KGB went under. None of it made sense. There was nothing there to protect. All the installations were empty. Absolutely no traffic in or out. But Intel agents were all over the place. It was almost like they also happened to be there looking around."

"When Marow arrived at the boat on the Turkey coast," she continued, holding out two photographs, "are these the two men who met him?"

"One of them," he answered, nodding toward the left picture.

"Just one?" she said, sounding surprised.

Commons smiled.

"What about this man?" she asked, holding up the other photo.

"What about 'em?"

"You did not see this man?"

"Look Carol, if you don't believe me, ask Marow."

"Mr. Marow is dead," she said calmly.

"How?"

"Gunned down while on the boat with these two men."

"Not with that one he wasn't," Commons snapped as he shot a finger at the right picture

"A fishing trawler found these bodies on the boat. The CIA identified both of their agents, and the Navy identified their man."

"The Navy?"

"One of the men was a Navy SEAL."

"Then they weren't previously acquainted, right?"

"Mr. Crenshaw, the Navy SEAL, had not met the other two," she answered.

Commons wasn't surprised. Spooks often carried "need-to-know" and "compartmentalize" policies to the extreme. Hence the need for passwords in the field, where agents frequently met for the first time.

"However," Carol continued, "the fact is you had to see these two men meet Mr. Marow in Turkey."

"No," Commons came back, "The fact is a fishing trawler may have found those three in the boat, but that doesn't mean the same three left Turkey. Someone pulled a switch."

"In the middle of the ocean, Arch?" she asked maintaining her calm voice. "And with three highly trained operatives present?"

"They were trained," Commons countered, "not bulletproof. The one I saw isn't in your pictures, but he was there in Turkey."

"What do you propose?"

"If none of the agents were aware of the others physical appearance, I would think someone broke security, killed the Navy SEAL and took his place. After knocking off the other two, he took Crenshaw off ice and flew the coop."

She studied him a moment, closed her briefcase and stood. "Guard!"

"When do I get out?"

"As soon as I leave," she responded, "the police will learn that the sales clerk, who reported the theft, didn't realize you had already purchased the shades—he was a new part-time employee."

"Glad I picked expensive ones," he said with a smile.

Ignoring his remark, she was spared a parting shot by the arrival of the guard.

It was almost an hour to the minute when the guard appeared and unlocked the cell. Commons was led to the claims desk where he signed an illegible scrawl for a signature of the false name he had given.

When he returned to the street, the evening lights were just coming on. He considered going for a drink, but the exhaustion suddenly swept over him and he opted for a cab home.

"Well at least I got something out of the deal," he chuckled to himself, removing the elastic-like derma-skin fingerprints he had utilized from his make-up kit. Once applied, the "artificial fingerprints" were virtually undetectable and provided a variety of identities—some real, others fictional.

He put on his new sunshades and hailed a cab.

12

Commons sat at his hotel breakfast table, an early morning scotch on the rocks remedy for the blahs sitting to the side of an opened newspaper. As was his occupational habit, he scanned the classified ads over his morning eggs. He had expected at least another week of inactivity, but a help-wanted advertisement directed otherwise. It read:

WANTED
Chaucey Inc. wants Archery
Expert. Locate & ID Russian
Exports. Start immediately.

He swallowed the last of his drink and stacked the dishes on a tray for room service.

After showering, shaving and a brief dialing stint on the telephone, he was in a rented car. By 10:30 he arrived at the apartment of a stunningly attractive black artist he had met a year earlier.

After mixing him a well-diluted drink, they sat on the sofa, and she listened to a description of the man Commons saw in Russia. When he finished the narrative, she picked up a drawing pad that was resting on the floor.

"Well, it isn't the most thorough description you've ever given me," she said with an airy English accent. "But I'll see what I can do."

As she drew, he moved over to the sliding-glass door leading onto a balcony.

"I know it was dark," she said suddenly, "but would you prefer brown or black hair?"

"Well, he's a bad guy," Commons mused.

"Black it is," she said with a grin.

He walked back and sat on the sofa. He noticed that her white satin gown snugly fitted her taut breasts and fell away into her lap. He enjoyed looking at her and often daydreamed about an affair. "I guess I should have called first."

"It isn't a bother," she assured him, placing a slender hand on his knee. She returned to sketching. "I've been sleeping in too late as it is."

"How's that boyfriend working out?" he asked in a conversational tone.

"Which one?"

"Uh, I think his name is Tony."

"I dropped him three guys ago," she answered with a slight smirk, still intent on the drawing. "They're really bozos, you know?"

"Who?"

"The jerks in the bar scene."

He shrugged.

"The last guy I went out with twice. He wanted to lay me, wed me and meet his momma—all in one night!"

He laughed.

"I even considered—" She paused, briskly stroking the pad, "dating you."

Caught off guard, he looked up to her passive face.

"Oh yeah," she answered his betraying expression—but never looking from her drawing. "I think you think about it, too."

She glanced at him.

"You're sharper than I gave you credit for."

"Thank you," she came back, holding up the sketchpad. "How's this?"

Staring from the paper was a squat face accented by a sparse mustache and a tangle of hair.

"That's him," he answered.

"Well, there you are," she said, tearing out the page and handing it over. "Have you any idea who he is?"

"No, I call 'em the Export."

"I hope it helps," she said, standing up with him.

"Time will tell. What do I owe you? The boss is paying."

She straightened up to her full five foot seven inches. “I’ll settle for a kiss.”

Again his face showed he was caught off guard.

“We could keep pretending we’re not attracted to each other,” she offered as an alternative.

“That’d be really dumb, wouldn’t it?”

“It would be in Saint Lucia,” she replied, referring to where she was born.

“Oh?”

She had moved over to him. “The island is so romantic it is difficult not to fall in love.”

He leaned down, giving her a tentative kiss on the cheek.

“I guess that will do—for starters.” She interlocked her arm with his and escorted him to the door.

“Thanks,” he mumbled.

“Any time,” she responded, opening the door.

“Uh, listen,” he stammered, “I was thinking... Well...”

“Any day would be fine with me.”

He gave a sheepish look. “7:30 tomorrow night?”

“I’ll be here,” she said with a warm smile.

He lightly kissed her again—on the lips this time—and turned away.

She smiled while watching him walk down the flight of stairs, whistling. She had never heard him whistle.

From there he drove to two local computer stores and entered with the story of being a computer programmer searching for a powerful home system. Asking for IBM compatible computers he operated the same system in each store.

In the first store he connected the computer to the internal modem and dialed a dedicated line into the CIA. Several codes later he had accessed a computer in the Central Intelligence Agency.

The computer responded and five minutes later he printed the CIA’s information regarding Alister Marow and his last assignment.

In the second store, he logged into a computer belonging to Naval Intelligence. In each instance he left saying he would think about the purchase. The salesmen were in such dazes concerning what had just passed before their eyes that they merely waved a half-hearted farewell.

Secretly laughing, Commons steered his car back onto the highway. Whatever the salesmen suspected, they would never know for sure. In each case Commons had deleted the computer's two types of temporary files, the history files, the cache files, the file content data, the print log and server log. He had further taken the precaution of using bubble ink jet printers in order to avoid leaving any image on a printer drum or dot matrix ribbon. Even the stores' phone bills would fail to reflect the long distance calls. Commons had simply dialed a phone number arranged to bill calls to a third party. In this case, the credit card division of a local bank would absorb the charges. For obvious reasons, they never questioned such brief, out-of-state phone calls—not to mention being unable to investigate the numbers even if they so desired.

That night Commons dropped off to sleep with several pages of computer printouts draped over him and his recliner. He was content in knowing he needed another slice of information—a slice about which he knew absolutely nothing. He required satellite surveillance records of Atlantic ship movements.

His contentment wasn't with ignorance, but in the fact he knew from whom to get the information.

Jim Austiff.

PART THREE

THE STOPGAP

July 10, The Present
Washington, DC

13

Austiff arrived at the Professional Building at nine o'clock. Once on the fourth floor he headed to his office.

He breezed through the gold lettered glass entry door, pausing to gather several folders from an auburn-haired girl sitting behind the name plate, "Jann Cassell."

"Ms. Kegley wanted you to drop by her office as soon as you arrived," she said in a chipper voice. Her hazel colored eyes had always struck Austiff's fancy. Instead of drab, her eyes seemed to sparkle. And any sparkle in his life was welcome.

"Thank you, Jann," Austiff mumbled and moved down the hall. A few feet later he glanced to his left to see the perpetually empty second waiting area.

He moved further down the hall, passing the usual people at computers and books. A clique of employees had gathered in the small break-room to the left—they were the actual law office personnel.

In a heated debate over law, no doubt, he thought to himself with a smile. Every time he had been in there, he had caught the end of someone damning attorneys to hell or some such. Although acquainted with some of the personnel, the majority could have been green extra-terrestrial for all he knew. And according to them, all attorneys were probably extraterrestrial.

He opened Kate Kegley's office door and stuck his head in. It was decorated in a range of earth tones accented by tasteful dashes of color. Kegley was reclining at her desk.

"Good Morning, Jim," she said.

"What can I do for you?" Austiff came back.

A dishwater blonde that Austiff had failed to notice rose from one of the couches in the office.

"You could tell us who John Wilson is," the blonde cut in.

Austiff opened the door wider, permitting him in. The second woman was Dana Masters. She had been the OCSTO Security Director during the last 18 years and possessed a timeless quality thought reserved for women like Elizabeth Taylor, Raquel Welch and Sophia Loren. She was the, "owner," of a company called Corporate Investigations. Like most of the businesses in the Professional Building, the first floor Security/ Investigation Company was another hatchling beneath Austiff's wing.

"Why, Dana," Austiff exclaimed, "you've been wandering around the personnel files haven't you?"

"And the War Department, Army, CIA, FBI, NIA—"

"I get the idea."

"John Wilson—" she started, then pointed toward Austiff's office, "or at least that John Wilson, doesn't exist."

"Oh," Austiff said, although wittier replies came to mind.

"As Security Director," Dana said, "I'm concerned for your safety. When Mr. Wilson popped up yesterday, I couldn't find anything on him. Who is he?"

"An old friend."

"Perhaps he's not—"

"Dana," Austiff interrupted, "you're an excellent Security Director, but trust me, John is no threat."

"Sir," she pressed, moving closer. Her heels brought her to 5 ft. 9, just an inch short of Austiff. He could see she was choosing her words carefully. "It is odd timing that this old friend of yours, who doesn't exist, should show up when relations with the Arabs are at their most sensitive."

"Don't worry."

"Not to mention the missing serum."

"Oh, yeah," Austiff came back with an exaggerated shake of his head, "he not only stole the serum, but also returned to give us a shot at catching him!"

Masters sighed: "The truth is, giving highly classified information concerning satellite surveillance of ship movements in the Atlantic is very irregular."

Austiff shifted the weight of the folders to his left arm. "Maybe I'm just getting old and stupid. Hell, tomorrow I'm giving out brochures on Blake's work with our EMS craft."

"Jim—"

His deadpan expression abated her plea.

"You're the Director," Dana conceded.

Austiff turned to Kate Kegley. "Was this meeting for her, or did you want something?"

"I wanted to let you know we haven't found the missing serum," Kegley responded.

"Any clues?"

"It was someone on the night watch," Dana offered.

"With high clearance," Austiff added.

"That seems to be the case," Dana confirmed.

"Of course, no one on the night watch has a high clearance," Austiff said. "Which is why they're on night watch."

He turned to leave, but stopped: "Oh, Kate, I'm taking an extra hour for lunch so you might plan around it."

"Thanks."

"You don't mind, do you?" he questioned Dana with a hint of playful sarcasm.

"No. I'll be sure your wife has plenty of warning."

"Touché," Austiff said, and left the office.

"That was a low blow," Kegley commented.

"He's got a low wife," Dana returned, opening the door and waving bye.

Austiff's private office had been expanded during the last several years and now included an outer office for his Adjutant. Although his own office door remained, he had changed the route to his office to include the Adjutant's office. This was more out of unspoken affection than necessity.

The Director's Adjutant was Laura Phinor.

And naturally there were rumors. The law office personnel thought he and his Administrative Assistant were seeing one another on the sly. Not that they minded. Between Laura Phinor and the gossip column reports of Austiff's wife, the office had plenty to distract them when lawyer jokes waned.

Austiff walked into Laura's office and stopped by her desk.

"Morning, Jim," she greeting with her gentle voice. Laura Phinor had matured to her mid-thirties without the loss of beauty.

"Morning, Laura. How was your weekend?"

"All right." she answered, pushing up her glasses. They were blue frames today.

"Thought you were looking forward to your son dropping in on you."

"Well, thanks to you, he won't be back for another month."

Austiff looked confused.

"That Navy captain was so impressed with your letter he had Steve transferred to ship duty."

"Well Steve's a fine young man. He deserved a break."

"I know," she said, abandoning her facade of anger. "And I really want to thank you."

"Really," Austiff came back, "the boy deserved it."

"Well, I'll take you out for lunch or something. Fair?"

"Fair," he agreed, and moved on into his office.

Laying the folders on his desktop, he withdrew the bug monitor from his pocket. Slowly walking around the room, he performed his ritual debugging routine.

He completed the circle, pocketed the device and moved to the wet-bar for his next order of business: a glass of rum. The glass filled, he sat down at his desk and began pouring over the files and a stack of yesterday's transactions.

Opening the top-most file, he set aside an Office confirmation for a night flight to Florida. The next file contained a report of the tropical storm forming just outside the Gulf of Mexico. The faxed report included copies of weather analyses from the Oklahoma Storm Prediction Center and the Miami, Florida National Tropical Prediction Center.

Along with Flight Advisories, the report concluded with impending doom to the on-going mission in Florida. Signed by the Projects Director, Blake Clines, the report suggested yet another delayed launch of the new flying sub built by Engineering Inc.

A quiet pulse drew Austiff's attention to the lighted **409** line of his phone.

He lifted the phone and pressed the flashing button.

"Yes," he said into the receiver. He listened a few seconds. "Certainly, we're on our way."

He switched to another line and waited for the voice of his Adjutant.

"Laura, I'll be in conference for a bit. Take any messages and have any appointments wait. If I run too late, keep me an hour open for lunch. Yes, that's correct, thanks."

He dropped the phone into the cradle, swallowed a gulp of rum and left the office through his private door. Just down the hall he tapped Kegley's office door and stuck his head in.

"Chancellor," he said with a note of urgency.

Kate Kegley, with the phone to her ear, looked up and nodded.

"Listen," she said into the receiver, "something just came up. I'll call you back... Yes, right, bye."

The phone went down and she left the office with Austiff.

They moved down the hall, past the murmuring office workers and through the door marked, **1109**. The outer office was an area of 12x15 feet. A young woman at a word processor looked up with a smile while continuing to type. She was Archer Commons' "lawyer."

"Hello, Mr. Austiff," she greeted, "Ms. Kegley."

"Can we go on in, Carol?"

She glanced to the copy from which she was typing then back to Austiff: "Certainly. He's expecting you."

"Thanks," Kegley said and they moved through one more door.

14

The Chancellor's office was dark.

Heavy blood-red drapes covered the four windows, screening away daylight. The matching carpet seemed to absorb Austiff's feet as he moved into the room, all the while fighting the urge to melt into the couch sitting to one side. The atmosphere induced a desire for sleep. The main lights were dark, replaced by four freestanding lamps glowing from the room's corners. Although the illumination wasn't weak, the 18x18-foot room seemed dim. Austiff was never sure if the rich dark colors drank the light, or if there was a genuine need for more. The one well-lit spot was the desktop beneath the ever-polished banker's lamp. Beyond its green glowing globe, the room swallowed light.

Austiff and Kegley were nearly to the chairs before realizing the Chancellor had company. Archer Commons peered up from the left of the four chairs facing the Chancellor's expansive desk.

"Morning, John," Austiff greeted.

"Jim," Commons returned with a smile.

The Chancellor, standing at a corner file cabinet, moved from the shadows to his desk. His white hair almost glowed against the dark backdrop of the office. Even his gray, pin-striped suit seemed black by comparison.

"Good Morning, Jim," the Chancellor said to Austiff and then looked to Kegley: "Ms. Kegley."

They sat down.

"I understand you have a few questions concerning Mr. Wilson," the Chancellor said to Kegley.

"Well," she said with hesitation, "we just didn't know if he was a security risk."

"Yes," the Chancellor said.

She wasn't sure if he agreed or only acknowledged her opinion.

The Chancellor leaned back in his chair. He said, "Mr. Wilson seems an incongruous element, because he is."

"Excuse me?"

The Chancellor gave a brief and rare indication of a smile. "It's rather lengthy. Suffice it to say that Mr. Wilson's kind are the oil in the engine. Without them everything grinds to a stop."

She looked to Commons, unable to fathom him or the Chancellor's meaning.

"He works exclusively for me; no one else. He is to receive your full cooperation."

"Yes, Sir."

"And Kate?"

"Yes?"

"Outside this room, you know nothing more about him than when you came in here."

"Yes, Sir," she responded, uncomfortable under the Chancellor's intense green eyes. She also realized Commons—who she still knew as John Wilson—must have arrived with the Chancellor by way of the rooftop heliport. That was the only way into the Chancellor's office without passing an Office security checkpoint and several monitors.

"We may have a problem developing," the Chancellor addressed them both. "There are enough of Kate's, 'security risks,' to warrant our immediate attention.

"Jim, what do you know of the information you gave John yesterday?"

"Content?" Austiff asked.

The Chancellor nodded.

"There was an obvious hole in the data available," Austiff answered.

"Meaning?"

"'Data unavailable,' can mean a lot of things."

"Suppose it meant satellite failures," the Chancellor offered.

"Considering that's practically impossible under normal circumstances, I'd say it meant someone would have had to use a fairly sophisticated jamming device."

"Who?"

"We're to believe someone in the CIS," Austiff answered with a knowing smile, meaning the Commonwealth of Independent States.

"I don't mean to be a wet rag," Kegley interrupted, "but I haven't the foggiest idea what you guys are talking about."

The Chancellor shifted in his leather chair, directing his attention to Kegley: "Some months ago there were numerous satellite failures over the CIS. Within hours the failure spread to a corridor over the Atlantic Ocean. Any orbital satellite entering these areas stopped functioning until clear of the regions. They not only stopped transmitting data, but also stopped receiving it. The problem wasn't discovered until a CIA employee attempted to run some sort of geological program through a NASA satellite. To shorten a long story, nothing but weather satellites are working in the mid-Atlantic region. Alert status for the area has been stepped-up and regular reconnaissance flights have been increased."

"And?" Kegley questioned.

"Nothing," the Chancellor came back. "The only activity is a highly publicized launching of a flying sub by the Office of Naval Research."

Which, everyone in the room knew, was an OCSTO cover story.

"I suppose everyone is claiming ignorance?" Kegley prompted. She didn't have to mention that, "everyone" really meant she suspected one of the former Soviet bloc countries.

"Legitimately, as it turned out," the Chancellor confirmed, surprising Kegley. "The various states of the CIS are as much in the dark as we are. The blackout area has also spread to a fairly confined region of Mexico, as well. The Mexico area is over some pretty rough terrain and recon planes haven't found anything there, either. We sent ground teams to both countries. The Mexico team vanished and the Russian team was executed. They were supposed to have vanished too, but a fluke prevented their boat from sinking like it had been rigged to."

"What sort of fluke?" Kegley asked, suspecting a feign.

"It drifted onto a sandbar," the Chancellor answered.

"I take it we're not really suspecting this to have been coordinated by any of the former Soviet States?" Austiff questioned.

The Chancellor nodded for Commons to take over.

"We hope not," Commons answered. "I followed one of the Company's men assigned to the CIS. Oddly, Russian Intelligence agents were thicker than flies."

"What's odd about that?" Kegley questioned.

"It's a political thing, really," Commons explained. "We were in Armenia, which puts on a democratic face but is really the seat for former communist party members—at least at the moment. The Foreign Intelligence Service wouldn't have such a presence in Armenia unless they were there covertly."

"Excuse my ignorance of Russian government," Kegley said, "but I don't understand. I thought their biggest problem now was organized crime."

"That's perfectly normal," the Chancellor cut in. "Beginning in the late 1990s the news began focusing on the Russian Mafia—as if all the cold war hardliners suddenly died or disappeared. Don't believe that for a second."

Kegley merely nodded.

"If it makes you feel any better," the Chancellor added, "even the boys at Langley haven't been able to sort out all the changes over there."

"I guess that puts me in good company," Kegley said, realizing the Chancellor wouldn't think her an idiot when even the CIA at Langley didn't have a clue.

"At any rate," Commons continued, "the independent Russian countries have tried damned hard to get rid of any vestige of the old regime. Part of that plays into the theory that the Foreign Intelligence Service wouldn't put agents in the State of Armenia—that would be like us putting CIA snipers in another country. Of course, on the other hand, everybody and their damned dog is likely to show up in Armenia. And those few members from the ousted communist party that are hiding there would sing, 'Yankee Doodle Dandy,' if it helped them get back the power."

"That all sounds pretty iffy," Kegley observed.

"It is," Commons agreed. "But those former party members want to keep a low profile—they don't want the attention inherent to the presence of the Foreign Intelligence Service. So we believe they were there for the same reason as we were—searching either for some kind of jamming station or something worth hiding."

"So who executed the team?" Kegley asked.

Commons handed them copies of the Export's picture. "He's the only clue."

"And you don't know who he is?" Austiff asked the obvious.

"Correct," Commons answered. "He passed himself off as one of the team."

"How?" Kegley asked.

"The team members were not previously acquainted," the Chancellor answered.

"The team left by boat with that man on board," Commons continued. "When they failed to rendezvous with a ship at sea, a three day search ended when the crew of a fishing trawler found the boat and the team shot to death—minus this man. Autopsies confirmed the time of death at around the same time as when I last saw them alive. The third team member was a Navy SEAL with the responsibility of providing the transportation. Being the odd man out, I figure it was his security that was first compromised. He was probably killed by this man, who then stuffed his body below deck and pretended to be him."

"No clue as to who he is?" Kegley questioned.

"None. We've nicknamed him, 'the Export.'"

"The Atlantic ship movements you requested," Austiff said. "An attempt to find some sort of tie-in?"

Commons nodded.

"And it gets better," the Chancellor added. "We had a tip that led to a yacht full of Russian weapons and cocaine anchored in the Gulf of Mexico."

The Chancellor handed folders to Austiff and Kegley. They opened the folders to see photographs of the yacht as well as the seized crates of guns and cocaine.

"I'm lost," Austiff admitted. "How does this fit in?"

"The tip was from a source which I have next to a known gun runner and drug dealer," the Chancellor said. "The dealer in question may be trying to open a line of business with someone in the CIS."

"And...?" Austiff pressed.

"That's the general dilemma," Commons commented.

"We don't know if these two separate things are connected," the Chancellor explained. "If our dealer was opening a line of business to the CIS, that would explain the presence of the guns and drugs in the yacht. It could explain the blackout of satellites and the presence of the Foreign Intelligence agents in Armenia."

Austiff dropped the folder to his lap. "Now how in the hell did you get to that, Robert?"

Surprised, Kegley glanced to Austiff. She had never heard anyone speak to the shadowy man across the desk in such a tone. And she certainly had never heard the Chancellor called, 'Robert.'

"Drug trafficking in the former USSR is reaching an all time high," the Chancellor responded calmly. "A definite structure of organized crime is in place as well. Throw in a powder-keg of politics, truckloads of surplus war machines and weapons—it's not only a free-for-all, but also a crime lord's dream. Access to military hardware—satellites included—isn't a grand leap in theory."

"Is this the only evidence we have?" Austiff asked, looking over the photographs. He was still trying to process a drug-runner tied to satellites

"Yes," he answered with a nod.

"Kind of seems—thin."

"Don't forget," Kegley put in, "the satellites—"

"Which could be the problem rather than hiding one," Austiff interrupted with a glance at Kegley then back to the Chancellor.

"I realize the satellite failures and the Mexico yacht may not be related," the Chancellor admitted. "But if they are I'm sure you comprehend the implications."

Kegley smiled sheepishly: "I'm afraid I don't. I mean, I'm still a little unsure of this satellite connection to drug trafficking. You actually think someone could jam the satellites just to cover up smuggling? That's pretty high-tech."

"Oh it's possible," the Chancellor answered. "And the answer as to who could do it is frightening."

"Take your pick," Commons added. "New government, old government, organized military crime—just to name a few."

The Chancellor continued: "You've got to realize that satellite coverage isn't just limited to what you're used to seeing on the TV weather forecast. We're talking about real time satellites capable of reading postage stamps from space."

"'Real time,'" Kegley echoed, knowing exactly what the Chancellor had meant even before he had explained it.

"As clear as reruns of M.A.S.H. and as immediate as a snap," the Chancellor answered, snapping his fingers for effect. "All our agencies depend on those satellites. With all the arms and equipment floating around in the CIS, certain people would pay dearly to be able to jam those satellites."

"So if illegal arms and drugs start flowing from the CIS into Mexico," Austiff said slowly, looking at the Chancellor, "no one would notice at first. The economy is all but shot and... Well, we're talking about a massive influx of drugs which could be bought for the price of bubblegum and spill over into Texas before anyone suspected a thing."

"That would be the first likely place," the Chancellor clarified. "But if it gets that close, planes will be delivering it to anywhere in America."

Kegley felt a chill pass over her. "My God, you're talking about a complete economic failure in Mexico and narcotics like manna from heaven."

"Exactly," the Chancellor intoned.

"The street price would drop like a rock," Commons said. "You think drug-related crime is bad now? If this is anywhere near true, we haven't seen anything."

Kegley looked dazed: "I guess DEA is in on this?"

"Yes," the Chancellor answered. "The technical implications and the other alternatives are the reason we're involved."

"So you see," Commons added "We may have a lot more on our hands than some dead satellites."

"That's why you two are here," the Chancellor said. "I want to know if anything is in Mexico, and I need your help. If satellites were jammed in the CIS, then the jamming stations were there. But jamming over Mexico, had to be done from Mexico, and unlike the CIS, that's our backyard."

"What about your drug and gun runner?" Kegley asked, echoing Austiff's private thoughts. "Drag his ass in and pick his brains."

"I'm watching that very closely," the Chancellor said. "We don't have any evidence, and I don't want to touch that yet. That aspect is something with which the Office need not be concerned."

"What about a stealth plane for Mexico?" Austiff questioned.

"The Company," the Chancellor said, referring to the CIA, "tried that and never got its plane or pilot back. That's why I've been asked to give it a shot—and that's why I'm asking you. I want the *Tiger-3*."

Austiff furrowed his brow. "The Florida launch is just a test run."

"I know," the Chancellor conceded. "But no one really knows the potential of the *TG-3*. I want to utilize that while it's still an unknown."

"If something runs foul, there'll be some hot Arabs on our hands."

"Investors can be pacified," the Chancellor countered. "Besides, if they knew about the things they aren't getting, they'd be a lot hotter than a screw-up this problem will cause—and you're already chancing that."

Austiff conceded with a slight smile. "I'll draw up the best approach for the *TG-3* and apprise Blake of the new parameters immediately—uh, you realize we can't replace the test pilot with a professional?"

The Chancellor nodded he knew. "Just make sure they understand the importance of this mission. I want every kind of recording and image that little sub can take."

"You got it."

"Anything else?" the Chancellor queried.

There wasn't.

The Chancellor gave an almost imperceptible nod, indicating the meeting was over.

The Director and the Deputy Director left the office.

15

The purring of a phone cut through the dark mist and Sarah Austiff opened her eyes believing she had fainted from hyperventilation.

"It's about a 15 minute drive," she heard Kalvin Reedy's voice say from the other room.

A quick inventory reminded her she was nude, face down and spread-eagled across the family's teakwood dining table, her limbs securely fastened with nylon ropes. Supporting her hips, an over-stuffed sofa pillow caused her buttocks to protrude above her head and feet. The position wasn't uncomfortable, she mused, nor undesirable. She was concerned, however, that Kalvin had answered the phone.

"Yeah," his voice drifted from the Den. "I'm about to give it a real test run. We'll see how potent this serum really is... Quit your bitch'in. It's just something to keep 'em runnin' in circles—I thought I'd get a little fun out of it, that's all."

There was a silence and Sarah looked around the room, her eyes roaming over her B.A. degree, her daughter's photo and a picture of her winning the hometown beauty contest eons ago.

Hair styles sure were strange then, she mused.

"Great. I'm ready," she heard Reedy say, followed by the phone dropping into the cradle. She turned her head to see him sauntering into the living room.

The perpetually grimy smile, sparse mustache and messy hair never changed. Kalvin Reedy looked the same as the day Archer Commons first saw him in Turkey.

"I thought you were going to undress," Sarah said, noticing his wrinkled T-shirt and faded blue jeans.

"I did," he said.

"Oh," she mumbled suddenly, seeing him nude.

"Your husband's on the way, just like we planned."

She chuckled: "I can't believe he thought I really wanted to reconcile our differences."

"He's an optimist," Reedy said.

"Yeah, well... It only takes him a short while to get here. You better untie me."

"It's okay, he won't mind."

The absolute absurdity of the statement was overwhelming—but she couldn't help but believe it. She tossed her head of long red hair to the side. "Are you sure?"

"Positive," he answered, moving to her and setting a black bag on the table.

She strained at her bindings to look. "You're using the bag I gave you."

"Of course," he said noticing her smile. "And I've modified your favorite toy."

She watched as he pulled out several assorted devices, all of which they had used before. Then he pulled out an object with which she was very familiar. It was bullet shaped and about fifteen inches long, not including a rubber handgrip with what appeared to be buttons on it.

"Modified it?" she asked.

"You'll see," he said nonchalantly, and laid it aside while pulling a large knife out. "By the way, I brought a friend with me today."

"Who?"

"Bob," he answered, pulling a name out of the air. "He's behind you."

She looked around to see an average sized man in a suit.

"He's black," Reedy described.

She realized thinking he was white had been a silly notion.

"He's about seven feet tall," Reedy went on.

She now saw that the man was towering above her.

"Oh yes, and he's built like Mr. Universe and naked as a Jaybird."

"Oh," she said under her breath, her eyes wandering down the large man's body. "God."

"He's saying that he's been waiting for you," Reedy said.

"I've been waiting for you," Bob said.

"I don't think I can handle that much," she said.

"He's climbing on the table," Reedy described.

Sarah felt his body touching her.

"He's saying he wants the same thing I always want," Reedy added.

Sarah heard Bob repeat Reedy.

"I can't," she gasped, "I think he's too big."

"He is," Reedy confirmed.

"Wait—please—"

"It's going in," Reedy said, watching her face.

"No, wait," she said frantically, "wait—"

She felt an explosion of pain jolt up her spine, causing her to gasp for air.

"Of course," Reedy went on in his same tone, "somehow or other you're not going to pass out—but the pain is still unbearable."

She opened her mouth to scream but could only gasp for air as she felt Bob's weight thrust into her.

Reedy moved to her side, brandishing the long knife.

"Oops," he exclaimed without inflection, dropping the knife to the tabletop where it stuck. "God, Sarah, sorry about cutting off your nipple like that."

Jerking back and forth, she glanced down to see a pool of blood spreading on the table.

"You won't pass out yet," he said quickly, "but the pain and the shock are more than you can really stand."

She could feel the blood throbbing at her temples. Each time she started to scream she was jolted by a spasm of pain. She felt as though she were being literally ripped. Through her tears she saw Reedy move away.

"Stop—" she managed to cough with a painful grunt. "Bob, stop..."

"You were right about your daughter," Reedy said impassively. "She ended-up being a slut just like you."

He watched her glance over at him.

"You mean I didn't tell you," he said, pretending surprise. "She's one good lay. It was hard at first, her being a virgin and all."

"Bastard," she grunted through clenched teeth, "You—" Pain stole her next words.

"Anyway," he went on, "she wants in on the action. She came in just a second ago. She's over there by the entry hall."

She turned her head to see her daughter Tammy.

"She's coming to you, and pulling up her skirt," Reedy described, watching Sarah's wide eyes. "She's on the table, and she says she wants you."

"I want you Mother," Sarah heard Tammy say.

Sarah felt her daughter's legs sliding over her tied arms.

"She's grabbing your hair and pulling your face down, ordering you to do it—to do it now!"

"Do it!" Tammy said, grabbing Sarah's hair, "do it now!"

"Tammy—" Sarah gasped. She felt her daughter's thighs lock around her head.

Noticing Sarah had clamped her mouth shut Reedy said: "Now she's digging her fingers into your cheeks, Sarah—forcing your mouth open."

As if on cue, Sarah haltingly and tensely opened her mouth.

"You should have expected this, Sarah," Reedy called, backing to the front door. "And if you smother to death, you'll be getting just what you deserve."

Sarah heard Tammy repeat Reedy.

"You are one deranged sick-o," Reedy added.

Again, Sarah heard Tammy repeat him.

The front door opened and closed. Jim Austiff moved through the entry hall and froze—completely shocked by the scene before him. His wife, tied to the table seemed to be in a seizure, her body violently rocking back and forth while she screamed, cried and violently licked at the air.

"Sarah?" he whispered, then heard the cocking of a pistol at his side.

"Don't even breathe," Reedy said quietly. "Hands up very slowly—don't look back—and carefully remove your pistol with your fingertips."

Austiff removed his service revolver from its shoulder holster.

"Hold it out with your finger-tips."

Austiff did.

"Good boy," Reedy said, taking the gun. "Now, your wife thinks she's being screwed in the ass by a guy built like a Shetland pony. She also thinks your daughter is making her perform oral sex. Let's see, oh yes, she also thinks she's had her nipple cut off."

"Who the hell are you?"

"One hell of a truth serum, huh?"

Austiff started to turn, but felt a sharp burning in his knee as Reedy kicked him. The pain shot up his leg and he went down. Looking up from the floor Austiff recognized Reedy as the Export.

"Get a load of this," Reedy said grinning and turned toward Sarah. "You don't need to eat Tammy any more."

He fired his gun into the ceiling and said: "I just blew her face away."

Sarah's eyes grew wide with terror as she saw the blob of flesh where her daughter's face had been. Tammy was sprawled on the floor, the carpet unable to soak up the gushing blood.

Sarah's eyes rolled back and she fell limp.

"The name's Kalvin Reedy," the Export introduced himself to Austiff.

Austiff tore his eyes from his wife. "What happened to her?"

"I forgot to tell her not to pass out," Reedy said, his expression reflecting a pensive mood. "I guess blowing away Tammy was too much. You know, you guys could make a bundle selling this stuff as a recreational drug—I mean the possibilities are endless. You can see anything you imagine!"

Austiff looked from the excited Reedy to Sarah. "You're nuts."

"What are you complaining about," Reedy snarled. "She's nothin' but a slut anyway. You wouldn't believe all the secret shit she's stolen from you—all in the name of the elusive ultimate perverted fuck—if you'll pardon my French."

Reedy trained his gun back on Austiff. "Hobble on up, old man."

Austiff rose, surprised that his knee felt twisted at the worst.

"You know, I'm not here just by chance," Reedy went on. "I mean, how often do you actually come home for lunch—once a year, maybe?

But on the very day you're wife asks that you come home to discuss the future, I show up."

Austiff only looked at him.

"Well, here's the thing," Reedy said, as if talking to an old chum. "She knew I would be here, and that we—you and I—would be having this little chat.

"Look, I don't care squat for you, Austiff," Reedy went on, motioning the OCSTO Director toward the front door, "but you deserve better than that trashy whore."

Reedy ordered Austiff through the door and waved at a plumbing truck across the street. The truck cranked-up and wheeled over into the driveway.

"Kidnapping?" Austiff questioned.

"Too bad you weren't as bright about women," Reedy came back. "Good night."

"Huh—"

Reedy's gun-butt came across Austiff's head so suddenly that he felt the nauseating blackness only briefly, then crumbled unconscious.

The plumbing truck rolled-up, the back doors opening to reveal two muscular Arabian men who leaped to the ground and whisked Austiff into the truck. Within seconds the truck turned around and headed back into the street, nearly colliding with a late model brown Dodge. After an exchange of horn blasts, the truck sped off, leaving the Dodge halfway in the driveway where it had slid to a stop.

Reedy returned to the living room to find Sarah regaining consciousness.

"Hey, Baby," Reedy said, "welcome back."

She swallowed. "What happened?"

"Well, that depends," he answered. "What's the last thing you recall?"

She bit her bottom lip, thinking. She then said, "You tied me here and said you were going to let me try out some coke."

"That's it?"

"Uh... I remember you injecting the needle..."

"You don't even recall my suggesting you wake-up believing you had passed out from too much sex?"

She laughed. "Yeah, right, like that could ever happen."

"I guess the stuff completely blocks the memory, or something. What a bummer."

"What are you talking about?"

"A goofed OCSTO truth serum."

She still wasn't following his conversation and stared at him hard.

"Forget it," he said with a wave of his hand and moved to the assortment of items he had lain out earlier. "How 'bout some real fun?"

"Like?" she questioned, watching him pick up the bullet-shaped object.

"Like the modified finale," he answered, captivated by the gleaming cylinder. He then remembered she had been under the influence of the so-called truth serum when they had discussed the modifications to which he was now referring.

"What?" she questioned.

"I modified it," he answered, waving the bullet-shaped object.

She smiled. "How."

"I supercharged it."

"You're joking," she came back, grinning.

"It gives off a lot more tingles."

"Come off it," she giggled. "A supercharged vibrator?"

"Really," he emphasized, moving around to her waist. "You'll be shocked by what comes next."

He slid his hand between her legs, shoving the vibrator into her. He flipped one of the switches on the handle and she felt a mild current pulsating through her.

"Wow," she purred, squirming. "That's great!"

"You like?"

"Yeah, can you turn it up?"

"It packs a punch," he warned.

"So do I."

"I was hoping you'd feel that way," he returned and began moving the sliding intensity switch.

"Yes..." she moaned, "oh yes... More..."

He increased.

"Higher..."

He increased.

"That's... That's—fine."

He increased.

"No, wait..."

"Come on, you like it."

"Yes," she moaned, her body jerking absurdly.

He increased the voltage again, turning her moans of ecstasy into screams of horror.

She begged him to stop.

Her pleas fell on deaf ears...

16

When Tammy Austiff found the bloody body of her mother spread-eagled across the dining room table, she threw-up, fainted, and ten minutes later managed to phone 911.

Dana Masters received a phone call as well. As the Security Director she had contacts inside the local framework of law enforcement and never missed news relating directly or indirectly to the Office. Before arriving on the scene, she notified her Deputy Director, Rusty Griggs, and ordered him to meet her.

Arriving at the Austiff townhouse, Dana and Griggs were greeted by the police. They showed identification listing them as police officers and entered the house to view one of the most sadistic sexual crimes in recent memory.

Although not formally acquainted with Sarah Austiff, Griggs had endured the ritual embellishments of her exploits in the society column from his wife. In this irritating, over-the-breakfast table reading of the newspaper, Griggs learned to hate Sarah Austiff. His ham and eggs were, it seemed, forever accompanied with Mrs. Austiff's latest flings.

Personally, Griggs wasn't interested in apprehending a killer, inwardly considering the affair a good dosage of Western justice. So shocked by the assortment of sexual devices surrounding Sarah's body, he found himself believing she had received her just deserts. However, he also pursued cases until solved or closed by the Office—no matter his personal disposition. But whatever the outcome, it certainly meant a peaceful breakfast from here on out, he mused to himself.

The following morning, Tammy was released from the hospital to Dr. Baker. Kegley, Dr. Baker and Dana Masters took Tammy to the Sound Room for questioning. It was a tremendous help that she was very comfortable with Baker—he was, after all, the family physician. She also looked to Kegley—her father's very good friend and coworker—for support.

Hoping to reduce further strain, Baker gave her a mild sedative and began the session with casual conversation about Sarah. Taken back in her memory, Tammy was encouraged to recount previous emotional events.

"I was almost five," the golden-haired Tammy said, looking from Baker to Kegley. Her voice sounded far away. "We—dad, mom and me—were at a big party: there were lots of them back then. It was a large house and Dad was off somewhere while we—mom and I—were on a balcony.

"Then a man walked up..."

She paused, thinking of how she remembered looking to see a man she had seen in TV shows.

"Commercials," Tammy mumbled. "The man made political commercials—of course I was so young, I thought I had seen him in movies..."

Her voice trailed off again as she recalled the man placing his hand on her mother's arm. He said something about hearing Sarah Austiff was an adventurous woman.

"When he said he heard Mom was adventurous," Tammy reported, "she told him it depended on what he considered adventurous. I remember he smiled and said, 'taking chances,' then left."

She thought how her mother was smiling. When Tammy had tried to look off into the direction her mother was staring, all she could see were trousers, silk-stocking legs and the skirts of evening gowns.

Taken by the hand, Tammy was suddenly stumbling behind her mother through the ocean of legs. A door opened and they were alone in a room with the man from TV.

"She followed him into a bedroom," Tammy said at last, looking to Baker. "She locked the door and walked over to him. He said, 'What about her?' And Mom said, 'What about her?'"

Tammy recalled looking up to see her Mother running her hands over the TV man. In turn, he had bent slightly and ran his hands up her legs, parting the dress's front slit. From her angle, Tammy couldn't see her mother's hands, but heard the short chopping sound of a zipper. Her mother widened her stance slightly by moving her feet out. Tammy heard her mother make a small gasping sound followed by the single word, 'Yes.'

"They started having sex," Tammy whispered. "Right there in front of me. I didn't know it then, but still..."

She could see the TV man slip his hands into the front of her mother's low-cut dress as if it had happened only yesterday.

"She acted like I wasn't even there. I even moved closer to watch."

Tammy remembered looking up to see her mother's parted lips—breathing as though she were jogging on the treadmill at home. Suddenly, her mother released a high-pitched whine and her knees almost gave way. Startled, Tammy moved back to her original place just behind her mother. She watched her mother step back from the man and smooth out her dress.

"'Thanks,' she told the guy," Tammy said. "She had just screwed the guy right there in front of me—then said, 'thanks.'

"After that, whenever Dad was at work or out of town, she started bringing guys home. And I always watched. It was almost like she needed it, and knew I wouldn't tell."

Tammy lapsed into silence, still remembering.

"Then when I was seven," she suddenly said, her eyes locked on one of the white walls, "She brought home two men..."

Tammy remembered walking down the dark hallway which emptied into the living room. There, sitting on the floor, watching TV, were two nude men. Her mother, who was standing at her side, slipped her night robe off and moved across the room. Even through the dim room, lit only by the flicker of the TV screen, her mother's perfectly shaped body seemed to glow.

"I guess she had already told them what she wanted and expected, because they just looked at me—as if my being there didn't matter."

She watched as the men met her mother in the middle of the room and eased her to the floor. Their soft motions shortly became rough and aggressive—then Tammy's mother straddled one of the men and sat down. The other man sat down directly behind her.

Leaning forward, her mother pinned the lying man's hands to the floor and then looked over her shoulder to the man behind her. No words were spoken until the man behind her lunged forward. Her mother gasped and through tightly clenched teeth grunted the familiar, "Yes!"

"All three," Tammy said, hardly above a breath. She remembered seeing her mother's tears and although she was crying that the man was hurting her, she kept pleading for him not to stop.

"Then the guy behind..."

Her voice faded as she replayed the scene in her head. The man behind made a loud noise and her mother leaned away, turned around, and sat down again—her head disappearing into the lap of the man who had been behind and now faced her.

"She called me," Tammy said, turning to Dana. "She wanted me to see her—to see her—"

"It's okay," Dana soothed, taking Tammy's hand and looking over to Baker. "Don't you think—"

Baker snapped his head *no*, cutting Dana's plea short.

Tammy, submersed in her memories continued watching the pictures in her mind, hearing her mother's muffled voice calling her and the moan from the man she faced. By the time Tammy moved to her mother the man had visibly relaxed and Sarah's head reappeared. She heard her mother's voice echoing saying she was sorry Tammy had missed it.

Sarah reached out to caress her daughter's face. Curious, Tammy reached to touch the strange moisture on her mother's face.

"It was all over her face," Tammy said, a grim expression clouding her placid appearance. "She licked it off my hand..."

Tears began flooding her eyes. She stopped, trying to gain control again. "Dad came home the following morning and I told him I thought she was seeing other men and we should leave her—run away.

"He told me he couldn't, that sometimes the people we love the most, hurt us the most. But that pain, he said, was better than losing the person you love.

"I think he knew she was a slut—but he really loved her—at one time, anyway. I couldn't tell him that she had been making me watch her have sex. If he knew now, it would kill him.

"Three days after that, mom brought home a lover—a woman."

Again Tammy paused.

"I found Dad's extra revolver and pointed it at her while they were in bed—but couldn't do it.

"She woke-up and saw me standing in the hall. I told her Dad loved her. She said she knew and then she cried. It was the last time I ever saw her cry..."

Rusty Griggs appeared at the table with a folded sheet of paper in his hand. Kegley followed him into one of the sound absorbent halls.

"You wanted all the updates," Griggs said.

"What have you got, Rusty?"

"It seems we can't find the Director because he was kidnapped."

"Oh?"

"We canvassed the block and found an old lady down the street who said she and a Smith Plumbing truck nearly collided in front of Austiff's driveway. There are three plumbing companies utilizing a variation of the name, 'Smith.' None of them had a truck in the area and we've personally confirmed none of them have a vehicle matching the witness' description."

"That would explain why no one saw him after lunch, but not why in the hell someone didn't mention he failed to return. I guess I'll have to ream Jann's ass for sloppy work."

"I don't think it's her fault for not mentioning—"

"The Director of the most secret agency in America—a man with God knows how many secrets doesn't come back from lunch and—"

"Jann was protecting him," Griggs cut in. "She thought he was having an affair with Laura."

"Oh?"

Griggs nodded.

"Why am I the last to hear this shit?"

Griggs shrugged. "I followed it up, just in case. Laura's son wasn't due to return from sea duty for a month. But there was a mix-up with his orders and he came in yesterday. Laura left about the same time as the Director and neither one returned. Laura was in such a hurry yesterday, she didn't explain the mix-up. Naturally it sounded like she was making up an excuse to leave. Jann was just trying to kill the rumors."

"Hmm," Kegley said.

"As for Austiff's house—it was wiped clean of foreign fingerprints. But there were three bugs—Nova stuff."

"Nova?" she questioned with surprise.

Griggs nodded. "We found an unidentified fingerprint on one of the bugs, and a .44 caliber bullet from Austiff's gun in the ceiling."

"I see."

"Also, we leaned on the Coroner and he burned the midnight oil for us. His report on Sarah says she died of electrocution. Bluntly, someone cooked her box. It seems she had a kinky way of popping her cork—if you know what I mean."

"Thanks, Rusty," Kegley said. "You're such a poet."

"I try," Griggs came back. "One other thing."

"What?"

"The Coroner found traces of an unfamiliar chemical in her blood stream," Griggs replied, handing Kegley a sheet of paper. "That's the chemical breakdown."

"I'm not a chemist."

"It's our expensive truth serum. The one that's suppose to be undetectable?"

She looked up from the paper.

"It's not only psychotropic, but also ubiquitous. Ironic, isn't it?"

"Rusty?"

"Yes?"

She started to speak, shook her head and then decided on: "Stay away from the dictionary."

Griggs smiled and faded into the soundless passageway. Kegley returned to the center of the Sound Room.

"—nothing else?" Baker was asking Tammy.

She shook her head *no*.

"She never saw the guy," Dana reported as Kegley walked-up.

"Tammy," Kegley said and then paused, trying to decide how to word the question. "Did your mother, in the last week or so, mention anything strange or different about—well, about electricity?"

"I don't understand."

"Anything abnormal—something relating sex to electricity?"

"No," she answered slowly, then, "well, sort of—I guess."

"What?"

"It was about batteries."

"Batteries?" Kegley questioned.

Tammy nodded.

"What did she say?"

"Yesterday she said something about having to get an, 'Evereedy charge.'"

"'Evereedy?'" Kegley quoted.

"Yeah," Tammy answered, wiping her eyes. "I told her, 'You mean "Eveready."' And she said, 'No, I mean, "Evereedy."'"

"What's that got to do with anything?" Dana asked.

"Everything," Kegley answered, then looked over to Baker. "We through here, Doc?"

Baker nodded, urging Tammy to her feet.

"What about Dad?" Tammy questioned.

"He's out of town, Tam," Kegley answered. "At one of our other offices—a management problem. As soon as we can get in touch with him we'll let you know."

Tammy nodded and allowed Baker to lead her out.

Dana turned to Kegley for an explanation.

"Sarah was electrocuted," Kegley explained. "I want the M.O. checked against the term 'Evereedy.'"

"Sounds like a real long shot," Dana commented.

"It probably is," Kegley admitted. "I want Griggs on the 'Evereedy' angle and you on the listening devices found in Austiff's house."

"What listening devices?"

"Griggs said three were found—Nova built."

"This is getting too weird."

"Just find out how they got from Nova to the Director's house. The last I checked they only sold that stuff to the military."

"Anything else?"

"Not unless you can hold the wind at bay," Kegley answered, moving toward one of the soundless passages.

"What gives?"

"I've got to convince our irate Projects Director that the *TG-3* flight plan is as good now as it was when Austiff faxed it yesterday."

"Why wouldn't it be?"

"You do remember the tropical storm?" Kegley asked sarcastically.

"Well, change the sub-surface approach plan—or even the flight plan."

Kegley stopped and turned. "Do you know anything about the storm brewing down there?"

"Not much."

"Well those in the know say there isn't a timely way around the storm—and I can't delay the launch."

"You're the acting Director," Dana came back, "why can't you delay it?"

Kegley started to explain that the Chancellor didn't want any delays, but then remembered that Dana knew little about the new Mexico mission and absolutely nothing about the Chancellor's real identity.

"Let's just say it would be a political mistake," she finally said.

Dana watched her disappear into the soundless hall.

17

A warm breeze rolled across the sea and onto the crowded shore. The sunbaked sand reflected the blinding heat until a majority of the onlookers moved under beach umbrellas or were enticed into the lapping waves. Consisting mainly of tourists and Pensacola bikini regulars, the audience had gathered to view the large naval ship anchored several miles offshore. Although such vessels were a routine sight, few were ever surrounded by as many news crews.

The event was a media blitz—if for no other reason than it had been a slow news week.

The CVT 16, USS *Lexington* was the only naval aircraft carrier still in service which was used primarily for qualifying flight students and Navy aviators in carrier landings. Officially, the *Lexington* was temporarily assigned to the Office of Naval Research. The ship's crew included OCSTO personnel, Clines' engineers and one Arabian of royalty.

In a bold stance against the balmy climate, the Arabian Princess stood among a troop of four apish Arabians employed as bodyguards. Although attractive, the tightly clinging sundress wasn't as cool as she would have liked. The dress's redeeming quality was the neckline plunging to her waist—allowing her the obvious convenience of fanning her ample breasts. Her black hair, fashioned in a sprightly version of the French twist, offset a dark complexion that was presently flustered with heat and frustration.

The object of her scorn appeared from a nearby ship hatch. With a man assisting, the awkwardly shuffling form moved across the deck while wearing a bulky pressure suit similar to those worn by astronauts.

The Princess abruptly broke through her guards and began an ascent to the ship's bridge, where she could once again voice her objection to the blatant disregard of common sense.

Protruding into the air from the starboard side of the *Lexington* was the *Tiger-3*, or *TG-3*. So named because it was supposed to be an aggressive and stealthy prototype: the third in an unequal effort between the Office of Naval Research and select Arabian investors. The venture was unequal owing to the fact the Arabians were to receive a less advanced prototype than that in which they invested. Conversely, they were to receive what was promised: a 15-foot oval shaped sub-surface-to-air vehicle, armable as a submersible weapon and airborne jet. However, the *Tiger* craft they would never know was also a VTOL craft with a neuro-avionics package. Equipped with nuclear power cells, the *Tiger-3* could generate a low intensity electromagnetic field (EMF), which permitted midair maneuvering that rendered helicopter comparisons obsolete. This, "thinking machine," tied directly into the pilot's neurological activity and translated thoughts into actual maneuvering. The "fully loaded" prototype had evolved from Blake Clines' 1979 MGAS craft and Dr. Debbie Allinder's synthetic intelligence research.

Debbie Allinder had become a pioneer in the, "theoretical application of synthetic synaptic research." Her published articles brought a monthly pile of letters from scientists seeking opinions at which her writing only hinted. But while she was the recognized authority in the recent rage of, "synthetic intelligence," she purposely reined in her knowledge. In reality, her published work regarding theoretical design had been tested in practical application long ago.

She felt the world was not ready for the things she conceived and Clines built. Nowhere was this more apparent than in the *TG-3*: the embodiment of her life's work. As a result, the "real *TG-3*" had been replaced in this launch by the "*TG-2*," a prototype incorporating the nuclear power cells in a more traditional propulsion system. In an even more convoluted sleight of hand, the *TG-1* prototype was the vessel actually destined for delivery to the Arabians. The *TG-1* neither utilized neuro-avionics nor an EMF drive.

The Princess, like the Arabian investors she represented, would never be privy to this information. They had contracted for a weapons platform that could multitask as aircraft and scientific research sub—they would receive no less and no more.

However, what the Princess did know, and she had made abundantly apparent, was that engineers had suddenly decided to ruin the culmination of all their time, money and effort. Launching into the face of a storm was more than she could fathom. She entered the ship's bridge under full steam, followed by her guards.

"Captain," she called, swiftly moving past the temporary computer consoles littering the bridge, "I would like to express my dissatisfaction with proceeding with a launch in the face of certain failure."

The ship's Captain held out his hand toward a stocky man with short-cropped blond hair. "This is Mr. Blake Clines, the designer and director from Engineering, Inc. The rest of this—"

"Mr. Clines," the Princess cut in, "I am Princess Fonna."

"Yes, I know," Clines returned in a relaxed tone. "I understand you're not too happy?"

"I am of the opinion we shouldn't launch."

"I agree," Clines came back with a friendly smile. "As a matter of fact, I think this whole shebang is a crock of shit. But I only built the baby; someone else decides where to deliver."

No one knew if her shock was because Clines agreed or because of the way he agreed.

"Pilot secured," interrupted a bridge speaker, saving international relations.

Clines turned his back on the woman and moved over to a mass of temporary computer consoles and Office technicians.

"All buckled up?" a man was saying into a microphone.

"Like a sardine," came Debbie's voice.

"How's it going?" Clines said into the mic as he leaned over the technician.

"Fine, Blake," she answered.

Another man came up behind Clines and handed him a teletype printout: "The latest aviation severe weather forecast."

"It's moving into the Gulf?" Clines questioned, glancing over the paper.

"That's what the NCEP and the Miami Center are saying," he answered, referring to the National Centers for Environmental Predictions and the National Hurricane Center. The man added: "It's not like our own satellite feed is lying, you know."

"Yeah," Clines mumbled looking at the printout.

"What was that?" came Debbie's voice.

"Tell her to stand by," Clines ordered while moving to a red phone on a nearby console. He lifted the receiver and waited a moment.

"Kate," he said after a pause, "have you seen the last weather reports?"

He listened a moment.

"This last update has gusts up to 80 knots," Clines said, writing on a clipboard and showing it to the man who had brought the weather report. Clines had written: *Get the last FA*.

"That ocean's going to be a blender in just a few hours," Clines said, watching the man slip away. He looked out the windows to the dark clouds southward.

"No, I don't like it," he said at last.

The man returned, handing Clines another teletype printout.

"I don't suppose you've taken a gander at the last Flight Advisory?" Clines went on, looking at the sheet he had just received. He listened for a passing second, nodding his head.

"Basically, it's going from terrible to all-out-hell. We should scrub the launch. The new course will take her right down the throat of that mess. It's just short of a hurricane. Trained pilots aren't even messing with it."

Clines waited, listening with the drum of his large fingers on the console. He finally asked, "Why the hell not?"

He listened.

"What'd you mean, 'gone?'" he asked. "I don't care if he fell into a black hole—"

He was forced to listen as Kegley interrupted with the facts.

"So we hope everything else just works itself out, right?" He paused.

"No," he answered, staring out at the *TG-3* and just beyond it, the Office Research yacht. "Other than scrubbing the launch, I haven't got a better—"

Interrupted, he broke off.

"Just because we've said it pilots itself is no reason to shove it down the throat of Montezuma's revenge," Clines said in a clipped tone. "I damn sure hope this little jaunt is as necessary as you think."

He made no pretense of liking the situation as he dropped the receiver into its cradle with apparent restraint.

"Commence countdown from last hold," he ordered through a tightly set jaw.

"Five minutes and counting," boomed over the ship's deck.

Inside the *TG-3*, Debbie adjusted her helmet as she listened to Clines update her on the storm she was to pass through.

"It seems," he continued, "that Jim-Boy has disappeared from the face of the earth, leaving the entire circus at the mercy of Kate and Dana."

"Disappeared?"

"Don't worry about it," he said. "You have enough on your hands already."

"No new flight plan, huh?" She questioned.

"Zip. Apparently a lot of people are real edgy about this whole Mexico satellite thing. Just run the *TG-3* deep until you absolutely have to surface for the reconnaissance."

"I know, Blake."

"I just wanted you—"

"You've been clucking over me like a mother hen," she came back smiling, "that's what you've been doing."

"If we build any more things like this, we're going to set up the computer to accept a second set of neurological patterns," he added.

"First of all, there isn't room in the database for two patterns. And second of all, I'm offended you don't think I'm a good enough pilot."

"Now you're calling yourself a pilot?" he came back. "You're only in this thing because you spent a few months in training and your neuro-patterns are the only ones it'll recognize!"

She laughed at his facade of indignation. She knew it disguised his concern.

"Blake..."

"Yeah...?"

"Get off the line so we can launch this thing."

"Good luck," he added.

"Thanks." She heard the line click as he released the communications button.

She glanced over the controls once more.

"SNAP on standby," a voice filtered through the helmet speaker.

"All green from TacCon," said the voice of Tactical Control. "How are you reading, *Tiger-3*?"

"All green," she answered.

A quiet moment passed.

"Blake," she said into the mic, knowing he hadn't signed off.

"Yeah?"

"I'll be fine."

The 30-second mark went by, then the 20. The countdown dropped into the teens...

"Ten seconds," boomed a voice over the deck of the ship.

Another deep breath.

"Five, four, three, two, one—you are cleared for launch, *TG-3*."

"Roger," Debbie confirmed into her helmet mic while grasping the locked control stick in front of her. She depressed a button on the stick, holding it down.

Launch she thought and released the button.

The engines roared to life and within seconds accelerated the craft out over the water. She depressed the button again, thinking the direction in which she wanted to fly.

The *TG-3* obeyed, changing its flight path. Moments later the craft followed her instructions and leveled off into a one-half mile circular pattern above the cloudless water. At the back of her mind she knew it wasn't cloudless where she was headed.

As long as she held in the Neuro-link button, the *TG-3* continued to feed off of her neurological pattern. In essence, it recognized the similar patterns stored in its memory and adjusted the flight accordingly. Anything unrelated to maneuvering or her physiological response was ignored.

The *TG-3* gracefully rolled and swept down toward the surface. With the nose slightly up, it seemed to glide onto the water, hydroplane momentarily, and then slip beneath the waves.

Debbie watched for a few moments and then realized she was holding her breath. She keyed-up the communications console.

"TacCon," she said into the mic, "this is *TG-3*. All systems are go—she's beautiful!"

On board the *Lexington*, a cheer went up. Even Princess Fonna smiled.

"Go to manual in two hours," a technician said into his mic, trying to be heard over the celebrating voices. "Sit back and enjoy the ride."

"That's a-copy," she returned. "Tell Blake and all the guys I've got a big wet kiss for them when I get back."

The control room broke into laughter—all except for Princess Fonna.

18

Debbie Allinder was only three hours into the mission. She glanced to the control panel for the fifteenth time in what seemed as many seconds.

The glaring red lights stared back like a futuristic Christmas tree. She hadn't expected to see one warning light, much less a panel-full indicating that nearly every on-board system was in jeopardy. The storm she was attempting to dive beneath was jabbing its deadly fingers at the sub—each jab a bruising jolt.

She had already activated the backup battery to fill in for the nuclear cells that were being unexplainably bled dry. The backup battery, however, wasn't much better. The power indicators hovered near dangerous lows.

From her left helmet speaker she was hearing a nasal-sounding meteorologist explaining the difference between the sustained violent wind of a hurricane and the erratic gusting of what was now a tropical storm.

She readjusted the communication dial and tuned in a military weather report, which announced the storm was entering the Gulf of Mexico.

"And taking me with it," she mumbled to herself, fine-tuning the reception.

Her helmet's right speaker crackled to life with inexplicable static.

"Tactical Control," she said into the mic, "this is the *Tiger 3*, over."

Static came back.

The power fluctuated as the craft was caught in a strong sub-surface current and rolled.

"TacCon, this is *TG-3*. I am losing power—"

The craft jarred as it scraped an outcrop of rock.

She glanced at the depth gauge just in time to see it rapidly increasing from 300 feet.

"Damn," she swore. "TacCon, this is *TG-3*, I—"

Another jarring impact knocked her to the side of the cockpit. The mass of system lights began flickering out. She grabbed the control yolk to avoid a collision with a sea floor outcropping of basalt.

The sub went into another spin, nose down.

"TacCon," she panted, fighting the control yolk. She had long-ago shut down the Neuro-link interface to conserve the dwindling power source. Now she could feel the electric-driven controls fading out, making maneuvering impossible.

This is not the way I intended to die, she thought to herself.

Mercilessly the sub cartwheeled, crashing down to the sea floor as though carelessly tossed by a spiteful child.

She blinked her eyes to clear away the dizziness and then shut down all the power. The cockpit went ink-black dark.

She sat back, accepting the situation was out of her hands. She didn't need to turn on the exterior lighting to realize the craft was sliding and tumbling along the sea floor.

After sweeping into the Gulf of Mexico, the storm methodically moved along the Veracruz coastline. Remaining just short of a hurricane, it jealously claimed the unprepared both above and beneath the sea. In its wake, very little remained. As far north as the Texas and Louisiana beaches, dead sea life and wreckage would wash ashore for days yet to come.

Lexington TacCon received only a portion of the *TG-3* distress transmission before the storm forced the airways into utter static. Moments later the computers confirmed the *TG-3* was shutting down its own systems. All contact was then severed.

19

The morning was gray.

Peacefully, the Gulf of Mexico offered a fine mist as its only hint of the raging storm that battled within its depths three hours before.

Like an immaculate ivory dagger protruding from the bloodless back of a great blue beast, a boat stoically rode the waves. A yellow sliver of light flashed as a hatch door on the vessel opened, allowing a form out onto the deck.

Walking almost the length of the 72-foot deck, the rain-slicker clad form stopped to stare off into the clearing horizon. Emerging from the deep pockets of the raincoat, the man's large hands withdrew a pair of binoculars.

Focusing the field glasses seaward, he stood braced against the ship's railing, mesmerized—as though searching for an ancient Spanish galleon.

In the distant seascape, a white speck seemed to perilously balance on the line where the dark sky met the ocean. The man finely returned the viewing glasses to his coat pocket and turned to retrace his path to the cabin.

He paused as if to consider the two large Navy ships anchored off the stern bow. With an audible sigh, he opened the hatch door and walked up a narrow passageway that dead-ended into another hatch door. Going through the second hatch, the drenched man was greeted by the buzzing of voices and glare of lights.

"Morning, Blake," said a second man wearing a headset similar to those worn by phone operators. Except for black hair and a Navy lieutenant uniform, Daniel Sanhurst could have passed for Clines' brother. Like the *Lexington's* official orders during the *TG-3* launching, Sanhurst was working for the Office of Naval Research. In reality, however, he was permanently on loan to OCSTO.

"How's it going, Dan?" Clines returned, his face appearing from beneath the dripping raincoat. He wriggled out of the slicker and hung it on a coat hook.

"One motorboat and a lot of muck," Sanhurst answered.

"That's slow," Clines mumbled as he moved over to the wall of black and white TV screens. In order to lead the search for Debbie, Clines had transferred to the Office's Research yacht some hours earlier. Calculating the currents from Debbie's last known position, Clines had led the *Lexington* south and into a proposed search area. At Clines' request, the Navy reassigned a research vessel to help in the search.

The USS *Boston* had arrived in time to commit their deepwater subs to the search. Between the three surface vessels, there were four search areas and eight one-man mini submarines. Further out, Clines had employed helicopters and sonar transducers. Primarily used in anti-submarine warfare, it was an unusual search tactic. But the equipment had been available, and Clines used it. Whatever advantage transducers might have provided, the process of using helicopters to dip the listening devices beneath the surface had been made difficult by the storm's disturbance of the sea.

"How deep are we out to?" Clines asked Sanhurst. They were monitoring the progress of the subs.

"One-hundred fifty-six feet," Sanhurst responded. He didn't need to mention that the *Boston* and *Lexington* were searching even deeper waters a mere half-mile's distance away.

Clines ran his hand through his sandy hair and looked out the large windows.

"How long has that boat been with us, Dan?"

"What boat?"

"That one," Clines answered with a tilt of his head toward the port bow.

"I didn't know it was there."

Clines moved closer to the window, gazing at the distant speck.

"What's the matter?"

"It's a charter for a cable-based news service."

"How'd you know that?"

"Something about the company's name on its bow," Clines answered with a smile.

"You're a real smart—"

"Contact," came a voice over the bridge speaker.

Clines moved over behind Sanhurst to view the small TV screens and computer-generated information.

"Coordinates?" Sanhurst asked into his mic.

"I'm sending them up now," replied the voice.

Sanhurst began typing the numbers that appeared on one of the small screens.

"Well?" came the voice.

"Hold on," Sanhurst said, still entering data into the computer terminal. After a short pause the TV screens jumped and wobbled—then took on a new picture.

"Is that it?" questioned the voice.

"I'm still zooming the camera," Sanhurst responded as he depressed a button and stared at the gloomy shape on the screen.

Several seconds passed.

"Well, snoopy," Sanhurst mumbled, "it looks like..."

"Like what?" the voice came back.

"A..." Sanhurst pressed another button and the picture lightened in contrast.

"What?"

"A metal ice chest," Sanhurst concluded as the picture cleared.

"Well, crap," said another voice.

"I'll second that," came yet a third voice.

"Keep looking guys," Sanhurst encouraged. "Sub-5 come on up for shift change."

"Will do," responded a fourth voice.

"We're never going to find the *TG-3*," Sanhurst surmised as he pushed the flexible microphone away from his face. He watched Clines move over to the window again.

"How goes the *Lexington* and *Boston* searches?" Clines questioned, still gazing out at the distant speck that was the news boat.

"Between our three ships we've found more junk than a salvage yard could hold."

Clines nodded, glancing back at Sanhurst in time to see him press the earphone to the side of his head.

"It's the *Lexington*," he said to Clines, then brought the mic in front of his mouth. "Roger, *Lexington*, But I'm still not showing any power loss..."

Sanhurst nodded. "I'll let you know."

"What power loss?" Clines asked, watching Sanhurst push the mic away.

"I don't really know. They called over a while ago saying they had a drop in power. Wanted to know if we had the same problem."

"Did they explain?"

"Nah. Although I tapped into their communications, and the *Boston* is having problems too."

"Hmm..."

"You have a theory?"

"No. It's just odd."

"They felt the same way."

Clines smirked: "Next they'll be asking how to rivet their ships back together."

"Moving out deeper," a voice came over the bridge speaker.

"Keep it on the floor," Sanhurst ordered into his mic.

"Will do," the voice responded.

"Nothing from the helicopters, I guess?" Clines ventured.

"A lot of background noise mostly."

Several moments went by, an occasional word or two between subs became the only break to the sleep-inducing drone of the computers.

"Contact," a voice rang out. "This is Sub-7, I have a contact."

"Coordinates?" Sanhurst requested.

"I'm sending it up now."

A moment passed.

"Hold present course, Sub-7," Sanhurst said. "You'll have visual in about five minutes."

"Roger."

"TacCon?" came another voice.

"Go ahead," Sanhurst said.

"This is Sub-5. I've got a loss of power here—like a short or something."

Sanhurst's hands flew over the control panel, keying in the telemetry and systems checks being transmitted by Sub-5.

"This is Sub-7," came a voice. "My sonar just went off-line. I'm blind down here."

"What'd you mean, 'blind?"' Sanhurst asked.

"I mean my search lights went with it," Sub-7 answered tersely.

"Stand by," Sanhurst said, then, "Sub-5?"

"Go ahead."

"I show you're down by 20 percent. Take it home and see what's wrong."

"Roger."

"Sub-7?" Sanhurst said after a brief moment.

"Go ahead, TacCon," Sub-7 answered.

"I'm running a check, hang on."

A long pause followed.

"Sub-7, reduce power and reverse course," Sanhurst said suddenly. "How'd you burn off enough juice to pass the PNR?"

"I didn't," responded Sub-7. "The power just bled off."

Listening in, Clines wasn't happy. Passing the Point of No Return meant one of the surface vessels would have to leave station to retrieve Sub-7 once it surfaced.

"Yeah, right," Sanhurst was saying.

"I'm telling ya' something's screwy down here," Sub-7 responded amid a wave of static.

"What the—" Sanhurst danced his fingers across the keyboard.

The wave of static filtering through the intercom was not a solid wall of noise.

"Sub-7," Sanhurst said, and then: "Watson!"

"What's the problem?" Clines cut in.

"We've lost Watson," Sanhurst answered, his voice nearly a whisper.

"What the hell do you mean, 'lost him?'" Clines snapped, moving to the instrumentation panel.

"It was like a power surge, then we lost contact."

"Who's closest to Watson?"

"Number 5, I guess. They're at the outer search grid."

"Have a helicopter do a dip," Clines ordered.

Sanhurst contacted the helicopter and ordered it to move to the last known position of Sub-7.

"TacCon," came the voice of Sub-5, "I'm—"

A burst of static came, then nothing.

Sanhurst looked up from the tracking computer. His face was ghost white: "He's gone."

"Where's that damned chopper?" Clines asked.

"Big Daddy," Sanhurst said into the mic, "are you at the drop yet?"

"Roger," came through Sanhurst's earphone. Sanhurst nodded to Clines, who picked-up a mic/earphone set and keyed the transmit button.

"Big Daddy, this is TacCon," Clines said in the mic, "we're down two subs in that area. What da' ya' got?"

"Popping noise," came back a voice, "air escaping."

"Roger," Sanhurst said, realizing that meant Sub-7 had just lost pressurization and the pilot might very well be dead. "Come west some and drop again."

Nearly three minutes later the helicopter reported in. "Nothing."

Sanhurst looked at Clines.

"Keep all the subs out of that area," Clines ordered. "Contact the *Boston* and have them make-ready the deep *Navy Diver*."

"You're going down?"

Clines nodded.

"Navy equipment," Sanhurst said. "You have to take Navy personnel down with you."

"Any suggestions?"

"I'll put these orders through and get my replacement before the dinghy's wet."

"I'll be waiting," Clines called over his shoulder, on his way out the door.

20

The submersible's official name was *XND-1*. Service personnel called it the *Navy Diver.* It was a winged, nuclear-powered three-man prototype, designed for the navy through collaboration between Engineering Inc. and a private ocean research foundation. With a depth range of 5,000 feet and a top speed of 12 knots, it was several times faster than traditional submersibles. Owing to the nuclear power-plant, it also boasted the new technology of waterborne molecular oxygen extraction; thereby prolonging its submerging time beyond the endurance of a crew.

Whereas OCSTO subs were one-man submersibles requiring a tactical control on-board a surface craft, the *XND-1* was completely self-sufficient. If the trial period continued being a success, there were tentative plans to construct slightly larger versions to replace outdated and larger American, "reconnaissance," subs.

None of this however, concerned Clines. What occupied his mind was the *XND-1* cockpit. Jammed with advanced instrumentation, he found the cramped cockpit uncomfortable after ten minutes, and the crane had only now lifted them off the deck.

The peculiar sensation of being off-balance momentarily hit Clines as the *XND-1* was eased into the water and the crane's clamp detached.

"Okay, *Boston*," Sanhurst said into his headset. "We're diving."

From the co-pilot seat Clines watched the side of the slate-gray Navy ship disappear behind a ceiling of water.

He looked over at Sanhurst, "Everything green?"

"Nothing goes wrong 'till you're a mile down," Sanhurst grinned back. "Don't you watch the horror movies?"

"I don't know why they let people like you into the service," Clines returned, shaking his head.

"They don't," came a voice from behind. "He paid his way in."

Clines looked into the small mirror to his side to see the face of a thin, bearded man peering through a hole in the mass of computers. The section was the domain of Buzz Johnson, a 30-year old electronic whiz and another Navy Lieutenant on loan to the Office.

"Figures," Clines joked.

The three lapsed into silence as the sub descended.

Fifteen minutes and two-hundred feet later, they picked up a sonar contact just beyond the last reported position of Sub-5.

"Roll cameras, Buzz," Clines ordered.

"We're rollin' cameras now," Buzz announced into his headset.

Clines imagined Captain Upchurch on the bridge of the *Boston*, impatiently listening with a grim face. Up until now he would have been leaning closer to the speaker, as if it would enable him to visualize the scene two-hundred feet below his salvage ship.

"Do you have a picture, over?" Clines asked.

"Affirmative," Upchurch said into the voice-activated intercom. The portable monitor sitting to the side of the speaker had flickered to life, bringing the view to the bridge officers of the USS *Boston*.

Sanhurst carefully guided the *XND-1* as close to the wreckage of the OCSTO submersible as he dared. With the current pushing from behind them, he had his hands full compensating with a steady reverse thrust just to maintain a constant and stable position.

Beneath them, bathed in the 1,200-watt halogen-mercury-iodine lights of the *XND-1*, Sub-5 sat dead on the seafloor: her ballast tanks damaged from impact with an outcrop of basaltic rock.

"I have visual on Joe," Sanhurst suddenly said, referring to the pilot of Sub-5. Clines activated an additional exterior light to see a face peering up at them from one of the sub's viewing ports.

"I see him," Clines reported. "Buzz?"

"Nothing back here," Buzz responded, meaning there was no communication from Sub-5.

Clines tapped his headset with a very animated gesture, hoping Joe would realize he should try his radio again. Instead, Joe returned a just-as-animated cutting sign across his throat.

"Drop a locator beacon," Clines ordered.

"Doing that now," Buzz reported, activating his panel and causing the *XND-1* to eject a baseball-sized locator beacon. The shiny spherical beacon created a small cloud of sand as it settled onto the seafloor. It then began to throb with a blinding strobe while emitting a constant directional radio signal.

"*Boston*, this is *Navy Diver*," Clines said into his mic, "over."

"Go ahead, *Navy Diver*, over," came the voice of a communications officer.

"Sub-5 appears to be completely powered-down but intact. We've dropped a locator beacon for you guys, over."

"Roger that," came the reply. "The Captain says help's on the way down, over."

"We copy," Clines replied. "We're moving further out to search for Sub-7, over."

Clines nodded to Sanhurst, who angled the *XND-1* over and past the stranded sub.

"At least he's okay," Clines noted.

"He's damned lucky," Buzz said.

"What's wrong, Buzz," Sanhurst said.

"Nothing," Buzz mumbled, turning his eyes out toward the dimly-lit seafloor.

"Have you heard the stories of how they used to bury hard-hat divers in their helmets?"

"I've heard," Buzz moaned.

"Well, I've seen it. Once, off the coast of Norway—about a mile down—"

"Knock it off for a sec," Buzz interrupted.

"What—"

"Shut-up," Buzz ordered, holding his hand to his headset. "I'm hearing something."

Clines and Sanhurst looked at each other with shrugs.

"Can you drop below or get above this current and cut the motor?" Buzz asked.

"What's the floor now, Blake?" Sanhurst questioned.

"It's at 250 feet."

"Deeper it is, then" Sanhurst said, then into the mic: "*Boston*, we're diving deeper. Over."

"Copy that and on standby," came the *Boston's* communications officer.

The sub slowly sank, fighting the current with teeth clinching vibration. A moment later, the sub fell out of the current and into calm cold water.

"There," Clines said, pointing a finger off to one side of the sub.

Sanhurst maneuvered the sub around, casting the full effect of the lights from the camera and exterior lamps.

As they moved in closer, they could see a gash in the side of the sub—easily explained by jagged outcroppings of sea-floor rocks.

"I wonder why he lost power in the first place," Clines mused aloud.

"Hey!" Sanhurst cried out. "Look!"

"Son-of-a-gun," Clines said grinning. "He's alive!"

In the viewing port of Sub-7, Watson could be seen wearing scuba gear.

"*Boston*, we have a visual on Sub-7," Clines reported. "Watson's okay."

"Roger," came the voice of Captain Upchurch this time. "We see 'em, over."

"Were dropping a beacon," Clines came back, nodding at Buzz to make it so. "It looks like the hatch has taken a hit and is probably jammed, over."

"We concur," Upchurch agreed. "You boys did okay, come on back and we'll handle it from here, over."

"I'm still picking up the noise," Buzz interrupted while ejecting the locator beacon.

"What are you talking about?"

"I'm picking something like static—it's further away than Watson."

Clines looked at Sanhurst who shrugged, then in the small mirror at the concentrating face of Buzz.

"Could you be more specific than just, 'static?'" Clines asked.

"It's coming from pretty far off and really weak. It sounds like an open com line transmitting static."

"It's not ambient noise?" Clines asked, meaning noise in the water.

"I'm getting a lot of background for certain," Buzz responded, "but I think we want to check this one out."

"We're talking Debbie, aren't we?" Clines pressed.

"Could be," Buzz admitted. "I mean you don't usually hear a communication line on the fritz out in the middle of nowhere."

"*Boston*, this is *Navy Diver*," Clines said into his mic, "Buzz thinks he's picking up an open com line, over."

"Stand by," came the Communications Officer's voice. After a moment: "We aren't picking anything up, over."

"It's an open line of static," Clines clarified. "Buzz says it's real faint, over."

"Roger that," the officer responded. "Stand by."

Upchurch came on the line. "I thought you only lost two subs, over."

"I'm guessing it's Debbie, Sir. Over."

"We copy," Upchurch said. "Proceed as you think best, *Navy Diver*."

"Roger that," Clines answered, then looked at Buzz in the mirror. "Which way?"

Buzz pressed a series of buttons, peered at his instruments, then said: "Down."

"What's the floor?" Sanhurst asked, slowly diving the sub.

Clines looked to the computerized data on the panel in front of him. "It's still dropping."

"*Boston*," Sanhurst said into his mic, "What's the floor in this area, over."

"Stand by," came Upchurch. Then: "300 feet. Over."

Looking at the depth scope Clines shook his head and keyed his mic. "We're reading 350 and rapidly dropping, over."

"I can hear it over our motors now," Buzz reported.

"*Navy Diver*," came Upchurch's voice, "are you certain of your depth reading? Over."

"Yes, Sir," Clines answered, "and we're still dropping, over."

Clines entered a command on his keyboard and the screen flashed a series of numbers overlaying a three dimensional representation of the seafloor.

"Looks like an abyss," Clines commented.

Sanhurst glanced over to the screen: "It's only about 40 feet wide,"

"What's it bottom out to?" Buzz asked.

"Too much signal bounce to tell," Clines replied, looking at the computer readouts. "I'd say there's a lot of metal mineral deposits down there—and plenty of nooks and crannies to spare."

"The *TG-3's* only pressurized down to three-thousand feet," Buzz interjected.

"Another one of those big, 'ifs,' in life," Clines remarked dryly.

"This is one hell of a hole in the sea," Sanhurst commented. "And it's not on any map I know of. I wonder how anyone ever missed it in the first place?"

"I don't know," Clines said. "The sea's a big place. It's not too hard to imagine."

"But this is right in our backyard," Sanhurst came back.

"It couldn't very well be a recent development," Clines retorted. "The geological upheaval would have been felt on the mainland, if it was."

"Hmm," was Sanhurst's only response, then he fell silent.

While the sub descended, Clines relayed their findings to the *Boston*.

The walls of the abyss began looming into the lighter water overhead. Twenty minutes and 1,600 feet later, any chance of sunlight vanished as the sub passed into the depth that sunlight could not penetrate. The *XND-1* became like a cocoon, its inner life of lights and exterior lamps the only points of motion in an ink-like liquid world. They continued to drift downward.

Nearly 23 minutes elapsed before the search lamps of the *XND-1* glinted across something man-made.

"There," Sanhurst called, seeing a dim shape resting on an out-cropping shelf. He slowed the *XND-1* and a vibration accompanied the reduced descent speed.

"A current?" Clines questioned.

"Yeah," Sanhurst said, fighting the controls, "a stout one."

The sub stopped descending and Sanhurst continued fighting the rushing current just to hold a hovering position to the side of the *Tiger-3* sub.

"That's the *TG-3*," Clines said in disbelief, then into his mic, "Debbie, this is Blake. I'm five yards from you. If you copy, tap out, 'O.K.' using your damaged comm line or the bulkhead."

Buzz put his hand to his headset. "She's using the bulkhead. The message is, 'OK.'"

"What's your status?" Clines asked into his mic.

Buzz began writing the coded message.

"'Leak, cells low. Need lift,'" Buzz read.

"Good spirits," Clines mumbled with a smile.

"Wait a sec," Buzz added, writing again. "'One hour of air.'"

"We'll have you up in no time," Clines said into the mic, then turned it away. "Buzz, load the lift cylinders."

"Give me a couple minutes," Buzz came back, "I'm having a slight malfunction here."

"What kind of malfunction?"

"It's like a short—"

"Just hurry it up."

"I'm not playing checkers back here, you know."

"Sorry," Clines apologized, and keyed his mic to update the *Boston*.

A few moments passed.

"Okay," Buzz said, "move in for the first cylinder."

Sanhurst pressed on the control yolk and the *XND-1* inched through the turbulent water.

21

The first four flotation devices were attached to the *TG-3* within minutes.

Sanhurst blinked as a trickle of perspiration stung his eye. He held the control yolk as though glued there. He scanned the mass of gauges on the control panel and then looked seaward, eyeballing the distance to the damaged *TG-3*.

"Would you hurry it up?" he called over his shoulder.

"I'm doing the best I can considering these damned robot arms are still screwing-up," Buzz snapped back, fighting a series of switches and buttons.

Clines leaned slightly forward to view the metallic arms of the *XND-1* erratically moving outward with the last flotation device. It looked like nothing more than a smooth, three-foot-long metal cylinder measuring three feet in diameter. A glowing arrow on its side indicated which end belonged up. Beneath, a stout but flexible cable with a self-locking clamp swayed in the current.

Equipped with a hydrogen accelerator and a microcomputer-driven pump assembly, each lift cylinder extracted hydrogen molecules from water with which to fill a deployable titanium-composite inflatable. As the lightest and most simple chemical element—containing only a single proton surrounded by one orbiting electron—the newly split-off hydrogen then adhered to a molecular bonding agent within the inflatable. This created a compound-hydrogen gas, which then deployed the inflatable upward. As a cylinder ascended, and the atmospheric pressure naturally expanded the compound-hydrogen gas, the inflatable vented unnecessary excess. Excess was determined by a surfacing duration programmed prior to use. In this manner, the rate of ascent could even be programmed to include decompression stops if necessary: thus preventing a case of aeroembolism—commonly known as, the bends.

"Did you run a systems check on those arms?" Sanhurst asked Clines.

"Yeah. I couldn't find anything wrong. It's almost as if there's some sort of minor power leak."

"How could that be?" Sanhurst asked. "The nuclear generator is shielded big-time."

"I'd guess a short of some sort."

"But nothing serious?"

Clines shook his head with assurance. "A few lost volts at best."

They looked out to see the last Lift Cylinder was attached to the *TG-3*.

"Okay," Buzz called out, peering at the damaged *TG-3* through his small porthole. "They're in place."

"Well?" Sanhurst said tersely. "Retract the arms."

"They won't retract," Buzz returned. "Just back us out."

"Just, 'a few lost volts at best?'" Sanhurst quoted, looking at Clines.

Clines shrugged.

Sanhurst eased back the controls and the *XND-1* propellers churned away. Once free, the retractable arms hummed to life and folded back into the sleek side bays of the *XND-1*.

"See, a minor problem," Clines mumbled to Sanhurst, then keyed his mic: "This is *Navy Diver*. Lift Cylinders are in place and we're clear, over."

"Hit the button, Son," Upchurch came back. "That woman's running out of time."

Unknown to Upchurch, Clines had already hit the button. The three men involuntarily leaned forward, watching the *TG-3*.

A burst of bubbles exploded around the perimeter of the oval-shaped flying-sub. Five sphere-shaped inflatable spheres suddenly expanded under the lights of the *XND-1*, each as if a featureless clown from a child's jack-in-the-box toy.

The inflatables quickly grew to sizes roughly equaling fifths of the *TG-3*, displacing only the volume required to achieve positive buoyancy commensurate with the programmed ascent of one foot per second.

"It's working," Buzz reported.

"Can you see it, over?" Clines said into his mic.

"We see it, over," Upchurch responded.

As the *TG-3* drifted into a level plane with the *XND-1*, Sanhurst began pacing their ascent at approximately the same speed.

"So," Sanhurst said, relaxing back in his chair, "what's our surface ETA?"

Having already calculated the data for input to each of the lift cylinder computers, Clines answered: "We're at three-thousand feet, coming up at a foot per second. We'll see the top-side in about 50 minutes."

"Providing your James Bond toys don't give us any problems," Buzz said.

"True," Clines put in.

"True?" Buzz came back, startled by Clines sudden agreement.

"We've had Cylinder failure before."

"Cylinder failure?" Sanhurst cut in, casting a sideways glance at Clines.

"Yeah," Clines mumbled. "We lost a sub a few months ago. The inflatable blew and the sub snapped the remaining cables. Headed to the bottom like lead."

"What caused that?" Sanhurst asked.

Deceptively nonchalant, Clines said. "Salinity."

"How would the salt in the water affect them?"

"More salt molecules," Clines answered, watching the *TG-3*. "It interfered with the hydrogen accelerator separating the hydrogen molecules from the oxygen molecules."

"When did it happen," Buzz asked.

"A few months ago."

A moment passed, then Buzz asked, "It only happened once, right?"

"Yep."

"How many times have you used them?" Sanhurst cut in.

"Not including this time, twice," Clines came back. He glanced at the mirrored image of Buzz, then at Sanhurst. "You know, we're only using them this time because Debbie has to be at the surface in less than an hour. No time for anything else."

The other two didn't even nod. Their attention on the *TG-3* reflected renewed anxiety.

It started 16 minutes later.

"I think we've got a problem," Sanhurst said.

The other two men looked out at the *TG-3*. One of the inflatables had slowed the venting process. It was growing noticeably larger than the others.

"What are we at now?" Buzz asked.

"1,070," Clines read from a gauge.

A minute passed.

"1,010," Clines read from the gauge.

"Come on," Sanhurst growled, "vent..."

"990," Clines reported, his eyes alternating from the sub to the gauge.

Four of the inflatables continuing venting and even began venting faster as the *TG-3's* ascent perceptively sped-up.

Clines looked to the depth gauge, then at the *TG-3*: "Vent, you son-of-a—"

"Look at the size of that bag," Buzz cut in, astonished at the swelling sphere.

"950," Clines read out.

As the one inflatable continued to swell, the disproportionate rate of ascent increased. The *TG-3* began tilting at an angle.

"This isn't good," Clines mumbled.

"What?" Buzz questioned, his face almost against his viewing port.

"The four other computers are compensating by venting faster," Clines explained.

Even as Clines was speaking, four of the inflatables seemed to be in an obliterating mass of venting gas bubbles. Having measured the pressure and ascent speed, the four computerized cylinders attempted to compensate and were vented for an inner pressure that had yet to build. As a result, the faulty cylinder was pulling the *TG-3* upward into a 45-degree angle.

"940," came Clines' voice.

"Come on, vent" Sanhurst whispered through clinched teeth.

"920."

Look!" Buzz cut in. "It's venting."

"No it's not," Clines shot back, staring at the swollen inflatable furthest away. A small stream of bubbles had begun a steady out-pour.

"It's separating from the cylinder," Sanhurst guessed in a clipped voice, and glanced to Clines for confirmation.

"890," Clines reported while nodding his head in agreement to Sanhurst's assessment.

"Come on," Buzz chanted, "come on..."

"880..."

"If it doesn't vent," Clines began, "It's going to—"

A Sudden rumble jolted the *XND-1* as a mushroom of bubbles completely engulfed the *Tiger-3*. The three men grabbed at anything that was bolted down as their sub careened sideways.

"Shit!" Clines yelled as the lights flickered to dark.

The *TG-3* was suddenly below them and appeared to be rapidly descending.

"She's gone now," Sanhurst said in the dark.

The lights winked back. The *TG-3* was gone, replaced by the trailing debris of one Lift Cylinder. There was a stream of bubbles descending into the dark beneath them.

"Oh God," Buzz moaned.

"Wait," Clines snapped, looking to his gauges. "We're the ones moving."

Sanhurst pressed down on the control yolk, now realizing the shock wave from the faulty Lift Cylinder had blown them upward.

"What the hell's happening down there?" Upchurch's voice filtered through, throwing protocol to the wind.

"Well?" Sanhurst questioned, looking at Clines.

Clines smiled. "It's coming up."

"Report!" Upchurch was ordering.

The *TG-3* was just beginning to rise into sight.

"*Navy Diver*," came Upchurch frantically, "report, you sons-of-a-bitches!"

"Should we tell 'em, or let 'em suffer a bit longer?" Sanhurst said with an evil smile.

"*Navy Diver*, here," Clines said into his mic, grinning at Sanhurst as much as from relief at the averted disaster. "The *TG-3* lost a Lift Cylinder, over."

"Is she gone?"

"Negative. You'll get a visual as soon as she's in camera range, stand by."

The *TG-3* slowly drifted into sight, its drooping aft section slowly leveling out.

"I hope she's okay in there," Buzz whispered.

"Glad I used five instead of four," Clines mumbled.

"How's that?" Sanhurst asked.

"The required number of cylinders for something on the order of the *TG-3* is four—"

"But you used five," Sanhurst finished, nodding. "Smooth move."

"This time," Clines qualified.

"Shit," Buzz said from the back. "My heart hasn't slowed down yet."

"Mine either," Clines said and looked to the depth gauge. They were at 807 feet.

The *TG-3* continued its ascent, resuming one foot per second. Eleven minutes later, the shapes of the search and rescue ships appeared above them.

When the subs broke the surface, emergency cables and cranes were attached to the *TG-3* while a medical team boated over to the work platform and opened the hatch.

Up to her neck in water, Debbie Allinder gulped in a breath of fresh air and looked up into a blinding sun that had burned away the morning clouds. She smiled faintly and shook her head in the classic, "that was a close call" gesture.

"Dr. Allinder?" said one of the medics.

"Jones to you," Debbie said, "Davy Jones."

22

The ember glow of morning splashed across the white helicopter as it touched down on the USS *Boston*. Painted in aqua-green along the tail rotor were the words, **ENGINEERING INC**. The, "C," was depicted as a cog.

Humming into a muted whooshing sound, the blurring mass atop the helicopter slowed into visually distinctive blades. The pilot scrambled down, looking around suspiciously while doing so. He walked around to the side and opened the hatch. The Chancellor stepped down, his black London Fog coat flapping in the breeze. He moved from the chopper, leaving the pilot to wait.

Separating from a group of uniformed men, Captain Upchurch walked out to meet him.

"Mr. Jones, is it?" Upchurch greeted with a handshake.

"Yes," the Chancellor returned, "Captain..."

"Upchurch," the Captain supplied: "Simon Upchurch."

"Pleased to meet you, Captain," the Chancellor came back. "And I apologize for the inconvenience."

"Hell, Mr. Jones," Upchurch said affably, "I couldn't miss the chance to meet a man who stopped the Navy dead in the water."

"I just cashed in a favor," the Chancellor explained.

"Must have been a whopper," Upchurch said, directing the Chancellor across the deck. "They wouldn't let me pull-up anchor until you gave the word."

"I would have preferred to explain the situation in person, but Mr. Clines' message didn't leave much time for that."

"Yes," the Captain replied without much meaning one way or the other.

"I take it you're not privy to what this is all about?" the Chancellor questioned.

"I was hoping you might remedy that."

The Chancellor smiled as best his face would allow. "Well, Captain, believe it or not, I don't know either."

Upchurch appraised the authoritative figure beside him, trying to determine if he was telling the truth.

"The message I got was to make sure this ship didn't move an inch until I got here," the Chancellor added.

"I see."

"We'll get this squared away just as fast as we can," the Chancellor assured Upchurch.

"It must be damned important," the Captain grumbled.

"I've been an investor in Mr. Clines' company for a couple of years now," The Chancellor came back. "If anything, I've learned he's no dullard."

They walked on, climbed a set of metal steps and entered the ship. Men were rushing to and fro, busy with their duties.

Reaching the dining compartment, they found Clines putting away a second helping of eggs and Debbie pushing a slice of sausage in circles on her plate.

"Here I am thinking you're near death, and you're both stuffing your faces," the Chancellor said in undertones.

Clines looked up, his burly chest seemingly dwarfing the table. He smiled. "Why Mr. Jones, I'm even glad to see you."

"I'll get back with you later," Upchurch said, excusing himself from the compartment.

"Well?" the Chancellor asked sitting across from Clines and studying the bandage on the side of Debbie's temple.

"Where would you like me to start," Clines countered.

"'Mr. Jones,' is a good place," the Chancellor replied, referring to the code name they had agreed upon long ago. While Clines' message did indeed request an extension of the *Boston's* assignment, by addressing "Mr. Jones" the Chancellor had been alerted to an issue involving national security.

"Debbie," Clines said.

The Chancellor looked to her.

"I'll have to show you," she answered the Chancellor's look.

"Show me what?" he asked.

"This," she answered, pulling a CD from her denim shirt pocket.

The Chancellor looked from her to Clines.

"It's the hit of the year," Clines commented.

"How interesting," the Chancellor replied without inflection.

"It's data from the *TG-3* sonar and radar" Debbie elaborated. "No one has seen it except Blake and myself."

"An absolute must for the, 'Mr. Jones,' in your family," Clines dryly joked, sounding like a TV commercial.

"I give," the Chancellor said. "What's on it?"

"Come on," Debbie came back and stood. "You'll have to see it to believe it."

With Clines bringing up the rear, the Chancellor begrudgingly followed Debbie out onto the *Boston's* deck and they ferried over to the floating platform to which the *TG-3* was anchored. Only the OCSTO research yacht, still under the guise of belonging to the ONR, floated nearby. The *Lexington*, having received new orders the previous evening, was miles away.

Debbie walked out onto the grill-like catwalk and lowered herself into the now dry cockpit of the sub. Unbolting a small viewing screen from its place in the instrumentation cluster, she lifted it onto the sub's open hatch. Standing in the pilot seat, she was out of the sub from waist up. She inserted the CD into a slot atop the screen and pressed a button.

The Chancellor walked-up and knelt down to view the screen.

"While down there," Debbie explained, "I took readings on the entire abyss."

"Abyss?"

"The trench the storm dumped me into." Debbie answered.

"It turns out," Clines put in, moving in behind the Chancellor, "there's an unmapped crevice below us."

The Chancellor watched as the picture bounced around until a computer enhanced replica of the terrain below took shape.

"That spot there," Debbie said, pointing to a dark area on the screen. "It's about 4,500 feet down. I had the computer enlarge and enhance the picture."

On the screen the replay zoomed in on the dark area. After a moment, animated colored squares formed a solid picture resembling a cartoon.

The Chancellor leaned forward, staring at the image.

"I wasn't sure either," Debbie reflected, noticing the lines of concentration etched on the Chancellor's face. "So I increased contrast and ordered the computer to make it into the likeness of a photograph."

The shape on the screen suddenly became brighter, assuming the texture of a laser photograph.

"My, God," the Chancellor whispered almost reverently. "That's part of *Skylab*!"

"The same part that housed FORBS," Debbie added, looking up at the astonished Chancellor.

"But it didn't even go down in this hemisphere," the Chancellor protested.

"Well it's here now," Clines came back. "Frankenstein's monster returns."

"What you've described could be the ultimate weapon," Upchurch remarked.

The Chancellor nodded, looking out at the OCSTO research vessel. Glancing over the Navy ship's nearly empty deck, the Chancellor reassured himself no one was near enough to hear the conversation.

"Maybe now you understand why it must remain under wraps."

"Why wasn't it just completely dismantled?" Upchurch asked.

"It was a government contract," the Chancellor explained. He had discarded several possible explanations, deciding upon the one that offered the least facts with the most satiating elements of truth. "They wanted to study it more."

Upchurch looked down to the deck. "And so Mr. Clines' company took over as gatekeeper when the previous company went belly-up?"

"Well, Engineering Inc. bought the patents. Mr. Clines never gave it a moment's thought. We thought it ancient history."

"Hard to believe it turned-up here," Upchurch pondered.

"I guess NASA's telemetry was slightly off."

"I'd say," Upchurch agreed. "I recollect it was to fall near the Indian Ocean."

The Chancellor nodded, then: "I'm telling you this so you'll understand the danger involved. I wouldn't ask you to send your men down if it wasn't important."

Upchurch glanced into the squinting green eyes of the man before him.

"FORBS is at about 4,500 feet. The *XND* is the only available submersible which can retrieve something that deep."

Upchurch nodded, then said: "Or about 8 minutes from being crushed to death."

"True," Chancellor came back. "If there were any other way, I'd take it. But every sub capable of making this dive is being utilized right now. And we've got to bring that thing up and re-seal it."

"Have you thought about destroying it?"

"If the *XND* can't get close without losing power, that's what we'll do."

Upchurch moved away a few steps and looked back at the Chancellor: "That's one hell of a yarn."

The Chancellor nodded in agreement.

"The power drain on our ships—the one we can't trace. FORBS?"

"I would say so."

"It seems to me, the closer you get to the thing the more power it can pull."

"That's why we'll need to spend about seven hours re-shielding the *XND*."

"You know, you don't have to ask my permission to get the *Navy Diver* down there."

The Chancellor knew the Captain was right—at least technically. One call to Washington and Upchurch would dance if so ordered.

"Yes I do," the Chancellor said. "This is potentially a very dangerous assignment, and no decision for a bureaucrat in Washington."

"Tell ya' what," Upchurch said. "I've got four people qualified to take the *Navy Diver* down. If two volunteer, it's a deal."

The Chancellor agreed. He believed it was more than he had a right to expect.

Captain Upchurch wasn't overjoyed about sending the *XND-1* back into the uncharted abyss, and he said as much to the prospective volunteers.

As if probing an unknown trench that was at least 4,500 feet deep wasn't enough, knowing why, didn't make it any easier to volunteer.

And yet, seven hours later Sanhurst submerged the *XND-1* into a deep region of the abyss with Buzz riding shotgun from his electronic domain. They were the most qualified, they had rightly argued. While they were trained on the *XND-1*, they didn't point out that their, "on-loan," status to ONR was a disguise for working for OCSTO. It was something Upchurch didn't know and it was something the two Navy men didn't realize, "Mr. Jones," knew.

At 4,500 feet and 75 minutes after leaving the surface, they saw it—*Skylab*.

"We have it in sight, over," Sanhurst announced.

"How's your power reading, over?" came Clines' voice through the intercom. There was the slight, "fizz," of static.

"It looks okay, over," Buzz reported, glancing at a gauge.

"The picture up here is crap," came Clines' voice. "What do you see, over."

"From what you told us, I'd say this thing is the Power Converter, over," Sanhurst said.

"Roger that," Clines came back. There was a slight increase in background static. "Is the container compromised, over?"

"I'd say so," Sanhurst responded, studying the ripped Spacecraft. Resting on a ledge, it looked as if a huge beast had bitten off a portion of the craft and left it with the Converter exposed to the open sea. The Power Converter itself was hardly visible in the cocoon of the cracked protective containment sphere. The small portion of the Converter that was visible was dish-shaped and crusted over. Sanhurst also noted the device seemed to emanate light from within the darkened recesses of the downed spacecraft.

"Standby," came Clines' voice.

"Roger," Sanhurst responded.

"You know," Buzz said to Sanhurst. "I really don't like this."

"I've had better feelings myself."

"*Navy Diver*," Clines came back, "what's your power loss, over."

"I show a very minor drop," Buzz reported to Sanhurst.

"Same here," Sanhurst agreed. He keyed the mic: "We show a minor power drop but the shielding holding fine, over."

The line fizzed with static.

"Repeat, *Navy Diver*, over," came Clines' voice.

"We show a minor power drain, over," Sanhurst reported.

"We copy," Clines came back. "All the...back...for..."

Static filled the speakers.

"*Boston*, repeat your last message, over," Sanhurst said into the mic.

"*Navy Diver*...off," came Clines' static-laced response. "Repeat, back off, over."

"Roger that," Sanhurst said, then to Buzz: "Only too happy to oblige."

The *XND-1* sluggishly began to ascend, its motor moaning.

"My sonar just went out," Buzz said, pressing several dead buttons. He looked to the power gauge and furrowed his eyebrows. He reached over and tapped the gauge. "Oh, shit."

"What?" Sanhurst questioned, fighting to force the sub upward. The ballast tank wasn't responding.

"The power gauge," Buzz said, "look at it."

Sanhurst glance over at his gauge. It was about the same as when he last checked: "Looks fine."

"Yeah?" Buzz said, tapping his again. "I think it stopped because there's no power to it. I mean, it shouldn't just stop in the middle like that."

"*Boston*...this is *Navy Diver*, do you copy?" Sanhurst said into the mic.

Static.

"Don't like this," Sanhurst mumbled. "Don't like it at all."

"Look," Buzz ordered, pointing toward the downed spacecraft.

The dark water inside the spacecraft had begun glowing an eerie blue-green.

"Bad," Sanhurst mumbled. "Definitely bad."

Sanhurst redoubled his efforts on the control yolk and ballast tank. Nothing happened. They seemed suspended, as if the last few feet had been obtained upon momentum only. Sanhurst re-adjusted the control panel and tried again—a sluggish moan answered as the sub started upward.

"Look at this," Buzz called from behind.

Sanhurst glanced around to see Buzz's controls awash in what appeared to be a glowing light. Small sparks flickered like fireflies in an aura surrounding the control panels.

A spark arched out, striking Buzz.

"Shit," he gasped, jolted back in his chair.

"It's up here too," Sanhurst said, looking over at the glowing empty seat to his side.

The entire cabin seemed bathed in the eerie glow. Sparks of light crackled as they seemed to slipped in and out of the controls.

The motor ground to a halt, and refused to start despite everything Sanhurst tried.

With a jolt the sub was descending.

Still fighting the dead controls, Sanhurst frantically attempted to restart the motors.

Buzz screamed.

Sanhurst turned to see a control panel erupting in Buzz's face.

A flash of light and fire burst to Sanhurst right side, singeing his shirtsleeve and catching the control panel as if it was a conduit of electrical power. Behind him, Buzz was caught in an arc of electricity, shaking uncontrollably while the panel consumed both itself and him.

Sanhurst realized that the Converter was pulling the *XND-1*, draining the nuclear power-plant with each foot they drew closer.

"If you can't get out of there," Clines had told him on the surface, "for God's sake don't let the Converter get a-hold of the *Navy Diver*. I can't even describe the horror that could happen."

Ever the professional, Sanhurst manually adjusted the diving planes and set the small *XND-1* wing-flaps at a maximum dive angle. Slowly at first, then by degrees, the *XND-1* began descending just short of the outcropping ledge on which the Converter sat. Dropping past the shards of *Skylab*, the *XND-1* banged against the wall of the trench, then drifted back and downward.

The *XND-1* continued swirling into the darkness below. As the sides began crushing in and the rivets popping under the water pressure, Sanhurst looked around to see Buzz charred beyond recognition.

It was the last sight Sanhurst was to see. The water sliced though the hull like a knife. Sanhurst never saw, felt or understood another thing.

His lungs gave way like tissue to the obliterating pressure and he was forced into the same fate he had seen off the coast of Norway.

24

"We lost them," the words echoed.

"What?"

"There goes cabin pressurization."

"My God..." gasped a voice.

Captain Upchurch moved across the Bridge to the monitoring station. He glanced over the vacant readouts then looked at Clines.

Clines shook his head. "They're gone."

The Chancellor glanced out toward the sea, as if he knew Clines was mistaken and the Navy Diver was surfacing...

"Sir..."

The Chancellor looked toward the voice.

Clines was seated across from him in the sound-cushioned Engineering Inc. helicopter. He said, "You did the best you could."

The Chancellor looked out the window, unable to fight the hour-old memory. He too-easily visualized the *XND-1* caving in like paper. He remembered ordering the depth charges and then watching—as if expecting pieces of flesh to bubble to the surface in the boiling seawater.

The setting sun outside the helicopter's window lit the liquid-red horizon—as if sizzling in an acrylic-amber sea of blood. The chopper bobbled as it rose from the deck of the *Boston* and banked into a north-westerly flight—leaving a watery grave. The *Boston* and the OCSTO yacht, with the *TG-3* now mounted on its aft deck became specks in the watery distance. The Chancellor finally turned his head to see Clines and Debbie.

"You can't blame yourself," Debbie said in a small voice.

"I've sent people to die before," the Chancellor responded, "but needlessly...?"

Debbie remained silent, remembering something he had once told her: *Death is a very obscure line of duty.* While she never believed he was completely fathomable, she felt his remorse was greater than he showed. She believed that his many faces, each necessary to his occupation, masked a man trapped by his circumstances; that the dark secrets eroding away his life was the price for being one man able to make a difference in the world. The differences he made were those of a stage director never seen, but applauded through the actors.

Having known him since she was 15, she realized he was sort of the director in her life. Opening doors for her that remained closed to others, the Chancellor had molded her into one of the differences he had made. She had long ago realized that her success had found expression only because he provided a means to the end. Their relationship was a two-way street of his design—and she did not begrudge him that.

He had always been there for her—professionally and personally. She had never heard him utter a harsh word in anger or resentment. Her father had died when she was 13 and she had since grown to think of the Chancellor as the fatherly figure in her life. Despite the darkness in which the Chancellor was veiled, it was a testimony to his character that he had earned her respect.

Now, like times before, she wanted to console him—to convince him that he was wrong about the *XND-1*—that it was not a needless tragedy. But like the Chancellor, she knew otherwise.

"By all logic the Converter shouldn't have been active," Clines commented.

"It doesn't really matter now," Debbie countered.

"That's what we thought years ago," he came back.

"You're being morbid, Blake," she accused.

"He's right," the Chancellor interrupted.

"So, uh, what's the point?"

"I don't like unanswered questions," the Chancellor replied.

"I see," she said with doubt.

"Loose ends," Clines added, "have a way of unraveling in the future."

"And there are plenty of loose ends here," the Chancellor said.

"Like?" she pressed.

"Like why was the Power Converter active?" Clines asked rhetorically.

She started to answer and then realized the implications. She could have answered practically any question about the inner workings of FORBS. But the Power Converter wasn't her specialty.

"You think FORBS survived the *Skylab* crash?" she questioned incredulously.

"Think about it," the Chancellor said. "The Converter can be activated remotely by anyone with its coordinates. The only reason to activate the Converter was to power-up FORBS."

"Which means," Clines added, "someone has to know where the Converter and FORBS are, as well as the access code."

She looked from one to the other. Without conviction, she said: "That's crazy."

"Hardly," the Chancellor came back. "If you recall, Blake spent nearly seven hours adding additional shielding to the *Navy Diver* because it was nuclear powered."

And nuclear power, Debbie knew, was the power-up source for FORBS.

"Don't forget all the minor power losses from the ships and subs," Clines noted.

"But how—where—I mean who—"

"It's all speculation," the Chancellor interrupted, still uncertain how the non-nuclear power drains belonged in the equation. Clines had speculated that in searching for nuclear power, the Converter interfered with other power sources. Whatever the case, it was just one more loose end.

"Damned good speculation," Debbie was saying to the Chancellor. "I mean, do you have any other way of explaining it?"

The Chancellor nodded his head *no*.

They sat in silence for a moment and then Debbie suddenly looked at the Chancellor.

"You're bringing Karns in on this, aren't you?" she asked, staring at him.

"Yes."

She looked at Clines—Karns' only friend. "You knew?"

"Yeah," he answered with a nod of his head.

"When?" she pressed Clines.

"Karns only called me last week—"

"I mean, when is he due back?"

"Oh," Clines said. "Actually, he should already be at the yacht."

The Chancellor looked at her. "Debbie..."

"What?"

He shook his head as if to say, *never mind.*

The subject was an old one never broached. The Chancellor looked back out to see the gray storm clouds below the chopper.

25

The helicopter Shuttered as it dropped below the rain-drenched clouds covering Washington DC. Whipping through the drizzle it eased to the pavement near a large hangar located adjacent to the International Airport. The nearby floodlights pierced the mist, creating cone-shaped areas of visibility in the dark.

The Chancellor stepped to the ground followed by Debbie and Clines. Clines then retrieved two suitcases and closed the hatch. A black limo was pulling around to meet them as the helicopter drifted upward and toward the hangar. The large doors echoed as they slid opened, accompanied by the hangar's lights activating.

The driver of the limo hopped out to open one of the passenger doors.

"I'm, uh, going with Blake," Debbie announced, looking to Clines. "If you don't mind."

"I can guess where we're going," he said.

She smiled and faced the Chancellor. "I'll see you in the morning."

His features were hidden in shadows but she saw him nod as he said, "Take care."

"I will," she responded.

He disappeared into the waiting car and they watched the backup lights flicker as it dropped into gear. The car pulled away.

Clines looked to Debbie. "The yacht, right?"

"Please?"

He sighed. "Let's go."

They moved across the pavement, passing the hangar as the tall doors were sliding back together. Clines used a pocket remote to deactivate the alarm on a glossy black 1960 Studebaker Lark Convertible that was parked off to the side. While Debbie slipped into the passenger side, Clines removed a plastic model boat from his suitcase and tossed the baggage into the trunk.

Within moments they were pulling away from the hangar.

"Why in the world is Zelda letting you drive her car?" Debbie asked, referring to Clines' current girlfriend.

"It's a trade," he answered, slowing down at a guard gate. "She's driving Karns' Dart."

He rolled the window down and held out his license.

The security guard shined a light on them: "Oh, Mr. Clines, glad to see you back, Sir."

"Glad to be back, Skip," Clines replied.

"Hey that was some rescue you pulled," Skip came back, oblivious to the moisture accumulating on his slicker and the Studebaker's opened window frame.

"Good grief," Clines moaned, "they didn't run some kind of special on it, did they?"

Skip smiled: "Cable did. Got to tell my wife and Skip, Jr. that I personally knew the rescue-man in charge."

"Did you tell them the rescue-man was responsible for launching the sub in the first place?"

"No point," Skip said, leaning over, "I figure it was the stupid government dopes who pushed for the launch anyway."

"You got that one right," Clines agreed.

"You Engineering Inc. guys are okay," Skip said.

Smiling, Clines produced the model boat and handed it to the guard: "For little Skipper, as promised."

"Thank you, Mr. Clines," Skip said, and waved for his partner to open the gate.

"Hope he enjoys it—it's straight off the *Lexington* herself."

They waved and drove on.

"Skipper?" Debbie questioned.

"Skip Jr., his son. Good kid."

"Oh," she said. Then: "Now, why are you letting Zelda drive Gray's Dart—I didn't even know you had finished restoring it."

"We only finished it out about a month ago. I wanted to make sure it was sound, so Zelda's been driving it around town."

While the '63 Dodge Dart GT convertible was indeed what might be termed an American classic, Clines doubted it really held any interest for Debbie. He knew she was using the subject to discuss Gray—not that he minded, but he felt the car deserved better attention than that.

"Blake," she said, "How's he been doing?"

Clines considered her a moment, wondering why it had taken her so long and what he should say in reply.

"Karns is Karns," he finally contributed.

"Blake..."

"He's private, you know that."

She did, but her expectant gaze was unperturbed.

"He doesn't tell me how he feels, Debbie," Clines said at last.

She was quiet a moment, then: "Does he still get flashbacks?"

"No more than me, I suppose," Clines answered. He thought a moment longer. "He has the one about Jay every now and then."

"Jay?"

"A man in our unit," he answered, "in 'Nam. He was half-a-step from a section 8 when his girl wrote him a, 'Dear John' letter."

"Pushed him over the edge?"

Clines was silent, remembering the night as though it were yesterday.

"Blake?"

"Huh?" he said, pushing the mental picture away.

"What happened?"

"He blew his brains out," Clines answered bluntly. "It was a mess... Blood and brains... Just a horrible mess."

"God!" Debbie moaned, repelled as much by Clines' tone as his words.

"Did Karns see it happen?"

"We both did."

He glanced at her, realizing she wanted more detail.

"We had been in a helicopter which was shot down by a captured American chopper," he explained. "Somehow five of us got together on the ground..."

Clines saw the crazy air chase in his mind. He watched through the hatch as he realized they were losing altitude and going down. The chopper shuddered and Gray was thrown sideways—his head slamming against the bulkhead. Clines grabbed him and forced him to jump the remaining 12 feet to the ground.

Clines came up, firing at the Vietcong—yelling at Lieutenant Gray to get up. Groggily, Gray managed to pull out a weapon and start firing. At first Clines had thought the lieutenant too dazed to realize what was happening. Lieutenant Gray had started firing his weapon in the wrong direction—or so Clines had first thought. Clines had then glanced around to see that the "dazed" Lieutenant Gray had just mowed down five Vietcong who had been rushing them from another direction.

"So what happened?" Debbie said.

Clines focused on the road again. "The five of us regrouped and started a march back. Just before dusk it started raining and the damned VC were hot at our heels.

"One of us—Mickey Rand—fell into a pit of spikes."

Debbie grimaced.

"Being a lieutenant, Karns was in charge. He ordered us to climb into the pit with Mick."

"For God's sake, why?"

"The Vietcong were having trouble tracking us, but weren't too far behind. Karns figured we were far enough ahead that the rain would help hide our trail..."

Clines smiled a moment. "We're standing there in the middle of the jungle, having an argument no louder than whispers. I told him I didn't care if he was a fucking General, we needed to take advantage of the rain and run like hell. Karns—and I barely knew him them—seemed to just stop listening to me. He just looked off in the direction we had been heading. And then, just as suddenly, he looked at me and said 'We are taking advantage of the rain, it's covering our tracks. All we have to do now is disappear.'"

Debbie smiled. "What'd you say?"

"I told him that's exactly what I was going to do. But when I turned to take off, he yanked me back by the collar and told me that I'd be 'disappearing' right into the guns of another squad of VC about a mile away."

"He heard them, didn't he?"

Blake nodded his head with a smile. "He said as much too, but I didn't believe 'em."

"So what happened?"

"I told him that was the biggest bunch of bullshit I'd ever heard. So he told me that even if he was wrong—and he said that he wasn't—we couldn't disappear unless we were nowhere to be seen."

"That convinced you?"

Clines shrugged. "That, and he put his hand on my shoulder and told me to trust 'em. For some damned reason he seemed so absolutely sure of himself, I agreed. So we hid in the pit."

Clines smirked. "Of course, I told him that if the VC found us, I would kill him first."

Debbie smiled. "So where did Jay fit into all this?"

"Oh, yeah," Clines said, becoming somber again. "We covered ourselves with the grass and bamboo and parked our butts for a few hours. It was right at sundown—I mean we could just barely see to the other side of the pit—when Jay pulled out this letter he'd been reading for a couple of days..."

Clines watched Jay Casper gripping the wrinkled letter in his hand. It was too dark to actually read the letter, so Jay merely crumpled it tightly in his fist. Clines turned his attention toward Hollender, the other soldier.

"Yeah, it feels real good," Jay mumbled in a whisper.

Clines looked over to see Casper with the letter in one hand and his gun in the other. The gun had a silencer screwed onto the barrel—standard equipment for the mission on which the Chancellor had sent them.

"Jay..." Gray whispered, "You okay—"

"So what happened?" Debbie asked again.

Clines blinked his eyes, as if seeing the road in front of him for the first time. "He said something about his girlfriend leaving, put the pistol to his face and blew out his brains."

"Oh, my God..."

"Hollander vomited and kind of lost it—started trying to climb out of the pit. I had to knock 'em out."

"And Karns?"

"It was ghoulish. When I finally sat down and looked over, he was picking up a chunk of Jay's brain from his lap... Then he handed it to me..."

Clines remembered the two of them sitting with the near headless Casper and Mick Rand beneath them, the spikes poking through him like pins in a cushion. Hollander lay unconscious, covered in his own vomit. The blood was everywhere—some of it having spattered all of them. The blood was pumping from Casper's body forming a red pool at their feet. And there they calmly sat.

"What for?"

"Huh?"

"Why did he hand it to you," Debbie asked.

"He said, 'Here Blake,'" Clines quoted. "'Her name is Bonnie. Mail it to her... Tell her she should have lied a little longer.'"

It was silent in the Studebaker for several moments and Clines drove on. She hadn't asked about the fifth team member, and it was just as well. He had not even survived to see the pit in which they had huddled.

The sound of the tires on the pavement and the swish of wipers seemed loud. Debbie thought back to the times Gray had mentioned having flashbacks that were, "as real as being there." What she thought she had understood, she had never even come close to visualizing until now.

"It took us two weeks to get out of that jungle," Clines said finally.

"Karns never said anything—he never told me... I mean, yeah, he said he had flashbacks, but..." Her voice trailed off.

"It's not a pretty memory," Clines said. He glanced at her. "We saw things that were so gruesome they didn't even look real."

"Why hasn't he ever tried to get help?"

"You mean like a therapist or something?"

"Yeah."

"He did. Twice."

"What happened?"

"They said they could only help him through heavy duty medication or worse. He didn't want to risk it. I wouldn't either."

For several minutes they rode in silence again, listening to the wipers swishing back and forth.

"Blake?"

"Huh?"

"I feel like time is really slipping away. How do I reach him?"

"I don't know."

"What about Gail James?"

"What about her?" Clines questioned, looking at Debbie. He could see she was really in an emotional turmoil. He looked back to the road.

"He's not mentioned her in ten years or more," Clines answered one of the questions he was certain she wanted to ask. "I can't say he got over her in the traditional sense. I mean, it isn't like he's slowly come to love her less. It's more like he's matured. She had too much turmoil in her life in the first place. It was like she was never able to get her act together—even when she was swearing to your face that she was fine, you knew she wasn't. I think Karns has finally outgrown her."

Debbie looked over at Clines.

"Don't misunderstand me," he quantified. "He never stopped loving her. I think he's just learned that love is more than butterflies in the stomach. It's respect and honesty as much as it is sacrifices and flowers."

Debbie nodded.

"I asked him once if he thought about her much."

She waited, knowing Clines sometimes thought long before speaking. In that respect both he and Gray were occasionally alike.

"He kind of laughed," Clines finally continued, "and said, 'you're thinking when you're trying not to.'

"For the longest time," Clines said slowly, "the worst thing he did was to not talk about her."

He looked over again, ensuring he had eye contact. "Kind of the same way you usually don't talk about him."

She didn't immediately respond and then: "What did he say about my getting married?"

"The same thing he said about your divorce: 'Sometimes it happens that way.'"

That ended the conversation and they drove in silence again. The lights of the city had faded behind and an occasional lamp post flashed their features into view. His—thoughtful. Hers—lost.

Moments later the car came to a halt at an old river dock. A short stroll across the road and down a set of rickety steps was a port of what was now, low-rent boat slips.

"You want me to wait?" Clines asked.

"Nah," she answered. "You need to get home for some rest."

"You want your suitcase?" he asked, a thumb stabbed toward the trunk.

"I'll pick it up when I see you at the office tomorrow."

Clines looked toward the darkened dock for a moment, then to Debbie: "It has been a long time. What're you going to say?"

"'Hi,'" she offered.

Clines shook his head with a slight smirk on his face.

She stepped from the car, clutch purse in hand, and leaned over to peer at him. She noticed the same forced reserve that she had notice on the Chancellor's face.

"Blake... I realize you probably don't think this is a good idea. But I just need to do this."

"I know."

"Thanks," she said with a smile.

He returned a smile. "Sometimes you do whatever is necessary to get by and be comfortable with your conscience."

"Sounds philosophical."

"I have my moments," he responded. "Be careful."

"I will. Thanks, Blake." She let the door close.

Watching her move across the road, Clines realized he had ceased to exist in her mind. She was thinking about Gray.

Clines shifted the car into gear and turned around for the city.

26

The misting air was fresh and cool. Although partially shrouded in a mist, shiny surfaces loomed sharply out of the dark: it was a ghost-clear midnight.

Debbie stood in the vague mist, staring at the rickety dock and old boats anchored among the many empty slips. The once pristine dock was now decrepit—the white paint worn away. With only a handful of lamp posts working, the area was reminiscent of a rundown prohibition-era wharf. Absent were the yachts of previous years, replaced by cabin cruisers, flat-bottomed boats and inexpensive pontoons.

Debbie audibly sighed and moved down the creaking steps. She slowly made her way to the 48 ft. motor yacht. The once flawless work of sailing art fashioned by Elco Cruisers in New York, now sat in the stagnation of dim haloed dock lights—a spectra of the past; its dingy white paint flaking with age. Emblazoned across its stern, the italicized *Paige Alexandra* was faded and stained.

She walked across the gangplank and onto the deserted deck. The canopy was gone, leaving the open sundeck, a couple of empty chairs and a cup of coffee on a table. It was cold.

She considered calling Gray's name, but it seemed inappropriate in the surrounding stillness. For the same reason she dismissed knocking on the heavy oak door of the deckhouse. Instead, she felt along the lintel, retrieving a key she knew was there.

Unlocked, the door yielded noiselessly, opening on well-oiled hinges. Groping along the dark wall—or rather the *bulkhead*—she found a lamp switch. With a click the corner lamp came to life and she turned to face a .25 caliber Wafffnfabriken Simson pistol. At the other end of the German gun was Karns Gray.

"Wow," she said with a sheepish smile. "Déjà Vu."

"You know it may be just a boat to you, but it's still my house—ever thought about knocking?"

"I uh, thought I'd surprise you," she explained lamely.

"You did," he responded, his voice smooth. His dark brown hair was well-combed and she assumed he had not been in bed, despite his wearing a gray housecoat. He rose from the chair and surprised her with a hug.

"It's nice to see you, Deb."

She had mapped out a number of conversational lies in order to sound flippant and casual. But with his arms around her all she could manage was, "I've missed you."

Gray stepped back at arm's length. "You still look beautiful."

"Just shoot me now," she said with a tilt of her head to indicate the pistol he was absentmindedly holding. "I'll die happy knowing you said something sweet."

"Oh, sorry about that," he said of the gun, and moved to the dining table where he returned the pistol to a suit jacket hanging from a chair. His other gun was in a shoulder holster draped over another chair.

"I guess you're wondering why I popped in," Debbie said.

"You weren't just in the neighborhood?" he asked, a faint smile on his face.

She smiled back, remembering the excuse she had used a number of times years earlier. Her bravado wasn't what it used to be.

She handed him the key. "The Chancellor said he was bringing you in, so I thought...I'd just...drop in."

He nodded with an understanding expression. "I see."

"I suppose I should have waited until morning," she said, watching him walk over and open the door.

"I wasn't sleeping anyway," he commented, returning the key to the beam above the door. "Let's get some air."

She followed him out onto the deck, laying her purse on the table. "How's it been going?"

"Fine," he answered automatically. "Yourself?"

"Okay," she said with a lilt in her voice. "Blake and I just flew in from the Gulf."

"That explains the Navy duds," he commented, indicating her denim shirt and jeans. "The *TG-3*?"

She nodded, watching him lean against the yacht's railing.

"It was all over the news," he said.

"I've heard."

"Of course everyone had it pegged as a Navy project. It's a good thing the Office's research yacht was registered with the sailor boys."

"Yeah," she agreed, moving over to the railing by him. "Imagine an OCSTO Navy—the press would go crazy."

"Did the *TG-3* pilot survive?"

"I'm here, aren't I?"

"You?" he said, mildly surprise.

"Bingo."

"I didn't realize you were a pilot?"

"I'm not."

"Then how—"

"That's the beauty of a neuro-link and synthetic synaptic computer components," she said. "The craft does what you think it to do. Besides, my synaptic pattern was the only one in the system—no one else could have made it move one inch."

"I'd call that job security."

"Yeah."

"So what happened out there?"

"An old friend of yours tried to sink my sub," she answered elusively.

"An old friend of mine?" he asked.

"Well, a part of an old friend of yours. I came across the FORBS Power Converter."

"That's the thing that powered-up FORBS, right?"

"Yeah."

"What about FORBS?" Gray asked.

"It was just the Power Converter."

"What does that mean?"

"I'm not sure. The Chancellor and Blake are worried that it means FORBS has been recovered from the ocean.

"Recovered?" Gray questioned. "After all this time?"

"They say there's no reason for the Converter to be active unless someone used the activation codes."

"So its been sitting out there waiting for power to just float by?"

"The surface ships did detect minor power drains—but not enough to power-up FORBS. However, the closer our subs got to the Converter, the greater the power loss. The Navy lost their deep-sea submersible because of that."

"Hmm."

"Frankly, I'm not sure what to think of it. And I don't think it really matters, either. The Chancellor dropped depth charges and blew it to kingdom come."

"That's one way to solve a problem—remove it."

Debbie flickered her eyes between Gray and the distant city lights. The lights were so obscured by the weather they appeared only intermittently, like spiritual apparitions.

"Karns..."

"Yes?" He looked at her, realizing she was suddenly struggling with what she wanted to say. He also realized she seemed even more sensual than he remembered.

"You know, I didn't come all the way out here, in the middle of the night, to talk about FORBS."

"Oh, I had that much figured out when you said, 'Wow.'"

"Am I that transparent?" she asked, feeling embarrassed and silly. She couldn't believe the way she was feeling, what she wanted to say, or the way she wanted to act. It all seemed so ridiculous. Being unable to verbalize it made it even worse.

"Well," he stumbled with a vague shrug.

"I, uh, just felt I needed to see you again," she finally managed to say. "I really meant it when I said I've missed you."

He stepped back a pace, buying time. It wasn't an obvious gesture to thwart her, but she was aware of it nonetheless. A momentary silence filled the space between them—an awkward emptiness.

"I don't know what to say," he said. That he found her exciting, alluring and desirable was meaningless in the shadow of what she wanted.

"I shouldn't have done this," she said in almost a whisper while gazing out over the water. She looked over at him, realizing he was completely unreadable. And that was when something clicked and fell into place.

She didn't have to read this man to know his torment—not now. Clines had provided the insight that she had been selfishly ignoring, even though it was staring her in the face. Whether she was the right woman for him was insignificant in comparison to the inner battles he fought daily. She realized she had wanted him to love her, when she should have been offering to love him. She recalled Clines' advice from years earlier: *Be his friend first and you won't have to be careful*. She had been too young, or perhaps too preoccupied with her desires to understand the nuances of that advice.

She turned to look at him—seeing him in a whole new light.

"It's okay," she said quietly. "I didn't mean to put you on the spot or anything."

"I'm the one who should apologize," he came back.

She moved closer to him, looking up into the unfathomable void of his dark eyes. "Do you know what one of the best things about you is, Karns?"

His face was calm, his eyes slowly moving from the river to her. She had to admit he had become a master. There was absolutely no indication of any sort of battle behind the solid face before her.

"What?" He asked.

She glanced off a second, a smile flirting for attention on her pouty lips. She hoped he was still enamored with her beauty: "It's that you're nothing like my ex-husband."

He laughed—music to her ears. She didn't realize that her laugh was received in much the same way.

"I hear you've had a rough go of it," he said at last.

"You mean the flopped marriage?" she questioned.

He nodded.

"Doomed, I tell you," she almost cooed. "Completely doomed from day one."

He smiled, enjoying her playful intimacy. It was as if in that once sentence, she had parted a curtain of femininity, offering everything and demanding nothing but his audience.

"That bad, huh?" he said.

"Completely," she assured him with a slow closing of her eyes. She looked up, hoping they were now past the terrible awkwardness of moments before. "If everything bad ended as quickly as my marriage, this would be a good life."

Gray grinned, basking in her charm.

Looking up at him, she wondered how he concealed so much, so well. She had helped him divert the conversation—to avoid the heart of his thoughts. Only moments before she would have wanted to grab him by the collar—to tell him about her feelings. She would have asked him how he handled the silence—the pain—the loneliness he imposed on himself. She still wanted to know all those things, but now she didn't intend to indulge her selfish frustration whereas she would have before.

"Did you care for him?" Gray asked.

"No," she answered simply. "I was looking for a quick fix."

"I'm sorry," he sincerely said, realizing what she meant. "If I could have changed things—"

She interrupted him with a shaking of her head, and stepped closer to him. She said, "Don't be. I made that mistake by myself and tried to blame it on you."

He didn't have a response, and she wasn't expecting one.

"Listen," she said, inching even closer. "I'm not here to force anything—"

He started to interrupt, but she placed her hand on his chest and said: "Wait."

He nodded.

"Vietnam was horrendous: I understand that now. The things you feel aren't always easily handled or fixed. I won't waltz in here after all these years and tell you how to feel—you don't need that shit and neither do I."

She paused, her hand still on his chest. "I'll never be a Gail James—and however you deal with that part of your life is something I can't make myself a part of—and I shouldn't."

Again she paused, feeling her stomach tense up: "I'm probably more screwed-up in the head than you. But, I'm willing to talk about it. I'm willing to listen. Sometimes that's all that's left... However you choose to work through these things, I'm here if you need me.

"I made a mistake," she whispered, "a huge mistake. You were right—I was too young—and I made all the mistakes of a selfish little girl. I just didn't understand what you were going through. I'm sorry, and I'm here now."

He put his hand on hers, searching for words.

She carefully touched his arm. "It's alright. You don't have to say anything. Just know that I'm here, okay?"

He nodded, his expressionless face seemingly softened.

Leaning against him she kissed his cheek and whispered: "I'm going to leave now—I'll see you tomorrow."

She didn't wait for a reply. She turned, sweeping her purse off the table and he watched her move across the deck to disappear down the gangplank.

By the time she reached the road, the knot in her stomach felt as though it were in her throat. She wanted to go back but knew it wasn't of any use. Just realizing she might never have him made her sick to her stomach. So much so, she actually stopped to throw-up. When she didn't, she straightened and looked around.

She emitted a sound somewhere between a sarcastic laugh and moan.

"No car," she mumbled with a shake of her head and wondered what cab fare would cost.

27

The Sound Room.

Drumming his fingers, Karns Gray patiently sat at the table in the center of the room. Per the Chancellor's instructions, he had phoned in to arrange a briefing with the OCSTO Deputy Director. Clines had dropped by the Yacht at 10:00 a.m., drove him in and helped him find the center of the Sound Room.

Gray pushed a cup under the coffee urn's spout and drew a mug-full. Leaning back, he loosened his tie and stared at the cup. Debbie's appearance on the yacht hadn't been the only case of déjà vu. He had sat in this same room—drinking coffee—20 years ago. He looked to see if it was the same coffee urn, but it didn't look all that old.

His mind drifted to the previous night. Actually, he had been thinking about it—about Debbie—all morning. He had spent the last 20 years waking up alone in isolated and exotic places all over the world. He had witnessed panoramic views and breathtaking vistas, but always with emptiness inside.

But this morning had been different. He awoke thinking about Debbie. Not that he hadn't thought of her often. They had loosely stayed in touch, whenever his assignments permitted a letter or postcard. There was a period of about three years when they lost contact during her courtship, marriage and separation. Her letters, cards and calls always brightened his outlook, but he had distanced himself from feeling more.

Perhaps, he thought, *that had changed.*

He had showered and shaved while humming some tune of which he could neither remember the title nor words. He had finished shaving when it occurred to him that he was feeling literally good. Not just okay. Not just all right. But good. He actually laughed at the face in the mirror.

"Did you fire your lawyer or something?" Clines had asked when he picked up Gray.

"How's that?" Gray responded, still preoccupied with his thoughts.

"You seem very pleased with yourself," Clines had said.

"I think I am," Gray had told him.

It was true that he felt a certain new spring to his step, but it was something about which he was naturally laconic. On uncertain ground, he was acutely diffident about a next step. For that reason alone, he had asked Clines, rather than Debbie, to lead him to the center of the Sound Room—Gray had never committed it to memory.

"Mr. Graham?" came Kate Kegley's voice.

Gray looked over to see the OCSTO Deputy Director coming into the room with a brief case.

"Ms. Kegley," Gray greeted, standing to shake her hand.

"Please, call me Kate."

"All right Kate," he said. "Just call me, 'Jack.'"

"Jack. John. You Chancellor agents certainly use sturdy names."

He smiled, liking her. "We each wear red and blue long-johns with an, 'S,' on the chest, too."

She flashed a smirk; "For, 'Superbull,' no doubt."

Getting down to business, she sat across the table from him.

"The Chancellor gave me a brief run-down of what you needed to know," she explained, opening the briefcase. "He said you'd probably have a number of questions as well."

"That's almost a given."

"Several months ago, all satellites failed over the CIS. Shortly thereafter, the pattern of blackouts extended over the Atlantic and Mexico.

"Just a few days ago, the Chancellor was thinking this tied into a yacht full of Russian weapons and drugs anchored in the Gulf of Mexico. He's less sure of that now, thinking it might have something to do with FORBS."

She looked up from one of the folders.

"I only learned about the FORBS Power Converter not burning-up with Skylab this morning, Jack. I can hardly believe it."

"Really?" Gray came back. "Why?"

"If FORBS had been fully operational, it could have been like some sort of Big Brother right out of Orwell's *1984*. It not only would have been self-sufficient, but also would have had unlimited learning capacity."

"That's a fair assessment," Gray agreed.

"The potential is incredible. It could have broken any programming language or code—I mean, a computer with human insight... That's—that's scary. With that kind of ability it could have accessed any database—"

"You're preaching to the choir, Kate," Gray interrupted.

"I'm sorry. But it just amazes me how irresponsible scientists can be."

"Well, FORBS was originally intended as a tool to help study the human brain."

"You know what they say about the road to hell?" she came back. She didn't mention having been here when NASA brought Skylab down or her knowing about his participation in Project Hacksaw.

"Anyway," Gray said, returning to the subject at hand, "the Chancellor's thinking the satellite blackouts have something to do with the FORBS Power Converter, right?"

She responded with an affirmative nod. "One of the blackout areas coincides with Debbie's flight plan and where she went down."

"And satellite jamming to cover Russian weapon and drug smuggling is a sight more improbable than a major CIS operation to recover the FORBS Power Converter?" Gray speculated.

Kegley leaned back. "It's a question of what is the greater coincidence."

"There's been a flow of black market weapons in and out of Mexico for years," Gray countered. "It started with the feud between the government and the wealthy land owners—weapon shipments are a common occurrence."

"True enough," she agreed.

"What about recon planes?"

"Regular stealth flights over both countries. Just the usual petty stuff for the most part. But then, they did lose one the stealths over Mexico."

"Who knew the access codes to FORBS and the Converter?"

"That's where it gets interesting," she replied, looking to her notes. "Dr. Farrell, Dr. Baker, Jim Austiff and Steve Andrews."

"E.H. is dead," Gray commented, "And Jim's missing—a good reason for his disappearance. Who's Steve Andrews?"

"He was Dr. Farrell's lab assistant."

"Was?"

"Or is."

He looked at her expectantly.

"Steve Andrews disappeared from the face of the earth about eight months ago."

"His affairs?"

"Nice and tidy—which doesn't tell us a lot with the possible exception of his credit card."

"Where I come from, 'tidy affairs,' means an expected disappearance."

"The thing is," Kegley pointed out, "up until his disappearance, he was very up-to-date on all of his affairs. The only quirk is that he canceled his one credit card."

Gray looked pensive. "I thought anyone who knew anything about FORBS had died."

"FORBS, yes," Kegley put in. "Mr. Andrews helped Dr. Farrell in the design of the Power Converter. He knew substantially less about FORBS. According to the records, he moved into the private sector before Dr. Farrell finished designing FORBS."

"Well, Steve Andrews aside, there's a few minor glitches."

"What?"

"The Atlantic blackout began before the *TG-3* launch. Assuming the satellite failures were cover for a salvage, why was the Converter still there?"

"It was too deep to recover," Kegley offered.

"And what are the chances, in all the thousands of miles of ocean, the *TG-3* would pass right by it."

"Well it was actually the storm that forced her off course—which makes it fairly coincidental in my book."

Gray shook his head *no*. "This morning Blake said he found the *TG-3* within a quarter mile of its flight plan. Essentially, Debbie held it on course."

"I thought it was further off course than that."

"No," Gray confirmed. "And there's about a half-mile to a mile play in that number if you're pinning down the location of the Converter."

"And that means what?"

"It would mean the Converter was within the *TG-3's* planned route."

"I think you're concentrating too much on one aspect that is a coincidence," Kegley countered.

"Oh?"

"We have blackouts over the CIS, followed by blackouts over the Atlantic, followed by blackouts over Mexico," Kegley said.

"Go on."

"We have a boatload of Russian weapons and drugs in the gulf, near Mexico. And there is that stealth plane that disappeared over Mexico."

"And it all means?" he asked, using her approach.

"An operation moved from the CIS to Mexico."

"And the FORBS Power Converter?"

"No relation to the blackouts," she answered.

"Well, that's possible."

"Good," she said. "Because if it came down that way, that means Jim's disappearance, whether related to FORBS or not, hasn't anything to do with the blackouts. The same goes for Steve Andrews, who may have decided to disappear on his own—which substantiates his canceling his credit card."

"Why do I get the feeling your trying to sell me a bill of goods?"

"Excuse me?"

"You obviously favor your theory. Why?"

She slid a nearby coffee cup under the Urn's spout.

"Well," she said, bringing a full cup back, "there's a couple of complications that connect the weapons, the blackouts and Austiff."

"That's completely contrary to your theory, isn't it?" he said with a smile.

"Sort of," she admitted, adding a package of sugar to the coffee.

"But you have a rational explanation," he added.

"Even if I'm wrong, there are other scenarios," she said, pushing the folders over to him. "Personally, I think there are three or four things happening here, none of which are related. The Chancellor, on the other hand, says to give it all to you for your evaluation.

"I'm honored."

"Take your time," she said, standing up and then casually pointed to a button on the tabletop. "Press that when you're ready to leave. It buzzes Austiff's Adjutant, and she can lead you out of here."

"I know the way," he assured her, realizing she doubted him. She had no way of knowing he had memorized the path when Clines had led him in earlier.

"Okay," she said. "But this room covers nearly this entire floor—about two thirds of it. You could be lost in this maze all day and we'd never hear or find you."

He nodded. "I'll remember that."

She picked up her coffee. "Later, then."

She walked into the maze and the room was completely silent.

28

If anything, the Office was thorough, Gray mused.

The reports spread across the tabletop had required two hours of studying.

The trouble had begun when a nondescript scientist on the CIA payroll was unable to activate his geological program through a NASA satellite. The satellite stalled somewhere over the CIS. Attempting to run the program through an alternate satellite passing through the same area netted the same result.

"And that started the ball rolling," Gray had remarked to himself, while looking over the papers. It was only a matter of hours before the establishment realized every satellite orbiting through that specific region of the globe went on a hiatus. Naturally, no one tended to believe that the various CIS counterparts were equally baffled.

Just as satellite failures over the Atlantic began, reconnaissance flights were stepped-up and numerous agencies went on alert. While repeated recon flights revealed nothing of interest, a region over Mexico fell prey to the mysterious blind spots.

The CIA was called into action and with the help of highly trained military specialists, teams were sent to the affected regions of the CIS and Mexico.

At that point, the Chancellor was asked to assist—probably by someone within the CIA or pentagon, Gray knew. The Chancellor sent John Wilson—the alias was unfamiliar to Gray—to keep an eye on the CIS team. Wilson's report read like an obituary column. Four apparent Foreign Intelligence agents killed by Alister Marow and half that again by Wilson himself.

A fishing trawler came across the CIS team shot to death, and with enough explosives attached to their boat to sink a battleship. The explosives were to ignite when the boat was partially sunk from holes blown through the bottom. Only, the boat drifted onto a sandbar and was unable to sink to the point where the water-level-trigger activated the explosives. An examination of the explosives and the triggering device did not yield additional clues. The method, while unusual, was not indicative of any known modus operandi.

Wilson was assigned to locate a lead but references to that were apparently redacted—a form of compartmentalizing "need to know" information. Gray flipped through the pages, ensuring they weren't out of order, then flipped through the second folder. Obviously the Chancellor had something brewing elsewhere.

Returning to the first folder, Gray read over a report regarding the existence of a yacht-load of drugs and surplus Russian weapons in the Gulf of Mexico. Oddly enough, the tip had come to the Chancellor who in turn had sent an agent to the yacht for a near death escape and photos of the contraband. There followed a DEA report concerning the same yacht and cargo. The DEA report, a thorough piece of investigation, explained that the weapons were part of a shipment lost shortly after the Armenia coup of '91.

The yacht's owner-history included an obscure investment counseling firm in Alaska which later sold it to a company called World Pleasure Cruises. The second company filed bankruptcy and auctioned off the boat to an Arabian buyer. The Arabian buyer was untraceable, and the report concluded a false identity had been employed in order to secure the yacht for purposes similar to those for which it had now been impounded.

Gray hit the button Kegley had explained would alert Austiff's Adjutant.

Returning to the two reports, and reading between the lines, Gray decided a stool pigeon was the only reason the Chancellor would have received a tip regarding the yacht. Logically, he would have sent an agent to document the yacht's cargo only if he wanted to tie it to someone under investigation. The near-death escape meant the agent had failed to keep the reconnaissance a secret. The DEA was then asked to seize the cargo, thus making the failed recon of the 1109 agent appear to be the first prong of a two prong DEA investigation.

"Not a bad example of covering your ass," Gray thought aloud.

"Pardon me," came a whispering voice.

Startled, Gray looked up to see Laura Phinor. Being so acclimated to hearing the faintest of sounds, Gray had forgotten he could not hear through the absorbent walls of the Sound Room .

"I was thinking to myself," Gray explained, appraising the attractive woman. She had a profusion of blonde hair that cascaded over her shoulders, accenting a fairly tall and slender frame. She wore a gray suit —tailored for women to include a skirt hemmed just above the knee.

"Are you ready to go now?" Laura asked, her voice barely overcoming the sound absorbing quality of the room.

"Actually," Gray responded, "I was wondering if you could track down anything on a defunct corporation called World Pleasure Cruises."

"Anything particular?"

"General stuff. Owners, notable stockholders—that sort of thing."

"Well," Laura came back, "a major stockholder in the company was called Consolidated Investments. They actually held some sort of legal controlling interest through one of their subsidiary companies, called North investments, or some such."

Gray's eyes went wide and he held up an index figure as he flipped back through the pages he had been reading.

"North Alaskan Investments?" he suggested, re-reading the name of one of the seized yacht's previous owners.

"That's it," Laura answered.

"And how do you know that?" Gray asked, surprised that she would just happen to know such a tantalizing piece of data. The information meant that two of the previous owners of the seized yacht had been the same company.

"Because Dr. Charlton Trenton was on the board of Consolidated Investments—that was his big start."

"Trenton?" Gray echoed, recognizing the name.

"Yeah. There was a big write-up about him in the last issue of *Time*. He has a Ph.D. in linguistics and a Masters in some area related to aerospace. He was one of the driving forces behind the government selling of NovaNet back in the 80s. Recently, he's put Nova back in the spotlight by gearing the company's research and development toward aerospace instead of defense."

"Wow," Gray said, realizing he sounded silly saying it—kind of like Debbie.

"It was really interesting," she replied with a smile.

"Any details worth remembering?" Gray ventured.

"Well, let's see. It was built in Nevada around the late 50s and was abandoned when one of the administrations went budget crazy. Dr. Trenton managed to put together a group who purchased the complex and turned it private. There was a big deal about the computers that ran the place. The government had left a ton of classified information and had to go back after the sale to purge the system."

"You're amazing!" Gray said smiling.

"Thank you. Anything else, Mr. Graham."

"Not right now."

"Well, buzz if you need anything else."

"I will, uh . . ."

"Laura," she offered, "Laura Phinor."

"Yes," he agreed, "I imagine you are."

She threw him a playful smile and turned to leave. He watched the sway of her hips as she seemed to glide from the room.

With a shake of his head he returned to the reports.

He flipped over to the data regarding Jim Austiff's disappearance. Rusty Griggs contributed a copy of the city coroner's report with exhibits indicating Sarah Austiff died of electrocution and had been injected with a stolen Office truth serum. Her death coincided with the disappearance of the Director—an obvious connection.

Griggs also contributed a paragraph to the finding of three cybernetic listening devices in Austiff's home.

Cybernetic, Gray noted. The report indicated that a routine security sweep would not have revealed the devices owing to their emitting a bioelectrical signature. Griggs had correctly deduced that Austiff was security conscious at home as well as at work, and that only cybernetic listening devices could have avoided his detection.

Must have been pretty high tech bugs, Gray thought. Further down the page he saw the name of the listening device manufacturer—

"Son-of-a-gun," Gray mumbled to himself. The file indicated the bugs were state-of-the art Nova design.

Kegley had ordered Security Director Dana Masters to follow-up and she had requested a federal search warrant for the Nova complex in Nevada. The warrants were expected in a couple of days.

Gray set that sheet aside and opened a folder regarding the *TG-3* incident. After briefly scanning the information he closed the file and formed a temple with his fingers while in thought. A few moments later he gathered the documents and made his way through the maze and out of the room.

Entering the law office, he stopped at the front desk.

"Graham," he told Jann, the receptionist. "To see Ms. Kegley."

Jann Cassell pressed a button and then into the headset mic she wore, she said: "Ms. Kegley, Mr. Graham is here to see you... Certainly.

"She's on her way up," Jann told Gray.

A few moments later Kegley appeared.

"I didn't expect to see you," she said surprised.

"Not today, anyway, huh?"

She smiled and indicated for him to follow. They made their way to her office and sat down.

"So, what do you think?" she asked him. "I'm right or wrong?"

"I think you're a little right," he said, then slightly smiled. "And I think you're a little wrong."

He could see she was curious regarding his opinion. He said, "I'm going to have to check a few things before I'm absolutely certain. There's some unusual elements I need to look over."

"I see."

"What I'd really like, is to know exactly when the warrants are going to be served on Nova."

"The warrants will be issued by tomorrow morning and we're having the FBI serve them later in the day—near sundown."

Gray looked puzzled.

"We figure there will be less people and suits to deal with during the evening shift."

Gray nodded in agreement. "Makes sense. What are the chances I can get a copy of Nova's floor plans and security arrangements?"

Kegley opened her desk drawer, withdrew a folder and tossed it across her desk. Across the cover were the words "NovaNet: Proposed Construction and Security Design."

"The information is old, but it's the only thing we can find. The FBI agents are receiving the same copy."

"May I keep it for a while?"

"It's yours."

"Thanks," Gray said, standing.

"What next?" Kegley asked.

Gray unnecessarily glanced to his Rolex: "Lupper, or linner—depending upon your preference."

"Huh?"

"Late lunch, early dinner or—"

"Late lunch early supper," She finished.

"See ya' later," he said with a smile and a wave.

Gray took the elevator down to the third floor, reading the Nova folder as he walked through the hallway. He found Clines where he expected, in Engineering Inc., immersed in a pile of computerized diagrams.

"What does it say," Gray joked, referring to Clines' diagrams. "'See Spot run?'"

Clines looked up smiling: "No, it says, 'Blake hungry, Karns late!'"

Gray laughed: "Where to?"

"There's a deli downstairs," Clines said, leading the way. "What took you so long?"

"I was reading about an old buddy of ours," Gray answered, following Clines through the frosted entry door and into the hall.

"Which one would that be?"

"Trenton."

Blake shook his head in amazement and as they came to a halt, pressed the elevator button. "He's living the life of Riley, the bastard."

"I guess you read *Time*, too," Gray noted.

"Yeah," Clines said as the elevator sounded and they entered the lift. "He was also in one of the money magazines last month, and *Newsweek* the month before that."

"It should be illegal for a man like that to prosper," Gray came back.

Clines nodded, agreeing with his friend's sentiment. "I wonder if any of it ever bothered him?"

"He enjoyed it, Blake," Gray came back.

The doors opened and they walked across the rotunda, each thinking back to Vietnam and the black operations orchestrated by Charlton Trenton. Units of CIA sponsored mercenaries had raided friendly South Vietnamese encampments, killing everything that moved. North Viet-cong bodies and weapons were then planted so as to point a finger at the enemy. It had been a desperate and immoral attempt to drum up support and sympathy.

They sat at a table and ordered dinner.

"So," Clines finally said, "what's the deal with Trenton?"

"The office is having the FBI serve search warrants on Nova tomorrow," Gray answered, waving the Nova file then laying it down.

"Why?"

"Nova listening devices were found in Jim's house?"

"Hadn't heard that one," Clines remarked.

"I'm sure the Chancellor thinks he's clean," Gray came back. "And he may be. But Gizmo says something's not quite right."

"Uh-oh," Clines responded. "What are you up to?"

"I'm thinking of paying a visit through the back door of Nova while the FBI is going through the front door."

"Wait a minute," Clines said, leaning toward Gray. "You're thinking about breaking into a place with highly secretive government aerospace contracts, while the FBI is there?"

"Hey, if something goes sour, I'll have a safe escort out."

"And straight to jail," Clines added.

The waitress brought the food.

"By the way, ever heard of John Wilson?" Gray asked.

"He's 1109, isn't he?" Clines said.

"Yeah. I think he's been working on a crossover."

"I haven't heard anything," Clines said, chomping down on a salad drenched in Ranch dressing. A, "crossover," was an assignment that tended to cross the path of another agent's assignment.

"Any idea where we might find 'em?"

"Try the Chancellor?"

Gray shook his head *no*, causing Clines to look at him.

"What?"

"I don't know," Gray said. "I think the Chancellor knows a bit more than he's saying."

"Sounds like typical, 'need-to-know,' procedure," Clines commented.

"It sounds like it," Gray admitted, "but it's not."

Clines chewed a couple of bites and swallowed: "I don't follow."

"I don't have the answer. I just know there's a hell of a lot more going on than just the stuff we think we're not seeing."

Gray attacked his steak with determined concentration.

"I know how to get a-hold of Wilson," Clines suddenly said.

"Yeah?"

"I understand he was brought in just before Austiff disappeared. Check with Kate."

"Because she's supposed to cooperate with me," Gray said smiling.

"Exactly," Clines said.

"That only leaves one more little problem."

"What?"

"I'm going to need some of your engineering genius for this one," he said and pulled a pen out. He quickly drew a diagram on the Nova folder.

Clines looked at it then at Gray. "It looks like a shock absorber."

"It should be able to extend from two or three feet to several feet," Gray explained.

"Into a pole?" Clines questioned.

Gray nodded. "I'll need five of them—six just to be on the safe side."

"It would help if I knew what they were for."

"Jumping."

"What kind of, 'jumping?'"

"The pole vaulting kind."

"You're joking."

"Hey, I was pretty good in high school."

Clines reached over, picked up the folder on Nova Security and glanced inside. He looked at Gray. "You're not kidding."

Gray confirmed his friend's misgivings with a nod.

"Wouldn't it be simpler to have the Chancellor pull some strings and go in as one of the FBI?"

"You can bet Nova Security will be watching them like hawks."

Clines looked to the folder again, then: "Well, fly in behind the FBI. The airnet will be down for them."

"I doubt radar will."

"Jeez, Karns," Clines said, looking up. "Seems there'd be an easier way."

"It has got to be quick, on the opposite side of the FBI's approach and something so unusual as to not merit a manned response."

"I can easily build the telescoping poles," Clines said, "but this is pretty risky. You've got to be quick, balanced and fast."

"Well I—"

"Shit," Clines exclaimed, looking at the information again. "Even if you make it over the first two, you'll have to beat nine—at the least—computerize silos! And they only have a time lag of one to three seconds from sensor contact to active firing—that's assuming none of the equipment has been updated."

"If it makes you feel any better," Gray came back, "I'll be practicing my skills later at an athletic field—just to make sure I can do it."

"You damned well better, you lunatic. Gizmo ought to be screaming at you."

Gray smiled at Clines' reference to the inner voice of wisdom. "Believe me, Gizmo's not all fired-up to go, either."

Clines pushed his unfinished salad away. "I've lost my appetite."

"Sorry about that."

"You ought to be," Clines grumbled. He tossed out money enough for both meals plus tip. "Let's go."

"But I'm not finished yet," Gray protested.

"You've got to find John Wilson, figure out how to monitor the FBI's insertion and practice getting yourself killed. You don't have time to eat."

And with that the two men left the table.

29

Kalvin Reedy was an unkempt, uncouth bourgeois man, with the moral standards of a sewer rat. The fact he had lived 45 years without so much as a traffic citation or blowing himself to pieces was a miracle of the worse kind.

Always sporting a black mustache and a ragamuffin hair style, he had maintained only two aversions throughout life: he hated bars, preferring to drink in solitude, and he hated waiting. For Reedy, waiting was the worst. He imagined all sorts of deviltry could destroy him at any idle moment wasted in waiting. He absolutely abhorred waiting.

Unfortunately for Reedy, his contact had left a voice-mail message to wait for a phone call at the crowded tavern where he was now sitting. He leaned forward, lifting his hand. A waitress appeared.

"Another beer?" she asked politely.

"Nah," he answered, pushing an empty mug toward her. Both she and the mug vanished into the crowd.

The bartender sat a phone on the table to his left: "You Kalvin Reedy?"

"Who wants to know?"

"The robot," the bartender answered, indicating the phone.

Puzzled, Reedy lifted the receiver and pressed the flashing button. "Yeah?"

"Reedy?" came the familiar sound of an electronically altered voice, clearing-up the bartender's allusion. The bartender walked away.

"It's about time," Reedy growled. "Do you know how long I've been waiting?"

"Sorry," the voice replied. "I've been—"

"I detest waiting."

"Well, I—"

"This had better be good," Reedy cut in for the second time.

"It depends on what you call 'good,'" the voice returned.

"Get on with it."

"I think they're on to us."

"You, 'think?'" Reedy questioned.

"I know," the voice affirmed.

"And who are, 'they?'"

"Who do you think?" the voice came back, without infliction. Reedy had never heard the voice change in anger or pitch. He could never decide if the voice was synthesized through a computer that removed all emotional subtleties, or if the contact was really that self-controlled. The voice went on to clarify whom Reedy should think was after them: "The Chancellor."

"Why the sudden worrying?"

"There's a new Chancellor agent involved. He plans to initiate some sort of infiltration or assault on Nova during the scheduled FBI search."

"So?" Reedy came back flatly, as if this information was an everyday thing.

"Some of the older research is still there and—"

"Look, the warrants only cover computer databases and paper files," Reedy interrupted impatiently. "Our stuff is on old NCR tapes—it's years old, most of it."

"Perhaps the Chancellor agent suspects as much."

"Nah," Reedy assured the voice. "He's probably smart enough to know nothin' incriminating's goin' to be laying around just for the FBI to breeze through and take. He probably wants to slip in unobserved for a look around."

"If he keeps digging, he's going to wonder why I had a major chunk of stock in World Pleasure Cruises."

"So, what's the problem?"

"'What's the problem!'" the voice echoed without change. "You idiot. This guy's unraveling things faster than we can put them together."

"Okay," Reedy conceded coolly, "I'll kill 'em."

"Whatever this guy knows, the Chancellor knows—you can't blow-up everyone. Hell, you can't even blow-up a boat full of dead men right."

Reedy all but growled at the contact's reference to the fiasco involving the CIA boat failing to explode after he had rigged it. Reedy had been especially proud of his workmanship in that particular venture. With jagged holes in the boat's bottom, and explosives wired to everything, including the dead men, the, "accident" would have been perfect. Reedy figured boats were either scuttled or blown-up, but a combination of the two would confound any investigator in the unlikely event the hull of the boat was recovered. He had deduced that any investigator worth his salt would finally conclude the boat had struck something, and blown-up while sinking. In the meantime, the fish would have been feasting on body pieces and the bullets would have been fish shit.

Reedy had thought it his best work yet—especially the, "fish shit," part.

Having made his getaway in a turbine helicopter, Reedy had no way of knowing the boat hadn't sunk until some days later when the smart-ass with the synthesized voice phoned him.

While he might have failed at blowing-up the boat, Reedy was certain he would need only one bullet to shut up the contact. If only the contact hadn't been so damned important to everything.

"All right," Reedy conceded. He knew from experience how hard it was to even find a Chancellor agent, never mind trying to kill one. "But I want the receivers from Austiff's house."

"They became evidence after you axed Sarah, dumbass," the voice responded, then rhetorically added; "Why do you think they want to search Nova in the first place?"

One of these days, Reedy thought.

"Listen," said the synthesized voice, "I'm concerned about the new Chancellor agent—"

"So how's this new Chancellor agent supposed to be breaking in?"

There was a pause on the other end of the line. "On foot."

"I mean, how is he planning to get past the fences? As if it matters."

"I told you, on foot."

Reedy laughed. "That's the most asinine thing I've ever heard. Nova can withstand an army, you know that."

"He doesn't think he needs one."

"He'll think differently when he's dying, won't he?"

"Just see to it he doesn't pull anything off."

"I won't have to do anything," Reedy said. "You know about Nova defenses."

"You had better hope so," the voice warned. "As fantastic as it sounds, Blake Clines thinks the man can do it."

"Just out of curiosity," Reedy said, "what's the name of this superman, anyway?"

"Graham something," the voice answered.

"Graham what?" Reedy probed cautiously.

"Uh, Jack Graham," came the answer.

"About 6-foot, brown hair, dark blue eyes?" Reedy pressed, his heart rate up.

"Yes, that's him."

Reedy clinched the receiver, "What the hell are you tryin' to pull?"

"What'd ya' mean?" asked the voice.

"You know damned well what I mean," he rumbled through clenched teeth.

"The hell I do," came back evenly.

"I killed Jack Graham some 22 years ago," Reedy hissed. "He's damned well dead!"

"Well he's one hell of a live ghost now," the voice responded. "Get a grip."

The phone clicked into a buzz. Reedy dropped the receiver into the cradle as though it were a snake about to strike. He was still staring at it when the bartender returned and took it away.

Reedy's thoughts however, had wandered back in time—years away—to the particularly difficult job of killing a Chancellor agent named Jack Graham. Or at least, that was one of his names. They had never met face-to-face, but Reedy was familiar with seeing his victim through the scope of a rifle. Graham always seeming to know when a gun was trained on him from nearly a block away had baffled Reedy. So much so, that after several such attempts, Reedy masterminded a more subtle approach—a simple car wreck. Reedy remembered the moment his truck accidentally interlocked bumpers with Graham's Mercedes. He recalled the sick feeling that came to his stomach as his truck bashed into a wall of dirt and rock, then rolled down an embankment.

How Reedy survived was a mystery—without a scratch he kicked open the door and escaped into the woods just as his truck exploded.

He had left on foot, covering nearly a mile before the backwash of an unmarked helicopter—flying at treetop level—nearly blew him off his feet. A nagging doubt overcame him and he hiked back to make sure Graham was dead.

And he was. He hadn't found much of the body—but it was a body. The charred remains had caused him to throw-up.

Reedy exhaled deeply—unable to shake the news. If Jack Graham were alive, that at least explained the mysterious helicopter...

"But he's dead," Reedy mumbled to himself. "Jack Graham is dead."

30

By 5:15 p.m. of the following day, Karns Gray—alias Jack Graham—was slipping a black canvas knapsack over his shoulder while sitting in the passenger compartment of the Engineering Inc. helicopter. The pilot, Archer Commons—alias John Wilson—was monitoring the air traffic control chatter as well as an encoded frequency directly linked with a viewing room at the CIA in Langley, Virginia.

In approximately five minutes, the FBI helicopter would enter the Black Mountain region and request from Nova a landing clearance to execute the search warrants. At the same time, and unknown to either party, an orbital satellite's course had been altered to pass over and transmit a, "real time," video feed to the CIA. When the FBI entered Nova airspace, the CIA would confirm that the defense net was down. Gray would then exit the chopper.

The entire arrangement seemed unnecessarily complicated to Commons. He had been ordered to transport Graham to an insertion point at the outer perimeter of the Nova Complex. Commons was then to retreat to the desert and wait for Graham to infiltrate the complex, and then return for a pick-up, all the while avoiding radar by flying within mere feet of the ground.

As any competent pilot could have performed the service, Commons had been informed that his presence was merely to answer Graham's questions, which—after an initial barrage—had been few and far between.

Jack Graham wasn't what Commons expected. He looked younger, taller and frighteningly intense. Graham had thoroughly quizzed him regarding his mission into the CIS and the unknown Export. Neither agent could decipher the reason behind the Chancellor's file redaction of information regarding the Export.

And now, here they were waiting. Gray had been watching the swirls of dust thrown up by the hovering helicopter when Commons suddenly tensed-up. Commons glanced over to Gray and tapped his earphones to indicate he had just heard the FBI requesting clearance at Nova.

Gray looked up the slope he was about to climb, as if he could see the FBI helicopter. All things being equal, anyone could have. Nova only occupied a few square miles on top of the mountain—well within the range of average eyesight.

Commons keyed his mic, activating the encoded line to the CIA: "This is Eagle Eye, I have one rooster heading for the hen house. Do you confirm, over?"

He nodded his head. "Roger, that."

Commons turned to report that the CIA satellite feed indicated the FBI chopper was still outside the protection of the Nova defense grid.

"I heard," Gray assured him.

"But—" Commons was about to protest that was impossible, but was interrupted by Nova Air Traffic Control, announcing that the defense system was down and the FBI was cleared for landing. About a second later, the CIA confirmed that the FBI chopper had moved into the Nova defense grid.

Commons turned to see Gray turning to face the hatch: obviously, somehow, he had heard.

"Take her down," Gray ordered.

Commons did as told. As soon as the skids touched the ground, Gray climbed down. The helicopter rose a few feet upward, and began its ground-hugging retreat down the mountainside.

Black Mountain towered six thousand feet over the Nevada desert floor. It was selected from the surrounding mountain range as the most advantageous and strategic location to build the Nova complex.

Secretly constructed in the late '50s, it was approachable only by air. At the time of its construction, Nova maintained the most advanced security system offered by technology. In the same league of secrecy as Dreamland, which was the government's classified Nevada testing grounds, Nova had been an alternate site for running the country in the event of nationwide nuclear strikes. While Nova was nowhere near the full-scale importance of the North American Defense complex in Colorado (NORAD), it could, for all intents and purposes, repel an army of men and machines.

And on that Karns Gray intended to gamble his life. He shifted the knapsack on his back and trotted up the sloping gradient.

With the sun balanced on the horizon off to his side, he came to the first of three 12-foot fences surrounding Nova. He held his hand as if to sense the electrical charge: not that it was necessary—large signs warned of high voltage.

Reaching into the small knapsack, he withdrew a two-foot rubber insulated cylinder that vaguely resembled Blake Clines', "shock absorber." Grasping the ends, he extended it outward with a twist. After repeated motions, it became an insulated shaft meeting Olympic competition standards for pole vaulting.

Gizmo, that little voice of warning, was nearly screaming.

"Well, Gizmo," Gray said to himself, "this isn't an athletic field with a soft airbag on the other side."

He moved back several yards and turned to face the fence. He concentrated on relaxing his suddenly cramped toes, feeling as though he was aware of every pebble beneath his shoes. He took several deep breaths then lunged toward the fence.

The pole jammed into the dirt. Throwing his weight into the effort, he was hurdling through the air and over the electrical barrier.

Falling to earth, he released the pole as it thudded against the fence. He crashed to the ground and tumbled to a stop. Sitting up in the dirt, he looked back and grinned.

He stood, dusted his black clothes and started for the next obstacle.

"Forty-thousand volts down and 84 grand to go," he mumbled to himself, taking off in a trot.

Inside Nova, several hundred feet beneath the mountain, a man sat at one of dozens of computerized panels cluttering the main control center. A high-pitched beeping tone accompanied the flashing red light on the desk before him. He reached to a built-in phone receiver and lifted it to his ear.

"This is station one," he said, "I've got an intruder in section 4-E."

He listened a moment, pressing several buttons on the panel. A monitor flashed to life with a video replay of Gray pole vaulting while another screen zoomed in as he currently jogged.

"No, I don't think it's related to the FBI... The intruder, uh... He pole vaulted over."

He listened again.

"I don't know, Sir. He looks like the man we've been expecting. Should I—"

He stopped mid-sentence.

"I realize it's—" He paused for an interruption.

"Yes, Sir. I'll wait."

Gray had been jogging only for a short time when he slowed to a stop and held his hands out again.

His research indicated the area was free of defenses. The ground on which he stood was intended as a, "no man's land."

Perhaps that was why he stopped. Something was wrong, but he couldn't put his finger on it. Cautiously, he moved forward a few steps, then again stopped. A faint memory of a fellow soldier came to mind. The soldier was young, inexperienced and excited about something he had found. Gray remembered warning him to wait—but the warning was drowned in an explosion and the young soldier never returned from the Vietnam jungle.

Gray focused his eyes on the ground before him, realizing what was wrong: weeds. Browned by the heat of the sun they filled the area ahead and intermixed with the tall dry grass were patches of much shorter weeds and barren spots of sand.

Mines. Randomly scattered beneath the ground—beneath the patches of shorter dead grass and barren spots of sand were mines. Now that it was clear, the unmapped field was obvious.

Concentrating, he carefully and unhurriedly moved though the 100 yards of mines. Fortunately, the minefield stopped 15 yards before the next fence—and so did Gray. He methodically scrutinized the ground until he felt sure it hid no more surprises and then moved to the fence to study the stubby four-foot tall silos on the other side.

Equally spaced around the Nova perimeter were supposed to be motion sensitive machine gun turrets. Given their placement, an intruder could expect to pass no less than nine of them. Then of course after that, was the third and inner fence.

The Nova defense plans indicated each turret was capable of striking any moving object within a 360-degree circle of each silo-shaped unit. The turrets were made with electronic shielding which protected—or rather prevented them—from damaging each other with their own gunfire.

But when Gray walked to one side to examine the nearest turret, something was amiss. Although the general appearance was correct, there were no machine gun barrels visible. True enough, Nova was to have removed the guns when the government sold the facility, but Gray hardly expected them to abide by that rule.

The nearest turret on the other side of the fence was sitting 15 feet away—and it was humming.

It was a generator of some kind, Gray concluded. He pinpointed a minute shape in the slit of the turret. Whatever it might be, it wasn't a machine gun. Gray looked about the ground for a stone. Finding a rock roughly the size of a man's head, he heaved it into the air and over the fence. It thudded to the ground without incident.

"Hmm."

He reached into his knapsack and withdrew a grenade. Unlike grenades of old, this one was equipped with an electronic timer. He flipped open a guard-cap covering the timer and dialed the delay to five seconds. He snapped the cap back, pulled the pin and lobbed the grenade over the fence. It rolled near the turret and stopped.

Five seconds later it exploded.

The nearest silo zipped around and fired a thin beam of laser light.

Surprisingly, the laser flashed past the place of the explosion and sliced into a second silo. Gray frowned, smiled, then frowned again. The bad news was lasers. The good news was they obviously had never endured a field test and were subject to self-destruction if they missed their target. Of course there was one other piece of really bad news. He didn't see any room for a mistake on his part.

Inside Nova, both the man at Station One and his supervisor were staring in disbelief at the monitor.

"—I don't know," the man at Station One was saying, "he just walked through the minefield like it wasn't there!"

"Who is he?"

"How the hell should I know," the seated man snapped. "Whoever the hell he is, he just disabled a laser."

"Zoom in on him," the supervisor ordered. "Maybe the computers can ID him. Man, this couldn't have come at a worse time. The FBI is landing right now."

"What the hell is he doing?" the seated man mumbled, zooming the camera in on Gray's back. He was on his knees, repeatedly reaching into the knapsack. He then stood, dropping a crisscross of webbed grenade belts onto his upper torso. Turning, he faced the fence and withdrew another of Clines' telescoping poles.

He extended the pole.

"He's gonna' do it again," the Station One man reported, staring at the screen.

"He'll be dead when he hits the ground," the supervisor retorted smugly.

Watching the small monitor, they saw the pole jam into the dirt...

After having set the remaining grenade timers to one second each, Gray was once again hurdling over a fence. The pole banged against the fence, and he let go.

He heard the increased generator hum of a nearby laser turret. It had detected him. Only seconds would pass before something happened.

Gray broke concentration from his weight, speed and leverage to focus attention on the already activated laser turret.

He felt a tingling sensation flashing by while he plummeted to the ground and another flash pass within inches of his face as he rolled to a landing. He was now certain that each turret housed a thermal tracking system for each laser. In the moment it took the computer to assess its two misses and readjust its aim via a new tracking signal, Gray had reached his feet and tossed his hand out in a rapid motion as he pulled the grenade pin. A blur flew through the air.

An explosion rocked the ground, sending dirt flying.

The second laser silo whirled and fired multiple beams in the direction of the blast. Debris clouded like landscape with a pall of smoke and dirt.

Gray slipped another grenade from the web belt, pulled the pin and tossed the grenade.

The second turret's signal made contact with the thermal signature of the second explosion and fired another laser.

Gray was on the move when a blast roared to his left. Thrown off balance, he tumbled to the ground while pitching another grenade. The third silo's laser hit the exploding target.

Rolling to his feet, Gray was close enough to throw a grenade at the fourth turret. The blast shook the ground as the turret crumbled, bursting to flames beneath the surface.

Faltering logic circuits caused the third turret to again fire at the last tracking fix, allowing Gray to concentrate on the two upcoming turrets, which were at that moment swiveling to fire.

He ran at a dead heat.

The fourth and fifth silos fired, striking first at his feet, then singeing his left arm. Having re-evaluated and re-acquired the target, silo number four fired almost immediately after silo number five grazed his arm.

Gray, however, took another fall as he recoiled from the pain of being grazed by the high-intensity burn. The rolling stumble saved his life as silo four bolted a beam over his head, striking the sixth silo. Relieved of watching silo six, Gray came up from his fall tossing grenades back at silos four and five. He made a dash past silo six, which erupted into flames. The explosion of silo six shook the ground. The unexpected vibration forced Gray to stagger, fall and roll as he was being grazed again—this time by the laser of silo seven. He was up on his feet even as silo seven was attempting to re-acquire its target.

Inside Nova, the two men sat watching the monitor in dumbfounded, rapt attention. As the shrill of an alarm sounded in their ears, they watched Gray avoid the eighth turret and destroy the ninth. He had maintained an almost straight path and was now clear of the lasers' search range. Gray had pole-vaulted over the third and final fence before the supervisor shook off his disbelief and reached for the phone.

"That's not human," the Station One man was mumbling. His control board was ablaze with warning lights and damage reports.

"That's right, patrol," the supervisor was saying into the phone, "shoot to kill."

"Look at 'em go," The seated man said in complete amazement.

The supervisor slammed the phone down: "Unless he's Clark Kent, he won't outrun bullets!"

"Why the hell not?" came the other's response. "He just out-ran lasers!"

31

Nova was like an iceberg with less than one-third above the ocean of Black Mountain. Aside from the above ground airplane hangar, the, "main building," was little more than a pretentious reception area. Housing the, "Club Med," features visiting dignitaries and military personnel enjoyed touring, the visible signs of Nova were mere window dressing. The remaining two-thirds of Nova comprised the seldom seen control center, data centers and equipment production facilities—all located beneath ground. While card key passes permitted access to above ground facilities, subterranean areas required fingerprint scan approval. Voiceprint and retinal scans regulated the most classified areas.

By the time Gray approached the airplane hangar, his laser burns and minor cuts from flying debris had congealed. He squatted next to a wall, catching his breath. According to his research, an elevator inside the hangar could take him to a subterranean monorail—a tunnel that offered the most obscure path into Nova.

A squeal of tires on pavement grabbed Gray's attention in time to see a jeep roaring around a corner with guns blazing. Bullets sprayed the cement and he dove through a window for his life.

He sprung to his feet inside a cool office barely bigger than a U-Haul trailer. He automatically pulled the .38 pistol from his shoulder holster —then shifted it to his left hand. From his knapsack, he withdrew a pistol with a slightly longer barrel. He dropped the knapsack to the floor and rushed out the door.

At the far end of the hangar, the jeep was skidding out of the sunlight and into the hangar entrance. Even while they were firing again, and Gray was ducking for cover, he had to admire their marksmanship. The volley that had nearly found the mark and sent him scurrying into the cramped office had been fired from outside the hangar, from the back of a jeep—a good 75 to 100 yards away! The latest rounds forced him behind an ominous black machine. He heard the bullets ricochet off the machine instead of tearing into it.

He looked up to find himself staring at a sleek-shaped helicopter of a design considered conceptual by the aerospace community at large. Gray was certain of this because Clines had shown him numerous theoretical designs employing orbital exhaust and blade configurations similar to the one now sitting before him.

If this was indeed one of those concept helicopters made real, he was impressed. The concept helicopters of the future were intended to attain extremely high altitudes, enabling their turbine engines to boost them into a low orbit. It truth, the spacecraft of tomorrow, was the helicopter of today.

The screech of tires brought him out of his revere and he pressed to the floor to see the jeep coming around the front of the helicopter. He started to aim his .38 pistol, then reminded himself to use the other gun. He raised the pistol, aimed and waited.

The jeep skidded around the front of the chopper, its wheels failing to hold fast. Gray squeezed the trigger just as the jeep slid into his sight. The shot was perfect—at least for Gray. The man operating the mounted machine gun bolted back limply, a bright colored dart protruding from his chest.

The driver was bringing a handgun up to fire—but Gray had rolled under the chopper and to the other side. The driver only caught a glimpse of Gray coming around the chopper's nose before a dart to his chest ended the chase. Gray moved over to the jeep, amazed as ever that men would sacrifice themselves for such foolish causes. These two, however, were extremely fortunate. He checked to ensure the darts had drugged them into unconsciousness as Clines had promised, courtesy of a chemical nerve agent—among other things. Out of curiosity he lifted the eyelids of one of the men and checked his eyes.

Clines hadn't exaggerated when he had said the gun delivered eight hours of sleep in one dart. Whatever the darts held, the man was practically comatose.

Death was one of the things he had tried to avoid since 'Nam, but every once in a while... He shrugged off the introspection, knowing it to be self-destructive. He quickly moved across the hangar and retrieved his knapsack. Returning to the jeep, he dropped the dart pistol into the bag and re-holstered his .38. He bent down, checking that his .25 was still in the leg holster. Satisfied with that, he pulled the machine-gun operator from the back of the jeep and within moments had slipped the machine-gunner's gray security uniform over his own black clothing. He then removed a two-way radio from the jeep and clipped it to his belt.

Hefting the unconscious machine gunner over his shoulder, Gray moved toward the set of steel lift doors at the far end of the hangar. Above the doors a light flashed to life as he stepped into an invisible beam.

"Fingerprint Identification please," a soothing recorded voice said. A hand-sized panel to the right of the door illuminated.

Gray pressed the unconscious man's hand on the panel.

"Fingerprint Identification confirmed," the voice said after a considerable pause. The door slid noiselessly open and he carried the man inside.

The door hummed shut and the car began descending.

Gray dropped the body and reached into his knapsack. He pulled another pole out of his pack and extended it a few feet. He then pressed it against the trap door of the ceiling and pushed it open. After collapsing the pole he returned it to the knapsack, which he shifted to a more comfortable position on his back. He then jumped to catch a-hold on the edge of the trap door. He pulled himself up onto the top of the lift just as it slowed to a stop. Quietly, he closed the trap door.

Beneath him he heard the doors open and several voices.

"He's not here," said a voice.

"What'd you mean," came another voice, filtered through a transmitter, "I just okayed the computer to allow him in. He was carrying Frank."

"I guess this is Frank laying here," replied the voice. "He's unconscious and his uniform is gone. No Jack Graham, though."

Gray wrinkled his brow. *How did they know?*

"The elevator have a way out?" asked the voice through the transmitter.

"I'll check."

Gray frantically scrambled up the metal rungs on the shaft wall and slipped into a crawl space. Behind, he heard the trapdoor open.

"There's a trap door, Dr. Trenton," the voice said.

"Find Graham, then. He's probably wearing Frank's uniform."

"There's dozens of work tunnels: we'll need more men."

"I'll send them. In the meantime you and Wales start looking."

"Yes, Sir."

"Who the hell is this Graham guy anyway," came Wales' voice.

"I don't know. Here let me help you."

Gray inched out to look down on the men struggling through the trap door. He backed out of sight as they straightened up.

"I'll start on that one," the first man said.

"I'll take this one," Wales replied, sounding nearer.

Gray heard their grunts as they started up the metal rungs. Momentarily, a head poked into Gray's crawl space.

"Wales?" Gray asked, nonchalantly.

Surprised, the man stood holding the rungs. Although he saw Gray's foot snapping out, he only had time to blink and accept the blow. Wales fell to the elevator ten feet below.

Gray scrambled down the shaft's ladder and dropped into the elevator car.

The elevator was now out-of-service, the doors locked open onto a view of the waiting area. The rock of the mountain served as the wall on the other side of a monorail track. A monorail-car hummed around a bend and stopped. Fifteen men in gray began clamoring onto the platform beside the track.

"He's up there," Gray called to them, pointing toward the ceiling of the lift. "We think he drugged the guy in the elevator. He just now knocked Wales down."

"Who the hell is this Graham guy, anyway?" asked the man in charge. He was waving his men on to the elevator.

"Beats me," Gray answered, although wittier responses came to mind.

They rushed past, looking silly as they crowded into the lift and began climbing up through the trap door. He moved in behind them, waiting until only one man was left, then stepped out and to the side of the lift.

"Hey," Gray said, just loud enough to get the man's attention. "Look at this."

Unable to see Gray, the man stepped out of the lift and was rewarded by a gun butt across the back of the skull. He crumpled to the ground unconscious.

Gray lifted him and moved to the waiting monorail car. The sensor above the door flashed on.

"Fingerprint Identification please," the recorded voice said. Another hand-sized panel to the right of the door illuminated.

Gray pressed the unconscious man's hand on the panel.

"Fingerprint Identification confirmed," the voice said after a moment. Gray dragged the man on board.

"Destination please?" said the automated voice.

"Monorail Car Repair," Gray ordered, remembering that was the last destination on the rail's route.

He eased the guard to the floor and settled back into a cushioned seat.

Even though he had an excellent mental record of time, he consulted his watch out of habit—a habit born out of an exacting effort to imitate the commonplace. It confirmed what he already knew: thirty minutes had elapsed since he cleared the first fence. He removed the knapsack from his back and pulled out a few supplies. Using bottled water he cleaned away the dried blood on his arm and employed a small mirror to clean the minor scratches on his face. He put everything back in the pack and looked up just as a tone sounded.

"Approaching Rail Station 8," the automated voice announced as the car began slowing.

He knew the car had traveled downward for half a mile and would continue slowing for another quarter of a mile before stopping at Station 8. Not that it mattered. Gray's real destination was nowhere near what he had told the computer and he had doubts as to how long he could remain in the rail car.

Glancing ahead he saw the boarding area of the next stop.

He stood and moved to the door.

Gray reached into his knapsack and pulled out a hunting knife. Inserting it between the door and the frame, he used the knife to pry open the door. He braced his back against the door frame and pushed until it opened enough to allow him to squeeze out.

Leaping, he hit the ground and rolled several feet. By the time he had stood, he heard the rail car seriously braking as it entered the narrower tunnel beside the waiting platform. When it came to a halt, there was a sudden onslaught of men.

Concentrating, Gray filtered out the voices of the men until he isolated the one coming from a two-way radio. As he listened in on the heated exchange between the group leader and Trenton, the others quieted down.

"—the computer doesn't show a stop for the car so he jumped while it was moving," came Trenton's voice through the leader's transmitter.

"So where does that leave us—searching all the tunnels?"

"He had to jump in the last 50 yards," Trenton came back. "That's when the car slows for the stop."

"There's dozens of work tunnels—"

"Then you best get started," Trenton cut in.

"Okay men," the leader called to the others. "He's in the tunnels. Let's go."

Gray turned, searching the walls and roof. He worked his way backward, passing three work tunnels. Then he spied what he wanted an overhead ventilation duct.

Once again he withdrew a, "shock absorber," and extended it. After a short jab, the vent facing came loose. Inserting one end of the pole into the duct, he sat the other on the ground and climbed the pole. Once in the air duct system, he retracted the pole and replaced the vent cover just as the security team passed beneath.

Inching around, he began crawling through the air vent system. His destination: the Cray computer room.

32

In the mid-1970s Seymore Cray introduced the United States Department of Defense to the Cray-1 and later the Cray-2. Prior to the explosive market growth of computers during and after the 80's, the Crays were the fastest computers extant. Receiving the nickname, "bubbles," due to the bubbling sound created by their coolant liquids, the Crays had cost over 17.6 million dollars per system, and housed more processors, faster computing speeds and larger memories than the public realized.

The Crays belonging to Nova had been tailor designed to the specific task of early warning and first strike launching of nuclear weapons. Obviously, when Nova became a private corporation, it possessed the most powerful computing abilities in the free world.

At the heart of Nova were three such Cray computers. Their ceaseless beating poured data throughout the Nova network of computers and terminals like life-blood to vital organs. Requiring other computers to front-end, or access the Crays, each system fulfilled a different task. One was tied into global information networks, a second, the security and functions of Nova and the third filled in as a backup and overflow, ensuring the first two systems were maintained and supported in the event of failure.

It was because of the second system that Gray had jumped from the monorail car. If everything automated was tied into the massive computer, as Gray suspected, then contact with any Nova system would be reported. For that same reason Gray now crawled through the air duct, instead of risking exposure to the ID scans at doors and elevators.

The very fact that Nova was considered a leader in aerospace designs also lent to the possibility that the aging Crays had been relegated to merely monitoring Nova itself. If that was so—and Clines had thought it likely—then the defenses Gray had encountered and now avoided, might be control by more recent computer technology. It was relatively safe to assume synthetic intelligence had yet to be discovered or utilized to the degree Debbie Allinder had privately achieved. But stand-alone, thinking computers were readily available to entities like Nova—and Gray had no desire to match wits with one of those.

Along similar lines of thought, Gray began rehashing the Office's investigation of Nova. He came to the same conclusion as before: namely that OCSTO, through the FBI, was wasting time by expecting anything incriminating in the Nova databases. Even if such evidence had been stored in the systems at one time, the fact that Gray's intrusion was expected meant someone probably tipped them off to the FBI's "surprise" visit.

When Gray finally reached a vent for the computer room, he found that massive changes had indeed been made.

The hum of computer drives drifted upward like the sounds of a miniature hydroelectric plant. The room, a large area of 7,500 square feet was filled with computers, employees, FBI agents and lawyers.

There had definitely been a tip-off.

Gray worked his way past two more air vents before finding one in an unobtrusive hallway connecting the computer area with a smaller room.

"—there is no way in hell this is legal, Mr. Voit," an irritated voice drifted up.

Gray looked down to see two FBI agents; one a tall dark-haired man and the other a petite Mexican-American woman with dark shoulder-length hair.

"Let me put it to you this way," agent Voit responded, wasting a double entendre on an unappreciative lawyer, "we can drag your butt in with the rest of this bologna, if you want. Either way, we'll have copies of all this crap and I'll be working on something else tomorrow."

"Look, Mr. Crown," the female agent said without a trace of an accent, "it's going to be a long night. Why not make it a little less lengthy?"

Crown sighed: "I'm just telling you what my clients will tell me."

Crown was pulled away by a Nova employee in a white lab coat. Gray watched Crown being led to another agent several feet away.

"Well he didn't act like it was for a show," the female agent was saying to her partner.

"Plausible denial, Esmeralda," agent Voit said. "I doubt he knew if we'd show up for certain—but whoever sent him, knew."

"So he comes off real indignant, because he really is, huh?"

Voit nodded his head.

"Agent Carrasco," came another FBI agent's voice, I was wondering if you could help me with something?"

"Sure," the female agent said, then to Voit: "Be back in a few."

While Carrasco walked off in one direction, Voit moved off in another. Gray figured that was his cue. He removed the dart gun from the knapsack and secured the weapon in his waistband. From the knapsack he also removed a self-adhesive, half-inch photo of himself. He then used the image to cover Frank's picture on the photo ID attached to his shirt. After then clipping to his belt the Nova transmitter he had taken from one of the guards, he pried the vent loose and brought it into the duct. He wormed his way out of the air duct and dropped the remaining four feet to the floor. He glanced around, making sure no one had seen him. Casually, he moved into the computer room and behind a nearby Nova employee—a leggy dark tanned woman with raven black hair cascading to her waist.

"Excuse me," Gray said.

With a start, she turned.

"You gave me a fright," she said. She stood a mere two inches shorter than Gray.

"Sorry, Ms. Carter," Gray apologized, reading her photo ID. He lowered his voice. "Mr. Trenton ordered me to drop in and pick up some old records."

"Oh?" she questioned, putting her hands in her pockets.

"The stuff they're not checking," Gray added almost in a whisper and with a tilt of his head toward the numerous FBI agents scattered about the room.

She glanced nervously around. "Why now?"

"He's as nervous as you, I suspect."

"Just a moment."

She disappeared into an adjoining room and reappeared shortly. In her hands was a spool of what appeared to be giant recording tape.

"I think this is it," she said.

"You think?"

"There's several old tapes mixed in," she answered, handing it to him.

"This is for microfiche, isn't it?" he asked.

She nodded *yes*.

"Is there a place I can check it—to make sure it's the right one?"

"Right now?" she questioned, exasperated.

"Unless you want to be the one to take him the wrong tape..."

"Okay, right," she said, taking back the tape. "Come on."

She led him past several agents who were intent on downloading copies of a database onto disc.

They passed through the hall where Gray had climbed from the air vent. The dark gaping hole where the vent cover belonged seemed obvious to Gray. He glanced at the girl, and over his shoulder. No one seemed to notice.

The adjoining room was cluttered with castaway tables, coffee and coke machines and several lop-eared magazines. It was obviously a break room.

On one side of the room was an archaic computer console. She snapped the tape onto it, reeling the tape onto another spool, then hit a *start* button, followed by an *online* button.

Gray watched her type several keys on a yellowed keyboard.

She turned to face Gray. "This'll run for about ten minutes. When it gets to the end, on the printer at the keyboard it'll print on the paper the word, 'filemark,' and a question mark. Type a, 'Y,' each time and the tape will rewind at the end—and pray the FBI doesn't want to look at it."

"Tell ya' what," Gray said, "Go back out there and find that lawyer—Crown's his name. Tell him to make enough noise to keep the Feds away from this room."

"Good idea," she said, looking at his photo ID, "Mr. Martin."

Gray smiled. "Just call me Frank."

"I'm Christine," she responded, and left the room to carry out his instructions.

He turned his attention to the computer, watching the spool slowly inching around. At one end of the machine 4x5 sheets of microfiche began slowly dropping into a trap. Gray took one and inserted it into a view projector attached to the console.

There were names and dates of money transactions—mostly Arabian. The name Fatima Qabazard-Fonna appeared several times. He remembered news coverage of her tradition-breaking marriage to an American several years back. The name clicked in place as he recalled reading she was representing her father's interest in the *TG-3*.

He pulled the fiche out and inserted another. Crown's voice rose in a vehement objection from the other room.

Christine had done as instructed.

Turning his attention back to the, "pages," that were separated into blocks on the fiche, Gray was certain he was studying chemical notations. There were numerous references to a Russian-American Fur Trading Company. Although there were no dates, he was certain this was historical information. The random notes didn't seem to have a bearing on his goal.

He changed to another fiche. It was data on synthetic intelligence. Gray leaned in to read more closely. Some of it was highly technical, but sounded vaguely and uncomfortably familiar.

The next fiche was filled with names, addresses, a few notations on military weapons and—

"Shit!" Gray mumbled to himself, looking at the fiche. There was a California address for a Mr. and Mrs. Seth Ŝulok. Gray felt as if he had been hit between the eyes with a hammer. A known drug and weapons dealer, Ŝulok had avoided being linked to illegal operations as far back as Vietnam. People knew he was involved, they just couldn't prove it. Ŝulok had always been one step ahead. Ŝulok was the reason for Gray's undercover assignment to a college in Texas—which was how he had come to know Gail...

Gail... Somehow, at the most peculiar moments, she popped into his head. He shook off the thought and returned the fiche to the others in the group. He didn't feel like reading any further—his mission had just altered course somewhat.

Two computer operators came into the break room.

"Christine says you're with Security," said the one with the name McGruder on his ID.

"Yeah," Gray responded.

"What's been happening with that intruder?"

"We're still searching the monorail tunnels," Gray answered.

"What beats me," said the other, a bald short man by the name of House, "is how he got in—did he come in with the FBI?"

"He pole vaulted," Gray explained.

"No shit?"

Gray nodded, looking to the printer. He typed a, "Y," to the prompting "Filemark?"

It again printed, "Filemark?" and Gray entered another, "Y."

"End of reel, more?" it printed.

"What do I do now?" Gray questioned.

"Get an, 'End of reel,' message?" McGruder questioned.

Gray nodded, *yes.*

"Type, 'N,'" McGruder instructed.

Gray did, and the reel began rewinding.

The tape reel stopped and Gray pulled it down, securing the protective plastic rim around the outside.

"Gotta' get this to boss man," Gray said and passed them.

Christine Carter walked into the room carrying a clipboard, while Crown continued a din of noise in the adjoining area.

"Finished?" she asked.

Gray nodded *yes*. "Thanks."

"No problem," she said, smiling.

Gray put on his best debonair look. "Let me buy you a cup of coffee upstairs—a kind of *thanks* for helping me."

"You don't have to do that."

"At least give me a chance," he said, taking the clipboard from her and tossing it to a nearby tabletop.

She blushed.

"Christine and I are taking a break," Gray announced.

"Okay," House said, noncommittally.

Gray held his arm out in an animated gesture and effected an English accent: "This way me lady."

She smiled and looped her arm with his and they started for the door.

"You really are a flirt, Mr. Martin," she said.

"Frank," he corrected.

House and McGruder followed them to the doorway of the break room, watching them work their way through the crowd of people and to the exit door.

"Frank Martin..." House echoed abstractly.

McGruder, seemingly absorbed by the missing air vent, only mumbled.

"Did you hear me, Tom?" House said, moving over to the other man. "Frank Martin is the guard that was knocked out by that Graham guy."

House looked at the missing air vent grill and then into McGruder's eyes.

"That was...him!" House gasped, his eyes wide. McGruder was already at the phone calling security.

33

Gray waited until the elevator scanner requested fingerprint identification.

"Oh," Gray exclaimed to Christine Carter. "Would you get that? I've got to report in."

"Certainly," she replied, moving to the lighted panel.

Gray moved to the side, going through the motions of talking on the transmitter in a low voice. He nodded his head a couple of times, as if answering questions. When the computer confirmed Christine's fingerprint pattern, the doors opened. Gray, "signed off," and stepped into the lift with her.

Once inside the elevator, he reached across and pressed the Ground Level button.

"Security must be really fascinating," Christine remarked, immediately.

"It has its moments," Gray said, wedging the computer tape and radio transmitter between the banister and the wall of the elevator.

"So what's the deal with the FBI and the trespass alert we're under?"

"I'm not so important they have to tell me any of that," he replied smiling, then: "Been with Nova long?"

"About three years."

"Do you see much of Mr. Trenton?"

"I've only met him once," she answered frankly.

"I see."

She suddenly realized he had been unfastening the gray security uniform.

"What are you—"

"Pardon me a moment," Gray interrupted, removing the gray shirt. He tossed it to the corner, removed his .38 pistol and placed it on the floor. He tossed his shoulder holster to the corner and then pulled his own black shirt over his head. For a brief moment Christine found herself admiring Gray's muscular physique. Just as quickly, he turned the shirt inside out and pulled it back on.

Christine was surprised to see the, "inside-out black shirt," was now a white shirt, black tie and black coat. Even a close examination hardly revealed that the "coat" portion was actually sewn onto the "shirt." A Nova photo ID was already attached to the lapel, although Christine didn't realize it was inscribed with yet another alias. Gray bent down and the sound of Velcro accompanied the removal of what had been dark sneakers. Beneath them was a shiny pair of black oxford dress shoes. After discarding the "false" sneaker covers, Gray completed his formal attire by removing the gray uniform trousers and discarding them to the mound of items in the corner. He dusted off his black, "suit," pants and retrieved his pistol, which he pocketed, "inside," the, "suit coat."

Christine watched him run his hand through his hair, casually primping.

"What..." Christine began, but faltered. "I mean—"

"It's part of my job," Gray said with all the aplomb of a man doing what was natural. He picked up the computer tape and the radio. Resisting the urge to turn on the radio and monitor Nova's search for him, Gray leaned against the lift wall and smiled: "We've certainly had some hot weather of late, haven't we?"

Suspicious, Christine was about to ignore his caviler attitude in favor of questions regarding his quick-change, but the elevator opened at the next level and two women wearing business suits boarded.

"—I told him I'd rather die than date him," the younger redhead was saying.

"That'll teach him," the taller brunette commented.

The elevator continued up, the two women chattering away.

They stopped at two more levels, picking up seven people and letting off one. Reaching the ground level, the doors opened, and everyone filed past a watchful security team.

Inwardly smiling, Gray knew they were still searching for a man in a security uniform.

"A lot of guards are up here today," Christine remarked.

"We still haven't found that intruder," Gray explained. They walked down a short hall that opened into a dome-shaped area resembling a hotel lobby. Passing a circular fountain, they followed a sign indicating the way to the restaurant. Off to one side, large glass doors marked the official entrance to Nova. Through the doors—in the distance—he saw the airplane hangar: an equally risky, but quicker ticket to freedom than the original plan of slipping out the way he had come in.

Two guards were at the glass doors, meticulously checking IDs. Owing to the number of people milling about, they had their hands full. Gray couldn't fathom why so many people were here in the evening and was hard-pressed to look a gift horse in the mouth. The larger the crowd, the easier to hide.

The doors abruptly slid open, admitting a man in gray security clothes. Just beyond the door was a dingy jeep. The guards checked an ID card clipped to the man's shirt, and waved him in.

"About that coffee," Gray said to Christine, taking her by the elbow, "I'd like to show you something first."

"What now?"

He directed her to the main entrance.

As they approached the door, Gray slipped his photo ID into his pants pocket and said aloud: "Really, Miss Carter, if I'd known security was so picky I'd never have flown all the way in from Las Vegas just to replace a stupid transistor."

"What?" Christine asked, confused.

"ID please," said one of the door guards.

They looked up to see the expectant face of an entrance guard.

"Not you too?" Gray nearly howled, catching the attention of several passersby. "I'm not going to wait another ten minutes just to have you confirm I left my pass in the damned toilet!"

"Sir?" the guard questioned.

"Why the hell do you think she came all the way up here with me?" Gray snapped at the guard, reaching over and jerking Christine's ID card from her lab coat. "Just to see me off?!"

The guard scanned the card Gray shoved into his hand.

"Frank, what are—"

"What am I raving about?" Gray snorted indignantly. "See if I make any more house calls!"

Gray started through the door.

"Uh, Sir?" said the other guard doubtfully.

"Talk to her," Gray growled, stabbing his thumb back at Christine Carter. He stormed through the door.

The three watched him jump into the jeep and roar off, the tail lights glowing in the dark.

Confused, the two guards looked to Christine.

"Don't look at me," she said. "He was perfectly normal a second ago."

"I take it he's an outside Computer tech," said one of the guards with a smile.

"He's security," she corrected, furrowing her brow.

"But he said—"

The other guard nearly knocked the first guard down. "That was him!"

"That was who?" Christine asked, now even more confused.

The first guard was on his transmitter. "Main Entrance to Security, we just sighted Jack Graham. He's in a jeep headed to the airplane hangar, over."

"Roger," came back.

"Oh, my God," Christine mumbled, looking past the guards to see the trail of dust thrown up by the distant jeep.

She was too shocked to realize one of the guards was handcuffing her.

34

For the first time since breaking into Nova, Gray felt he was at least dead-even, if not a step ahead, of security. He tapped the jeep's brake and wheeled into the hangar. At the far end, near three black choppers, two men stood together. Driving nearer, he saw that the one with a two-way radio to his face was wearing a gray Nova Security uniform. The other was in a black flight suit.

Gray slammed the brake and sharply cut the steering wheel. The jeep slid around to them sideways. Gray fired the dart gun at the security man before he could bring his pistol into play. The man dropped like lead. In one fluid movement Gray sprang from the jeep.

From his pocket Gray replaced the dart pistol with his .38 automatic and fastened the barrel on the temple of the remaining man.

"You a pilot?" Gray asked, appraising his catch. The man was balding, in his mid-thirties and possessed the presence of mind to remain calm. His photo ID read Gary Hodges.

"Yes, Sir," Hodges answered.

"Good. Which of these beauties is tanked and ready?" Gray questioned, indicating the three sleek Nova helicopters.

"All of them," Hodges answered.

Gray reached into the jeep and lifted the computer tape. "Let's go."

"You mean—"

"I certainly do."

Hodges opened the hatch on the nearest helicopter and it hissed oxygen while the hydraulic mechanism hummed.

"Inside," Gray prodded, tossing the stolen two-way radio to the ground. He followed the pilot into the helicopter and pulled down on the hatch, which sighed as it sealed shut. It was a confined cockpit overflowing with computers and instrumentation. Behind the cockpit was a second area designed for three to four passengers. In the middle of this second area was a small door on the deck marked, "storage bay."

"A quick lesson," Gray said, still holding the pistol. "Weapons, radar and any particulars you might remember."

"Engines on," Hodges said, addressing the computer console. "Flight Systems on."

The cockpit hummed to life with lights and minute throbbing sounds.

Hodges pointed: "That's the ignition. These buttons activate the computer console manually. Just about everything can be operated manually or by voice command. To activate a system, identify it and follow with the word, 'on.'"

Gray caught the sight of two jeeps approaching the hangar door.

"Weapons?"

"Here, on the stick," Hodges answered. "Also on the panel here—missiles."

"Any particular way of addressing the computer?"

"Huh?" Hodges asked.

"Voice avionics usually has a very select and limited vocabulary. Like, 'Vic-on,' in place of, 'Voice on.'"

A loud beeping noise accompanied the flash of a green light beside a computer screen at eye-level. Across the screen appeared:

Interactive Voice System activated.

"Interactive voice is activated," said an automated voice, and then responding to what it thought was Gray's repeated command, the automated voice said: "Interactive voice is on."

Hodges looked at Gray with surprise. "That's true. But this system is way ahead of anything on the market. It recognizes technical as well as vernacular terms."

"Good boy, Gary," Gray said. "Now get us out of here!"

"Sir?"

Gray waved the gun toward the doors.

Taking the hint, Hodges brought the engines to full power as the muffled sounds of bullets sang off the hull. He activated the remaining systems necessary for flight.

"Don't worry, Gary," Gray said, reassuringly. "If we do make it out of the air defense net, I'll put you down without harming a hair on your head."

Being bald, a concerned Hodges looked at Gray.

"It's a joke."

The eye-level screen in the center of the console printed that all systems were online and engines were ready.

Hodges grabbed the controls and the chopper gracefully floated upward and forward. The hangar seemed to drift by as they moved out into the moonlight.

"Blast the corner of the hangar," Gray ordered, once outside.

Hodges turned the craft around to see jeeps roaring out of the hangar. Sand was swirling like a storm. Useless bullets pelted the chopper, hardly reaching their ears. Hodges pressed the missile-targeting button on the yolk and fired.

The corner of the hangar collapsed in flames, the reddish yellow lighting up the night in a brilliant display of pyrotechnics.

Gray smiled. "Good job, Gary."

The screen in the middle printed out a warning accompanied by the computer's voice: "Warning: Nova defense net activated. Targeting now."

"Nova defense net deactivate," Hodges said into the intercom above his head. "Test flight authorization code, Hodges five seven, zero."

"Deactivation confirmed," the computer responded. "Nova control attempting manual override."

"Now would be a good time to go," Gray suggested.

Hodges needed no encouragement. The chopper leaped-out over the mountain.

Several miles later, Gray ordered Hodges to land the helicopter.

"Now, what about communications?" Gray asked, once the chopper was safely on the ground.

"All we need is the frequency and band to tap into just about anything."

"How about Directory Assistance for California?"

Hodges pressed a button on the console and a dial tone filled the cockpit.

Gray smiled.

Hodges entered a command on a keyboard and a map of California flashed on the screen, followed by an overlay of the area codes.

Gray pointed: "This one here."

Hodges entered the number on a nearby keyboard and a phone rang, followed by the voice of a directory assistance operator.

"I'd like an address listing for Seth Ŝulok," Gray responded to her prompting.

"Just a moment, Sir," the directory assistant replied, then: "I'm sorry, Sir, but that's a non-published number."

"But you do have a listing for him?

"Yes, Sir."

"Thank you very much."

"Have a good day, Sir," the operator said.

Hodges disconnected the line.

"Well, Gary," Gray said, "this is the end of the road for you."

Hodges looked up with panic on his face.

"Relax. I'm not going to kill you."

As promised, Gray let the pilot out and the black machine returned to the air. A few moments later, Gray spied the Engineering Inc. helicopter sitting out in the middle of the desert. He angled the machine's flight path and thundered through the thin air just over the white helicopter. The ground shook as the Nova helicopter threw dust clouds into the air. Bringing the Nova chopper into a banking turn, Gray piloted back around until the two helicopters were nose to nose.

Inside the other helicopter, Gray could see Commons wiping something off his shirt.

Tuning in a frequency, Gray heard Commons cursing.

"—the hell do you think you were doing?" came the tail-end of Commons' cursing.

"Like my toy?" Gray asked back into the unseen mic.

"Great! When do they come after you?"

"After they clear away the building I dropped on them."

"Well let's get out of here," Commons said.

"Negative," Gray responded. "I've got a little detour to make."

"What detour?"

"California."

"Cali—" That was all Commons got out. The black Nova chopper flew straight up and literally boomed as it roared over the desert.

"Tell the Chancellor I found a very old lead," Commons heard Gray over his earphones. "As soon as I can, I'll be in touch."

"Jack," Commons said into his mic, "Jack..."

"And static played back," Commons mumbled to himself.

Commons started the helicopter engine. Adjusting the radio he imagined his signal bouncing into space and off a satellite.

"This is Eagle Eye," he said into the head-set, "come in Eagle Nest, over."

"This is Eagle Nest," came the voice of the Chancellor's assistant, Carol. "Go ahead Eagle Eye, over."

"Patch me through to Mission Control, over."

In Washington, the Chancellor leaned over to his ringing bedside phone and picked it up. "Yeah?"

"A priority patch through from Eagle Eye," came Carol's voice.

"Send it through," the Chancellor ordered.

The phone clicked and a crackling noise filled the receiver as an electronic countermeasure was activated to ensure privacy.

"Hello chief," Commons' voice came through.

"Have a problem with the party?" the Chancellor asked, consulting his watch.

"We left a bit early," Commons answered. "My drinking buddy found another ride."

"I see."

"He really had a blast," Commons commented. "He was so loaded he didn't even head home."

"Where then?"

"He said something about an old lead—in California."

"Well I guess that answers that question," the Chancellor mumbled to himself and then to Commons he said: "Stay with him."

"Are you kidding?" Commons came back. "He drove away in a souped-up jalopy that I'll never catch."

"Standby," the Chancellor ordered, "I'll get you the address."

The Chancellor, now sitting on the edge of his bed, hit the hold button and dialed a phone number. He waited, then; "Carol, John's still on the other line."

"Yes, Sir?"

"My hearing's not what it used to be, you know," the Chancellor added.

The static burst of the electronic countermeasure was activated.

"Is that better?" Carol asked.

"Much," the Chancellor replied, knowing she was smiling. "Anyway, John's playing catch-up with Jack, and Jack appears to be heading straight for Ŝulok."

"How did he find out?"

"I'm guessing Jack found a pretty solid connection at Nova."

"Ah."

"Give Ŝulok's address to John," the Chancellor went on, "but first scramble my other line."

"Yes, Sir."

He waited until the third green light on the phone glowed to life, indicating that all three lines were now practically impossible to monitor.

"Thanks," he said to Carol and clicked the receiver. He switched to the third line and entered a telephone number. The line picked up after several rings.

"Alex, this is Jonathan Smith," the Chancellor said into the phone. "May I speak with your Mother? Yes, I'll hold..."

35

The California moonlight flickered off the incoming ocean swells, transferring a subtle calm to a lone figure standing on the beach.

He was in his mid-50s, but still vigorous as could be discerned by a muscular build. His white dress shirt accented his tan—a tan which spoke of many years toil and leisure under the relentless sun.

Further ashore he had heard the high-pitched ringing of a phone. The last few phone calls had been disturbing news and the past he thought long-dead had experienced an apparent resurrection.

His mind full of troubles, he finally turned toward the path of marble steps graduating up the beach to the only house in view. It was a large house with marble statues surrounding the walkways and a swimming pool overlooking the beach: the house of a not-too-pretentious well-to-do man. That was the image he strove for. The truth was another image.

The truth, he thought, walking toward the steps, was that he was wealthy beyond his wildest dreams and now facing the twilight of life. He had accumulated his wealth, lived a full life and now faced the one thing he dreaded most. Old age.

Even though he was healthy, with at least another ten to 15 years of good mobility left, he hated the idea of succumbing to the ravages of time. In fact, some years earlier, his entire focus in life had shifted from the gaining of wealth to the search for youth.

Seth Ŝulok wanted to live forever. Not that anything had proven feasible in that regard—at least not yet. But he sincerely believed he was closer to his goal than anyone could have imagined, had they known. Only two people—Charlton Trenton, and a well-placed informant—knew the full extent of his plan. Trenton was the only man he trusted—the only man with the capacity to grasp what others would pass off as fantasy and the wherewithal to help obtain it. Ŝulok knew he only needed a little more time. Time to find what he wanted, or in the alternative, who he wanted. And—he was having to again consider—time to rid himself of a wolf: Jack Graham. The man was supposed to be dead, but instead he was silently circling again, looking to make the kill.

Ŝulok covered the distance to the two-story house at an easy pace and was about to enter when a noise in the shadows distracted him.

He turned, his eyes trying to adjust to the darker area of the large veranda.

"I'm sorry," said a sultry voice, "did I frighten you?"

"Not really," he answered. "Did I hear the phone?"

A shapely young woman in her early twenties stepped into the moonlight and looked up with intense blue eyes. Wearing snug jeans and a white oxford shirt, she was as perfectly dressed as she was beautiful. Her hair—so black it looked blue—smoothly draped well past her waist. Her eyes seemed perfectly spaced. Her lips were delectably full and perfectly shaped. Her flawless skin was perfectly silky. Someone not the least bit attracted to her features would have been hard pressed to say she was less than perfect.

Holding a cordless phone to her chest, she remained at a curious distance. Ŝulok had never fathomed those secretive eyes and had seen eyes like hers only once before. Even though he loved her, those eyes haunted him with the past. He knew he would never know her inward thoughts by the chance of an insightful glance.

"It was for me," she said, her voice resonating alluringly. She was sensual without even being aware of it—or perhaps she was aware and doled out only what men could endure.

Changing the subject, she said: "Mother said you were leaving for Mexico tonight?"

"That's right," he lied. He was leaving, but not for Mexico. Moving to her, he touched her shoulder with fatherly kindness. "I was just on my way out."

"You're off to meet that awful Kalvin Reedy, aren't you?" she said, her voice modulated—which he recognized as scorn, this time.

"Now Alex," he said with a stab at control, "Mr. Reedy works for me—has since before you were born. He's a good—"

"He's an animal," she sliced with calculated aloofness. "You should see the way he looks at Mother and me."

"You're both very lovely—"

"Mr. Ŝulok," came a harsh voice from the door. A large Arabian appeared from inside. His over-sized hands held two suitcases. "There's one more bag."

Ŝulok nodded, reaching for one of the suitcases. "I'll take this one."

The large man stepped back into the house.

Alex moved back. She didn't like the way his voice—even his manner—changed when he gave orders. She knew he would never harm her. She knew he loved her—or at least wanted to please her. But she also knew at least one of his dark secrets—and it was something for which she would never forgive him. She had lived with her silent animosity since childhood, and it would never change.

It was what prevented her from accepting him as her father. As a child she had been leery of him. When she grew older the boarding school saved her from having to call him, "father." Time had not healed her wound—only caused it to fester in silence. He had been very patient with her, and she knew it. But that did not change anything.

"—did you phone Reedy we were leaving?" Ŝulok was asking.

"Yes, Sir," came the answer from just inside the door.

Alex watched him nod as she smoothed her jeans. Glancing off into the seashore she felt the sudden desire to take a late night swim.

"What about the Princess?" Ŝulok asked.

"She will be there."

"Where's your mother?" Ŝulok said, turning to Alex.

"She left earlier."

"She knew I was leaving," he said in an irritated voice.

He leaned over and kissed her on the forehead.

She gave him a slight hug.

"Alex..." he started, then paused. He didn't know how to tell her he may not see her again. He knew anything he might explain would ultimately turn any affection she had for him to anger: justifiable anger.

"Take care now," he finally said, and leaned into the house.

"Let's go," he called.

The large man re-appeared with another suitcase. The two of them moved down the steps and were swallowed in the night.

As she heard the car engine turn over she lifted the phone.

"Are you still there," she said into the phone and then, "I'm so terribly sorry for the delay—if you'll hold a moment longer..."

Alex moved into the house.

"He's gone," she called toward the stairs.

The sound of heels came from the upstairs hall. A woman wearing a wrap-around skirt and a white long sleeve blouse elegantly moved down the marble steps.

"He's off to see that Reedy guy," Alex said with a toss of her shining hair.

"I know dear," the woman commented, her voice a mixture of southern accent and sultry lilting.

"Let's leave," Alex suggested. "We'd be gone days before he would even know it."

"We have to wait," the woman returned, embracing the young woman. "When Mr. Smith is ready to press charges we'll be protected."

"You've been saying that for months," Alex said as she held out the phone.

"Who is it?"

"Smith," Alex answered, emphasizing the last name. "Or Jones. What's the difference?"

She took the phone apprehensively.

"Hello?" Then sure of the voice: "Isn't this against your rules of secrecy."

She listened, and then: "Yes, he just left, why?"

The voice at the other end answered by framing his words with concern.

"Aren't you being a bit melodramatic?"

She nodded with a worried look on her face and moved to a chair in the foyer. "Okay. I'm sitting down—what's wrong?"

She patiently listened a short moment.

"What's that got to do with us?"

Another pause drifted by.

"I see," she said, listening. "Okay, he broke into Nova and has been after Seth for years—so has half the government. That doesn't—"

She glanced up at the ceiling, her rusty green eyes darting about with impatience.

"On his way here?" she questioned.

She looked at her daughter then at the floor. "So? Seth isn't here."

She listened again.

"Prepare me?" she echoed realizing the man on the other end of the phone was doing something he had never done before. He was dancing around what he really wanted to say. "What for?"

Her face suddenly became sheet white.

"Oh my God... But he's...dead..." she mumbled.

She numbly held the phone to her face, not really hearing the Chancellor's voice.

"Yeah, I'm here... Why didn't you tell me...?"

She listened, not really following the conversation.

"No," she said at last. "I—I... We'll wait."

Visually shaken, she dropped her hand into her lap, shutting the phone off.

"Mother..."

With a vacant stare the mother looked at the young woman kneeling at her lap.

"Mother, what's wrong," Alex asked with concern.

She looked into Alex's eyes, the rich blue now more intense than ever.

"Mother..."

Gail Ŝulok could only shake her head slightly and lose herself in the dark blue eyes of her daughter.

36

The whining engine ebbed silent as the black helicopter landed on the desolate beach. The huge blades atop its rectangular ridge slowed into a muffled sound. The black machine seemed to swallow the soothing moonlight covering the radar-absorbent tiles with which it was armored and painted. Only the front hatches reflected light.

Opening the mirrored cockpit hatch, Karns Gray dropped to the sand and gazed over the meandering ribbon of beach. After a moment of thought he became aware of the cockpit vents hissing feverishly to replace the lost cabin oxygen.

He pulled down the hatch, and the hydraulics allowed the door to smoothly seal shut.

For a moment Gray stared at his image in the reflecting hatch. He sighed and turned, starting his trek toward the only house in sight.

The huge two-story house rose into the dark sky as though it alone commanded the waves to rush the seashore. While the house wasn't mammoth in size, it demanded attention.

He found the marble steps on the beach and quickly covered the distance to the house.

Surprisingly enough the security system was not activated and the door was unlocked. With trepidation, he carefully eased the door open. Satisfied it was safe, he slipped inside the house, locking the door behind him.

Reaching to his calf holster he retrieved the well-worn .25 caliber Wafffnfabriken Simson pistol.

He considered using the larger gun, but had learned long ago that a .25 caliber, used correctly, was an effective killing weapon. He had known one sniper who preferred a .25 caliber to anything else. Of course, that man performed only proximity kills—kills in close quarters. The secret, the sniper had explained, was to put the bullet through the eye-socket.

"It'll bounce around inside the skull," the sniper had said. "Kind of scramble the eggs..."

Gray had been his spotter—responsible for locating the target, pointing out any new variables and filling in should the sniper fail the mission.

And the missions...

A parade of faces suddenly danced by. Dead faces. At one time they had been merely numbers—an enemy to terminate. But now, in retrospect, it didn't matter if they were Vietcong and it was war. They had been living, breathing people. All dead now.

Gray shook his head, fighting back the memory.

Those faces were why he had chosen Clines' dart gun for the Nova mission and why he had easily resisted killing for the past 20 years. People did a lot of stupid things, but it didn't mean he had to kill them for it.

Except for Ŝulok.

It was a jaded perception. Even a perverted perception. But realizing this made it no different.

He took a deep breath to relax and forced himself to concentrate on the job at hand.

The house was gloomy: a canvass of impressionistic shapes. A brush of blue-white moonlight from an overhead skylight blended onto the foyer staircase. He became part of the painting, disappearing into the muted colors of French doors and closed-off rooms. Checking the house, he locked the first floor entrances then merged with the shadows of the foyer staircase as it feathered into darker blues.

By carefully stepping on the left and right edge of each step, he distributed his weight to the solidly supported areas of wood beneath the marble staircase. In so doing, he ascended the flight of steps without the slightest of sound.

Upon reaching the second floor, he moved down the hall, pausing to listen at each door.

He had ruled out three rooms, including the master bedroom, when he came to a door behind which he could hear shallow breathing and a clock ticking.

Slowly, he closed his hand around the doorknob and turned it.

When the handle stopped, he eased the door open and crouched down with the small gun darting back and forth. He could just make out a form wrapped in bed sheets. He felt the wall for a light switch by the door: there wasn't one.

Had he been unable to depend on his heightened senses, he doubted he would have approached the room this way. He doubted it, but not with certainty. He had practiced a rather self-destructive brinkmanship over the last few years, with each successive situation more likely to fail than not.

He could hear the racing heart of the person on the bed—their heart was pounding, as was his.

He took the plunge, sounding loud in the dark room: "Do not move."

"I won't," said a woman's voice. She had a slight southern accent.

"Is Ŝulok in the house?" he asked, realizing she'd probably lie if he was.

"No," came her soft voice.

So much for that, he thought. *Now what?*

"I won't make any sudden movements," the woman said in a small voice. "I know you're after Seth—I know you have a gun."

Her frankness surprised him.

"He left a while ago," she added. "And yes, I'm telling you the truth."

"Where and exactly when?"

"He said Mexico," she answered slowly, "an hour or so ago."

He thought over her answer. Gizmo was nagging at him. He felt as if he were missing something—not seeing the whole picture.

"How many are in the house?" he asked after a moment.

"Just my daughter," she whispered.

"Where?"

"Down the hall."

"Okay. Stay put and neither of you will be hurt—understand?"

"Yes."

He turned, knowing his full profile was dark against the contrasting shades of moonlight in the hall.

An excellent target for anyone with half a brain, he thought.

For some reason he felt an incredible anxiety. He felt he was missing something important—something to do with the woman, maybe.

Or perhaps I'm just slipping a bit, he thought, reaching for the door handle.

"Karns..."

Gray stopped, his mind racing even faster.

For the first time since entering the room the ticking clock seemed actually loud. The brass doorknob felt warm in his hand. The moonlight spraying through the large skylight at the end of the hall caused the door frames to cast vague, shadowy hues along the walls.

It seemed as if the clock was a bedlam of ticking, intent on assaulting his hearing. The woman slowly moved from the bed.

"I thought you were dead," she whispered.

She clicked on a table lamp.

When she straightened, her hair fell away from her face. Gray dropped the gun to his side in shock—absolute soul-stopping shock.

"Gail...?" he mumbled. Numbness was spreading through his body.

She straightened her posture, causing the full-length white satin gown to cling to her figure. Her large eyes seemed to physically pierce him.

She glanced away, nervously looking to the floor, then at him again.

Gray tried to say something, but his mouth moved without words.

"Long time," she said softly, moving over to him—again looking in his eyes. "Karns..."

He reached out, touching her arm lightly, then pulled back. *Was this real?*

They stood staring at each other.

"Mother," interrupted a voice—filling the shocking void.

Startled, they both turned to see Alex barefooted and standing in the hallway wearing a gray housecoat.

"I heard voices—" Alex looked down to see the gun in Gray's hand and then up at his face. A pair of deep dark blue eyes like her own gazed back.

"It's all right, dear," Gail said. "Come here."

The young woman glided across the floor to her mother.

"Alex," Gail said, gently caressing her daughter's long hair, "this is Karns Gray."

Alex moved her eyes from her mother to Gray, lightly biting her bottom lip.

"Karns," Gail said, nervously straightening Alex's hair. "This is my daughter, Paige Alexandra."

"You're...my father?" Alex said with an almost nervous reverence.

Shock upon shock, Gray glanced at Gail who simply nodded, *yes*.

He looked back to Alex—his own cobalt blue eyes gazing back at him.

37

The mantle clock chimed once and resumed ticking. The three of them stood as if statues.

Mechanically, Gray slid the pistol into his jacket. He didn't notice Gail studying him. He didn't see the dark blue interior of the room, the heavy wood furnishings or the balcony doors. He saw only the beautiful younger version of Gail and himself standing before him. The gray robe failed to hide the voluptuous curves of young womanhood. Flickering his eyes between the two women, Gray was struck by how they might easily pass for sisters, even though Gail was in her early 40s.

"Alex?" he finally said, questioning the familiarity of the name.

"Or, 'Paige,' if you prefer," she came back in her throaty voice.

He nodded, if only to offer a response. "You uh, favor your mother."

She smiled softly—a demure expression he found enthralling.

"I—uh..." He was too stunned to think clearly.

Alex smiled. "I guess a daughter is something of a shock."

"You're so...so beautiful," Gray practically whispered.

Again her modest smile. "You are too."

No one would have thought it, but Gray blushed.

"Alex," Gail interrupted.

She looked to her mother, then shifted her perceptive eyes back to Gray: "I'm sure you two have a lot to talk about. Although I'm not going to be able to sleep."

She glanced back at her mother. "I'll grab a snack downstairs."

Gail nodded, relieved of the awkwardness of asking her daughter to leave.

Alex moved to Gray. She was only a couple of inches shorter than her father. She reached out and gave his arm a gentle squeeze. Her touch was warm—almost hot. "I never believed... Well, I always hoped we would meet."

She left the room.

Gail moved over and closed the bedroom door. She leaned against it with her hands behind her back.

"I guess you'll hate me for this—you have every right too."

"I don't hate you," he said, then laughed in disbelief. "Though, I'm shocked as hell. I'm actually talking to you—I've got—we've got...a daughter...?"

Gail remained silent, drinking in his presence as only someone fearing the delicate reality of life could. She was most amazed at how Gray looked exactly the same as the last time she had seen him. It was as if time had simply stopped for him.

Gray looked at her—or perhaps feasted his eyes upon her. She had matured without really aging and was one of the most satisfying things he had ever looked upon.

"I'm sorry for everything," Gail said at last. "I lied—told you our daughter was another man's."

"And disappeared," he added.

She moved over to him, her familiarity natural.

"I over-estimated my worth," she said, looking up at him. "When I learned Seth wanted to kill you, I thought he would stop if I hated you. I was too young—too stupid to realize I was nothing. I don't even know... I can't say I ever really reasoned any of it out. The most honest thing to say is I was stupid."

"Does Alex know all this?"

Gail nodded, *yes*.

They silently stared at each other again, both enjoying the moment.

"What about us?" she asked at last. "You and I? Now?"

"Is there—can there be an, 'us?'"

"Oh yes, God yes," she said without hesitation.

"What about Ŝulok?"

"Seth is nothing," she answered, then looked more intent. "Or am I over-valuing myself again? Are you only interested in catching him?"

"I have to catch him."

"For yourself or Mr. Smith?"

"Who?"

"Your boss," she answered. "That's what we know him as."

"You know the Chancellor?"

"Balding, white hair, green eyes, real intense?"

Gray nodded. "That's him."

"He's—"

"You're the tipster," Gray said, putting it together.

"What?"

"You told the Chan—Mr. Smith—about the boat full of guns and drugs in the Gulf, didn't you?"

"Yeah," she admitted. "I've been feeding him information for years now. I was responsible for... Well, I had to do something to make right what I'd screwed up. I figured getting my husband jailed for life was a start."

"Husband..." The word rolled from Gray's tongue like an, *amen*, spoken in a tomb.

Gail nodded. "I've paid for it—dearly."

Gray didn't have a response.

"Karns," she said, placing a hand on his chest in much the way Debbie Allinder had. "If you'll just give me one more chance..."

He didn't respond, unable to voice the emotions boiling within.

"God knows I don't deserve it," she said, her voice trembling, "but Alex does. At least take Alex away from here."

"It isn't safe."

"Karns—"

"Gail, I—"

"I've lived 20 years with a fatal mistake. You can't know what it's like to know you've ripped out the heart of someone you love..."

Tears began forming in her eyes.

"When I thought you had died, I died," she said, struggling to hold back the tears. "The only thing I really lived for was Alex."

He nodded with understanding.

"You've got to give me another chance."

"You're married, Gail," he came back.

"Ha," she came back with tearful scorn. "My marriage is a fucking farce. I don't have a marriage. I have a wedding ring, that's what I have."

He wanted to yell, *yes!* She was everything he had ever wanted. And yet now, when he could see and touch her, she belonged to another man —an enemy, no less. Further still, at some point or another, he had begun looking back into the past with more analytical eyes. What he finally saw, he hadn't liked—in her and in himself.

With tears still streaming, she slipped her gown from her shoulders.

The cool satin whispered downward and delicately clung around the curve of her hips.

"I'm not a slut or a whore, Karns," she said through tears, "unless that's what you want. No man has the right to me that you have."

He stared. Not so much because of her nudity, but because of her words.

"I'll do anything," she said tears streaming. "Say anything, be anything you want. There isn't anything I won't be, say or do for you. Just don't turn me away."

Gray tried swallowing, but felt a lump forming in his throat. He realized she had absolutely nothing left to offer. On the one hand, it seemed like the ultimate offering. On the other, it was the saddest of offerings.

"I don't know what else to say—what else to give..."

"Gail..." His voice was that of defeat.

"I've made such a mess..." she whimpered, her voice breaking.

He reached out, barely touching her warm shoulder.

She leaned against him, her head down, weeping.

He carefully pulled the gown back up, covering her.

She looked up at him.

He lightly touched her face, tracing an imaginary line along the curve of her jaw and over to her full lips.

"It's okay," he said at last, realizing he was saying the words of another woman who could soon be hurt by a wrong decision here. "I'm here, you're safe now..."

She rested her head against his chest—listening to his heartbeat.

∞∞∞

A sound like earthquakes vibrated across the ocean surface, rebounding off the California shore 30 miles away. The two black turbine helicopters streaked at Mach speeds just feet above the calm ocean, tossing walls of water in their wakes. The Pacific Ocean was slashed open into a chasm which would send pounding waves to the shore for another quarter of an hour.

The unmarked helicopters groaned as their pilots suddenly throttled back the power and switched the huge engines into the almost silent drones of stealth modes. Skimming over the water, they continued reducing velocity until reaching the shore, where they hovered over the cold metal mass of black on the beach.

Silently the two machines eased into a landing beside the dark helicopter reeking of the same parentage. The cockpits and side hatches of the new arrivals hissed open and several men wearing camouflage khakis dropped to the beach. The last man out moved over to the cold helicopter and fatherly patted its black surface. He motioned the other five men to him.

They gathered around as he withdrew a cigar from his breast pocket.

Producing a lighter, he clicked a small flame into life and brought it up. Even in the flickering flame, there was no mistaking the cold face of Kalvin Reedy.

"Remember," he said through a puff of smoke, "don't touch Ŝulok's wife or daughter. All we want is Jack Graham."

The others nodded.

He took a long drag on the cigar then tossed it down. "Let's do it."

They began a march toward the beach house and Karns Gray.

38

Gray suddenly looked to the balcony doors.

Gail moved her head from his chest. "What is it?"

"I'm not sure," he answered, watching the curtains fluttering in the breeze. Everything seemed quiet, cool and safe. Too safe.

Trying to dismiss the feeling, he glanced down at Gail. The feeling didn't pass.

"What?" Gail whispered, sensing his tension and watching his face.

"Gizmo's yelling his head off," Gray whispered back.

"What?" she came back.

He shook his head as if to say, *Never mind.* Easing across the room, he moved out onto the balcony. As the room faced the beach at an angle, he could clearly see and hear only one section of the shore. The waves were splashing onto the sand and little else moved or made a sound in that direction. The moon was high in the sky and the view across the beach was nothing short of spectacular. He turned into the wind, enjoying the coolness on his face. The nearby palm trees rustled in the breeze.

"Karns..."

He turned at the sound of Gail's voice. Her tears had gone away.

"Is something wrong?" she asked, moving out of the shadowed bedroom and touching him—as if to reassure herself he was still with her.

"I guess not," he said, appraising her with an approving gaze.

She smiled, his attention stirring emotions she thought long dead. She moved into his arms.

"So," she whispered, "What now?"

He shook his head.

"What does that mean?" she questioned.

"It means I can't believe I'm here."

"We're together," she said softly.

He considered her for a long moment. "You know, the last time we spoke—"

"Please don't," she interrupted, fear gripping her chest. "Don't you think I haven't played that over in my head a million times?"

He nodded. He certainly had.

He was distracted by a noise in the hall.

Or was it downstairs? he thought to himself. He put his finger to his lips, motioning for Gail to keep silent, and then moved over to the bedroom door.

Opening it, his gun materialized in hand.

Alex was coming from the back staircase with a sandwich. She smiled.

He relaxed with a sigh and then tensed again.

Gail was at his side.

"What?" she whispered, now with more concern.

Gray waved Alex to them, motioning for her to be quiet.

"I heard the front door tumblers," Gray explained in a hushed voice.

"Come on," Gail whispered, "no one hears that good."

Alex's eyes were wide. "I heard 'em too."

Gray and Gail looked at her.

"Well, I'm sure it's my imagination again," she added in a whisper, and then to her mother: "You know I'm always hearing stupid things."

"Concentrate Alex," Gray instructed. "What do you think you hear now?"

"Your heart," she answered.

"Tune that out. Concentrate on downstairs."

Mildly surprised, Gail looked from one to the other. Alex had always claimed to hear the most outlandish things—impossible things. Everyone had written it off to her imagination. Now, here was her real father saying it was all perfectly normal.

"I hear the water dripping in the sink," Alex said with her eyes closed. "I hear—I hear something that sounds like a key in the door. It's scraping the inside of the lock."

Gray agreed with a nod. "Someone's breaking in."

∞∞∞

Reedy and his henchmen stole through the front door and were poised in the shadows of the moonlit foyer. Reedy motioned two of his men down the dark hall leading to the rear stairwell.

After giving them time to get in position, he led the remaining three men up the front staircase. They moved along the second floor hall and stopped outside of Gail's bedroom.

Reedy rammed the door and they stormed the room. As Reedy was turning on the light, one of his men rushed to the bed and threw the covers back from a lump of pillows. Empty.

Reedy checked the closet while the others searched the adjoining bathroom and under the bed.

"Where the hell," Reedy growled, hurrying to the opened balcony doors. He looked down to see the blank wall of the house was a sheer drop. He whirled out of the room.

Down the hall, he ducked into Alex's room to learn she was gone as well.

Returning to the hall, the others joined him and they rushed toward the back staircase.

Lying unconscious at the foot of the stairs, with brightly colored darts protruding from their chests, were the two guards.

"Where'd they go?" hissed one of the men.

As if in answer, the house shook violently and the wailing screech of a turbine helicopter rushed overhead.

"Damn!" Reedy yelled bounding down the stairs and out of the house. Out on the beach he looked skyward to see one of the black choppers arch upward and turn into a strafing run.

Leaping to the side, Reedy just escaped a spray of bullets. The chopper then rolled over and angled out over the ocean.

Reedy jumped to his feet, sprinting toward his helicopter.

Moments later, two black turbine helicopters were streaking across the glimmering water—mechanical beasts after their prey.

39

The helicopter howled southward along the Vietnam coastline, just feet above the floor of white foam-crested waves. The cargo area rattled with the sounds of machinery and wind as the chopper blades pounded out a kissing-suction noise to which the soldiers had grown accustomed. The sounds were as familiar to war as any weapons—and as absolute as the graveyards to which many would be sent.

There were ten of them this trip—introverted and silent. Crowded together they sat as if one man, the mission plunging them deeper into a private hell.

At the edges of Karns Gray's mind were the faint memories of his parents' motor yacht in Corpus Christi, Texas. He could almost hear the flocks of seagulls, their wings beating the air, sounding like—

The beating of helicopter blades. Gray mopped the clinging sweat from his forehead with his shirtsleeve and looked out.

They were nearing the beachhead and the liquid floor beneath changed to a murky green: like the color of their stained camouflage uniforms.

Sweat rolled down Gray's face, stinging his eyes. Wiping his forehead, he again turned his attention to the miles of undulating seashore heat waves.

A staccato of gunfire ripped a procession of holes above their heads.

When their helicopter veered to one side, a pursuing American chopper came into view. Another round of bullets confirmed that Americans were no longer piloting it.

"He's hit," screamed a voice. One of the men was trying to revive a soldier who had been hit by the last volley of weapon fire. The man's brains were splattered on the bulkhead behind him.

"He's dead, George," Thomas Hollander was saying, shaking George by the shoulder.

"No—no," George was insisting, "he'll be okay!"

Their own helicopter swung to the opposite direction, and Gray felt a sudden increase in altitude. The pilot was saying something about giving the VC a target of their own making.

"After all," came the pilot's voice, filtering from up front, "they love to shoot at U.S. birds, no matter who's in 'em!"

The copilot grunted an agreement.

Gray wasn't sure what they meant as he saw the beach passing beneath give way to the foliage of jungle treetops. A crescendo of gunfire from both the pursing chopper and the thicket of trees began bouncing around their ears.

"Karns..."

Gray snapped his head around to see what the pilot wanted.

"Karns?"

Gray blankly stared at Gail.

"Are you okay?" she asked.

Looking past her and out of the cockpit he saw the walls of ocean water thrashing upward—almost enclosing the black turbine chopper. The Vietnam coast had become California and the Army choppers, computerized fighters. Looking at Gail, he half expected her to be wearing camouflage fatigues instead of her satin nightgown.

"They're gaining on us," she repeated what he had not heard her say. "And something else just came onto this screen you told me to watch."

Shaking the flashback away, he looked down to examine the screen separating the two front seats.

"What're we going to do?" Alex asked from the back.

Gray pressed a series of buttons and looked to the console screen as it began flashing various diagrams of known ocean-going vessels. After a moment the screen stopped with the display of an aircraft carrier.

"That's what we're going to do," he finely answered. "We're going to give our friends back there a new target."

"What do you mean?" Gail asked, glancing from the screen to him.

"We shoot at that," Gray answered, pointing at the diagram, "and they'll shoot back at any black chopper in the air."

"Are you out of your mind?" Gail raised her voice.

"It was a good idea in 'Nam..." His voice trailed off and he brought the chopper into an attack approach with the naval ship. He began firing every weapon he could find—aiming to miss the Navy ship but shake them out of complacency.

The two pursuing turbine choppers flew into a mad hornet's nest of weapon fire.

Not being a pilot himself, Reedy was forced to watch as they took evasive action in order to survive the barrage of Navy firepower.

Off to one side, the other chopper took a blast to the cockpit and screamed over belly-up into a dive that exploded in the ocean.

Reedy's helicopter made its escape by out-climbing the Navy jets. Reaching its altitude ceiling, the rocket booster kicked in while the rotors retracted into the concealed blade compartments. As they achieved a low earth orbit, Reedy savored the last image he had of Gray's helicopter.

Erratically swaying as it strained to reach the safety of land while undetected, it had extensive damage by way of a hull-piercing gash.

Reedy only hoped the Navy had finished the job for him.

40

Oblivious to the fact their fellow countrymen were in the pursuing helicopter, the Vietcong shot down both aircraft. Not that it mattered in the way of numbers or percentages—at least, not in Gray's way of thinking. There were so damned many VC that a chopper-full certainly wouldn't be missed. And, truth be told, since the whole mess was little more than a proxy war with the Soviets, the downed chopper was just as likely to have been piloted by Russians.

Either way, it didn't do to start thinking of the enemy in any context other than simple numbers. They weren't anybody's fathers, brothers or sons. They were just numbers—a helicopter-full, in this case.

Gray had slammed into something—he wasn't sure what—and didn't really care. He just knew his head hurt with blinding pain. He wasn't gushing blood, though, and he figured that was good.

It was during this self-examination, when the helicopter was a mass of tangled bodies, that two strong arms had wrapped around his chest and he was forced into the 12-foot jump to the ground—which didn't help the throbbing in his head.

Pounding into the ground, the other man—Blake Clines as it turned out—came up firing his machine gun, giving Gray the time to grasp the situation. Clines was yelling at him to pull his gun—to start shooting.

"Shoot the bastards, lieutenant, shoot the bastards!" Clines was yelling, his machine gun blazing away.

Gray watched in rapt fascination as the helicopter, a mere 12 feet overhead, drifted away and downward, the blades seeming to slow into individually visible objects. Magically, it thudded to the ground a scant 30 feet away without exploding. Four VC soldiers scrambled toward it.

Oh shit, Gray thought, pulling his machine gun up. The VC were everywhere.

He fired off several rounds, cutting down the enemy who were running up from behind Clines.

The VC pouring out of the surrounding trees forced Clines and Gray to separate and run for protection.

Then the helicopter suddenly exploded—from an America grenade, no doubt. Clines and Gray were blown off their feet by the force of the blast.

They immediately began crawling into the jungle cover.

Some weren't as quick, or lucky, and were cut down.

Gray made it to the protection of a tree, but was having trouble remaining alert. His head wouldn't stop throbbing and he fought to maintain consciousness. He was sure he had blacked out at least once.

Through the bushes he could see the enemy shaking their heads over the burnt-out helicopter.

A twig snapped.

Gray looked around to see a VC soldier approaching.

The blackness at the edge of his vision swept over him again.

With a shake of his head, he fought his way out of the darkness within seconds—seconds that felt like hours. The soldier was leaning over him!

Gray started to lunge out—but the soldier suddenly looked like an American—then the enemy again.

Gray weakly thrust his fist out.

Archer Commons simply blocked the pitiful blow and caught Gray's head before he fell back to the sand. He eased Gray down.

"American?" Gray quizzed, vaguely aware of consciousness.

"Yeah," Commons answered, "USA's full of us."

"How many made it?" Gray asked, looking to see Commons' wet Hawaiian shirt.

"The lady's still zapped, but the girl seems okay."

"Lady?" Gray mumbled. "Our unit didn't have any..." His voice trailed off and he forced himself up on one elbow.

The ocean swells cascaded into the sand just a few feet away. Further out, the burnt-out army chopper was actually the damaged black turbine helicopter that Gray had managed to land just short of the beach. It was now cockpit-deep in water. It was still a dark sky, but without the interference of streetlights, the starlight and moonlight were incredibly bright.

"It worked," Gray mumbled. "Sort of...'bout the same as 'Nam, I guess."

Gray pushed up, gaining his feet with a wobble.

"John?" Gray said surprised, touching the cut just above his left eye.

"It has taken me the better part of the night to catch up with you, Pal," Commons came back.

Disinterested, Gray moved past him and over to Alex and Gail.

Alex sat stroking her mother's wet hair. Alex looked up. "She'll be okay, won't she?"

"Gail," Gray said, softly shaking her shoulder. "Come on, Babe."

She moaned.

"She'll be fine," Gray assured Alex with a smile and knelt down.

"Mom?" Alex said.

She opened her eyes.

"Mother?"

"My head is throbbing," Gail whispered.

Gray helped her to a sitting position.

"How long have we been here?" she asked, still dazed.

Gray looked at Commons. "About an hour—right?"

Commons nodded.

Gray stood again, ignoring the banging in his own head. He moved over to the surf and stared at the black machine, its cockpit surfaces reflecting the moonlight like two eyes. Leaving Commons on the beach, Gray waded out to the helicopter. He climbed into the cockpit for a short moment, and then reappeared with the reel of computer tape he had stolen from Nova.

"That was some escape," Commons remarked, as Gray trudged back toward him.

"You've been on my tail since Nova?" Gray asked, walking out of the water.

"Yep," Commons said. "Those other guys zipped past me about two miles out from the Ŝulok house."

"You know whose house that was?"

"Sure," Commons said, and then decided to lay out the cards. "I called the Chancellor to give him your message and he's the one who told me where to find you."

Gray nodded. "That's why information about the Export was redacted from the files I examined."

"I must have missed something," Commons said.

"We're in the middle of a crossover," Gray explained. "The Chancellor has been using Gail to get info on a gun and drug runner I was chasing some years ago—her husband now, actually."

"I see," Commons said, although he doubted he really understood.

"And from your general description of the Export, it sounds like Ŝulok's right hand goon, Kalvin Reedy."

"Kalvin Reedy, huh?"

Gray nodded the affirmative.

"Well, Jack—"

"Gray's the real name," Gray said to the other agent and held his hand out. "Karns Gray."

Commons looked apprehensive.

"I'm 1109 all the way to the bone," Gray added.

"Archer Commons," Commons said, shaking hands.

"Archer Commons?"

"That's the real name."

Gray smiled.

"I don't suppose you'd be willing to tell me why we're even in California," Commons said, changing the conversation.

"It's a long story."

"I've got time."

"I suppose you do at that," Gray replied, looking off into the distance, then back to the two women.

"Well," Gray said to Commons. "This is Gail Ŝulok, and my—my daughter, Paige Alexandra."

Commons greeted the women curtly then looked to Gray, "Your daughter? I thought she was *her* daughter?"

"Now that you're thoroughly confused, where's Blake's helicopter?"

Commons shrugged and led them around a bend and into a cove where he had landed the Engineering Inc. helicopter.

Pulling a six pack of beer from an ice cooler, he offered drinks to them. Gail took one and popped the tab open.

"Well, what now?" Commons quizzed.

"I think we ought to go fishing," Gray answered.

Commons did a quick mental analysis and could only come up with the satellite blackout area to the south.

"Mexico?" Commons ventured.

"I was thinking Padre Island," Gray returned.

"Whatever for?" Commons asked, steadying his balance by bracing against the helicopter.

"I told you," Gray said, helping Gail into the chopper, "fishing."

"I don't like the sound of this," Commons mumbled with a belch.

Gray took Alex's hand to help her up, and she turned to him, giving him a kiss on the cheek.

They locked dark eyes, communicating their isolated feelings in the simple act of being near one another. When she turned to step up into the helicopter, Gray caught Gail's eye. Her expression was a mixture of pride, happiness and sympathy. Gray had no way of knowing how much she had wanted Alex to have a father she could trust and love. Alex moved over and sat by her mother, laying her head on Gail's shoulder and practically falling asleep as she did so.

Looking at them both, Gray finally realized the pleasure his own father received by his occasional visits. He winked at Gail and she smiled back while gently caressing her daughter's hair.

Gray turned to Commons: "First, we need to call Blake to have the Nova helicopter picked up and repaired pronto. We're going to need it."

"Yeah," Commons agreed in a tentative tone. "What for?"

"That's the best part yet," Gray answered. "I'll explain on the way."

"I hope it's nothing like the visit you paid on Nova," Commons said, and climbed into the helicopter. He looked down at Gray and didn't like what he saw.

Karns Gray was smiling.

41

Despite Texas highway billboards advertising to the contrary, Padre Island wasn't much more than an elongated version of Galveston Island—which was, also contrary to billboards, trying to recover from having gone to seed.

Running in a downward arch, Padre began just 20 miles south of Corpus Christi and continued slightly over 100 miles south, dead-ending into Port Isabel.

Even though Gray had visited his father in Corpus Christi during the last few years, he had not driven the short trip south to Padre Island. His memories of the place were more than 30 years old. Like anything half-decent and empty, Padre had long since suffered at the hands of resort builders and spring-break college students. Hotel developments crowded the northern half of the island and were peppering what had been the island's southern section of nothingness and inexpensive coastal motels.

People had moved there in droves and the island was nearly a solid mass of buildings and play areas. Whereas this surprised Gray, it was just as Commons remembered.

However, any billboard notions of, "bikini pleasures," were far from Commons' mind during the dark morning hours in which he sat down the helicopter. Exhausted by hours of flying, he landed on the fog-shrouded beach-front property of the Sea Resort Motel—a remnant of years gone by.

At the office, he graciously accepted a room key and wobbled off to bed. Alex took her key and disappeared into the room next to Commons.

Gray and Gail took the room to the right of the others. He went straight to the phone.

"Why don't you turn on the air," he said to her, while dialing the phone. She pulled herself off the bed and clicked on the window unit.

Leaning back, Gray watched her disappear into the bathroom.

The phone at the other end stopped ringing and a sleepy voice slurred into the line: “It’s your dime—better be important.”

“It is,” Gray returned.

“Karns,” came Clines’ suddenly alert voice. “You at the Motel?”

“Just got here,” Gray replied “Did you send a crew to the helicopter?”

“You mean the Blacktooth?” Clines questioned.

“The what?”

“The helio you radioed about: that’s the official short version of its name.”

“Yeah, well...”

“I sent a repair crew as soon as you called—and per your instructions I didn’t tell a soul.”

“Great. Has it been repaired?”

“Hardly,” Clines answered. “They only got there a couple of hours ago. You neglected to mention that it was half-sunk in the ocean.”

“Oh, sorry about that. How long do you think it will take?”

“Well...” Clines stopped to think a moment. “We had to rent a hangar space to move it to, and I’m flying out some additional parts in the morning—the damage was mostly structural, you know. I’d say 24 to 38 hours.”

Gray nodded. He said, “I want you to personally bring it here, okay?”

“I guess I’m going to take a little time off?”

“If you would. Pack for a few days and brush up on your Spanish.”

“Oh.”

“What about the helicopters?”

“Oh yeah,” Clines said, remembering Gray had asked him to check on the number of Nova Blacktooth. “They built seven of them. And from what my repair foreman tells me, they’re beauties.”

“Hmm,” Gray grunted, thinking.

“Yeah,” Clines went on, “somehow or another, they managed to make than stealthy without using composite bonding or the usual radar reflective angles. Part of it is in the paint job of the tiles, of course, but it’s a mystery. They’re really something, I gotta say. You know, if we could replace the rotors with the *Tiger* EMF drive and incorporate the neuro-avionics package, that'd be something. Heck, we might even be able to turn it into a sub-surface to orbital craft. Now that would be something!"

Gray could tell Clines was only just warming up to the subject.

"So what was it you couldn't tell me on the radio?" Gray interrupted, trying to derail Clines' engineering tendency.

"Oh," Clines came back, remembering he had been fairly short when Gray had radioed in from the Engineering Inc. helicopter, which did not have a secured radio. Clines said, "A certain Seth Ŝulok is real popular around here."

"Really?" Gray replied, watching Gail emerge from the bathroom with a towel wrapped around her. She kissed Gray on the cheek and crawled under the covers of the king size bed.

"Yeah," Clines was saying. "Seems the Chancellor had a tipster primed for the federal witness protection program.

"The tipster I just picked-up, you mean?"

"She's the one. He called me in, laid out the story, and asked if I had heard from you. I lied, of course."

"All I want to know," Gray said, "is why he didn't tell me about her. She still thought I was dead—up 'till today when he called and told her."

"He didn't discuss that," Clines responded.

"Figures."

"About this Mexico thing..." Clines said.

"Yeah?"

"The Chancellor says the recons still haven't found anything."

"My hunch is they didn't know where to look," Gray returned.

"And you do?"

"Pretty good idea."

"Why not just pass the information along?"

"Listen, the bad guys have a man on the inside. The Nova people were expecting Jack Graham—someone in OCSTO or from 1109 tipped them off. I'm not taking any more chances that way."

"The Chancellor's going to want both our asses," Clines came back.

"I knew you'd see it my way," Gray said with a tired smile. "Just get out here as soon as you can get some teeth back in the Blacktooth."

"I should've seen that one coming," Clines said dryly.

"I'll see you then," Gray said. "And Blake?"

"Yeah?"

"Thanks."

"No problem—I'm going back to bed now."

"Good night, bro," Gray said, and replaced the phone receiver.

He looked over and saw Gail sleeping soundly. With a tired effort, he crossed the room and clicked the light out.

He was asleep when his head hit the pillow.

42

Early morning darkness had veiled the beach in a suffocating mist—as though the shore was compressed beneath burlap textured lead. An easterly dawning in the overcast brought daybreak as a glow of sea on the horizon. Slices of hazy moisture were peeled away to reveal thin lines of white foam rushing the shore. Slowly climbing above the water, the sun finally burst into the morning by splashing the sky in a celebration of colors.

Gail awoke in Gray's arms and stretched. Groggily she looked over to see he was still soundly sleeping. She lifted his arm to look at his watch, and then kissed his cheek.

He mumbled something sounding incoherent and she kissed him again.

His eyes remained closed and she sighed, thinking of allowing him to sleep longer.

"I'm still asleep," he whispered. "You'll have to keep kissing me to wake me up."

She smiled, a thrilling happiness running through her.

"I can't believe I'm here," she said grinning.

"It's only 11:30," Gray came back, opening his eyes to look at her.

"Not that, you clown."

He chuckled.

She climbed from the bed and staggered to the bathroom, re-wrapping the towel of the previous night around her body.

Gray heard the shower and threw his legs over the side of the bed. He moved to the window and stretched. On the beach, the lolling tide forced a group of seagulls to jitter up and down while scavenging for food.

He stood there for a long time—thinking. There were so many questions he wanted to ask Gail. And possibly many answers he didn't want to know. He had bottled-up 20 years of questions. He wondered how to approach her. While she seemed more accessible now, she had been subversive enough to hide plenty of secrets from Ŝulok during the last few years. Perhaps she was more like the Gail of old than she realized herself—or cared to admit.

So many unanswered questions...

And the main question: why? Surely not so simple a thing as thinking she was sparing his life.

He heard the bathroom door and turned to see her emerge wearing her satin nightgown. She had obviously washed it in the sink the night before, as it was now fairly clean. Seeing her in the daylight, he was even more attracted.

"I suppose new clothes should be one order of business," he said.

"I was hoping you'd say something like that," she came back, her southern lilt sounding more pronounced.

"You sure are country," Gray said smiling.

Suppressing a smile, she sat on the vanity chair in front of a mirror and pushed her clinging hair from her face. Even without makeup, her cheeks were blushed with color and her Cherokee features enhanced her natural beauty.

"You've been standing there wondering how to talk to me, haven't you?" she asked with a knowing smile.

He nodded.

"No more secrets. I promise."

"We've a lot to catch up on."

"Yeah," she agreed.

"Let's eat and buy those clothes first, what 'da say?" He had waited 20 years and a few more hours would make little difference.

She playfully grinned. "This country girl would say anything for new clothes, darlin'."

They awoke the others and joined them for breakfast at the motel restaurant. Afterward, Commons was elected cab-pilot. They took the helicopter lazily down the coastline, landing whenever Gail or Alex saw a seaside shop that caught their fancy.

The day was perfect. The sun was bright in the sky and the temperature was a mild 72 degrees. For Gray, there was something incredible about the day. Perhaps it was the weather—or perhaps the sheer absurdity of window shopping by helicopter. Whatever the reasons, he felt younger—more alive—fresher. He tried not to analyze it.

By 3:00 they returned to the Sea Resort, Gray having purchased two entire wardrobes for the women and a couple of changes of clothing for himself. Alex changed into a breezy thigh-length white sundress which laced up the front to a scooping neckline. Gail had slipped into a flowing gauze skirt and denim bustier that caught Gray's appreciative eye.

"You like?" she asked, twirling for him just outside the motel room. She put on a pair of Ray-Ban sunshades that matched Gray's.

"Those laces might take a little too-much time," he replied, playfully flirting and pulling her near.

She nuzzled her face into his neck: "It has a zipper hidden in the side seam."

"You guys coming?" Commons called from across the yard.

Gail looked over to see the agent in a T-shirt and jeans. He had just come out of the next door café.

She looked up to Gray. "I thought he was still in the room."

"Is Paige with you?" Gray called.

"Yep," came the answer.

Gray and Gail walked over.

They sat down to lunch, laughing about their morning shopping excursions. The usually sedate Alex hopped up from the table and caricatured the royalty she just knew everyone thought they were when landing the helicopter at the shops along the seashore.

"He even asked if I wanted on the, 'establishment's mailing list,'" Alex laughed, pretentiously emphasizing the word *establishment* while quoting a store proprietor. "I was like, 'Ooh, establishment, how ritzy.'"

The others began holding their stomachs, laughing as much at the usually sedate Alex delivering an uncharacteristic persiflage, as at the story itself.

"And mom," Alex went on, tossing her hair out of her face, "she's over there sounding like some hick: 'Hey y'all, look at this pretty thingy with shells in it—ain't it a hoot!'"

"Paige Alexandra!" Gail scolded through her tears of laughter.

Near the end of the meal, Commons excused himself and went back to his motel room.

"Mom says you were reared in this area," Alex said to Gray.

He nodded, swallowing a shrimp. "My Dad lives about 30 miles north of Padre."

"Mom says he's a shipwright?"

"Uh-huh."

"I'd really love to meet him."

"I'm sure you will."

"What about your mother?" Alex asked.

"She died about ten years ago."

"Oh, Karns," Gail said softly.

"I'm sorry," Alex added.

"It's okay," Gray reassured them with a smile.

"What happened?" Gail asked.

"She just went to sleep and didn't wake up. The doctor said her heart stopped—no reason for it."

"How terrible," Alex said sympathetically.

"There are worse ways to go."

"Your parents loved each other so much," Gail came back. "Your dad must have been devastated."

"It was pretty rough going for a while," Gray admitted. "But Dad said he preferred her to go like she did than any other way."

"Has he re-married?" Alex asked.

"Nah," he came back. "My dad—your grandfather—"

Alex smiled at that.

"—said that he couldn't find anyone to put up with him like mom. So it's just him and old Master Yen Hwúi."

"Who?" Alex asked.

"He's an old Chinese T'ai-Chi master that Blake and I met in Vietnam during the war. We brought him back and he has lived at Dad's ever since. When Mom died, Dad had him move in from the guest house."

"You never did explain to me what a Chinese man was doing in 'Nam?" Gail pointed out.

"It was some kind of political thing," Gray answered. "He got stuck over there."

"You were in Vietnam?" Alex asked. "In the war, I mean?"

Gray nodded his head. "Yeah."

She looked to her mother then back to Gray.

"You would have to be in at least your 50s right now," Alex said.

He shrugged, non-committal.

Both the women looked at him hard.

"You're joking?" Gail said.

"Really?" Gray came back.

"But you look like you're maybe 30 at most," Alex protested.

"Good genes, I guess," Gray said. He certainly didn't feel like going into the whole Project Hacksaw story.

"You know," Gail said, shaking a finger at him, "You purposely avoided telling me how old you were when we first met."

"I was undercover," he explained. "I was supposed to be in my 20s."

"Well you could probably still pass for your 20s," Gail admitted incredulously. "You look amazing!"

"I'm not falling for such an obvious pick-up line, lady," he came back.

"How about a less obvious line?" Gail asked playfully.

"Just as long as it's over the head of the child here," he came back.

"Hey," Alex said, feigning indignation.

Shortly before 4:00 they returned to their motel rooms and changed into swimwear. Going out onto the beach, they found Commons sitting in a lawn chair he had planted some 40 yards from the water. On his way to getting well sauced, he cheerily waved to them.

"To look at him you wouldn't think he spoke Russian fluently and had traveled the world over, would you," Gray remarked, waving back.

"He looks pretty plain," Gail said, also waving.

While Gail and Gray laid out a beach blanket, Alex dove headlong into the waves. In no time at all she had swum so far that she was barely visible.

"She's a bit far out," Gray observed.

"No further than you used to swim out in the lake," Gail responded, casting a seaward glance.

"There's a big difference between a lake and an ocean," he protested.

"I swear, I think both of you are fish," she countered. "She goes under for three to four minutes at a time, just like you used to."

He squinted his eyes, watching Alex.

"She's an adult, Karns," Gail said in an almost chastising tone.

He looked at Gail.

"You obviously would have been a great father," she added, stretching out in the evening sun.

Gray glanced seaward once more, noting Alex was now swimming closer. Feeling better about her safety, he turned his attention to Gail.

Wearing a black bikini, she seemed to burst forth with sensuality. His attraction wasn't so much to a perfect body, but to her confidence and sexuality—something she had always projected. Measuring 34-27-34, she was more appealing to him than any fashion model. He carefully soaked in every detail, all of which had existed only in his memory during the last 20 years.

Her rounded chin with a squarish curve graduating into high cheekbones still accented the fullness and softness of her lips. Her nose, having been broken in her youth, had an almost undetectable tendency to angle left—something he noticed only because she had pointed it out once. It seemed to add to her alluring appeal.

She opened her subdued eyes and looked up at him. There was a rusty brown hue to them that dissolved into the darker edges of green.

"Are you mentally undressing me," she asked coyly.

He shrugged. "I was thinking what a shock it was seeing you again."

She agreed with a movement of her eyebrows and a nod of her head.

Gray glanced away, looking at Alex for a moment. He looked back at Gail, remembering the years he had spent wanting to see her—longing to talk to her. Now that he could, he didn't know how to start. The questions, the reasons—he didn't know how to begin.

"You know," he finally said, looking at her, "it was such a long time ago, it seems a dream—like a hazy vision."

She knew what he was talking about.

"I was so stupid I wish it were a dream," she admitted, sitting up.

He nodded. He wouldn't admit a lot of it was a hazy dream for him. He wouldn't tell her how hard it had been. How he had fallen over the deep end. How he had started with simple sleeping pills and then started drinking. He hadn't wanted to get drunk exactly—just to escape. He couldn't remember a lot of it because he had been so near the brink of... Of what? Suicide?

"It was a bit rough," he said.

She looked at him carefully.

"Gail...?"

She waited.

He fought with the question. Love had become an obsession. How do you ask if you were alone in that crazy world?

"Did you... Did you love me?" he managed to ask. It was the question that had plagued him for years, and for a startling moment he thought her silence was that of someone about to hurt him yet again.

She looked unflinchingly into his dark eyes—peering into his soul. "I loved you, Karns. I never stopped loving you."

"So, what happened?"

She glanced out at Alex then back to Gray. Her voice came slow, earnestly: "What happened? I could blame it on Seth, but I don't know. I really don't know. I didn't realize Seth was the drug runner you were after until too late."

Gray listened, showing no expression.

"I messed up, Karns. I went too far, too fast, When I learned it was life and death between you two... I thought..."

"What?"

"I thought I was hot shit back then," she said. "I thought Seth might be more apt to settle down with me than go after you. I didn't love him, and I can't say that I thought it out that way. Hell, I didn't think much of anything out. I knew I was pregnant and I did think he might slow down if he thought the child was his."

"You're kidding," he said deadpan.

She nodded with a look of embarrassment. "Was I a dumbass or what? I didn't see beyond my own nose. I didn't realize everything he was into—you didn't tell me a lot before I met him and he sure didn't tell me anything. And then I was too busy boozing it up, kicking up my dancing boots and sashaying my butt around for cowboys. Like I told you last night, I just overvalued my merchandise."

He appraised her noncommittally.

"I'd like to think I did it for you," she said. "But, you know, that's probably a crock of shit. Sometimes..."

He waited, watching her look seaward again, and then down at the sand.

She sighed. "I just don't know any more."

He watched her glance out at Alex, then back to him.

"Listen. I know I hurt you that last day. I didn't want to. I just didn't know any other way to make you leave."

"Yeah, well it worked," he said plainly, knowing exactly to what day she was referring.

"I'm sorry," she said with the shake of her head. Looking at him, she wondered now how she could have been so foolish. She remembered the two months leading up to that day. How they had been a whirlwind she never expected. The shining engagement ring was a constant reminder of how carefully planned events had gone out of control. She hadn't wanted to fall in love. She didn't want to believe Seth could kill him. She wanted to marry Karns. And then she didn't want to marry Karns. She didn't want to hurt him—but did.

"That day was a bitch," she said to Gray. "I wanted you to feel—to feel—"

He could see she was fighting back tears again and he felt bad for making her face the memories. He said, "It's okay."

"I want you to hear it from me," she insisted. "I need you to know."

He nodded, waiting for her to continue.

"It was a fucking shitty thing to do," she said, wiping her eyes. "But I wanted you as far from me as possible. I figured if I hurt you badly enough, you'd drop that assignment.

"And it fucking worked," she cried with a humorless laugh.

She bowed her head for a moment, trying to compose herself. She remember sitting in front of the mirror that was above the bathroom countertop—the forsaken ring before her, shining like a beacon. She hardly recognized the face in the mirror.

Can that really be my face? she had thought. It was so haggard. She distinctly remembered running a nervous hand through her limp hair, the tears welling up in her eyes.

"Stop it!" she had ordered the pathetic face in the mirror. "Just stop it!"

She had pressed her hand against her chest, trying to stop the literal pain her emotions were causing.

Wiping away the tears, she had opened the door and crossed the hall into her bedroom. She collapsed onto the unmade bed and stared at the TV without seeing or hearing it. Then heavily sighing, she reached down and lifted the phone from the floor.

It had been as if her fingers were detached and moving under their own mind. Slowly she dialed Gray's number...

"It was like wading through glue," she said to Gray, coming out of the memory and looking up at him, her tears freely flowing. "When I called you, every movement took every ounce of power I had—you know?"

He nodded.

She paused again, unable to voice her thoughts. She remembered he answered her call on the third ring. She told him to come out to the house because they needed to talk. She told him it had to be in person. She told him not to expect good news.

The receiver went down without further conversation. She returned the phone to the floor and leaned against the headboard of the bed, gazing at the blank wall to her right. The air had suddenly become difficult to breathe.

"God," she mumbled through her tears, looking at Gray. "When you came over—I knew you had been crying. When you went in the bathroom—don't you think I heard you breaking?"

He shook his head *no*, feeling a lump come into his throat. He recalled wanting her to hurt—to feel pain. He now regretted it. "I didn't think about it."

"No," she agreed, "how could you? When you came out of there, I treated you like something on the bottom of my shoes. But it hurt, Karns—I was fucking dying... And of course you—shit, you were the perfect gentleman..."

Her voice trailed-off again. She remembered waiting for him to leave the house—waiting for the sound of his car to drive away. She wanted to look out the window—a last look. But she didn't dare. At last the car started, backed out of the driveway, and pulled away, fading into the distance.

She buried her face in her hands—sobbing until all that remained were dry heaves, and not stopping then. The depth of her sorrow went beyond what she was physically able to express, and she found herself on the floor gasping for air—hoping to just die.

Sitting on the beach, she wiped her eyes again. "I'll never forget the day Reedy said you were dead..."

It was one of those perfect days. She and Seth were seated in a restaurant. She was looking out at the beach when she felt Reedy's presence. Looking around, she saw him walking up. He was wearing black jeans and a black T-shirt. He looked as though he hadn't shaved in three days. He tossed a newspaper the short distance to the table and it landed in the cluttered space between her and Seth. One edge started soaking up the syrup from her plate. She lifted the paper to see it was opened to page five. Midway down a circled headline jumped out:

MAN DIES IN CRASH

"That's the last of Jack Graham," Reedy said triumphantly.

Gail caught her breath, feeling a sharp pain in her stomach.

She remembered calmly excusing herself from the table and managing to navigate the short distance to the restroom. Once there, she began crying and vomiting. After several minutes she began vomiting blood.

"I thought I was going to die," she said aloud, looking at Gray through her watery eyes. "I literally vomited blood. All I could think of was what I had done to you and what our last words were. I felt like a piece of shit— I *was* a piece of shit.

"I don't know how I lived—I really don't. I was so ill for days. The doctors said it was psychosomatic. I felt like telling them, 'No shit, Sherlock. I just destroyed a part of me...' After everything I'd done, I really wanted to die—but I didn't want to lose the baby, either."

A flood of tears strangled her voice. "I'm sorry," she apologized, sniffing and wiping her eyes again.

"It's okay," he comforted her, caressing her arm.

"You know," she went on, "from the beginning, Alex couldn't stand Seth as a father—and I don't know why. He did right by her—gave her everything, including love. She rejected it. So when she was about 13, I started telling her bits and pieces about you—about how stupid her mother was. It was a relief to tell somebody the truth. I told her everything and you know what she said?"

Gray shrugged.

"She said you weren't dead, that the body they found in the car wasn't yours. I tried to explain that even your teeth were identified. She said, 'Mother, he's a government agent—they're not gonna' tell anybody anything.' She never accepted your death."

Gray smiled. "She was right."

"Yeah," Gail agreed sheepishly, looking out at her. "She's the most important and dearest thing I have. She's so much like you, I used to cry."

"I'm that bad?" he said teasing.

"Yeah," she whispered. Her smile broadened, showing the minutely chipped tooth. "What about you?"

He shrugged. "Time marches on."

"I'm so sorry for hurting you, Karns."

He didn't respond at first. "You made your decision that day you said we were through. I had hoped you'd change your mind..."

She was looking down again. "I loved you, Karns. Maybe I didn't know the meaning of love, or how to define it. But I felt it. And turning you away was the hardest thing I ever did."

"But you didn't have to do it."

"I know that now," she said, tears flooding her eyes again.

"And you didn't then?" he said, fighting back his own emotions.

She shook her head, tears streaming and hands outstretched: "Dammit, I was wrong, okay? And then it was too late. I thought you were...were... I didn't know you were alive. Hell, even if I had known you were alive, I wouldn't have believed you'd ever want to see my face again."

She bowed her head again, hiding her face.

"I'm sorry," he said.

"No," she said, regaining control. "You're right. I should have had the common sense to know better."

They were silent for a while.

Alex came struggling out of the surf.

"Hey," Alex greeted, approaching.

"Hi, baby," Gail said, wiping her eyes.

"I'm going to get a lawn chair and bug Archer. Something tells me he's a riot when he's drunk."

Gray and Gail looked around to see several empty beer bottles scattered on the ground around Commons' chair. Commons, with a sloppy, goofy grin on his face, was waving at the people walking by him.

He was too far away for Gail to hear, but it was clear he was either talking to himself or the passersby.

"I wonder what he's saying?" Gail mused.

"He's singing," Gray reported, listening.

"Yeah," Alex confirmed, laughing. "He's singing, *Secret Agent Man*."

Gail and Gray joined in the laughter as Alex left for another lawn chair.

Gray turned to Gail: "I love you."

There it was. Plain. Simple. Truthful.

She reached up, slipping her hand about his neck. "How can you?"

He slightly shook his head, as if words didn't matter. "How could I not. You did all the wrong things, but you did them for all the right reasons."

"Karns..." She brought him down into a tight embrace. "I love you, too. I always have—always will."

He softly kissed her cheek, then her lips. He kissed her gently—enjoying the softness and wetness of her mouth.

Her tongue came back forcefully.

He pulled back.

"What?"

He only shook his head *no*. He wanted to sweep her from the blanket, take her to the room and passionately make love. Smoothing his hands upward, over her body and breasts—to her arms—he directed her hands into her silken hair. He crossed her wrists above her head, feeling her taut body next to him—warm, firm and expectant.

Having pinned her wrist with his left hand, he easily held her in a grip that slightly pulled her hair. Subtly, she thrust her pelvis—an undulating pressure, pressing, then pressing again. Back and forth, pressing, and then pressing again...

Perspiration beaded on her brow and her breathing became panting. "Let me touch you!"

"If you touch me," he said in a throaty voice, "I don't know that I could stop."

"Then let me touch you," she pleaded. "I want you to take me—right here on this beach if necessary."

She looked into his eyes, seeing his inner turmoil. The one man in him desiring her and the other man—the man of integrity who she had wounded—holding back.

"I am yours, Karns," she said earnestly. "Your woman. My marriage was a piece of paper and I won't believe that a piece of paper is more valuable than our love. So don't tell me we're not together because I'm married—because of a piece of paper."

She could see the tears forming in his eyes as he looked away.

"You have to know I love you, and I know you love me," she whimpered.

"Yes," he managed to say, turning his eyes from the ocean to her, then up toward the beach—as if avoiding eye contact. "But it isn't the right thing to do."

"The right thing to do?" she echoed, tears of her own forming. The love and desire were crushing her—as if physically tearing her heart. She was certain it would rip apart. She could see he felt the same. *If I can just find the right words*, she thought. *Show him that we belong together—that it doesn't matter if it seems wrong, it's right.*

"Karns," she whispered, "let me touch you, baby."

He relaxed his hold and she reached up, touching his face. She directed his eyes to her.

"I know it's wrong," she agreed. "But I'm not strong enough to fight something I don't understand—something that drives a wedge between us—something without meaning to me."

He remained silent, tears on his face.

"Tell me something I understand... Or make love with me, baby."

She pulled him into an embrace: "Please..."

The lapping waves filled the silence for several moments while they held each other. It was Gray who finally spoke.

"What would my daughter think of a father who holds only his desire, sacred?"

It was not what Gail expected, and the importance of it caused her to catch her breath. When truth had been something she would not accept, he had given her something she could not deny.

"Oh, baby," she said in a small voice. She realized that through some miraculous twist of fate, he loved her in spite of who she really was. Her tears of solitude renewed as she chastised herself for being so inferior—for having felt such inferior love.

"Your daughter wouldn't understand a father like that," she finally managed to say. "Which is why she'll always love and respect you..."

Gail loved him as if they were one—perhaps, even more.

43

At 9:00 a.m. the following day, Alex finished her morning swim and waded out of the surf.

Wearing a black-trimmed white bikini, her full breasts supported the small strapless top even though it was threateningly weighted down with seawater. Like the top, the bikini's bottom piece was sparing. French cut over the hips, the bottom exposed her shapely derrière while covering just enough to pass for more than a thong. Enticingly proportioned, she was a virtual Venus arising from the waves.

Her audience, three appreciative young men and two envious girls, watched on as she tied a matching pareo around her hips—dernier cri's most recent name for the sarong. Daintily, she held her hair back with both hands while looking down to slide into a pair of beach sandals.

With the diaphanous skirt fluttering in the breeze, she returned to the waters' edge. Draping her hair over one shoulder with an unconscious sultriness, she slipped a long shapely leg outward to rinse sand away from her foot. She repeated the pose with the other leg and then turned toward the Motel café.

Long used to adoration and envy, she paid no attention to the on-lookers, while the swaying-swish of her hips caused the young men to openly gawk. The girls, teenagers at best, stared in the hopes of learning some clue to Alex's nebulous eroticism.

Entering the restaurant, she found her mother and father laughing over breakfast. Gail was wearing a white ankle-length spaghetti-strap tank dress of rib-knit. Baring her shoulders and back, the neckline dipped to a tantalizing hint of cleavage.

Having crossed her legs, the dress had separated at the thigh-length slit, gathering in folds to either side of her supple legs. Casually rocking her leg, she, "flip-flopped," a flat-heel sandal with the apparent ease of habit.

Like the previous day, Gray had stuck with blue jeans, a white oxford shirt and penny loafers.

Seeing them—Gail with her Ray-Ban shades propped on her head and him with his hanging from a cord—Alex realized they really had been a close couple at one time. There was a natural easiness between them: an amiable comfortableness hiding an intense passion brewing beneath the surface. It was most obvious in Gail's inconspicuous gestures—a touch on his hand, or a slight brush at a stray lock of his hair.

As Alex approached the table she felt almost giddy at the prospect of having Karns Gray around as her father. Thinking of him as her father—her, 'Dad'—had been ridiculously easy. Perhaps, she reflected, it was a combination of the love and integrity her mother had always attributed to him.

But it went beyond that, she was sure. It was something in the way she felt about him. She hardly knew him and yet felt completely safe and trusting of him.

"So," Alex purred as she slid into a chair at their table, purloining a strawberry from Gail's plate, "what's on the agenda today?"

"What would you like to do?" Gray asked pleasantly, still thrilled by just her presence. "Shopping? Sunning? Site seeing? A little of this, a little of that?"

"I was kind of wanting to go to Corpus," she said with false thoughtfulness.

"Really?" he said, his tone rhetorical.

"Uh-hm," she drawled out in a girlish pitch then bit into the strawberry. The juice ran down her chin and she laughed while grabbing a napkin. "Oops."

"Any place particular?" Gray pressed, glancing to Gail, who innocently smiled.

"Oh, I don't know," Alex replied sweetly. She reached for another of Gail's strawberries.

"Get your own," Gail scolded playfully and slapped at Alex's hand—too late to save the strawberry from theft.

"I was thinking," Alex said, "I've always wanted to see boat-building."

Gray looked to Gail. Again she was the picture of innocence.

"Say," Gail said, as if the thought had just occurred to her, "your Dad builds boats!"

"Oh, that's right," Alex joined in with over-acted enthusiasm and a mouthful of strawberry.

Gray looked from one to the other. "You two think you're hustling me, don't you?"

"What?" they came back in shocked unison. "What da' ya mean?"

Gray was trying not to smile as he looked to Gail.

"You did say last night," she reminded him, "that you were going up there today. Didn't you?"

"I was planning to take both of you anyway," Gray came back.

"Does he know we're coming?" Alex asked.

"No," Gray said. "I only told him I had a surprise."

"What should I wear?" Alex asked. "Do you think he'll like me? Is that Chinese guy there? How long can we stay? Does he really—"

Gray raised his hand, his index finger pointing up.

Alex stopped rambling in mid-sentence.

"What you have on is fine," Gray answered, "yes, yes, and a few hours..."

An hour later, Gray eased the helicopter into the air. He waved at a few of the lingering curiosity seekers that had steadily streamed by since they had first arrived at the motel. He then banked the helicopter northward, following the shoreline toward Corpus Christi.

Gail was in the copilot seat, looking off into the distance. Gray almost reached over to caress the side of her leg exposed by the dress slit. Reunited just over 24 hours now, he was surprised at how her presence felt completely normal. It was as though sitting next to him was where she had been since they had first dated—as if she belonged there.

It was the same with Alex. He certainly had never been a father, and even now couldn't foresee meaning more to her than a father-type of figure. Nonetheless, he felt himself growing more attached and enjoying her company. She may have looked as if she should be gathering seashells on some exotic island, but her very nearness felt eerily natural.

He stole a glance back to the passenger cabin. She too seemed absorbed in staring off into an unknown distance. He turned back to the controls, smiling as he thought about her. She had been so concerned about making a good impression upon his father, that she had immediately left the lunch table to blow-dry her hair. She had also considered a change of clothing.

"You look fine," Gray had said when he found her staring at the closet of clothes bought the day before.

"A fine judge you are," she had retorted. "How do you think he'll respond to a girl in a bikini, huh?"

"He's always liked them, as best as I recall," Gray had answered.

"I just don't know if it's appropriate."

"It's in the heat of summer," Gray had then pointed out, "you're on a beach, you've got that skirt thing going—I don't see a problem here. Except that it might take you another hour to decide what else to wear."

She finally settled on simply exchanging her beach thongs for a pair of black sandals with nylon jute trim and 2½ inch wedge heels. As an afterthought, she had put on a pair of small white shell earrings and a delicate matching necklace.

He was impressed. The minor changes were elegant, and he told her so.

Gray came out of his reverie and pointed downward: "There she blows!"

As he brought the helicopter down, they saw a large two-story log cabin house in the distance. Next to it was the guesthouse, which was actually a log cabin garage apartment.

Several boats, yachts and sailing vessels littered the property—all in various stages of construction or refurbishing.

"Oh, look," Alex cried out, pointing through the canopy. Two black and white Siberian Huskies loped across the beach toward them. Stumbling behind was a litter of six pups not more than three months old.

"That's Kesh and Nick," Gray said, killing the engine after having gently landed on the sand. "The pups are news to me."

"They're so adorable," Alex cooed.

"That's because you haven't raised huskies," Gray retorted. "Oh sure, they're friendly all right. But when all the books tell you they have an independent nature, just remember it means they're stubborn as the day is long."

"Oh, Dad," she chastised. Realizing it was the first time she had called him that, she glanced over to see his response. All she could see was the back of his head.

"Well they are," he replied, busy shutting down the controls.

Relieved, Alex moved over to the door and opened it.

"Hello, puppies," Alex called down. Subdued puppy whines drifted up.

Gail looked at Gray, noticing his smile. Reaching over she got his attention by running her hand through his hair.

He looked up.

"Did you like that, Daddy," She whispered with a pleasant smile.

He winked at her.

"Why aren't they barking?" Alex asked.

"Husky's rarely bark."

"They'd be great in a townhouse, I guess," Alex thought out-loud.

"Ha," Gray grunted, moving up behind her. "You'd think a whole pack of wolves were loose when they start howling at being left alone."

Gray hopped down to the beach and then helped the women down. While the dogs were vying for attention, Gray glanced toward the house.

His father, Samuel Alexandra, was making a beeline for them. Wearing a beat-up fedora, sneakers and matching khaki shirt and trousers, the older man nimbly navigated a flight of steps that brought him down to the beach. In his 80s, Samuel Alexandra had strong aristocratic features and a full head of straight salt-and-pepper colored hair.

"Good to see 'ya, boy," He called in a robust voice.

"Hey, Dad," Gray came back, smiling, reaching out to shake the older man's hand. They gave each other a hug and stepped back still smiling. The lines etched in the older man's face were those of a man with a pleasant disposition. At 6 ft 1, even Gray looked up to him in more ways than one.

With apparent reluctance, Samuel allowed Gray to direct his attention to Gail.

"I believe you two have already met," Gray said in his usual equable tone.

"Gail?" Samuel mumbled. "Good Lord..."

"Hello, Sam," she came back, her voice shaken.

"What's with this, 'Sam,' nonsense," he said, his eyes growing misty. "Come here, you good-lookin' thing."

The two embraced and she kissed him on the cheek.

"We've sure missed you, young lady," Samuel said with a sniffle.

"Oh, Dad," she whimpered, unable to control the tears.

"Now—now," he comforted her and fatherly patted her on the back.

After a few moments they separated and the older man looked her over from head to toe. "You're still a mighty handsome woman, Gail James."

She laughed, embarrassed and happy.

"Aren't you a sight for old eyes," he added.

"There's never a tissue when you need one," she said, laughing and crying at once. Unable to clearly see, she leaned against Gray.

"Uh, Dad," Gray said, reaching to Alex who had squatted down to pet the dogs and stayed there. "This is Paige Alexandra—"

"Gray," Alex finished for her father while standing.

The old man pushed his hat back on his head, glanced at his son and Gail, then back to Alex.

With his eyes glassing over with water, he stepped up to Alex.

"Mr. Alexandra?" She said in a concerned voice.

"Would you do an old sailor a favor," Samuel said, a tear rolling down his cheek, "and let a grandpa hug his granddaughter."

Her lip quivering and tears filling her eyes, Paige Alexandra melted into the older man's embrace.

"Thank 'ya, Lord," he whispered. He patted her, holding tightly. After a few moments he held her out. Her blushing cheeks were moist with tears.

"I'm sorry," she apologized, "I don't know why I'm crying."

"Young lady," Samuel said smiling, "you're an oasis in this old deserts' heart."

He hugged her again.

Having instantly attached themselves to her, the puppies had followed Alex and were whining at her feet.

"Look at that," Gray said, swallowing to control his own emotions. "Now you've got the bloody dogs crying."

The others laughed.

Samuel stepped away again.

"Boy," he said, looking at Alex, "you're as pretty as that Caribbean beauty I married."

Alex smiled, wiping the moisture from her face.

Samuel looked to Gail then at Gray.

"That's some surprise, there, Karns," he said, taking his new granddaughter under his arm. He reached out for Gail and she joined him on the other side. "Come on, let's go to the house."

44

The group walked through the middle of Samuel's, "shipping yard"—20 acres of beachfront property—most of it in pristine condition. Samuel had invested well during youth and now built boats and yachts strictly for the pleasure. Of course his pleasure paid exceptionally well.

In the shipbuilding community he had earned a reputation as an unequaled craftsman and a meticulous artist. Unlike competitors, the vessels he designed and built incorporated an innovation of two watertight inner-hulls, each comprised of numerous individual watertight compartments. It was widely held that any vessel bearing a "Samuel Alexandra, Shipwright" plaque, was made from the finest wood and tenaciously weathered the trials of any waterborne tribulation.

"Blake says you haven't fixed the old girl up yet," Samuel commented as they neared the steps of the house.

"I've been on one assignment after the other," Gray came back.

"For ten years?"

"Well...no."

"Ah," his father said with a dismissive wave. "She's yours. It's none of my business."

"No, you're right, Dad. I should pay her more attention."

"I hope you're not talking about another woman," Gail said.

They were on the wide porch now, and Gray opened the door.

"No," Gray answered. "Dad's talking about the *Paige Alexandra*."

"First boat I ever owned," Samuel said, leading them into the house.

"I remember," Gail said, recalling Samuel's stories of years gone by. "You bought it when you were working for that company in New York."

"Elco Cruisers," Samuel supplied.

"That's it," Gail confirmed, looking to Gray. "You let it go to pot?"

Gray shrugged.

"It was a gorgeous Yacht," she said.

"I still live on it," Gray countered.

"In complete squalor," his father added.

"Okay—okay," he came back. "I'll fix it up. Of course, I'll need some help..."

"This is so neat," Alex said, looking at the logs of the house. They had come to a stop in an entrance area filled with old photographs of sailing vessels. Seeing the pictures hanging from actual logs had surprised Alex, oddly enough. Having never been in a log cabin, she was not used to seeing walls made of something other than Sheetrock.

"I had one almost just like it in Virginia," Samuel responded, moving over to where Alex was testing the texture of the mortar between the logs.

"He had a beard then, too," Gray said. "Everyone in school said my dad was Abraham Lincoln."

Alex laughed.

"Which was kind of an insult," Samuel added.

"How so?" Alex asked.

"Well, heck," Samuel answered, "Abe was nothing but a snot-nosed kid back then."

Samuel turned to Gray: "Why don't you make yourself useful and make us up some sandwiches with the lunch meat in the icebox."

"Yes, Sir," Gray said with a salute, and headed for the kitchen.

"I'll help you, Dad," Alex said, smiling at how the word sounded.

"Nah, that's all right."

"You go right ahead and help him, Paige," Samuel ordered. "Karns isn't all that special in the kitchen."

She grinned, following her father down the hall.

"I like your dad," she said to Gray, her voice drifting back.

"What," Gray retorted as they disappeared around a corner, "that old geezer?"

Samuel snickered and turned to Gail. "Come on."

The two of them walked into the den.

"You used to send him off when you wanted to talk," Gail pointed out.

"I still do," he said, walking over to lean against an empty fireplace.

Above it was a painting of his wife in her youth. She wasn't too much different in appearance from Debbie Allinder.

"Gail, I'm really happy to see you again," Samuel said.

"But you're worried about Karns—or what I might do to him again," Gail ventured a guess as she sat down on a love seat. She toyed with the hem along her dress slit. She had forgotten Samuel's habit of bypassing decorum and going straight to whatever was on his mind—no matter how much time had elapsed since he had last seen you. When Paige had been alive, they were a great tag team. One would grill a person while the other ran entertaining interference with whoever might interrupt. If merited, they even switched off, doing a sort of, "good cop, bad cop," routine. Samuel—the most abrasive—was usually the, "bad cop."

One thing was certain about Samuel Alexandra; you didn't have to guess where you stood with him—he let you know.

The older man nodded solemnly, confirming Gail's assessment. He wanted to know what she had in mind for his son, and what kind of woman she had become.

"I am so—so sorry for what I did," she said shaking her head.

"I never doubted you thought you loved Karns," Samuel came back. "And I'm sure you had your reasons for what you did, but that don't change it much."

"I know," she admitted in a small voice, looking down.

"Gail, I love you like you're my own. But I told Paige that Karns had bitten off more than he could chew when he started dating you. And I'll tell you straight, he got over you—but never got over the damage. He found a way to live with it, but that ain't really living."

"Dad," she said, looking up.

"No wait, hear me out."

She nodded, feeling a lump come into her throat.

"Karns wouldn't let that happen again—but God knows how much colder he'd become."

"I know," she said, fighting back a flood of emotion.

"I'm willing to bet you don't," he said, moving to sit near her. "That boy never touch a drop of alcohol until you two broke up. Then between the booze, pills of no telling what kind, and that job of his, he nearly killed himself."

Her expression told him she hadn't known. Too nervous to find distraction, she had allowed the dress slit to part and fall away again. She clutched her hands tightly together in her lap.

"He didn't tell us anything when it happened," Samuel said. "He wouldn't talk about it. He just slept and worked. Then one day Blake showed-up with bad news. Karns was so messed-up that he volunteered for some fool experiment—some kind of artificial intelligence project. Some nonsense like that. He ended-up in a coma for two years."

"He—he didn't tell me," she mumbled in shock. Her hands felt hot next to the cool skin of her legs.

"You know how he is—he just doesn't open up. Some people open up, some don't. Karns is the *don't* kind."

She nodded, biting her bottom lip.

"He's my only son, Gail. You know that's not my blood flowing through his veins, but that doesn't matter. He's my boy, you understand me?"

"I do, Dad, I do," she said sincerely, unable to prevent her eyes from watering.

"I just want you to treat him right," Samuel said, his voice tightening with emotion. "Don't hurt him any more."

"Oh, Dad," she cried, no longer able to hold the tears back. "I'll never hurt him again. I am so sorry..."

"Now-now," he said reaching over to pat her on the knee. "It's okay. Just do my son right, Gail. That's all I ask."

"I will," She promised in tears, unable to regain her composure. "I know... I made the mistake—that was wrong. I was so... I—was—so—terrible to him..."

Samuel retrieved a box of tissues from a nearby shelf and brought it to her. He sat beside her.

"I've told him I'm sorry," she said, wiping her eyes. "But I just feel—so—so..."

Her struggle for words faded into nothingness and he patted her gently.

“Just take care of the here and now,” Samuel said.

She nodded, wiping her nose. She reached over and hugged him. She said, “Do you forgive me?”

“Heavens yes, Sweetheart.”

Holding Samuel she could see the painting of his wife. Gail started weeping again.

“It’s okay,” Samuel said.

“No,” she managed to say, heaving with tears.

“For goodness’ sake—”

“Paige,” Gail cried, breaking the embrace and pointing to the painting. “Mom, she must have—thought—I...” She couldn’t continue, but tried anyway. “Now she’s—she’s—she died—thinking I...”

Gail tucked one arm under the other and hid her face with her right hand.

“I won’t lie to you, Sweetie,” Samuel said. “She was hurt by the whole thing. But she always thought you’d come back.”

Gail looked up, her eyes soaked and red. “She—did?”

Samuel nodded. “After Karns kind of moved on with his life, she thought you’d eventually come back. She believed it all the way to the end.”

“Oh, Dad,” Gail moaned.

“She really never stopped believing in you, Gail. I never saw anybody pray so hard for two people as she did for you two.”

Gail used a new tissue to wipe the tears away.

“Maybe that’s why you’re now here,” Samuel added.

Gail managed a smile.

“It’s okay now,” he soothed her, and then broke into a sly, crooked smile. “Of course, now you have a little competition.”

She looked bewildered.

“A fine young cutie named Debbie,” Samuel clarified.

“Now you’re being mean,” Gail pouted with a girlish smile.

He patted her knee. “Well, maybe.”

“Lunch is served,” came Alex’s voice, and she walked-in carrying a tray of sandwiches.

Gray followed, balancing a serving tray loaded with a pitcher and drinking glasses: "Fresh brewed tea anyone?"

Gail moved to him, still wiping her eyes. "Come here."

"What?" he asked.

"Come on," she said, having already taken the serving tray and sat it on the coffee table.

"Be back in a minute, Dad," she said, practically towing Gray out of the room.

In the hallway, just around the corner from the den, Gail gently pushed Gray against the wall. She wrapped her arms around him and pulled him down into a deep, French kiss. Surprised and pleased, he wrapped his arms around her small waist, enjoying the natural sway of her back against his hands.

She pulled back from his lips a fraction.

"I love you," she whispered.

"I know, baby," he said, surprised by her outburst, "you don't have to—"

"No, it's really important for me to say this, okay?" she said.

"Okay."

"It's, uh, it's not enough to—to tell you I love you... It's not even enough to—to show you that I love you..." Her voice faltered. She wasn't even sure if words existed to express what she felt. After all, one spoke with words but one didn't feel with them.

"Karns... I'm—I'm so—saying, 'I'm incomplete without you,' isn't even enough. I wish—I wish you could just take my heart—my feelings—and feel what I want you to know."

Her eyes had begun tearing up again.

"Oh, damn" she said, wiping away the tears.

He ran his hands through her hair and for the second time that day he was fighting emotions buried long ago.

"I'm just such a simpleton, I don't have the words, you know?"

"I know," Gray said. "It's hard to feel with words."

She half-laughed, realizing he really, truly, understood. "Yes."

"You don't have to apologize, Gail. We're on a clean slate, now."

She grinned through another wave of tears and waved her hand uselessly. “If I could just stop all this blubbering I’d be happy.”

He laughed and hugged her.

“Don’t laugh at me,” she managed to say.

“Silly woman.”

It was several minutes before either of them were inclined to break the embrace—and even longer still before they stopped touching and caressing. When they finally returned to the den, they were so emotionally intertwined that they felt awkward and clumsy in the presence of others.

Does it show? Gail thought, catching Gray’s attention with her eyes. She could see he felt the same.

The corner of his mouth upturned into a smile and he shrugged, as if to say, *I think so.*

She mouthed the words, *I love you.*

Gray picked up a sandwich and poured two glasses of tea. He handed one to Gail.

Seemingly oblivious to her father and mother, Alex was listening to Samuel explaining aspects of boat building while he pointed out various boats in the yard.

“Hey, Mother,” Alex said, looking around, “did you ever meet Mr. Hwúi?”

“Once,” she answered, unsure if she even sounded normal.

“He’s right down there,” Alex said pointing out the window with her glass of tea. The ice clinked in her glass.

Gail and Gray walked over to the window and looked.

Sitting on a small barrel, in the shade of a half-sanded boat, was a man with a pipe in his mouth.

“What’s he doing?” Gail asked.

“Waiting for Dad to come back to work,” Gray answered. “Or sundown—whichever comes first.”

“Seriously?” Gail said.

“He is serious,” Samuel responded.

She looked from one to the other: “What’d you mean? Shouldn’t we invite him in?”

"Old Yen only leaves that barrel when nature calls."

"I don't understand."

"That's just the way he is," Samuel admitted. "He goes out with me in the morning and sits down by whatever boat I'm working on. He'll stay right there until sundown.

"Does he speak English?" Alex asked.

"Oh sure," Samuel said. "Some days he talks my ear off."

"Come on, Paige," Gray said to Alex, setting his glass down and gulping the last of his sandwich. "I'll introduce you."

They went out the back door and crossed the yard. As they approached the boat—a 35-foot cabin cruiser, the old Chinese man looked up.

His face was weathered thin, and he was so small as to seem dwarfed by everything around him.

"Ah," Hwúi said, looking up at Gray. "Slow One, you visit father."

"How are you, Yen?" Gray said, looking down.

"Good," the old man answered in a heavily accented voice. "Your daughter, very pretty."

"Hello, Mr. Hwúi," Alex said, wondering how he knew who she was.

He bowed a nod to her. "Much of Karns Gray in you."

"Thank you," she said, for lack of anything more appropriate.

"It's good to see you, Sir," Gray said.

"Good to see you," Hwúi said to Gray then pointed his well-chewed pipe at Alex while still addressing Gray. "You are fortunate in your happiness."

Gray nodded, having heard the old man say this before.

"But happiness is a measure, not a measurer," Gray finished, familiar with the words.

The old man nodded, pleased: "It's so."

"Karns," came Gail's voice from the house some 40-yards away. "Phone call."

Gray looked to Alex.

"I'll stay here," she said.

"Later, Yen," Gray said and trotted to the house. He climbed the back steps, two at a time, and met Gail holding a cordless phone at the door. He smiled, took the phone and pulled her to him tightly.

"You are so beautiful," he said and kissed her passionately.

"Oh," she purred with a smile when he pulled back. Her eyes sparkled in the light. "You're beautiful, Baby."

Grinning, he lifted the phone to his face: "Gray here."

"You're not bad lookin' yourself, honey," came Clines' voice.

Gray laughed.

"You certainly sound like you're having a fine time," Clines added.

"Actually, I am," Gray responded, moving to the steps to sit down and watch Alex and Hwúi.

"Sorry to interrupt," Clines went on, "But Wilson said I could find you there."

"Who?"

"John Wilson?" Clines reminded him, "1109..."

"Oh, Yeah," Gray said, remembering that was one of Archer Commons' names.

"You *really* must be enjoying yourself."

Gray laughed again, accepting another glass of tea from Gail. "You didn't call me just to shoot the breeze, I suppose?"

"No," Clines came back. "I was going to give you an ETA, but with this new flippancy you've acquired—"

"When?"

"About 6:30 this evening—your time. Motel or Dad's?"

"Motel. And I need you to arrange something for me."

"Okay."

"I want to put a couple of people under protective custody." He looked to Gail as she sat beside him, resting her head on his shoulder. The dress had parted, as usual, and he lovingly squeezed her knee. Into the phone he said: "I don't trust too many people right now, so ask Debbie to personally see to it. She can stash the witnesses on my yacht."

"Is one of those witnesses who I think it is?"

"Probably."

"Do you think Debbie's a good choice for this?"

"What do you mean?"

"Karns, buddy, ol' pal," Clines said lightly. "Have you had too many beers in the hot sun? Debbie really likes you, if you recall."

"I just don't trust anyone but her," Gray came back.

"It's your funeral."

"Have her pick out a few guys she trusts. The witnesses will be leaving here in the Nova chopper after you arrive."

"Anything else?"

"That should do it."

"Consider it done."

"See ya' at about 6:30."

"That's cool," Clines said. "See ya'."

Gray clicked the phone, waited for the dial tone and dialed the operator.

Samuel came out onto the porch behind them.

"Well I'll be," Samuel said, squinting. "Old Yen just got up."

Gray looked over the boatyard. Alex and Yen were moving toward the beach.

"He never did that for us," Gray commented. The operator came on the line. "Yes Ma'am, I'd like to make a call to Mexico and charge my home phone..."

After Gray had left to take the phone call from Clines, Alex squatted down to be at eye level with Yen Hwúi.

"Mr. Hwúi?"

"Call me Yen, Pretty One."

She smiled. "Yes, Sir. Anyway, how did you know that I was Karns' daughter?"

"How could I not," he answered. "You have woman's lips, but they are your father's. You have woman's eyebrows, but they are your father's."

He reached out, gently touching her cheekbones: "And here, the shape of your father's face."

"I thought I looked a little like mom."

"You do," he said, "But your father, too. Especially the eyes."

"You remember what my mom looks like?"

Hwúi nodded gravely. "Great sadness for your father. I not forget her."

"They're getting back together," Alex protested.

He did not respond, but looked at the boat instead.

"Don't you ever do anything during the day?" she asked.

"Yes."

"What?"

"Read."

She looked around, seeing nothing but sand. Wearing simple tan trousers, sandals and a short sleeve shirt, Hwúi obviously had no place to hide books on his person.

"Read what?" she pressed.

"Many things," Hwúi answered. "Books, scrolls, manuscripts..."

He had seen her looking around for his reading material and anticipating her question he pointed to his head. "Here."

"You've memorized them?"

"Hard it is to believe, but I was young once," he said. "Much study then."

"Mr. Alexandra said you just sat here—doesn't he know?"

Hwúi shook his head, *no*. "He not ask."

She smiled, drawing the old man's gaze.

"What?" she asked, self-conscious under his renewed scrutiny.

"I am pleased to be in the presence of such beauty and wisdom."

She laughed.

"Come," he said, standing. "I will read no more now. We must talk of important matter."

Standing, he was no more than 5 feet 5 inches tall.

"Yen?"

"Yes, Pretty One?"

"Are you really a T'ai-Chi Master?"

"I am called that."

They walked a short distance in silence.

"What did dad mean a while ago," Alex said, "when he said happiness isn't a measurer?"

Hwúi pulled the unlit pipe from his teeth and looked at the beautiful young woman. She was attentive like her father, he decided. Her inquisitiveness had led right to the thing that weighed most heavily on his heart.

"Happiness is fleeting," he answered.

"You can't be happy all the time, if that's what you mean," she pointed out.

Hwúi nodded in agreement. "It is so. Why then do people search for happiness again and again."

"They want to be happy, I guess," she came back.

"And what is it to be happy?" he probed.

She looked at the old man, suspecting him of leading her to some point. "It's to feel good. To know everything is going okay—that you're content."

"And to be happy, means these things?"

"Well, yeah."

"Then happiness is a measurer of how you feel, is it not?"

"Well that's a way of looking at it, I guess."

"You guess?" he questioned.

"I could just as easily say that how I feel is a measurer of how happy I am—that happiness is the end, not the means to it."

The old man stopped walking and turned to her. "If happiness is the end, what has been gained?"

"Well..." She stopped, thinking it over.

He watched her closely, knowing she was coming to the conclusion to which he had led her. The American saying, *you can lead a horse to water but you can't make him drink*, passed through his mind, followed by the solution he had once heard that went: *But you can put salt in his oats and that'll make him thirsty.* It also occurred to him that he was thinking more like the Texans every day.

"I hadn't thought about it that way," she finally said.

"He pulled his pipe out and lightly tapped her on the collar bone: "Even the God your dad speaks of asked what is gained by having the world and losing the soul."

"I don't think Jesus was talking about contentment," she countered.

Hwúi looked up at her with the beginning of a smile: "That is so, Pretty One. It is apparent you know what *I* am saying, yes?"

He didn't wait for an answer, but urged her forward with a touch to her arm.

"I worry about the Slow One," Hwúi said, then looked to Alex as he realized she wouldn't recognize the name.

"Who?" she asked.

"Your father."

"Why—"

"Another time," he interrupted with a wave of the empty pipe. He went on as if no interruption had occurred: "You are like your father—before he took less traveled road."

She didn't know how to respond, and so remained silent.

"Like Karns, you are strong," Hwúi said. He tapped his own chest lightly and added: "In here."

She smiled at what she perceived was a backward compliment.

"But thinking does not—" he paused searching for a word, "*validate* feeling."

"What are you saying?" she asked, pushing her hair out of her eyes.

"Your father not yet achieve, 'being,'" Hwúi explained. "He very-very close. But now, I not sure."

Alex had leaned slightly forward, trying to follow his line of thought through the broken English. She said, "It's my mother, isn't it? You're like Mr. Alexandra. You think she's going to hurt him, don't you?"

The old man nodded.

"That's not going to happen, Yen," Alex protested, feeling that everyone was too angry with her mother. Earlier, Alex had stood by the doorway to the den, listening to Mr. Alexandra and her mother. Although Mr. Alexandra had been kind enough, Alex couldn't help but feel that he, like the old man in front of her, couldn't give up the past. They didn't realize what a good woman her mother really was.

"Mom isn't like that—not any more. She—we, love him!"

Hwúi's old face stared up unflinchingly: "The rice grower protects the crop against wild animals, but not his own oxen. The master guards against thieves, but not his own servant."

"Brutus plunged the first dagger into Caesar's heart?" Alex ventured angrily. She didn't expect the old man to grasp the Shakespearean reference, and she was too upset to care.

"It is so," he responded calmly. And then with the precision of a skilled surgeon, he added: "'The noble Brutus...'"

Abruptly, and dismissive, he turned and began the walk back to his barrel.

At first blush, she was angered by her own stupidity at referencing a literary example so appropriate to Hwúi's message. She had underestimated the old man. But then, she realized that from the viewpoint of her father's friends and family, her mother was Judas. She had done what none of them would ever dream of doing. She had betrayed Karns Gray.

How could they feel anything but distrust? Alex thought. *These people love my father and by hurting him, she hurt them deeply, too.*

She spurred herself out of her contemplation and caught up with Hwúi.

"I'm sorry," she apologized.

The old man continued walking, offering no response.

"I understand you guys are worried about Dad," Alex went on. "You've got every right to."

Hwúi stopped and looked up at her. "Did your mother do wrong?"

"Uh," Alex stammered, caught off guard. "Well, yeah."

"Why?"

"Well... She, uh, she wanted to protect—"

Ignoring her, Hwúi started walking again.

"Okay," she called and then caught up with him again. "I get it. It's the wrong answer."

Hwúi stopped and looked at her. "No reason for wrong, only excuse. Everything is black and white. The gray is not real. It is illusion. Parlor trick. You see gray only because someone says it is there—not because it is."

He took a step, and then turned back to her. "*Julius Caesar,* by William Shakespeare... You mentioned this, yes?"

Still digesting his last comment, it took her a second to shift mental gears. "Uh, yes, I did."

"You like Shakespeare's writing, yes?"

"Yeesss," she said, drawing the answer out slowly, wondering where he was headed.

"Why?"

"Because he writes beautifully. And he's so insightful."

"His words are of importance to you, yes?"

She nodded that they were.

"*Hamlet*, Act 1 scene 3: 'This above all, to thine own self be true / And it must follow as the night the day, / Thou canst not then be false to any man. / Farewell, my blessing season this in thee.'"

He leaned toward her, his eyes intense. "The last line means, 'Farewell, my blessing bring to maturity this in thee.'"

Despite her entreaties, the old Chinese master returned to his barrel without either stopping or responding with further conversation.

At 4:30 p.m., they said their farewells. The women climbed into the helicopter and Gray turned to his dad a last time.

"I always have these mixed feelings about your visits, Son."

"I know," Gray admitted. His father usually said the same thing each time. Gray was never certain if his pre-mission visits were more for his father's benefit, or for his own. Whatever the case, Vietnam had taught him well. Too many were the young men that left home—never to return—without realizing the significance of their final moments in the presence of family.

"You be careful now, boy."

They embraced and Gray climbed into the chopper. Within minutes the engine was up to speed and the helicopter lumbered upward. It banked and crept southward.

Samuel stood watching until they were a part of the endless horizon.

45

Blake Clines arrived at sundown.

The Nova Blacktooth smoothly landed beside the Engineering Inc. helicopter. The cockpit hatch hissed open and Blake Clines worked his large frame free of the machine. Pausing while the hatch sealed, he watched Gray approaching with suitcases in hand. Behind Gray, carrying more baggage, were two women, one of which he recognized as Gail. Commons—who Clines still knew as John Wilson—brought up the rear with even more luggage. Clines stuck his hands in his windbreaker, idly kicking a foot to loosen sand from his sneakers.

"Blake," Gray said, reaching Clines. Gray sat the suitcases down and clasped a firm grip on the shoulder of his friend.

"Just don't say it took balls to steal this thing," Clines said with a tilt of his head to indicate the Blacktooth. "I'm just glad I'm not 1109 any longer—the Chancellor will kill me mercifully quick. You, on the other hand, will have a slow and painful death from castration."

Gray smiled, knowing Clines probably enjoyed the chance to study the machine without interruption. He moved around to see a shiny patch of metal where once a gaping hole had been.

"How's it fly?"

"Great," Clines answered, following Gray around the back of the chopper. "They did a good repair job, given your time constraints. She's lost some of her stealth, of course. Oh, and here—"

Gray took the round yellow object Clines had removed from his jacket pocket.

"What's this?"

"That," Clines said, "is the reason they were able to track you all over God's green earth. It's a transponder—the thing that enables air traffic controllers to identify aircraft on their scopes."

Gray looked up from the device, his expression asking the obvious.

"Because," Clines said, long familiar with his friend's mannerisms, "each of the Nova choppers are equipped to monitor other Nova choppers."

"Ah."

"In fact, with the way that thing works, they could have followed you to the moon."

"I wonder if the other Blacktooths—or would that be, 'Blackteeth?'"

Clines shrugged, and Gray continued: "Well anyway, I wonder if they have something similar."

"Well it isn't like they knew to plant it on a chopper they didn't know you were stealing, is it?"

"Good point."

"I guess those are the, 'witnesses,' huh?" Clines asked, indicating the approaching women.

"Gail and Alex," Gray said.

"Alex?"

"Gail's daughter."

"Oh."

The two friends faced the women as they walked up.

"Blake," Gail said with a warm smile. She sat the luggage down. "It's good to see you."

He accepted her hug. He had always liked her, but now all he could think of was how Debbie felt. He had already crossed that bridge and hadn't liked being the bearer of such news.

"Blake," she repeated with a smile, while holding her hand out toward the young girl, "this is Alex, my daughter."

"Pleased to meet you," Clines said, appraising her with approval.

"I've heard a lot about you," Alex said smiling, and firmly shook his hand.

"None of the wolf parts are true," he came back with a personable smile.

"You're calling your best friend a liar?" she asked, a daring smirk on her face.

Clines winked at her: "In this case, yeah."

She laughed and looked to Gray: "You're right. He's a flirt."

Commons struggled up, huffing under the weight of two suitcases.

"So," Clines said, looking at Gray, "you want me to fly these beautiful ladies back?"

"Uh, no," Gray said, putting his arm around Clines' shoulder and walking him away from the group.

"No?"

"Archer—"

"Archer?"

"Uh—"

"His real name is Archer?"

"Well—"

"No wonder he goes by John."

"Anyway," Gray continued, "Arch will fly the women back in the Nova chopper and then meet us in Mexico."

"You mean I've stolen a helicopter and now I'm giving it away?"

Gray smiled. "We're lending it."

"Who's, 'we,' white man? And don't you think an Engineering Inc. helicopter will stand out like a sore thumb in Mexico?"

"We're not taking the helicopter."

"We're not... What?"

"We'll pick it up on the way back through."

"I see. Well, I'm not walking to Mexico, I'll tell ya' that right now."

"We're driving—I rented a car."

"To where in Mexico are we driving?" Clines asked, enunciating each word slowly.

"Just outside of Huejutla."

"Whawho what?" Clines came back, trying to sound out the name.

"Remember the preacher?"

"Buddy?" Clines speculated. Buddy Dawson was studying to become a minister when he was drafted into the army and shipped to Vietnam. He also came into a very important piece of counterintelligence just before being captured. What followed, after Dawson's rescue by Clines and Gray, was a grueling two weeks behind enemy lines. Dawson, whose health deteriorated during his three-month incarceration, rose to the occasion. He endured the two weeks of jungle hide-and-seek, offering as much help as his ailing body allowed and making no complaints. Clines and Gray held him in the utmost respect.

Gray nodded that Clines had guessed correctly. "We're going to meet him at some place easy to find, and he'll lead us to Huejutla."

"In the mountains of Old Mexico?"

"That's the place," Gray confirmed.

"Excuse me for sounding stupid, but why?"

"Because he's a missionary and we're a couple of church chaps who're driving down for a visit."

"And we're driving because...?"

"We want to keep a low profile."

"There's nothing low profile about gringos in Mexico," Clines argued. "Especially when one doesn't know a lick of Spanish and the other only knows how to ask for a kiss."

Gray smiled. "Hey, what can I say? You'll be real popular with the women."

"This sounds like a very long and drawn out trip."

"It's a perfect cover."

"Where exactly does the Blacktooth fit in?"

"After seeing the women are safely in Debbie's care, Arch will fly the Blacktooth into Mexico and meet us at Buddy's mission."

"And if we're not exactly sure where this Huejutla is, how's he gonna' find it?"

"He says he's pretty good with Spanish," Gray answered.

"Fine," Clines came back. "Why doesn't he drive, and we'll fly? We could all fly, for that matter. I mean, what are we accomplishing by splitting up?"

"For one, the women have to be delivered to Debbie for protection. Two, I suspect someone on the inside of keeping tabs on our movements. So, just in case someone does find out about Arch, no one will have a clue where you and I are. And three, Arch has got to bring me some satellite data that he has hidden in a safe deposit box. That data will be our map."

"Oh, Great," Clines moaned. "We're back to the satellites."

"All we have to do is shut down the satellite jamming."

"Oh, that's all!" Clines came back in a patronizing tone. "Never mind trying to get there nearly killed Debbie. Or that the most-qualified and well-trained military pilots and reconnaissance experts haven't found jack-shit—which means the jammers are probably mobile and moved daily... Never mind all that, Clines and Gray are to the rescue! Give me a break, Karns. I know you're the best but—"

Gray put a heavy hand on his friend's shoulder, halting the tirade: "Trust me."

Clines exhaled a long breath, then: "Please tell me you have a real good idea where to find them, and we're not going to end-up toast."

"I do, and I doubt it."

"You're going to get me killed one day."

Gray smiled and the two men moved back to the group.

"Ready?" Gray asked the women.

Gail and Alex nodded.

"Blake," Gray said, "You better run over some of the controls with Arch."

The two men climbed into the Blacktooth, leaving Gray with the two women.

"I'll be back as soon as I can," Gray said.

"I wish you wouldn't go," Alex came back.

"I have to."

"Do you think this will lead you to him?" Gail asked, meaning Ŝulok.

"Gail, I don't even want to do this."

"Really?"

He nodded. "As far as Seth goes, the Chancellor can get someone else to bring him in. But I still have to finish what I've started."

"I understand," she said dejectedly.

"Gail," he said, caressing her cheek. "There are people who've been hurt, maybe killed, because of your husband. He's into a lot more than drugs and guns, I'm afraid. No matter how much I love you and Alex, I've a responsibility to those people."

"People you don't even know," she said.

"And maybe one I do," Gray came back, thinking of Jim Austiff. "Look, I'll be through with this kind of work after this trip, okay?"

She gave a relieved sigh. "Promise?"

He nodded. "I promise. So, what do you want to marry? A boat builder who works for his dad or a troubleshooter for an engineering company?"

"I don't care," she said, "just as long as we're safely together."

They heard the Blacktooth engine whine to life.

"Please hurry back," Alex said.

"I will."

The women hugged him and then climbed into the helicopter with Clines' help.

"Got the tape?" Gray called.

"Got it," Commons answered over the noise, holding up the computer tape Gray had taken from Nova. "And I know, give it to Debbie. No contact with 1109. Trust no one but Debbie."

Gray looked to the women once more.

"I love you," he called up. "Both of you."

They called back the same, their voices disappearing in the turbine's whine. Gray stepped back, sealing the hatch shut.

Backing further away, Gray and Clines watched the machine float into the air and angle off over the motel. They remained until the Blacktooth vanished—only a matter of seconds.

"Alex's eyes," Clines said, looking into the dark blue eyes of his longtime friend, "I've seen them before."

"Let's call Buddy," Gray said, moving toward the motel. "I've got to firm up our travel arrangements."

Clines took a few steps to catch up.

"Alex?" Clines questioned, taking a couple of more quick steps to catch up. "What's that short for? Alexandra?"

Gray nodded *yes*, still moving.

"As in, Paige Alexandra?" Clines persisted.

"Yeah."

"Hmm, a daughter, huh?"

Gray stopped, turning to look at his friend. "Yes. Anything else?"

"Oh no—no," Clines answered offhandedly.

Gray started walking again.

"I guess that was a shock," Clines added, falling into step beside Gray.

"That's a word for it," Gray agreed.

Buddy Dawson was a missionary. Thin in both weight and hair, he stood for all the things a man of the cloth could, but without the usual black drape and white collar popularized by his television counterparts.

Dawson's objective for the last 30 years had been the spiritual conversion of the Mexican-Indian nation scattered throughout Old Mexico's mountains. The father of four fair-haired sons and an adopted Mexican daughter, Dawson had won favor with people whose society had hardly stumbled out of the 1800s. Between his efforts in bringing civilization to the mountains and ironclad belief, he was almost a legend—commanding respect from believers and non-believers alike.

It was a scant few minutes before dinner when he and his 13 year-old daughter rounded the dirt street corner and approached their house. It was an adobe and wood structure and surrounded by one of the few iron gates in an outer neighborhood of Huejutla. Dawson's success in Huejutla had led to a thriving church and an educational/medical facility. The village had grown from an unknown spot on the map to a town of some importance in the local community of villages. However, desiring to continue spreading the gospel, Dawson had begun traveling to outlying villages, hoping to repeat the Lord's success elsewhere. The villages, scattered throughout the mountains, consisted mostly of farmers growing their crops right on the mountainsides. It was a world without a place for the side-by-side extremes of wealth and poverty indigenous to the coastal tourist attractions.

"There's a man on the phone," came his wife's voice from inside the house. She came out onto the porch wearing a well-stained apron that might have been white at one time. A small woman of 5'6", Martha Dawson's sturdy frame revealed none of the hardships her 48 years had given her.

"He says he's that Army friend of yours" she reported, blowing a wisp of dark hair out of her face. "He's called three times already."

Smiling, Dawson rubbed his daughter's hair and bounded up the steps—kissing his wife once there.

"It's a great evening," he announced.

"Did you hear me," she said, failing to sound scornful.

"I see a night of love in your eyes," he came back and hugged her.

"Buddy!" she gasped with a giggle, reacting to his unexpected pinch.

Dawson sailed into the house with a laugh.

The living, kitchen and dining areas were a combination effort accented by a room to the left. To the right, a brief hall ended into two bedrooms and a bath. Moving a few steps through the living room, he picked up the waiting phone.

"Hello," he said, "this is Buddy..."

As he listened to the voice on the other end, his smiling face broadened into a grin.

"Well I'll be a blister in the sun," he roared with a laugh. "You tell ol' Blake to kiss señoritas, no señoras."

Still grinning, he bobbed his head several times like an absurd dashboard ornament.

"No problem—I can move three of the little rug-rats to the living room."

His grin faded to a smile: "Sure—sure... What time? Yeah, that'd be fine..."

A few minutes later Dawson replaced the phone receiver and walked out onto the porch where his wife and daughter were talking.

"Well?" Martha asked.

"I'm supposed to meet them in Tampico tomorrow, mid-day."

"I thought you said Karns was killed in action," she said thoughtfully.

"He was—sort of."

She looked at her husband.

"He and Blake were shot down near the city of Dá Nang. When they crawled out of the jungle, they were sort of drafted for a second time—they work for some guy the government hires when they need something done behind the scenes. I used to kiddingly call him, 'gray eminence.'"

From the look on her face he realized she was unfamiliar with the term.

"'Gray eminence', is a term for someone who exercises power behind the scenes," he explained to her. "It was a nickname for the 17th century French monk, Père François Joseph du Tremblay. His clerical clothes... were...gray...and..."

She was looking off into the now darkened sky. It was her way of letting him know he was rattling off more information than she cared to hear.

"Well, anyway," Dawson said, "that's what I called him."

"I thought you were just a regular grunt in the service."

"I was," Dawson answered. "I was also a prisoner."

"Yeah?" she said, already knowing this.

"Blake and Gray were the guys who got me out."

"Why haven't you ever really talked about them before?"

"I have," he came back. "You just weren't interested at the time."

She weakly smiled.

"I wonder why they're coming here?" she pondered.

"Karns didn't say."

"A 17th century monk, huh?" she mumbled, letting him know she did occasionally listen. She opened the screen door and went in, her voice trailing behind: "Supper will be ready shortly."

46

The next 72 hours were wearisome.

The only thing that went off without a hitch, was the border crossing.

Their trek began in a light drizzle of rain that steadily worsened into a downpour and slowed their progress by nearly two hours. By the time they were about 225 miles into Mexico, the thundering rain had tapered off to a drizzle. They passed though the town of Aldama and came to stop behind a line of cars halted by a low-water crossing.

"How nice," Clines mumbled as they got out and walked to the front of the line of cars.

"It's only another 103 miles or so to Tampico," Clines commented sourly, surveying the literal river crossing the road.

"By boat," Gray said. "That's what we'll need to cross this."

"Howdy," came an American voice from behind.

They turned to face a young man wearing a Texas A&M ball cap. In the headlamps of the cars he seemed almost a lanky stick-man of about 6' 2".

"American?" Clines asked, happy to hear something other than the Spanish radio stations.

"Yep," came a burdensome southern accent.

"How long da' ya' think it'll take this ta' go down?" Clines asked, effecting equally slurred English.

"Most likely 'till later t'night," A&M replied. "Y'all from Texas?"

"Yep," Clines answered with the appropriate twang. "Vistin' a preacher friend of ours down this-a-way. Didn't plan on this, though."

"Ah, this is ordinary this time of year," A&M commented with a wave of his arm. "Why, I came across water a-ways-back that flooded my car to the door handles!"

They glanced at the soaking interior of a nearby two-door mustang to which A&M pointed.

"Boy howdy," Gray exclaimed, maintaining the Texan ruse.

"Ain't it, though," A&M said. "It was root, hog or swim there for a while."

"Leastwise you didn't sink," Clines put in.

"Yeah, there was a guy got stuck out in this mess here earlier, climbed out on his truck and, SWOOSH—swept 'em clean away. He lucked-out and snagged a tree 'bout 50 yards down."

"Where's the truck?" Clines asked, glancing in the direction of the flowing water.

"Down that-a-way, somewhere," A&M confirmed, pointing in the same direction.

"Well, Slim," Clines said, turning to Gray, "I'd rather hold a greased pig under an oil-well than try a-go at this."

"I reckon you're right as rain, Bubba," Gray responded, doing his best to keep from laughing.

"Where you boys headed?" A&M asked.

"Huejutla," Clines answered.

"Hmm, don't recollect it," A&M said.

"It's jest a spit in the trail," Clines explained.

"Yeah," Gray chimed in, "we ain't bin there ourselves. We're suppose to meet our preacher friend in Tampico, first."

"Well gosh-darn it, I can hep ya' out, there," A&M said, producing a plastic-coated map from his back pocket. He laid it out on the wet hood of his car and pulled a flashlight from his other pocket.

"I'd backtrack here and go through Victoria to avoid low water," A&M explained, showing them an alternate route on his plastic-covered map. "Or ya' could jest hole-up and wait it out in Aldama."

"Any motels in Aldama?" Gray cut in.

"Well," A&M drawled, "not what ya' might be use to—but there's one there."

They thanked him and moved back to the rented car.

Closing his door, Clines turned to Gray: "One of our guys?"

"You mean an American agent?"

Clines nodded.

"Well he certainly isn't a Texan" Gray said with a smile. "Harvard grads—even those from Texas don't sound that southern fried."

"Harvard?" Clines questioned.

"The fool was wearing a college ring," Gray explained.

Clines laughed. "I guess I've been out of the field too long. I didn't even think to look."

Clines started the car and turned it around in the road.

"'A greased pig under an oil-well?'" Gray said, repeating Clines' earlier expression.

"What?" Clines came back with his jokester's grin.

"Good grief," Gray came back, "nobody wants to do that, Bubba."

Clines laughed and pulled out onto the road.

Not to be confused with Juan Aldama in the state of Zacatecas or Aldama in Chihuahua, the Aldama tucked away in Tamaulipas had only found its way onto maps some few years earlier. Up until then, it had been a dirt encrusted, one-phone village that turned into a mud gully during rainstorms. The Aldama they drove back into, however, had improved by two additional phones and just enough roadwork to retard mud.

Clines and Gray parked the car and divided their time between a meal and two phone calls. The first call went to Tampico, from where Dawson had already left, and the other to Martha Dawson for instructions to their house in the mountains. After a meal in a café that would have failed U.S. health standards, they loaded into the car and began backtracking in the rain.

The alternate route led them to Ciudad de Victoria (the City of Victoria) and a "hotel" for the night. Characteristic of Mexico, it was an old stone building with Spanish tiled open spaces. The best TV station available was airing three back-to-back dubbed reruns of *The Six Million Dollar Man*. While he didn't understand a word, Clines watched them all.

At the cloudy and misty crack of dawn, they shaved to the rhythmic snores of a pigpen outside their second-floor room and then took to the road. The day passed in a profusion of intermittent rain and mountains.

The unmapped Ciudad de Valles marked the end of civilized roads. Shortly thereafter, the setting sun was accompanied by the imposed speed of 7 mph—imposed by what they loosely termed a road.

Ever winding upward, the crater sprinkled gravel road narrowed and widened at will. Twists and turns that avoided trees or boulders often occurred, and just as often without apparent reason.

"Did she say anything about this?" Clines asked, while the car bounced through an unavoidable trough in the road. He was referring to Martha Dawson's instructions.

"Nope," Gray answered, jarred by another pothole.

"Wouldn't you think she would," Clines came back, straining to make out the next turn as it almost seemed to vanish in the car's headlights.

"You would think," Gray agreed.

"Maybe the sign was a joke," Clines suggested, referring to the handwritten wood plank that had indicated this was the road to Huejutla.

"I think these people have more on their minds than practical jokes."

Clines only grumbled.

It was nearing midnight when the road leveled into a smooth surface and they picked up a native who had found the use of his hitchhiker's thumb. With his assurance of an upcoming Huejutla, they drove blindly into the unknown.

An hour later, the dirt encrusted car pulled into the semblance of a town. The native continued to direct them whenever they used the word, *Gringo*.

The native finally found his own destination and bid farewell in the center of the town.

"I guess we can just drive around," Clines suggested.

"Why not," Gray agreed. "But I think Buddy lives a little further out from here."

"Just don't call it the suburbs," Clines commented dryly, turning down a dirt road.

Gray was too tired to fire off a repartee.

Fifteen minutes later they heard a loud voice shouting, "Hey!"

They slowed to a stop, looking out the window to see Dawson waving from behind a wrought iron gate. They backed up the car and pulled into Dawson's driveway.

Commons, who had flown in a day earlier, and the Dawsons had the laugh of their lives. Clines and Gray had missed the only paved road to Huejutla. They had spent the last 50 miles on an abandoned road the locals called, "the pig trail."

Martha fixed the men a late snack and then everyone went to bed.

The morning came earlier than Gray would have liked. His watch showed 7:30. He had slept only four hours. He turned in the bed—hardly more than a cot—and closed his eyes again.

It was of no use. The aroma of breakfast drifted in from the kitchen accompanied by a clatter of noise from the dirt road outside. Sleeping was a lost cause.

He fought his way out of the sinking mattress and inched through the cramped room to the bathroom—a small affair in which he might have been able to lie down had it been half-a-foot longer.

The light bulb was broken. The sink didn't work. The toilet didn't flush.

He forced the stuck door open and saw Clines trying to work his way out bed—an actual cot, in this case.

"Morning," Clines mumbled, bleary-eyed. The short blond hair on his head stood straight up.

Now that's funny looking, Gray thought.

"What're you grinning about?" Clines croaked groggily.

Gray moved to the door leading to the rest of the house and paused: "It's broke. It won't work. It doesn't flush."

Clines stared after him.

The remainder of the day was no less bizarre. Although most of Mexico was wading through the rainy season that had hindered Clines and Gray for three days, Huejutla was on a mountain range above the rain. In short, the sink didn't work and the toilet didn't flush because of a drought.

Following breakfast, Buddy led them to a nearby stream—Huejutla's answer to bathing during a mountaintop drought. After bathing in their skivvies they removed the harmless, but unidentified, waterborne larvae from their hair. They then filled buckets to restock the house's rooftop water tank. That done, the plumbing was of some use—if only sparingly.

The four men then strolled into town, where they availed themselves of an open grocery market. The best and freshest supplies, Dawson explained, were brought in by surrounding village farmers on the weekends. During the week, however, only the wives and children of Huejutla area farmers sold goods. Even less appealing than some of the questionable food produce, was what at first glance appeared to be one merchants' shaggy, flyblown rug suspended from a rack. It was Dawson who pointed out that the, "rug," was the lining of a cow's stomach.

They spent the rest of the day sightseeing. Along with the children, Gray, Clines and Commons piled into the back of the Dawson's station wagon and rode to Tampico—an hour-long trip that was remarkably relaxing owing to very well-behaved children. After a few pyramids and shops, they returned to Huejutla and a full-course dinner served-up by Martha.

As the sun dipped below the tree line, the men thanked Martha for another fine meal and relaxed around the table rehashing old times and swapping stories. The conversation eventually turned to the local economy and crime statistics, neither of which was spiraling in any direction.

"Nah," Dawson responded to Commons' concerns. "There's been a slight decrease in the price of drugs in the major cities, but nothing really outlandish. We've heard there's been a few larger supplies made available, but nothing on the scale you're suggesting."

"Well, I guess that's one less thing to worry about," Commons commented.

"It has been pretty easy around here for the last few years," Dawson said. "Now back in the 70s—" he whistled "—we just about had war on our hands."

"I remember," Gray said.

Clines looked at him: "I didn't realize you followed Mexican politics."

"I had to," Gray responded. "I had an assignment down here."

"You should've dropped in," Dawson said.

"All I wanted to do was get in, get done and get out," Gray said. "It was just a little bit too volatile here for my taste."

"Yeah," Dawson agreed. "They even hung a fella' just outside of town here."

"Sounds like it was pretty bad," Commons commented.

"It was," Dawson confirmed. "One of my men got caught in a fight and had his stomach sliced open with a machete."

"Ouch," Clines grimaced.

Dawson smirked: "He's a tough one—got so mad he wrapped his shirt around his belly to hold his guts in, chased the other guy down and beat the tar out of him. He said the Lord turned the other cheek, but there wasn't anything in the book about guts."

The men laughed. They had too. It was the things you couldn't laugh off or forget that did the most harm.

"The feud with the wealthy land owners was pretty messy," Dawson concluded. "Since then, things have really loosened-up.

"So now," Dawson said to them in a different tone, "what brings you boys down here?"

Commons looked at Gray, wondering how much he would say. He had found the man offered a lot more "need-to-know" information than did any other 1109 agent. On the other hand, Gray's judgment seemed a slight keener than most of those same agents.

"A hodgepodge of a mess, Buddy," Gray answered, crossing his leg and absentmindedly toying with a toothpick. "Mexico, along with Russia and parts of the Atlantic, has been under a satellite blackout of sorts for a while now."

"A blackout?"

"Someone's been jamming the signals. I've a pretty good idea who, but with the drug situation *not* being a problem, I'm at a loss to understand why."

"I can't say there hasn't been an increase in usage," Dawson said, "but it's not near as bad as Mr. Wilson here was describing a minute ago."

The conversation branched-off onto other avenues and before long both Clines and Commons went on to bed.

"Listen," Gray said after the others retired, "I was wondering if you might do me a favor."

"Name it."

"Unless John decides to drive back, we're all going to want to fly on home after—after we finish the job we came down here for. The problem is, we've got a rented car that can't drive itself."

"All you want is for me to drive a car back to Texas?"

Gray smiled. "Not even that far, Buddy. I rented it for one week and there's a branch office in Tampico. If you could—"

"Done," Dawson interrupted.

"Thanks. I'll have John leave you a note on where to find it."

"Okay. You know, after all I owe you guys, you shouldn't feel you have to ask."

"Buddy?"

"Yeah?"

"We—Blake and I—were happy to pull you out of that camp. But it was our job, too. The intel the Vietnamese girl gave you about that massive buildup was the thing that got you out. You don't owe us for that."

"Karns," Dawson said easily, "the intel was the reason you guys came. But it was you and Blake that got me out—not the intel. It was Blake that carried me on his back because I couldn't walk and you who cleared the booby traps, killed 31 VC soldiers and made us, 'disappear,' as you put it."

Gray couldn't argue with Dawson's facts.

"I paid the Army back by giving them the information, but I can't pay you guys back—nothing could equal what you and Blake did for me.

"If you and Blake were headed straight for hell, I'd have something to offer. But you're not— so I'm stuck owing you."

"Fair enough," Gray said, accepting the unavoidable and rising to go to bed.

"Don't worry about tomorrow," Dawson said with a yawn. "I always put in a good word for both of you."

47

The three agents slipped out at 4:00 a.m.

They drove three miles out of town and pulled to the side of the dirt road. The Nova helicopter was another two-mile hike across jungle-like terrain. It had been the most concealed, and as far as Commons could determine, closest landing site to Huejutla.

Killing the car motor, Gray turned in the seat to look at Clines across from him and Commons in the back seat.

"Uh-oh," Clines said, "here comes the bad part."

Gray smiled. "Look guys, I'm pretty certain there's some trouble waiting for us up there. There's no point in you two risking it."

"You know," Clines began, "I think I said something like this a few days ago. I'm pretty sure I did."

"I heard you," Commons agreed. "You—you did, yeah."

"I, uh, I thought so," Clines came back, shaking his head. "It seemed familiar like—"

"Like something you would say, right?" Commons joined in.

"Just like that," Clines came back, "I was thinking to myself—"

"Look, you clowns," Gray interrupted, "I can come back and pick you guys up after—"

"You forgot to say, 'if,'" Clines cut in. "'If,' you come back."

"What exactly do you think you're up against?" Commons asked, turning serious.

"Two, no more than three, Blacktooths," Gray answered.

"Why do you expect Nova choppers?"

"Because, they built seven of them," Clines said, looking at Gray to see if he had hit on the right track. "We've got one, one was destroyed at sea and that leaves five to patrol the blackout areas—four if you figure somebody's using one for more legitimate purposes. Right?"

"Close enough," Gray said, admiring the fact Clines was always right there with him—thinking ahead.

"If you're right," Commons said, "you'll be up against real pilots—not agents trained just enough to handle the job."

"That's why I'm giving you guys an out," Gray came back.

"Don't look at me," Clines protested almost indignantly. "You dragged me all the way down here—three damned days in a car—I'm sure as heck not driving all the way back. Besides, you'll need a RIO."

Technically, Clines was probably right. The voice avionics system could report all incoming bogies, but unlike a human Radar Intercept Operator, it wouldn't make maneuvering suggestions. Gray wasn't all that comfortable with the voice avionics system, anyway.

"You'll need a CIO, too," Commons added.

"A what?" Gray asked.

"A Communications Intercept Operator," Commons answered, proud of the position he had just created. "Hey, you're going to need somebody to listen-in to what the pros are doing. That'll be about your only edge."

Gray looked from one to the other. They weren't backing out.

"Well, gentlemen," Gray said, diplomatically clearing his throat, "to paraphrase General Patton, at least we're not shoveling shit in Louisiana."

Clines and Commons produced flashlights and the three men spent the next half-hour blazing a two-mile trail through the tall grass. When they reached the Blacktooth, Commons removed the camouflage netting and they slipped into flight suits from the storage bay.

The helicopter's systems were brought online while Commons strapped into the area just behind Clines and Gray. Although roomy enough for passengers, the area was a communications center.

Gray took the small CD Commons had brought back from Washington and slipped it into a computer drive.

"Help me out here, Blake," Gray said, watching the screen intermittently while checking the helicopter's other systems.

"What do you need?" Clines asked.

"Have the computer extrapolate the satellite ETA, flight path and duration in the blackout area."

Clines pressed a button and a small computer keyboard hummed outward, accompanied by a console screen winking to life. After a few moments of typing, the CD drive flashed a busy light followed by rows of data spilling onto the computer screen.

"I assume you're only interested in the LEO satellite," Clines prompted.

"The what?" Gray came back.

"There's only one Low Earth Orbit satellite running through this area, and its footprint—"

Gray interrupted Clines by an upheld index finger. "I don't have a clue what you're talking about. I just want to find the satellite that's being jammed."

"Well," Clines said, looking at the data on the computer screen, "we've got two satellites hitting this general area. One's on an Intermediate Circular Orbit and pretty far out there. I'm guessing it's the LEO jobber that we're after"

"Just do your magic and tell me what I need to know," Gray clarified.

Clines' hands danced over the keyboard briefly and then he pointed to a column of numbers. "Okay, this one has an orbit period of about 90 minutes and a local horizontal exposure of about 20 minutes."

When Clines looked up he saw Commons and Gray staring at him, both with the, *that means Greek to me* expression.

Clines consulted the list and his watch. "It should pass over in about 30 minutes."

"Whereabouts?" Gray asked.

Clines brought to life yet another computer screen; this one reflecting data from a satellite supported global positioning system. This particular satellite was in a geostationary orbit above the equator were it remained "parked" over one place on the globe.

"It'll come across here," Clines explained, pointing out a path on the computer-generated map. The location was a few hundred miles further away, directly over a mountain range.

"Thanks," Gray said while increasing power to the engine. Under his breath he added, "Like pulling teeth."

Clines smiled.

Switching the Blacktooth to stealth mode, Gray took the control yoke in hand. The helicopter smoothly and quietly lifted off.

"I think I've got something here," Commons said from the back, adjusting the communications arrayed across the panel.

"Let's hear it," Gray said, holding the helicopter just above the treetops.

Commons flipped a series of switches. A moment of static filled the cockpit, followed by crystal clear voices.

"—we copy you, Red Leader. Looks like another quiet night, over."

"Morning, Blue Leader," a voice came back. "Not night, over."

"Pick-pick-pick."

"Well, they're certainly cavalier, aren't they?" Gray commented. "Keep monitoring them."

"If they're in stealth mode," Clines said, "we'll have to light-up like a Christmas tree just to luck into any kind of return."

Gray glanced over, realizing Clines was right. Any active radar search might give them a position at which to aim but would serve as a beacon marking their own location.

"We have to hit them with radar to find them," Gray finally said. "It couldn't be much easier for them, either."

"Don't forget our patch job—it'll have to throw back some sort of signature."

"Well, fine."

"Wait a minute," Clines said excitedly, and entered several commands on the keyboard.

A blip appeared on the radar screen between the seats. To the side of the green dot a long identification number appeared, followed by altitude, speed and distance data.

Gray hadn't heard the squeal of a radar lock, and he looked at his friend for an explanation.

"It's a Nova transponder," Clines explained.

"Really now?"

"We're configured to monitor it."

"Kind of like an air traffic controller?" Commons questioned.

"Exactly," Clines answered. "Only these helicopters can pretty much choose who can see them."

"Well, if we can see them," came Commons voice, "can't they see us?"

"Perhaps," Gray said, thinking of the yellow transponder Clines had handed him on Padre Island. "But they're not going to see our transponder signal because Blake yanked ours out."

"I'm monitoring two choppers," Commons came back. "How come you've only got one contact?"

Gray and Clines looked to the radar screen again, as if doing so would rectify the problem.

"Well?" Gray asked. "Could they be out of range?"

Clines pressed a button and the radar coverage extended further, but still no second Blacktooth appeared on the screen. "I don't know—they could be. Or they could be in stealth mode and have their transponder offline."

"Red Leader says they have satellite contact," Commons reported, listening to his headset. "They're commencing to jam the satellite."

"Well we haven't got time to figure it out now, boys," Gray said, turning the chopper.

"So what's the plan?" came Commons' voice.

"Plan?" Gray questioned.

"What plan?" Clines asked.

"Oh great," Commons moaned. "Laurel and Hardy."

They were suddenly plastered against the cushioned seats as Gray engaged the afterburner at full force.

"Try not to test out our flight suits, okay?" Commons called from the back, referring to the flight suits they wore. Designed to constrict the body when G-forces threatened to pool blood in the lower extremities, the suits prevented blackouts due to loss of blood flow to the brain.

Approximately ten seconds ticked by.

"Trouble," Commons reported, flipping a switch and filling the cabin with the communications feed from the other helicopters.

"...bogie at the treetops," came the voice of Blue Leader. "We are engaging."

"We copy, Blue Leader. Happy hunting, over."

Commons shut off the cabin monitor.

"Uh-oh," Clines moaned. "We just lost the transponder signal. They're on to us."

"Cat's out of the bag," Gray responded. "Light 'em up."

Clines activated the radar, sending out a long burst of power.

A Heads Up Display, otherwise known as a HUD, appeared on the inside surface of the cockpit windshield. Projected in green, the HUD allowed them to view their surroundings while monitoring a flow of data transmitted from the helicopter's computer. Radar contacts, distances, altitudes and weapon status were all right there for immediate inspection.

"Possible contact," Clines reported. "Bearing 180, 100 nautical miles, angles 10... She's accelerating from 430 knots."

"Possible?" Gray came back.

"That's stealth technology for you," Clines responded.

"We must have passed right beneath," Gray commented, glancing through the HUD and into the starlit sky. Unaccustomed to the HUD, Gray had already decided to rely solely upon Clines' reports. To do otherwise, Gray reasoned, would be to lose precious time trying to decipher data that he needed to know immediately.

"What about that second bogie?" Gray asked.

"Can't find number two," Clines responded. "Our only contact is now at 83 nautical miles, angels 10. He's accelerating passed 450 knots."

Although Commons had piloted his share of miles, he always went through the mental process of multiplying 6,076 feet by each nautical mile in order to visualize the nautical distance. Although the actual footage included a fraction, he rarely considered it unless precision was necessary—and he had never been in a situation requiring it until now. By the time he finished calculating the information, Clines was sounding off new data.

"He's trying for a radar lock," Clines reported. A beeping tone accompanied Clines' warning.

"Where's the other one?" Gray asked, concern in his voice.

"Busy, I hope," Clines responded.

"If we can just get him out over the water," Gray mumbled to himself.

"What da ya' have in mind?" Clines asked.

"I don't want to drop bombs or dead people on Pedro and Julio," Gray answered, meaning he preferred to engage the enemy above an empty ocean.

"Roger that."

Short moments later, with Gray jinking the chopper up and down, they blasted over Puerto Vallarta on the western Mexican seaboard. Once he had flown several miles over the water, Gray brought the Blacktooth around into a northeasterly direction.

"Light 'em up again," Gray said, completing a gut-wrenching turn.

Clines sent another radar burst.

"Contact," Clines sang out again. "120 miles out, dropping from angels 9, 8, 5—he's noses on, steady at 400 knots."

Blue Leader had yet to obtain a solid radar lock on them but the sudden altitude drop from angels 9 to angels 5—meaning 9,000 to 5,000 feet—indicated he had a clearly defined course of action. At current speeds they would be within firing range in under a minute.

"Number of contacts?" Gray asked.

"Only one, still noses on," Clines answered.

"Noses on?" Commons echoed, realizing they were talking about a head-on collision. "Now would be a good time to run like hell!"

Following a standard Navy avoidance maneuver he had learned over 30 years earlier, Gray veered left by 20 degrees. He then forced the Blacktooth into a rapid 20,000-foot climb.

"Master Arm on," Gray called, arming their weapons system. The ready lights flashed on the board in front of them.

"Bogie coming on a right turn toward us," Clines reported from the scope. "He's climbing passed angels 18 at 430 knots... At angels 20 now —noses on at about 70 standard miles."

"Centering up on the T," Gray reported, more to assure them that he was maneuvering into a better launching position.

The Threat Receiver switched from a loudly repeating chirp to a feverish pitch. Blue Leader had just locked in his weapons.

"Inside 60 miles," Clines read off.

"Centering the dot," Gray reported, as he steered the Blacktooth into the optimum position for launching the onboard missiles.

"This is good," Commons moaned.

"Sparrows in the tubes and ready," Clines reported, assuring Gray the sparrow missiles were waiting for his launching.

Gray pressed the tracking button and the cockpit filled with a beeping sound, intermixing with the whining Threat Receiver that was now painfully constant.

"Lock 'em down," Clines all but whispered, as if by force of will the radar would lock on the other Blacktooth.

"No tone," Gray reported, meaning the computer hadn't locked in the target.

"Go—go—go," Clines said as the tone beeped to life, signaling the radar had found the target. "You've got him, on target."

"Fox 1," Gray called, pressing the firing button. The Sparrow missile sang away.

At almost the same instance, Blue Leader fired.

"Bogie veering away," Clines reported, then immediately, "incoming!"

Both choppers peeled away in opposite directions, each running from the other's missile.

"Look at that son-of-a-bitch go—he's up to 800 knots," Clines called out, reading from the scope. He might as well have been describing their own evasive maneuvers.

Gray arched the Blacktooth into a steep dive, then yanked the control yolk right, rolling the Blacktooth in an attempt to avoid the missile. They were literally flying sideways now. What had been a view of the dark horizon, was now a view of the ocean surface 50 yards away.

The maneuver had failed, and the Threat Receiver continued wailing.

"Hang on," Gray called, over the sudden roar of the chopper's turbine. He pulled back hard on the yolk and they rolled into a sudden vertical climb that practically smeared them to their seats.

The missile pursued.

"What the hell is that thing?" Gray growled.

Fighting the dizziness, Clines managed to check the status board.

"It's locked onto our heat signature," Clines answered.

"Hold on," Gray said, and jerked back on the stick while reducing turbine thrust by 90 percent.

For a few seconds the Blacktooth maintained upward momentum. After that, the effect was similar to having the ground open up. A klaxon sounded.

"Eminent rotor failure," Clines called, reading the computer screen, followed by, "flame out!"

Neither Gray nor Commons needed the report. When the rotor failed to compensate for the 90 percent loss of thrust, the helicopter reached an apex and fell straight back. The reduced output from the turbine engine coupled with cool, forced-fed air rushing into the afterburner's combustion chamber, caused a, "flame out." Much like the extinguished flame of a common gas stove, the engine was now spraying fuel into the "unlit" afterburner.

A second klaxon—the flame out warning—began howling and the chopper tumbled in a free-fall. With no frame of reference on which to focus, they closed their eyes hoping to fend off the dizzying disorientation, all the while being violently thrown about in their seat harnesses.

Even though the chopper was sound proofed, they could have sworn they heard the missile scream past after having lost its lock on their non-existent heat signature.

"We're clean," Clines reported, monitoring the missile streak away harmlessly.

Commons glanced out the cockpit—the ocean was a mere 3,000 feet away, and rapidly approaching.

Gray regained his senses and attempted to restart the engines.

"Two thousand feet," Clines called out from the altimeter.

"Vic-On," Gray nearly yelled, trying to hear his own voice over the klaxons.

"Interactive voice is on," came the computer's voice.

"Engines on," Gray ordered.

A short moan vibrated the hull.

"Insufficient recovery time from engine flame out," the computer replied.

"Engines on," Gray ordered a second time.

The moan came again—longer.

"One thousand feet," Clines called keeping the panic out of his tone.

"Insufficient—"

"Engines on," Gray interrupted the computer.

The vibrating moan lasted a fraction longer.

"Engines on," Gray repeated, not allowing the computer to report the last failed start.

They suddenly felt the air forced from their lungs as the mammoth chopper seemed to scream wildly—as if in pain from the engine restart.

Gray grabbed the wildly shaking control yolk, bringing the helicopter under control again.

"Vic-off," he ordered.

The screen confirmed the system had shutoff and Gray eased back in his seat.

Even in the cooled cabin, all three men were drenched in sweat. They had pulled out of the dive with barely five hundred feet to spare.

Clines looked over at Gray: "It's still better than a three-day car trip."

"So you say," Gray responded, veering the helicopter into a shallow descent. He brought the Blacktooth to the deck while coming around onto Blue Leader's last heading.

"Kill the radar," Gray ordered.

"Done," Clines said, shutting down the system, while Commons nearly came unglued behind them.

"Don't shut down the radar, you idiot!"

"Trust me," Gray said.

"Like I have a choice now," Commons retorted.

The starlit Pacific was now a sparkling display of glitter passing a mere seven feet beneath them. Dropping the altitude even further, Gray slowed the Blacktooth to almost a crawl.

"You know, I did say I thought it would make a good sub," Clines commented in an off-hand tone. They had drifted to a mere five feet above the surface of the water.

Commons was torn between looking at the water-drenched side hatch and looking into the front cockpit area.

"Anything on the air?" Gray asked Commons.

"Nothing," he answered. "Although I'm sure our collision with a motor boat will make the morning news."

A full two minutes passed in silence.

"He's out there," Gray whispered. "Back tracking. He's probably got his radar down to about a five to ten mile search pattern...and..."

Clines looked over. "You see him?"

"I got him dead ahead," Gray reported with an affirmative nod.

Clines gave a cursory glance out then looked back to the status board.

"Where?" Commons asked, straining to look up into the dark sky.

"Oh, I make it to be about angels 25, and seven miles out," Gray answered.

Knowing that it was ordinarily impossible to see that far, let alone with that kind of precision, Commons looked at Gray. "You're joking?"

"How's it going down?" Clines asked Gray, ignoring Commons' skepticism.

"We'll wait till he's dead overhead, then lock on as we climb up from beneath and just a bit to his aft."

"Just give the word," Clines said, "and he'll go to the grave in dirty diapers."

"You seriously think he sees 'em?" Commons asked Clines.

"Uh, no," Clines came back. "I seriously *know* he sees 'em."

"I'm going to die at the hands of lunatics," Commons moaned, turning his attention to the communications board.

It was several minutes before the two choppers passed each other.

"All right," Gray said, watching Blue Leader slowly pass overhead.

"I don't think he sees us," Clines whispered unnecessarily while grinning. The Threat Receiver occasionally chirped lightly, indicating they were being intermittently bombarded by Blue Leader's minimally powered-up radar.

"I wonder what sort of radar return that patch job is making?" Clines mumbled.

Commons glanced upward.

"My guess is he thinks we're a surface contact," Gray answered, watching the helicopter the others couldn't see. "He's too high to see us, and the beauty of our tail-end patch job is that our radar return isn't cataloged in his computer."

Clines looked at his friend. "Hey, that's right."

"Maybe he'll think of that," Commons offered.

"He's not that good," Gray said, bracing himself. "And it's too late anyway. Get ready Blake."

Gray threw the turbine into full afterburner, pulling on the yolk.

"Light 'em up!"

As the Blacktooth arched, 'head over heels,' Gray rolled it upright. Clines activated the radar at full power.

No one said a word. The radar lock tone sounded, and Gray pressed the firing button.

There was no possibility of missing. The missile this time, a Nova hybrid of the Navy-built Phoenix, locked its own radar onto Blue Leader. At a rapidly decreasing range of feet, rather than miles, the Blacktooth was a sitting duck. With its built-in guidance system, the missile homed in.

Blue Leader hit his turbine afterburner, but that only succeeded in causing a greater fireworks display. He fell to the ocean in a ball of flames.

48

Occupying the southern edge of the Central Mexican Plateau—an intermittent mountain range extending to the United States—the dormant volcano, Pico de Orizaba rises an impressive 18,696 feet skyward. Alternately known as Citlaltépetl—the Aztec word for, *Star Mountain*—the jagged snow-covered peak is the third highest of its kind on the North American Continent.

Although breathtaking in size, the three agents in the stolen Blacktooth placed Orizaba's grandeur second only to being alive to see it. Their cheers had hardly died, and the Blacktooth Blue Leader was still a fiery cinder in the Pacific, when Gray turned the helicopter land-ward, racing in at Mach speed.

Flying at the moderate altitude of 12,000, Orizaba rapidly expanded into a dark panoramic view, completely filling their vision in the early morning starlight.

It was Commons who first mentioned the other Blacktooth—the one that had not shown up on radar.

"I take it," Commons added, "that you think the jamming station and the other Nova helicopter are on that mountain."

"What makes you say that?" Gray asked.

"Oh, I don't know," he mused, "perhaps this hell-for-leather dash into the uncertain jaws of death—if you'll permit me a certain poetic phrase."

Gray smiled. Commons was sounding more like Clines every time he opened his mouth—which, he reflected, might have been too much art for art's sake.

"Actually I'm not too worried about the other Blacktooth."

"Don't invest too much faith in our press notices," Clines put in.

"Gentlemen," Gray said, "the other Blacktooth is too busy to look for us."

"Oh?" This from Commons.

Gray glanced to Clines: "Didn't you tell me, when you were ranting and raving about driving to Mexico, that the most-qualified, well-trained military pilots and recon flights failed to find the jamming stations?"

"Well, yeah, but—"

"I heard him," Commons said to Gray, then looked to Clines with a grin. "Yeah, you did—you said that—"

"That's what I thought I heard," Gray joined in smiling. "It was something like that—"

"Exactly like that," Commons added.

"Now who're the clowns," Clines finally said with false grumpiness.

Gray chuckled. "Well, you were right, sort of."

"What?"

"You said the jamming stations were most likely mobile."

"Well, yeah," Clines admitted. "It was kind of a spur-of-the-moment, off-the-top-of-my-head kind of thing. I mean, if the experts aren't finding them, they nearly have to be mobile jammers. But either way, I doubt we're gonna' find them—especially down there in the dark."

"Oh, we'll find one easily enough—but not down there."

They looked at him like he was nuts for a moment. And then it dawned on both of them.

"You mean—" Clines began.

Gray nodded.

"Up...there...?" Commons finished the thought, pointing overhead.

"I have to admit, it's perfect," Gray said. "You've got everyone looking all over the place for ground-based jamming equipment while you take up the world's first and only orbital stealth helicopters and knock out the eyes and ears of any specific satellite you want. You're safe because no one thinks to look up. And even if they did, they couldn't detect your helicopters anyway."

"That is pretty smooth," Commons commented.

"Any last words of advice?" Gray asked.

"Wait-wait-wait," Clines said hurriedly. "You want to go up there now—right now?"

"It better be pretty quick," Gray answered.

"What's the rush?"

"My guess is we just destroyed Red Leader's replacement. Once the satellite clears the area they want jammed, Red Leader will be looking to dust our butts. We were lucky the first time."

"Yeah but it's a whole new set of variables up there," Clines argued.

"That's true."

They looked at each other.

"Well," Clines drawled, sitting back, "in for a penny, in for a pound, I guess."

The Blacktooth swept upward, over the Peak of Orizaba and rapidly climbed spaceward. As the sky grew even blacker, Gray detected a slight sluggish miss in the engine.

"I hope this works," Gray said, reaching for the flashing button marked **Orbital AutoPilot**. He pressed it.

"Voice-avionics is now activated by the Orbital Automatic Pilot," announced the computer's voice. "Please stand by while orbital systems engage and sub-orbital systems disengage."

"Is this cool, or what?" Clines said with a grin.

Gray released the controls as he felt the Orbital Autopilot take control.

There was a sudden acceleration caused by a ten-second rocket-based engine burst. Intermixed with the sudden, but slight acceleration, was the hum of the engine rotors slowing to a halt. With a distinctive, "thud," the blades folded down into the ridge running along the topside of the Blacktooth.

"I wonder why it retracts them?" Gray pondered aloud.

"I'd guess to protect them from re-entry heat," Clines said.

"Orbit established," the computer announced.

They glanced out to see the world curving into the blue sphere that looked so artificial in movies and photographs. It looked the same now, only more so.

"Look!" Commons said, pointing. As he did so, he was suddenly very aware of moving slowly. Like the others, he hadn't been expecting weightlessness—although it was only natural.

In front of them, no less than 150 yards away, another Nova Chopper silently followed along behind a satellite. They had neatly managed to come up behind their prey.

“I guess that proves it,” Commons commented.

“Well I doubt they’re up here taking the satellite for a walk,” Gray responded dryly.

“Should we warn them?” Clines asked.

“I’d like to,” Gray said, “but no good would become of it.”

He activated the Master Arm switch, forgetting the voice avionics system was still activated.

“Master Arm, on,” Gray reported.

“Master Arm is on already,” the computer said.

Gray was about to order the voice avionics system to shutoff when it added: “Orbital Weapon on standby.”

Clines and Gray glanced at each other.

“What the hell is that?” Clines mumbled.

“Beats me,” Gray said. “How can I get it to identify what the weapon is?”

Clines scratched his chin. “Good question. Let’s try this.”

Gray watched him type on the keyboard:

ORBITAL WEAPON SYSTEM?

A line of type appeared on the large screen between them:

Orbital Weapon System: White light laser

“Oh-la-la,” Clines said.

“Orbital Automatic Pilot, off,” Gray said, taking the control yolk in hand.

“Orbital Automatic Pilot is off,” the voice avionics system responded as the Heads Up targeting display re-appeared above him—just as it had during the dogfight.

"Voice-avionics, off," Gray ordered.

The computer displayed the confirmation on the screen, which had previously listed the Orbital Weapon System.

"I wish I were as confident as you," Commons remarked.

"It isn't confidence," Gray explained. "I'm afraid I might say the wrong thing."

"Ah, I see your point."

"Centering on the T," Gray said, after having re-focused his attention through the HUD and on the other orbital helicopter.

He pressed the trigger.

"Fox...3...away..." Gray said, watching in amazement as the tail-section of Red Leader suddenly seemed to explode. An odd stream of ice seemed to come spewing out. There were no missiles, and no flash of light. The "white light" laser was just that, a laser which fired in the invisible spectrum of white light.

"There she is," Clines said, looking at the radar. The damage had eliminated Red Leader's stealthy cloak.

"Why isn't she turning for an attack," Gray pondered aloud.

"I don't think that's the way they work," Clines observed.

"What do you mean?"

"See that sudden red glow on the bottom?"

"Yeah?"

"She's re-entering the atmosphere. It'd take too much fuel to dogfight up here. That, and you might bounce right off the atmosphere."

"Anything Arch?" Gray asked.

"Nothing."

"They're probably dead," Clines commented.

Gray looked at him, about to point out the damaged tail rotor wasn't that bad, then: "The oxygen?"

Clines nodded.

"Oh yeah," Commons said, listening to their exchange. "It was probably sucked right out when you put a hole in it."

"Actually," Gray corrected, remembering the concept, "the pressure would have been blown out."

Commons raised an eyebrow.

"Space is a vacuum," Clines added. "Instead of a greater pressure on the outside—like when underwater—up here the greater pressure is on the inside.

As Clines finished speaking, Red Leader began glowing crimson red as it sliced into the atmosphere. It Rolled over, nose first toward the earth. Protected by the tiles covering it, Red Leader survived the fiery re-entry only to fall to a certain death in the ocean.

"Well that was sort of anticlimactic," Commons noted.

"We could orbit around to the CIS—knock out any orbital choppers there, I guess" Clines said.

"We aren't that good," Gray said. "Besides, if the blackout areas are hiding something, we'll now see it in Mexico. They can deduce what they need from that."

"Fair enough."

"Uh, guys," Commons said, listing to an earphone.

"What?" Gray asked.

"We might ought to consider, going back now."

"What's wrong?"

Commons flipped a switch and the cabin was flooded with momentary static.

"...Roger, SAC-Com," came a voice, "the object is still outside visual range and pulling away fast. Request permission to fire, over."

"Intercept 1, attempt radio contact first. That failing, weapons are free. Bring that bad boy down, whatever it is."

"Stratcom thinks we're a UFO," Commons unnecessarily explained. "Or something worse."

Gray looked at Clines: "What da' ya' think, Mr. Spock?"

Clines crocked an eyebrow up. "Well, Captain Kirk, I think we should get our logical butts out of here."

And they did.

49

Debbie Allinder was alone.

Completely. Totally. Utterly.

Alone.

Having spent her life as a scientist and a government agent—neither conducive to relationships—she was without someone to whom she could turn. There was no one in whom she could confide. No coworker. No friend. No one.

Surprisingly enough she had just come to understand this. In her loneliness of the past, she had hope—and that had been her companion. Even during her brief marriage—a tempest affair at best—her husband had not been her companion. Hope had.

She had led others to believe she marched forward with living. That life was a simple matter of taking the next step. In truth, however, life was a stumbling headlong rush toward one girlish hope.

A girlish hope of a future just recently within her grasp—but no longer. Her future had crumbled beginning with a phone call four days earlier.

Blake Clines, acting unusually mysterious, had called from his office, telling her to meet him in the Sound Room.

Once there, he prefaced the destruction of her future by saying Karns had specifically requested her help on the QT—that he trusted only her. She knew something dreadful had happened. The request, something in which she should delight, had been delivered in the tone of a death-knell.

"What's happened?" she asked, fearful. Blake had only recently told her of Karns' apparent exuberance following her visit to the yacht—and then this: a reversal of attitude.

"Jeez, Deb," Clines had said nervously. "I—I don't know how to tell you this..."

She reached over to touch his shoulder. They were sitting in chairs, almost knee to knee. She asked: "What?"

His sky blue eyes were troubled. "The Chancellor sent Karns to find out about the satellite failures..."

"Damn it, David," she scolded, using his first name as Karns—and only Karns—usually did, "what's wrong?"

He swallowed, and then took the plunge: "It's Gail James..."

Debbie sat back, as if physically sucker-punched to the face.

"The mission led Karns to Ŝulok," Clines began, and ended. The damage was done, how or why was just extra noise.

Debbie was looking at him—perhaps, through him.

"This is classified, but the Chancellor's been using her as a source of information on Ŝulok's operations for the past few years."

"They're together?" Debbie whispered no louder than a breath of air.

"Karns and... Gail?" Clines clarified her question.

Wide-eyed, she numbly nodded.

"Yeah... Debbie, I'm—I'm sorry. I know how much he means to you."

She pursed her dry lips. "What does he want?"

"He uh... The idiot wants you to provide protection for Gail and her daughter. He thinks there's a leak in either the Office or 1109."

Her mouth had fallen partly open and then came her voice still and small: "He wants *me* to protect *her?*"

"I tried to tell him—"

"It's okay," she said. "I'll take care of it."

Clines looked at her, unsure how to interpret her comment.

"I mean, I'll see to it."

"He said to pick some good Office security guys. Use his yacht as a safe house."

"When will they arrive?"

He hesitated. "This evening. By helicopter at the yacht."

She leaned over on the arm of the chair, her own slight weight almost too heavy to bear.

"Debbie, I'm sorry..."

So her future crumbled.

In an almost perfunctory daze, she mechanically made the arrangements per Clines' instructions. She took the rest of the day off, stopping by Corporate Investigations on the first floor just before leaving.

After telling the receptionist she wanted to speak to Dana Masters, she waited only a few moments.

"Whatever are you doing here?" Dana asked.

"We need to speak in private," Debbie answered.

Once in Dana's private office, a large white futuristic room, Debbie said that she required the services of several security agents. And then she added that it couldn't be reported up the Office chain of command.

"Debbie," Dana said, "all office-related assignments must go through the Director—which is Kate right now."

"It can't," Debbie protested.

"Well I certainly can't help you if you don't tell me what it is I'm supposed to be helping you with."

"I've got a couple of witnesses to safeguard until... Well, until another agent is available to move them."

"Witnesses to what?"

"Drug operations."

"This all sounds rather mundane," Dana commented. "Not exactly OCSTO's cup of tea. I don't understand why you don't want to clear it through Kate."

Debbie could see Dana preferred to go by the book—she always had.

"Look," Debbie said, lowering her voice. "I can't give you all the information you want, but maybe this will help. Do you remember that agent Kate brought in a few days ago?"

"Jack Graham?"

"Yeah," Debbie confirmed. "They're his witnesses. And as you know, Kate cooperated with him 100 percent."

"Well, who the hell is he?"

"He's kind of a freelance," Debbie answered, not exactly lying.

"That's supposed to make me feel better?"

"Will you help me or not?" Debbie asked, growing perturbed.

"You know, I've got a real bad feeling about this," Dana came back. "If something bad goes down, what's my excuse for unauthorized use of field agents?"

"You'll come out smelling like a rose," Debbie assured her.

That surprised the Security Director. "Really?"

"Trust me."

"Okay, how many do you want, when do you want them and where?"

"Whomever you can spare, starting this evening. There's a yacht on the Potomac River..."

That evening four agents reported to the *Paige Alexandra*. Shortly thereafter, the stolen Nova chopper dropped out of the evening sky and landed on the road beside the dock. The only woman Debbie had ever considered hating stepped down to the ground. Her daughter followed. Then a mountain of luggage came after that. As the helicopter drifted skyward, the Security agents carried the luggage onto the yacht. Impassive and numb, Debbie watched. Even as Gail produced a computer tape she was to pass along to the Chancellor, Debbie felt strangely removed from the reality of the moment. She heard Gail introduce her daughter and herself—Debbie even heard her own voice saying her own name—but it was all so unreal.

It felt as though she were dreaming—one big practical joke of a dream. Until now, Gail had never really existed—she had been only a name; a fading memory in Gray's tormented mind.

But now, Debbie realized, she herself was to become the memory. Gray had built Gail up to something the woman could have never achieved on her own. She had become the missed opportunity; she was the undying and eternal love. It didn't matter if it was untrue. It was the reality Gray had built for himself.

However artificial, however improbable, Debbie knew she was unable to compete with that.

She closed-off her emotions and spent the next 72 hours fulfilling Gray's request. At the end of the fourth day she was mindlessly tossing a playing card onto a table while staring at Alex's deep blue eyes. She moved her concentration to the yacht's railing—where Gail stood wearing a pair of jeans and cowboy boots. Gail was looking into the nightlights along the shore of the river—the same way Gray had often avoided confrontation.

"I'm thinking," Alex explained the delay, concentrating on her cards.

Debbie brought her attention back to the game and looked at the young woman. "Take your time."

Gail's daughter... No one needed to tell Debbie who Paige Alexandra's father was. Debbie knew it as soon as she had laid eyes on the young woman. It was in her eyes—the proverbial knife twisting in Debbie's back. The mother and daughter were obviously close, yet vastly different. Gail seemed much more outgoing without revealing a thing. Alex, on the other hand, was essentially a female Karns Gray. She rarely spoke, but in her silence her body language spoke volumes—when she wanted it to.

"Excuse me a moment," Debbie said and moved over to Gail.

The women stood in silence for a moment.

"You haven't slept in days, have you?" Gail remarked, suddenly looking at Debbie.

"A little bit."

Silence again.

"Listen," Gail said, turning to look at Debbie. "I know you care a lot about Karns—and I know I'm not exactly what you wanted to happen right now... I mean, I guess it has just been the two of you for some time now?"

"Not exactly," Debbie finally said, still looking out into the darkness, watching the lights reflecting off the river.

"Have you known him long?" Gail probed, pushing her hair back.

"Since I was 17," Debbie answered, glancing at Gail. She realized Gail could have easily passed for the older sister she never had.

"Quite a while..." Gail summed-up.

Debbie sighed, fighting a fury of accusations.

"Karns is a very good man," Gail went on. "But he's not put together like other people—he shouldn't have put you on the spot this way."

He's not the one who put me in this spot, Debbie thought, but didn't say.

"Debbie... I don't pretend to know how you're feeling and I know you must think I'm really a cold-hearted bitch—"

"Because you treated him like shit?" Debbie asked in a cool voice.

Gail looked at Debbie, unable to read the other woman's face. "Yeah, I know."

"That's a cop-out," Debbie said. "It's easy to say, 'I was wrong,' and move on. You don't have to feel wrong. You just have to pay it lip service."

"Look," Gail said, "I'm sorry if my being here upsets you—I can leave."

"'Fraid not, Sweetheart," Debbie came back without inflection. "Not until Karns says so."

Debbie looked her straight in the eyes and added, "It's my job and I accepted the responsibility."

"Meaning I didn't?" Gail questioned.

"You tell me."

"I don't have to tell you shit," Gail came back defensively.

"That's true," Debbie said, her brown eyes boring into the other woman. "But you fuck over Karns this time, and I'll fuck you over."

Gail started to say something, but then realized the woman in front of her was not just bluffing. Nothing about Debbie's posture had changed—she was still casually leaning against the railing, her black and white mini-skirt ensemble making her look like she had just stepped out of *Vogue* magazine. But Gail recognized a coiled snake when she saw one.

"I'm sorry I jumped at you," Gail apologized, pushing her hair back. "I've really been on a roller coaster the past few days."

"We all have," Debbie said.

Gail couldn't tell if the statement was an offering of peace or another angry jab.

"How'd you meet him?" Debbie asked after a moment of silence. She wanted to hear Gail's version of Gray's story.

"He was on an undercover assignment in my college. It wasn't anything dramatic, we just fell in love."

"What happened?" Debbie asked, looking down at the water.

Gail noticed the other woman's tight jaw line

"It just didn't work," Gail answered, trying a diplomatic way out.

Debbie glared at her. "Look, Gail, I'm trying very hard to understand you. I can't if you keep giving me this bullshit."

"Okay," Gail came back. "No bullshit. I was offered money to keep my eye on him—even lead him away from some of the drugs and weapons deals he was to watch. I fell in love and learned about good guys and bad guys. I pretended to love Seth—the man paying me—thinking he wouldn't harm Karns. It all went to shit."

"You made it go to shit," Debbie came back.

"That's right," Gail admitted. "And hardly a day passes that I don't think about that. I wasn't born some evil temptress, Debbie. I was just a naive smart-ass who thought she knew more than she really did. *I* fucked it up. *I* fucked it *all* up. I don't suppose you've ever made those kinds of mistakes, have you?"

"No," Debbie answered. "I haven't. I've made mistakes—and people were hurt. But I've never *knowingly* hurt anyone on *purpose*—and I wouldn't. Even if I thought I was protecting someone, I'd give them the chance to understand what I was doing."

"We can't all be as thoughtful, I guess."

"Or as thoughtless," Debbie came back and moved toward the table.

"Debbie..."

She stopped, facing away.

"I... I..."

"You feel sorry?" Debbie questioned, turning her head to profile, not even giving Gail the courtesy of eye contact. "Maybe even pity? Don't bother. That doesn't make you go away."

"I don't want to be enemies, Debbie," Gail said.

Debbie turned to face her. "You want to be friends?"

Gail nodded *yes*, fearing a trap.

"You know, when I look at you and Alex, that's the furthest thing from my mind," Debbie said. "You know what really goes through my mind?"

Gail didn't respond. She knew she would get the answer anyway.

"I think, 'what a waste.' You wasted years, Gail. All because you were too stupid to trust him."

"You have no idea what I went through," Gail came back, struggling with her emotions. She didn't want to appear weak in front of this woman. "I hurt Karns—alright. But I hurt myself, too. And I've paid for it. Boy have I paid! I wish I knew a better way to make all of this work, but I don't. I understand that you hate me—"

"It's not hate," Debbie interrupted at last. "I thought I hated you. When you stepped off the helicopter the other day, I *thought* I hated you. But it's not that at all. It's pain. Pain for me—pain for Karns. He worshiped you—I mean really worshiped you! And you're not worth it. All that you put yourself through, all the self-inflicted loathing and pain—and I assume you felt that—none of it means a damned thing. *You hurt yourself*, but you're entitled to do that. What you did to Karns though... Nothing excuses you for screwing up his life, too."

Gail didn't respond, and couldn't. It was all she could do to keep from breaking down and sobbing.

"And if you're thinking he had a choice in how he reacted—then you didn't know the man at all. And believe me, Gail, you didn't. You didn't take the time to know him."

Gail blinked and the tears began flowing.

"I can't feel sympathy for you," Debbie said, realizing tears of anger were forming in her own eyes. "You haven't seen friends blow their brains out right in front of you. You didn't get treated like shit after your country brought you back from a war you didn't want to fight.

"No, all you did was go to bed with a man who loved you, cheated on him, deserted him, and lied to him... That about covers it doesn't it?"

Gail bit her lip, her answer choked with emotion, "Yeah, that about covers it..."

Debbie turned to sit down, but moved closer to Gail instead. "When I think of never having Karns, my heart literally hurts.

"I love Karns," Debbie said to her. "But not like you."

Gail didn't respond, but looked down, unsuccessfully trying to hide her face and hoping Debbie would stop the onslaught.

"It's not how he treats me," Debbie went on, not waiting for the eye contact she now wanted. "It's not because he's handsome. And it's not because he's good in bed—we've never made it past just being friends. But I love him in spite of everything that haunts him and hurts me.

That's why I love him. Next to my own father, he's the most honorable man of integrity I've ever known—and that's something you know nothing about—can't even comprehend.

"Don't ever expect me to like you," Debbie added, "and we'll sure as hell never be friends."

Debbie returned to the table and eased down.

Gail turned her back, unable to face the truths and fears from which she had run for more than 20 years. Her anger was gone, replaced by a generous helping of self-loathing. All she could do was weep.

Alex remained motionless. When she looked up her eyes were glistening with moisture.

"Maybe you're right," Alex whispered. "But she's suffered enough. And she has changed."

"Or maybe she finally ended-up in the right place at the right time," Debbie came back, her face flushed with the anger and pain that had boiled to the surface. "Maybe she'll never put her life straight—always go from man to man looking for the emotional high. Or needing turmoil to feel loved."

"You don't even know us," Alex said, a tear falling down her face.

"I don't want to know your mother," Debbie quietly said, wiping the tears from her own eyes.

"Let me ask you this," Debbie said, just loud enough for Gail to hear. "We know what she did. I know what I would have done. What would you have done?"

For a moment Alex froze. She opened her mouth to answer, but then did not. Suddenly, she realized the meaning of Yen Hwúi's words: *The world is black and white*. The gray was merely people justifying their positions—like her mother. Her mother had turned her father away because she claimed he deserved better. But that was just something gray. Given the same situation, Alex knew what she would have done. It was as simple as black and white.

Alex looked at Debbie, the shock of this realization etched in her face.

"Me too, Alex," Debbie answered, seeing the sudden awareness in the young girl's face. "Me too."

Gail moved up the side of the yacht, toward the bow.

Alex reached over and gently took Debbie's hand in her own.

"We all love him," Alex said after a thoughtful pause. "You and I just understand what that means more clearly than mom. That doesn't mean she loves him less. It just means she understands less—and I think that hurts even more... I know you're suffering, Debbie, but you can't mend pain with pain... Please, don't be cruel..."

Debbie watched the young girl walk across the yacht and embrace her mother—both of them weeping.

"Shit," Debbie said, leaning back in her chair. Her anger expelled, she felt miserably empty.

Her attention was drawn away from the table by the sound of an approaching helicopter.

She looked back across the yacht to see the four OCSTO agents assigned to protect them looking up river.

Following their line of sight, Debbie noticed the hum of a turbine engine.

"They're back," Alex called over the growing thunder of a helicopter. All three of them trained their eyes at the chopper while a gust of wind abruptly whisked the playing cards into the air.

"That's them," Alex said over the vibrating noise.

Debbie scrutinized the chopper. Alex was right. Gray must have finished his Mexico mission and flown straight back. The original plan called for them to pick up the Engineering Inc. helicopter they had left in Texas and fly back to the Office's hangar. Of course, they probably did that already. Her eyes caught an odd movement near the rear of the Blacktooth. Another Blacktooth moved from behind the first one.

Damned odd, Debbie thought.

Debbie looked over the Blacktooths once more, realizing what bothered her. The helicopters were completely unblemished. There were no structural repairs on either machine.

This wasn't Karns Gray...

50

The four bullet-ridden OCSTO agents were corpses before hitting the ground. A searchlight from the sky blinded Gail as rushing wind and thunderous weapon fire screamed in her ears.

Gail was shocked into numbness anchoring her to the deck. She was hardly aware of Alex's weight being thrust into her by Debbie.

Gail looked over to see Debbie moving her mouth—her voice seemingly delayed.

"Damn it," Debbie was yelling over the roaring noises. "Get below!"

Alex grabbed her dazed mother, pulling her into the yacht.

Slipping a pistol from her nearby purse, Debbie fired several shots—one shattering the searchlight—and backed into the yacht's deckhouse. Another blazing light bathed the yacht in stark illumination.

"Whoever they are," Debbie grunted as she shut and barred the door, "they're not shooting back."

They moved through the deckhouse to a second door leading into the forward cabin.

A rumble shook the boat. As vibration shattered the cabin's 18 windows, Debbie looked back to see the barred door burst into sawdust. Whirling around, she slammed both Alex and Gail to the deck with one hand while raising her gun.

The first man rushing in never saw the woman who killed him—the second man did.

"Hurry!" Debbie ordered, reaching down and pulling Gail by the hair. She forced the women down the steps leading into the lower section of the yacht.

She then barred the second door and turned. The windows facing the bow remained intact, while those running the length of the cabin had been destroyed in the first salvo. She heard footsteps in the broken glass up on the deck to her right. Dropping to the right knee, Debbie fire two

9mm rounds through one of the shattered windows. The satisfying sound of a body splashing in the river followed. She leaped down the steps, securing another door behind her.

Having retreated just about as far as possible, Alex turned to Gail, her voice trembling with fright: "What are we going to do?"

"Go out the back door," Debbie answered, opening a storage closet.

"What back door?" Gail gasped.

"The one we'll make," Debbie returned with a grin, holding up a package of explosives.

"Are you crazy?" Gail objected.

"'Crazy?'" Debbie echoed, pulling three scuba tanks from the closet, along with an assortment of black hoses and three diving masks. "We can't out-gun them and down's the only way out."

Debbie moved over, stuck a blob of putty to the hull and wedged the explosives into it. She set the timer.

"You guys know about scuba gear?" she asked, picking up one of the tanks.

"A little," Alex answered. "A boyfriend of mine took me diving once."

"Better than nothing," Debbie responded and pointed to the two scuba tanks: "You guys grab those and follow me."

They moved into the next compartment—really a small adjoining sleeping cubical—and locked the door.

Setting down her tank, Debbie jerked a mattress from the bed and propped it against the door. She then spun around and knelt to attach the loose hoses to the scuba tanks. Turning the valves on each of the tanks she looked at the women.

"You first," Debbie said, lifting the tank up. After Alex accepted the tank, Debbie turned her and fastened the belt.

She lifted the other tank and slipped it onto Gail's back. While Gail fastened her own belt, Debbie slipped her tank on. She reached over and grabbed one of the hoses that was attached to Alex's gear.

A staccato of gunfire sounded, followed by the sound of one of the doors above being rammed open.

"This is the regulator," Debbie said quickly, pushing the purge button.

The women jumped at the sudden blast of air. Debbie said, "Stick it in your mouth and breathe."

Alex accepted the mouthpiece.

Debbie tested Gail's purge button and then her own. "If you get water in your mask, hold the top like this—" She slipped on her mask and pressed on the glass just above and between the eyes "—and blow air out your nose. That'll force the water out.

"And no matter what happens, don't take the regulator out of your mouth—"

They heard another blast and the tramp of feet in the passageway. The locked door rattled.

"It's locked," said a Middle Eastern accent.

"Nah," came back a sarcastic response, "What do you expect, a welcome mat—"

Debbie was suddenly aware of a dizzy pain—and darkness. She realized she was touching the deck and water was splashing on her legs. She shook her head—clearing the cobwebs.

The explosion to the hull had happened so suddenly, so forcefully, that they were blown across the few feet of the compartment and into the bulkhead before being aware of it.

Used a little too much dynamite there, didn't ya' Butch, ran through Debbie's mind, recalling what had been funny in the movie *Butch Cassidy and the Sundance Kid*. Pushing the mattress off of them—the only thing that had saved them from the shredding of flying debris—Debbie wasn't laughing. Having not had the benefit of a second mattress when she hit the bulkhead, her head was now hurting from the impact. To make matters worse, it seemed as if the explosion was still ringing in her ears.

Bulkhead damage exposed the flickering lights in the next compartment.

Debbie stood with the help of the nearest bulkhead for support.

"You guys okay?" she called.

Two feeble, "yeahs," came back through the flickering light.

Debbie noticed the rushing water was climbing her legs.

"Put your regulators in your mouth," she ordered, the lights finally going dead. "We'll be under water in a moment. Alex, hold your mother's waist so you don't get lost. Gail..."

Debbie groped about and found the other woman's arm: "You hold my waist. Don't anyone let go."

"I gotta' tell ya'," Gail said, her southern drawl very pronounced, "I'm scared."

"Me, too," Alex added.

"If it makes any difference," Debbie said, "so am I. Now, let's go."

The water was neck high.

"We're going under," Debbie said. "Breathe normal and stay calm."

Debbie bent her knees and slipped under the water. She moved along the deck, toward the place where a door and bulkhead had been, and now were gone. She bumped a soft, floating object and then realized it was one of the men killed by the explosion. She moved on, feeling with her hands.

She finally felt the inward flow of water and moved toward it.

Ahead of her the cabin was vaguely bathed in a dim blue-greenish light. At first she couldn't figure out from where the light was coming. The further into the cabin she swam, the more distinct objects were. Straight ahead was the gaping hole caused by the blast and the source of light. Streaming through the eight foot jagged rip were the river-filtered dock lights. She looked back, now able to clearly see Gail and Alex. She gave them the, "thumbs up," sign, hoping they realized it was a question. They both stuck their thumbs up in response. They seemed okay, so far.

Looking ahead, Debbie grabbed the edges of the blast hole and pulled herself through it and out of the cabin. As she slipped free of the yacht, Gail's tug loosened. Debbie turned to grab her, but too late.

She reached further back with no luck; then to her sides. No Gail. No Alex. No luck. The vague lighting wasn't enough by which to see, after all.

Gail and Alex had disappeared in the black inky water.

Reedy watched the assault from the first black Nova chopper and was leaning forward as if on the edge of his chair during a Super Bowl telecast. A whirlpool of bubbles suddenly swirled from underneath the yacht.

"The bitch!" he roared and then glanced to the stone-faced pilot. "Take us down. She's blasting through the bottom of the damned boat!"

The black machine dropped to five feet above the murky Potomac and cast its search light into the quickly dissolving bubbles. The yacht was listing to its port side.

"There," Reedy snapped, pointing at two dark heads breaking the surface of the river.

Debbie swam around, biting down on the air regulator in her mouth. She cursed herself for not roping the two women to a tether so as not to lose them—but there hadn't been time.

She circled, searching. She glance in the direction she thought was up, unable to see the bubbles from her oxygen tank.

Stupid, ran through her mind. *You can't even see an inch in front of you. How do you expect to find them? They could have surfaced—or be within arms' length.*

She stretched out her arms and legs, hoping she might find one of them. Again, no luck. She decided to surface.

As the blackness swallowed up any hint of direction, she held her hand out in front of her dive mask to feel the rising stream of bubbles. Keeping her hand in the bubbles, she slowly swam upward.

She popped into the night air, pulling the regulator and mask from her face.

"Gail," she called. "Alex!"

Her voice echoed back from the riverbank.

Realizing the choppers were gone, she turned around to see the top of the yacht slipping beneath the water. With a sizzling groan, the river swallowed it.

The night was deathly silent.

Part Four

FORBS

September 28, The Present
Aysien, Island

51

Situated in the South Pacific Ocean, Aysien Island was circumnavigated by the American fleet during the island hopping of Japanese strongholds in World War II. The military's preliminary survey flight of 1941 established the island to be roughly five miles in diameter and of no strategic value. In the inevitable distillation of the Military's observations, map makers came to believe Aysien was merely a temporary atoll and failed to record its position.

Near the center of the island, covered in unrestrained tropical vegetation, five buildings were clumped in a haphazard arrangement dictated by tree density. Barely covered with severely weathered coats of camouflaged-colored paint, the Japanese architecture of World War II was unmistakable. The Japanese had once thought very highly of Aysien Island.

Within the perimeter of the buildings, the growth had been cut back, which made for a clearing occupied by a few remaining climbing vines and a dozen or so trees. Leading away from the area were several recently blazed trails, all ending at meaningless locations on the island. The largest and most important path, of course, led down to the main beach. This one, well-trodden path, was also occupied by what could best be described as an insulated, two-inch fiber-optic cable. The cable ran the entire length of the path, covering a two-and-a-half mile stretch connecting the center-most building with a Nova Blacktooth helicopter sitting on the beach.

A woman attempting to find respite from the sweltering heat shimmering through the cloudless blue sky also occupied the beach. Unusually relentless, the heat was baking both the beaches and intruding islanders. In her effort to endure the suffocating heat, the woman wore a thong bikini, a large floppy hat and dark shades. With the exception of the Nova Blacktooth, her sunglasses and tan were the only dark blemishes on an otherwise stark white beach. Even her bikini and the lounger on which she reclined, blazed white. In contrast, the island jungle behind her was a near-solid green wall, juxtaposed to the vivid cerulean Pacific Ocean she was facing.

Lazily reaching into an ice cooler at her side she retrieved a tumbler-filled mixed drink. Balancing a glass and cigarette in one hand, she poured herself a refill. As she returned the tumbler to the cooler, the glass tilted slightly, spilling some of the drink across her surgically enhanced breasts.

Enjoying the cool wetness against her skin, she rubbed it about her neck and shoulders.

"Good afternoon, Fonna," came Seth Ŝulok's heavy voice from behind. "May I join you?"

The Princess gave a non-committal shrug.

Ŝulok planted a portable white lawn-chair at an angle to her left and sat. Stretching his large brown legs in a lazy posture, he mentally smiled. He had noticed the mixture of alcohol and perspiration trailing glistening beads down her neck and into the spacious valley between her lesser-tanned breasts. Scanning the length of her body as though she were a spirited thoroughbred, he was tempted to make a pass. Well-acquainted with the wiles of women, he knew the French-cut bikini was selected for both its bright contrast and revealing impact. In his opinion, however, the French-cut thong and matching strip of material barely concealing her breasts, were not worn in the interest of being "stylish" or comfortable. For her, he had surmised, everything was a power struggle of some kind. Her weapons were bloodlines, money and sexuality.

"You're very attractive today," he said, failing to sound superficial.

"The less covered, the more attractive?" she questioned with a glance at him.

He shrugged.

She smiled and flipped her cigarette into the sand. She found Ŝulok a very attractive man. Even in his 50s, he maintained a muscular frame that was complimented by his tailored shorts and loose-fitting shirt. Not that she would ever permit herself any sort of relationship with him.

She had learned relationships were only a matter of financial arrangements or political maneuvering—and she had learned it in a very hard and publicized manner. It was the one lesson in which her father had been unrelenting. Being the youngest of three sisters, she had been christened Fatima Qabazard, and grew up realizing she would never exercise the power of a throne. As such, she hadn't felt bound to the traditions of marital arrangement, such as her sisters. So when the dashing, wealthy and young American oil tycoon, Casey Fonna, visited her country, Fatima was stricken by love—completely, totally and without reservation.

Casey, being typically American, swept her off her feet and charged full speed ahead into a relationship of which her father knew nothing. Three months after Casey's arrival in Arabia, Fatima eloped. They were married in Las Vegas.

The marriage lasted all of a month. Fatima was in a clothing store parking lot when two of her father's Arabian agents forced her into a van and returned her to Arabia. Casey, who had been out of town visiting an oil site, was killed in a mysterious explosion on the following day.

"You are a Qabazard," her father had told her after the news of Casey's death became public. "You are a member of this royal house. Your marriage will be at my discretion."

"No," she had screamed at him. "I am a Fonna, and I could buy ten of your thrones if I wanted."

She stormed from the palace, and returned to America for the burial of her husband.

With her newfound wealth and status, she quickly and expertly took over Casey's business. His Majesty Qabazard, soon realized his youngest daughter was an important asset to the throne. As her connections with American industry were more valuable than his pride, he finally accepted her use of Casey's name as her own—an acrimonious statement of her disdain for everything Arabian. In an effort to reclaim and bind her to the family, he had the marriage annulled and the title of *Princess* restored to her—all only under Arabian law.

Having her cake and eating it too, she had finally begun using her title again. She saw no reason to miss the opportunity royalty presented. As the legitimate representative of the Royal family, and under American law the only heir to the Fonna Empire, she enjoyed a fastuous and powerful lifestyle. However, not one to forgive, she felt it was only a matter of time until she found proof of her father's involvement with Casey's death. She could afford to bide her time.

Love, she had come to realize, like filial affection was a Sisyphean task.

"So," she said, turning her attention to Ŝulok. "What are your plans now?"

"We wait."

"You make jokes?"

"Not at all," he replied, confused by her remark.

"On what do we wait? Mr. Andrews tells me there is no way to achieve the power-up without the final data from the Converter. And this, 'jump start,' idea of yours is also a waste, I think."

Ŝulok looked to the fiber optic cable snaking from the Nova helicopter and disappearing into the island growth. The, 'jump start,' idea had been the only option left, until his OCSTO contact had mentioned Gail and Alex were on a yacht belonging to Jack Graham, and his prisoner had revealed who Jack Graham really was. It was almost perfect, if not a little late in coming.

"You see how everything kind of connects? We take Austiff, and thanks to the so-called, "truth serum," his agency developed, we've learned that Jack Graham is also known as, Karns Gray."

"So you've already said," she came back.

"And that's why Kalvin picked up my wife and kid—well, my wife and *the* kid."

She sat-up on the edge of her chair. "I must confess, Seth, I haven't any idea what you mean. You always talk is if I know what you are thinking."

"Sorry," he apologized. "All I'm saying is we were completely out of options when we hooked-up the Blacktooth to FORBS. But now Gail and Alex are the bait we need."

"And this means?"

"It means that Jack Graham will come running to us," Ŝulok answered, scratching a non-existent itch on his scalp. His thinning salt-and-pepper hair had never been something about which he worried, but it was a constant reminder that time was running out.

The Princess waited, surprised to see Ŝulok grinning.

"Jack Graham was the one connected to FORBS years ago... All these years, and he was the one..."

"What are you talking about?" she asked, trying to snap him out of his recent tendency to lapse into some sort of silent introspection.

"Jack Graham was the experiment that didn't exactly work," he answered. "I learned about it a few years back, but no one knew the test subject's name—except for Jim Austiff and a few others who're mostly dead now. Ha! All this time I've been wanting to get my hands on Jack Graham and didn't even know it—hell, I thought the bastard was dead."

Looking at Ŝulok, Fonna got the distinct impression he was drifting in his memories. She said, "I don't understand how—"

"I'm getting to that," he assured her, the glassy look in his eyes suddenly evaporating. "Now, we know that for FORBS to activate, it must receive the boot-up signal that's programmed into the Converter. That signal—what we think of as the access codes—is the first thing that's transmitted in order for FORBS to activate. It is also the first signal that FORBS transmits when accessing another computer—the signal kind of adapts to whatever system is being accessed. According to Steve, if we duplicate the signal—the code, if you will—we can power up FORBS from the Blacktooth instead of having to pull power from the Converter. The access code—that signal—is the most important ingredient. The power can come from just about anywhere once FORBS is activated. That signal simply starts the whole process."

She was just as lost as before, and it showed on her face.

"Don't you get it?"

"No, I don't" she admitted. "Steve Andrews told me that the access code cannot be duplicated—that it's a one of a kind signal."

"That's right," Ŝulok agreed, "but synthetic or not, a biological imitation or not, FORBS is still a computer—a lot like the human brain. That signal is stored in any system FORBS accesses."

"Yeah...?"

"And apparently FORBS accessed Jack Graham," he concluded, still not used to using Gray's real name.

Fonna looked at the large man, understanding dawning on her face. "So, you mean the startup access code—this signal you're talking about—is in the brain of this man, Graham. Like a memory or something?"

Pleased with himself, Ŝulok nodded.

"How's that work?"

"I don't know," he said with a laugh. "Steve says we may have to physically connect Graham to FORBS."

"If it's as easy as it sounds, why didn't we just nab him in the first place?"

"Because the sealed OCSTO records only called him, 'the patient,' and, 'the test subject.' My contact had no way of knowing it was Jack Graham. Even after my first interrogation of Austiff, I had no way of knowing that the Karns Gray he talked about was Jack Graham. I thought Graham was dead, remember?"

Fonna made some sort of huffing noise to indicate she remembered, but felt it was something he should have known.

"Besides, Graham works for the Chancellor, and those guys are very hard to catch or kill."

"But Steve Andrews is certain we can connect Graham to FORBS and power the unit up, right?" Fonna asked.

"It's all pretty theoretical," Ŝulok admitted. "But yeah, that's right."

She noticed that he had that faraway look in his eyes again.

"The incredibly impossible thing," Ŝulok mumbled more to himself, "is that Graham will be the one to validate my life's work."

"Your life's work?"

"My little pet project—nothing with which to concern yourself."

"Does this have something to do with FORBS?"

"Don't worry, sweetie," Ŝulok came back. "You can utilize FORBS to your power-hungry heart's content. After I have what I want, it's all yours."

"You've been dancing around this subject for some time now, Seth."

"And I'll continue dancing, too."

She almost wanted to hit him, he seemed so smug with his secrets. She tried a different tact: "When are we going to find this Jack Graham, or Karns Gray or whatever the hell his name is?"

"Don't worry, he'll come to us."

"How do you know?"

"Because I've got what he wants."

"You mean your wife?"

"That's right."

She thought it over a moment. "When I think of the time and money we have wasted—"

"Why don't you go whine to daddy," Ŝulok interrupted, realizing she was starting to sound a tad haughty for his taste. "Of course you'll have to explain what you did to Dad's precious *TG-3* investment."

"You arranged that."

"I wouldn't have known about it if you hadn't told me. And of course, you had to personally oversee the operation—I'm sure Dad would love that."

She felt the anger growing.

"You could tell him about this whole FORBS business—but then, you don't want to share that, do you?"

Fonna glared at him.

"Face it," Ŝulok said, knowing how sensitive she was about this particular subject, "you're just a messenger-girl Daddy uses to show Arabian interest. You're a big-breasted, royal go-between. Dear 'ol Dad learns you screwed-up his investment and he'll probably drop you down the same hole he dropped your husband."

"You dare speak to me in this manner?" she snapped, standing up and tossing her drinking glass to the sand. She reached down to retrieve the large white dress shirt she had worn to the beach. "While you have been ferrying that slut of a wife back and forth, OCSTO, no doubt, is closing in on us. Has it not occurred to you, that by kidnapping your wife you have divulged the presence of your contact?"

"Oh, Yes," Ŝulok answered calmly. "But if I get my hands on Jack Graham, it's worth it."

"You almost sound as if you want to get him worse than you want to complete our project."

"He *is* our project, now," Ŝulok mumbled looking seaward and remembering the shores of a bloody land called Vietnam. His face had become the picture of obsessed rapture. "A ghost—a wolf—who's pursued me across the world and will not die..."

She stared at the big American sitting across from her, unable to comprehend his meaning and too insulted to care. She stormed back up the beach and toward one of the buildings. She didn't really need Ŝulok now. If Steve Andrews was right, all she needed was Jack Graham—Karns Gray. If Andrews was wrong, she didn't need anybody.

Either way she had sown the seeds of a disposable relationship that she planned to use against Ŝulok.

And it was harvest time.

52

Reedy watched the two trickles of sweat racing down his bald chest and mentally bet on the right side to win. As if on cue, the left suddenly faded into his belly-button and the right rushed on. He picked up a .357 magnum and pointed it at his stomach. He pulled the trigger without flinching, listening to the hammer click.

Tossing the gun to the foot of the bed he sighed, deciding not to re-clean it. His eyes wandered to the leather bag sitting on the floor off to his left. He smiled, thinking of Sarah Austiff's throaty description.

"It's a bag of tricks," she had told him, unbuttoning his shirt. "I bought it for you to put your play-pretties in."

One of those, "play pretties," Reedy reflected, killed her. She called it the ultimate orgasm. He called it the best way to get information and pass time.

A faint tapping at the thin wood door timed itself with the dim flickering light bulb, fighting for the meager electricity fed to it from the island's generator.

Before Reedy could answer the knock, the door opened and closed, admitting Princess Fonna.

As she moved over to the bed, he was smoothing out the sheets he had just pulled over his nude waist. When she sat down on the edge of the bed he noticed her large dress shirt was unbuttoned nearly to her waist—allowing him occasional glimpses of her untanned breasts. She had been giving him similar views since they had first met. Her hair hung loosely about her shoulders, framing her dark face.

"My," Reedy said with mock respect, "what an honor."

"How would you like more money than Seth is paying?" she asked abruptly, wiping the perspiration from her neck with the long tail-end of the shirt.

He glimpsed her thong bikini-bottom and another flash of her nude breasts. She had removed her swimsuit top before coming into the room.

"What's the job?" he asked.

"Taking over FORBS."

"We'd have to kill Seth first," Reedy jested, intending the comment as a joke.

"Then kill him," she said, touching his exposed knee.

Reedy looked at her, realizing she was serious. With a laugh he said: "Kill my golden egg?"

"Golden egg," she scoffed. "You are like me—much too hungry for the likes of Seth Ŝulok."

"How much money are you talking about, baby?"

"Half of everything."

"All I've seen of FORBS is a dull gray blob—where does the money come in?"

"Are you foolish as well as blind?" she snapped, then consciously relaxed her body language and inched her hand up his leg. She changed her tone to a more sultry pitch: "When Seth powers up FORBS, there is nothing we cannot obtain."

"Frankly, I don't see how sitting out here in the middle of the Pacific can make any money."

"It is an advanced artificial intelligence. It can launch any missile in the world; intercept any transmission in the world; reorganize any computerized data; access Swiss bank accounts—any bank accounts for that matter. FORBS can decode and access any computer anywhere. And I'm fairly certain there is something else it can do—something unimaginably grand."

"What?"

"I'm not sure, exactly. But Seth acts like he couldn't care less that FORBS can do all the things I've just mentioned. He has, as you Americans put it, something up his sleeve."

"Do tell."

"I don't know what it is. I'm just certain it's the real reason he wants FORBS."

"Unimaginably grand, huh?"

She nodded. "And half of everything."

"You make it sound like FORBS ain't that important."

"FORBS is important," she came back, "but I'm pretty sure it's just icing on a cake—really great icing, but still just icing. So, what do you say?"

"Half?"

"Yes."

"Why not use some of your own men?"

"They trust Ŝulok," she came back. "More so, since I am no longer of much use now that the Power Converter is destroyed."

"He's good at that stuff," Reedy said with a knowing nod. He felt her hand on his thigh. "Half of everything?"

"Yes," she answered and pursed her lips. "What was she like?"

"Who?" he asked, thrown off by the question.

"Sarah Austiff—was she a screamer or a moaner?"

"Both."

"What do you like best?"

"A moaner who starts screaming," he answered with a smirk.

"And she liked to be tied-up?"

"Sometimes."

"Did it excite you—knowing you could do anything you desired?"

"Yeah," he breathed out, the sweat pouring.

"And she begged for it, right?"

He nodded *yes*.

"But you," she said with a vague smile and tilt of her head to the side, "you only wanted to abuse her, right?"

He nodded again, completely caught up by her voice and eyes.

"The thing you killed her with," she added, slowly moving the sheet and looking down. She made an, "oh," expression with her lips then continued without looking up: "You can turn it down so it doesn't kill—right?"

"Uh, yeah," he said, feeling her hand move upward and grasp him.

"I like men who take charge," she said, her tone giving no hint of what her hands were doing.

"I try," he mumbled.

She looked up, "Half of everything, an incredible discovery, and all of me. How does that sound?"

Her hand came away, purposely scraping him with a fingernail.

He winced.

"You've wanted it since you first saw me," she said coolly.

Her hand suddenly appeared in front of his face with a loud click. Dangling from her wrist were handcuffs. She climbed onto the bed beside Reedy and ran the cuffs through the bars of the headboard. With a second click she handcuffed herself to the bed.

"The key," she whispered, "is in my shirt pocket."

"Is this trust between thieves, or lovers?" he questioned, removing the key.

"It's my last offer. Half of everything and all of me. Call it submission—if that's what you like."

He tossed the key to the floor and unfastened the last two shirt buttons. He then slid the shirt over her until it was stopped at her wrist by the headboard. With two slight pulls, the tiny bikini thong fell away.

"Isn't this degrading for a Princess?"

"Maybe," she answered calmly.

He leaned over, kissing her throat. "I could say, 'no deal,' and take you as much as I want."

"I know," she said, looking back at him as he moved around behind her. Resting on elbows and knees, she propped her head on her hands.

"You could be gentle..." she started to suggest.

Without warning she felt him launch into her and a pain rushed upward, climbing her spine. Too late she realized he preferred anal sex. She gritted her teeth to stifle the scream rising in her throat. It came out a muffled whine. With a panic she realized he had run his hand into her hair and pulled out her only hairpin. On the backside of the clip was a second key to the cuffs.

"You don't need this," he said softly, studying the key and then tossing it aside.

She felt another surging thrust and vainly tried to yield to it. Tears came to her eyes.

"You've got a deal," Reedy growled in a husky voice. "Get the point?"

She did and wasn't liking it. But the pain and panic were so great she couldn't voice an objection.

As he began thrusting, she was unable to stop screaming in pain. Between gasping sobs, she begged and pleaded for him to stop. Instead, he kept grabbing her breasts for leverage, ramming harder and calling her degrading names.

"You made the deal," he grunted, "I'm making sure you keep it."

53

Lost in the past, Ŝulok watched the waves splashing onto the Aysien shoreline, but in his mind's eye it was another shoreline—one forever bathed in blood. Even though that faraway place had given birth to the fate that brought him to Aysien Island, it was something he had wanted to forget. But the thing that molded him could not truly be exorcised from the very man it created. He was compelled to remember, shifting in time and space, without control.

Like all people, the tapestry of who he had become had once been delicate threads of infinite possibilities. While his reflections did not including such introspection, he had consciously twisted life's decisions. Unaware, he had fallen into the trap of believing that life was not always as clear as black and white, or right and wrong. He had bought the myth that life was full of gray areas, wherein he had lived his existence. He did not realize that everything was either right or wrong—that the gray areas were merely his attempts to justify his actions. Ŝulok's despair arose from his lack of faith in anything except the eventuality of death. He could not see light at the end of that tunnel—could not believe in what was unseen.

What he knew was this: he had witnessed a young Vietnamese boy, fleeing an unavoidable death, savagely slaughtered. One moment the boy was alive, the next he was dead. It was not dignified; it was not full of any promise of the hereafter. It was brutal and permanent.

That was what Ŝulok knew with certainty. That was the blood-soaked beachhead of his memories. Of all the atrocities he had witnessed, that one single event was the moment he unsuccessfully tried to forget. That was where he now found himself—not on a Aysien seashore, but on a Vietnam field of slaughter masquerading as a beach.

While it was youthful greed that had brought him there, he supposed it was the hunger for power that had brought Charlton Trenton to the same place. Back then, Charlton Trenton was a loose cannon and the only thing that held Jack Graham at bay. Graham may have worked for some vindictive contract Agency of the CIA, but as long as Ŝulok remained the unofficial middleman between Trenton and foreign weapon suppliers, he was safe. No one was interested in stirring-up the troubled waters of Black Operations. And Trenton was the master of Black Ops—missions so secretive that they would never know the light of day. That was, in fact, what Ŝulok had witnessed on that Vietnam beach: a horrid Black Operation in an attempt to gain public support for the war—or so Trenton had said.

This was done by placing enemy weaponry—which, Ŝulok provided at a tidy profit—at the scene of alleged enemy actions. The actions, slaughters really, were actually the work of mercenaries selected by Trenton and paid by the CIA. Until Jack Graham began snooping around, the CIA had held Trenton's reins rather loosely. With the winds of political change however, Jack Graham became the CIA's ambassador of plausible denial—or so Trenton had also said. By hiring the Chancellor, the CIA was able to say they were investigating Trenton's methods, rather than admitting they knew what those methods were. That was Trenton's explanation, too.

Ŝulok had witnessed one of the last examples of those methods. He had stood on a beach very much like Aysien's, listening to the screams of defenseless villagers being downed by weapon fire. The South Vietnamese were lambs to the slaughter.

One, and only one, young boy nearly escaped. He ran screaming out of the village, toward the beach. He was almost to Ŝulok when a grenade sailed into his path. The blast threw the boy into the air amid a splattering burst of red.

Ŝulok was knocked to the ground, coming to a stop within arm's reach of the boy. Surprisingly enough, the boy continued screaming, even though the majority of his face was missing.

His hands as well as his knees were shredded ribbons of flesh—yet instead of going into shock or dying, the boy went on screaming.

Fighting the sickness in his stomach, Ŝulok looked back to where the face had been. He was puzzled as to how the boy was still screaming... There wasn't enough face—no mouth, to scream with. What was he saying?

He was screaming for a Medic—that was it. He was yelling, "Medic! Medic! I need a damned Medic!" He shrieked it over and over. And in English. Why? More importantly, how?

The Medic appeared. But the fool wasn't listening to the boy—he wasn't even helping the boy. Instead, the Medic plunged a needle into Ŝulok's arm.

Ŝulok tried to tell the Medic to help the boy, but the Medic only nodded cursorily.

"He's dead," the Medic said over the screaming, "calm down."

The drug took effect, and Ŝulok began relaxing. The weapon-fire now sounded further away. In his growing state of numbness, Ŝulok realized the boy hadn't been screaming.

He himself had been screaming.

"Am I okay?" Ŝulok asked the Medic.

"Sure," the Medic answered. "You've just seen the insides of one too many men, that's all."

Ŝulok looked at the Medic, wanting to ask the obvious question.

"I've seen it before," the Medic assured him and patted him on the shoulder. "You're not crazy—not yet, anyway."

"Thanks."

"Medic!" a voice yelled.

"Stay put," the Medic said. "It'll be back in a minute."

Ŝulok remembered watching the Medic rush away—all the while wanting him to stay.

Shaking his head, as if to ward off the memory, Ŝulok focused his attention on the present—or at least he tried. He kept thinking back to that bloody beachhead and the sudden loathing of death which had then taken root. It was some years later, after he had made his fortune in wartime drug trafficking and arms trades, that his deep-seated fear of death finally drove him into a fanatical health regime and then into the realm of theoretical science and research.

The long chain of events that had brought him to this point in time—to this very carefully selected island—had evolved over a period of years. Years of prodding determination, followed by pure, unadulterated serendipity.

"Seth," came a voice.

Ŝulok looked around to see Steve Andrews, the 45 year-old electronics specialist who had assisted in creating the elaborate FORBS power-up system. Even though he was a mere 5 feet 10, Andrews' weight of 140 gave him the lanky look of a man several inches taller. Dressed in a pair of bluejean cutoffs and a T-shirt, he looked more like a 60s hippie than the electronic guru he really was. Behind his oval wire frame glasses was a man ordinary in every aspect except one: a specialized area of electronics. If something conducted an electrical charge, Steve Andrews could repair it, or make one better. Andrews would have been the head of a multi-billion dollar electronic empire had he not been plagued by two inescapable revulsions: he hated work of any kind, and he liked the human race only a slight bit more.

"How's it going, Steve?"

"Everything's ready," Andrews answered, "It's a bit crude, though."

"Just as long as it works."

"Let me put it this way," Andrews came back. "If it works, you'll probably need every damned precaution you've planned on..."

54

The white Engineering Inc. helicopter lumbered through the cloudless Washington sky and briefly hung over the endless stretch of runway. Touching down with a tired thump, its whirling blades began winding down with the fading engine. Directly behind it, the stolen Blacktooth smoothly eased to a landing.

A long shadow creeping across the landing strip swallowed the three travel weary men climbing from the helicopters. Commons carefully removed each of his bags from the opened side of the Engineering Inc. helicopter. The cockpit hatch hissed opened on each side of the Blacktooth and a couple of luggage bags were tossed down. Gray and Clines followed, re-sealing the hatches.

They gathered the luggage and started across the expansive pavement. In the distance behind them a passenger jet was leaving the National Airport, its wings glinting in the evening sun.

Just ahead of the three men, Debbie was leaning against the fender of a black limousine. Her clothing, Gray noticed, was unusually conservative. No short hemline or plunging neckline. Wearing a simple black, thigh-length tank dress, she moved away from the car to greet them with, "Hi, guys!"

"A limo?" Clines questioned, watching the driver step from the car and unlock the trunk.

"What's the Chancellor want?" Gray asked suspiciously.

"He said you guys did a fine job," Debbie answered. "The limo and hotel are on him."

"What's up?" Gray pressed.

"Who cares," Commons answered, throwing his bags in the trunk.

"I don't," Clines responded, turning toward the aircraft hangar. "I'm taking Zelda's car. Tell the Chancellor and Kate I'll be in about noon—after I wake-up from passing out."

With a wave, he moved off toward the side of the hangar on which he always parked.

"I guess it's just us," Commons said to Gray.

"Just you," Gray corrected, and then looked at the limo driver. "You can drop me off at my boat."

"I'll take you," Debbie said.

"Okay," Commons drawled and then glanced to the amused limo driver. "It's just me."

Commons climbed into the car, calling back: "See ya' later."

Gray merely waved.

"Hey," Commons said with a grin, sticking his head out of the still opened door. "At least my grandkids will be happy to know I wasn't shoveling shit in Louisiana!"

Gray laughed as Commons pulled the car door shut. Seconds later, the limo crawled away.

Gray turned to face Debbie. "Your car out front?"

She nodded.

He picked up his luggage bag and headed toward the front parking area, cutting through the partially opened hangar doors. In the quiet football field sized building, several private jets and helicopters were sitting in various states of readiness. Gray knew that the hangar was publicly recognized as being owned by the same conglomerate which owned the Professional Building—the Office's home. The aircraft inside the hangar were all part of that same usable window dressing.

The setting sun sprayed a yellow haze through the large windows near the roof, casting the surroundings in a sepia tone reminiscent of an old motion picture. Gray looked over at Debbie—realizing something seemed wrong. Her heart was pounding.

"Debbie?" he questioned, noticing she looked worn-down; tired. "What's wrong?"

They stopped walking and she diverted her eyes to the floor, then back to him: "Karns..."

"What is it?"

"I... I... They're gone, Karns..."

His face drained of color.

"They, uh, they took them."

Gray looked at her, the words on his lips unsure: "Gail...?"

She nodded. "And Alex."

This time Gray was the one feeling as if someone had sucker punched him in the face. "Who?"

"They came in Nova helicopters..."

He looked down, realizing he had either dropped or sat his luggage bag on the hangar floor. He didn't remember doing either.

"I'm sor—" she began, but broke off as her throat seemed to constrict on her.

"When?" he asked softly.

"Last night." Her voice came with a tremble.

"'Last...night...'" he repeated her, not knowing why and having no point. Even speaking felt suddenly strange—as if it required all his concentration.

"I tried," Debbie said.

He said nothing.

"I really tried," she emphasized sincerely, not knowing what else to say. "They cut us down like—like swatting flies."

He watched her run a nervous hand through her long hair.

"You've got to believe I tried," She added, realizing she was losing control of her emotions again. Remembering how much she had thought she wanted something like this to happen only amplified the guilt she felt.

"Why shouldn't I?" he said at last—calmly. His voice was cool, modulated evenly.

"I don't want you to think..." She didn't finish. "Never mind."

He nodded, as though dismissing the whole affair, and reached down for his luggage bag: "Just take me home."

"You're staying with me," she came back.

He didn't retrieve the luggage and straightened up to looked at her, expecting an explanation.

"I—uh—I sank your yacht."

"You—sank—my...? This ought to be good."

"We were trapped below deck," she explained. "I blasted the hull to get out."

"Gail and Alex were with you?"

"Yeah," she said with a shake of her head and rubbed her forehead briefly.

"How did you... How did you lose them?"

"We were separated in the river."

He rubbed his beard stubble and looked at the sunlight gleaming into the hangar.

"It was dark, Karns. Maybe they were confused—"

"'Maybe?'" he snapped.

"Okay," Debbie said, realizing there could be no candy coating the truth—not with this man. "They were scared—confused I'm sure. I—I didn't have time to tether them to me."

"Skip it," he ordered in a weary voice and picked up the luggage bag. "Let's get the hell out of here."

She watched him moving toward the exit, not looking back. His footfalls echoed across the void.

"Damn you," she yelled, her voice bouncing back, "I tried!"

He continued walking until reaching the door.

"What more do you want from me?" she screamed louder.

He stopped, turned and walked back.

"I wanted you to protect them," he growled.

"What the hell do you think I tried to do?" she came back, unable to keep the anger, panic and the guilt under control.

His breathing was shallow as he struggled with controlling a rage just beneath the surface. He waved his hand as if to dismiss her and walked away.

"Karns!" she called, her voice echoing, *Karns, Karns, Karns...*

He faded through a doorway, the hushed clicking of the latch lingering into a loud echo.

She stood alone.

As always.

55

Gray turned off the shower and stepped onto the white tiled floor. After briskly drying off, he moved into the adjoining dressing area where bottles of perfumes and colognes crowded the sink. Picking up a can of shaving cream he lathered his face and pulled his razor out of the open luggage bag sitting on the cabinet.

A clean shave later, he rinsed the remaining traces of lather from his face and donned the floor length robe hanging from the door hook. He walked through the bedroom and into the living room.

Debbie was sitting on the sofa with a mixed drink in one hand and an ice pack on her eyes. Having kicked off her heels and exchanged her dress for a robe, she was resting her feet on the coffee table. Gray moved to her and took the ice pack.

"You need sleep, not ice," he said.

"I need to be drunk," she retorted, taking back the ice pack. "Want a drink?"

"No."

"That's right," she said with a sigh and took a sip from her glass. "You don't drink anymore."

"Razor blades, shaving cream, well-worn shoes and suits, pictures, colognes. Do you expect your ex-husband to walk in anytime now?"

"No, he's gone for good."

He moved over to a chair and sat down. "Where is he?"

"Who cares?" she asked rhetorically, leaning her head back again and covering her eyes with the ice pack.

"You never were the heart-broken wife."

"No," she agreed, "I wasn't."

Gray stood and moved to the patio doors. He looked up, sighting the evening's first star, flickering in the hazy skylight of the setting sun: "You shouldn't have married him."

"What's it to you?" she snapped, taking the ice pack off of her eyes to look at him. "You've got Gail."

He looked back, locking eyes with her defiantly.

She broke the look, pretending aloofness. In truth, she couldn't bear the loss of his faith in her. She looked down into her empty glass, uncertain when she had drained it.

"I'm sorry," she said, then tried to pick up his line of thought: "I married Bill out of sheer stupidity. I was undercover in a fashion show in Europe..."

"You're lucky you worked for the Office," Gray put in. "The Chancellor would have given you hell for mixing with civilians—I know."

"Yeah, well, I think Jim just pitied my ignorance."

"So, why the marriage?"

"Look," Debbie said, getting up and moving to the wet bar. "You must be tired—and I know you'll want to get an early start on finding Gail tomorrow—"

"Debbie," he interrupted her.

She looked over.

"I know you did your best. I didn't mean to come down on you the way I did."

She looked down, finished pouring the drink and re-corked the bottle. She felt too guilty to find solace in his apology. Suddenly, the conversation she had just purposely avoided seemed more comfortable than this old, new one. She took a long drink, carefully deciding what to say.

"I married Bill because you didn't want me, Karns," she said, and thought, *there!*

He didn't respond, so she tried again.

"You were so fucking wrapped-up in Gail, that you wouldn't even consider me. So I found a replacement."

That should do it, she thought, and drained her glass again.

He remained impassive.

"We weren't husband and wife, really," she went on with a fake laugh. "More like animals in heat, or something..."

"Debbie, I... You don't need to tell me this."

"Do you know why we've never talked about it?" she questioned, and then went on without his answer: "Because you never gave a shit one way or the other. That's why. It was always her—Gail."

She could see he was growing uncomfortable. *Good*, she thought.

"That's why you and I never made love," she continued. "I didn't want you using me in bed and thinking of her. And now that I've met her, she almost is me! Do all your women look alike or what?!"

"Hush."

"I will not," she sassed back. "I want you to know how I feel. I want you to understand—" She abruptly stopped, tossing her empty glass onto the sofa and moving to him. "I want you to understand I tried every fucking thing in my power to prevent Gail's kidnapping—and as guilty as I feel right now, I still hate her."

"Shut up," he ordered, losing patience.

"No," she said with a shake of her head, "I hate her, do you understand that?"

"Debbie—"

"I hate her," she yelled. "And you—you bastard, you asked me to protect her!"

"Deb—"

"Just fuck off!" she said in a tired tone, her words slightly slurred.

"You're drunk."

"I hope so."

He reached out to touch her, but dropped his hand and moved to the bedroom—closing the door behind him.

Debbie moved to the wet bar and poured a shot-glass of tequila. After downing the drink she started to pour another but changed her mind with a brushing aside of the glass. She picked up the bottle and moved out onto the balcony.

Upturning the bottle she took a lingering drink. The burning vapor spread through her chest, causing her to stifle a cough. Carelessly holding the bottle she turned around and leaned against the balcony railing.

She knew she had just angered and wounded him. It wasn't that she really wanted to, but his kindness in the midst of her storming guilt was more than she could bear.

And now she had practically done the same thing as Gail: she had purposely hurt him. *Damn*, she thought.

She looked out over the manicured lawns of her townhouse community, her stomach churning.

"Damn it," she cried, her tears suddenly gushing. "Damn..."

She turned the bottle up for another long drink and then wiped her eyes on the sleeve of her robe, smearing her makeup. For the millionth time, she wondered why Gray had become so important to her. It was an obsession.

But even obsession must have a limit, she thought.

The bottle went up again. After swallowing, she limply dropped her arm to her side and looked over her shoulder at the last vestige of the setting sun.

"Another day..." she mumbled, staggering back to the living room.

Falling to the sofa she took another drink and sat the bottle on the coffee table.

"Gail-Gail-Gail," she said in a singsong voice. "Fuck you Gail and the horse you road in on."

Sadly laughing, she picked up the remote control and switched on the TV.

Maybe I don't hate her, she thought. M*aybe I just don't like losing...*

She switched channels.

Karns... She remembered how helpless he had seemed when she was 17 and had pulled him from his burning car.

She switched channels again.

It was as though she were drawn to him from the moment she looked down into his blood-streaked face. She might have believed it was only a girlish whim, but it was based on more than just that. It was all the things she had told Gail—and more.

She pressed the remote button, changing channels.

My feelings for him almost approach his obsession with Gail.

"Oh, God, not that," she moaned.

She switched channels and took a drink.

Had she really mothered Bill, as her mother had suggested? She thought about the summer in Europe when she met him. He was sweet while Karns had seemed vague. He was so, "there," while Karns seemed like a specter with no roots or feelings. And of course, Bill was very interested in her, while Karns...

The comparisons were absurd, she knew. She had learned just how absurd when Blake had told her the story of Jay Casper and their ordeal in Vietnam. She had realized then, just how absurd her petty, selfish concerns had been.

Debbie looked at the television without noticing the changing channels. She took another gulp of tequila.

"Revenge," Debbie thought out loud, her mind wandering to a slightly different subject. *Maybe Ŝulok was after Karns, instead of Gail and Alex.*

Nah, she thought, *Gail said Ŝulok thought Karns was dead.*

"Are you stoned out of your mind," a voice suddenly intruded.

Debbie looked up to see Gray grabbing the TV remote from her. She realized she had been holding the channel selector down for the last few minutes as well as having the volume at maximum.

Gray lowered the volume as the TV stopped on a news report.

"Sorry," she said with a slurred voice, "I was thinking."

"You mean you *weren't* thinking," he corrected.

She laughed. "If I didn't adore you, buddy, I'd swear you were a stick in the mud."

"Hush," he said, turning up the volume slightly. On screen was a file tape of *Skylab*.

"—so whether the famed *Skylab* was actually found has become immaterial," an unseen commentator was saying. "Our sources tell us that the Navy dropped depth charges on whatever it was that they have denied was there. If the, 'flying sub,' had gone down on this very spot, why would the navy drop depth charges?"

A commentator standing on the deck of a yacht had replaced the *Skylab* tape. On the side of the deckhouse was the news station emblem of W.E.S.E. In the corner of the screen a local Washington news network logo appeared, followed by a line of type indicating the file tape was a re-run of exclusive W.E.S.E on-the-scene coverage.

The commentator had paused, looking out over an expanse of ocean while the camera zoomed out to take in his view.

"Chalk it up to another mystery of the sea," the commentator said, facing the camera again. "Who knows, maybe we should all start wearing our *Skylab* avoidance hats. Back to you Ted."

The screen changed to the W.E.S.E. newsroom and a newscaster who started off about aspects of *Skylab's* destruction some years earlier. The local live newsroom interrupted that.

"So they never did figure out what all the hubbub was about, right Marsha?" asked a tailored looking news anchor in the live broadcast.

The camera backed out to show a well-dress red-haired woman setting to the newsman's left.

"No, Dan, they didn't. The aftermath of the storm kept all the local stations busy and W.E.S.E. was the only news service that actually responded to the reports. By the time they followed-up on the lead, the Navy had packed-up and gone home."

"A very odd story indeed," Dan commented, straightening the papers on his desk.

"Made more so by the Navy's denial," Marsha pointed out. "W.E.S.E. claims their source inside the Navy department wouldn't even speak to them after the first airing of the story—and this was the very person that had told them about the *Skylab* connection."

"Didn't *Skylab* actually fall into the Indian Ocean?" Dan asked.

Marsha nodded. "There was nothing ordinary about the whole story."

"Hmm," Dan said with implied subterfuge, and tapped his pen on the desk.

"That's what they said," Marsha retorted with a smile.

Debbie smiled: "Talking about old news."

Lowering the volume again, Gray picked up the cordless phone and dialed a number.

"Yeah, could I speak to Blake?"

"What—" Debbie began, but Gray motioned for her to be quiet.

"Hey, Davo—" Gray said into the phone, then waited a short moment. "Yeah, I know. I'm fine... No, she's okay, too. Listen, didn't you say an independent news service shadowed you during the *TG-3* recovery?"

Gray looked at Debbie, who was looking back at him.

"Was it W.E.S.E?"

Another pause.

"Well it definitely wasn't W.E.S.E., then... Nah, you had your hands full, no one can fault you for that—don't sweat it. Get a good night's sleep—we're going to be busy again..."

Gray gave a short laugh at something Clines said and then hung up.

"Well?" Debbie asked. "What was all that about?"

"Just a theory I've been working on."

"Which is?"

"Later, when you're sober."

"'Sober,'" she echoed, standing up weakly, "Listen, bud—oops!"

Gray caught her before she fell onto the coffee table.

He lifted her and carried her into the bedroom.

"Whoa, Silver," she laughed.

He placed her on the bed.

"Get some sleep," he said softly and started to leave.

"Wait—wait—Mr. Stopgap." She giggled. "Really—just sit here with me—at least until the room stops spinning."

He moved back and sat on the edge of the bed.

"I'm sorry about Gail," she said, suddenly serious.

He nodded.

"I don't like her," she added, flatly, "but I tried."

"I know," he responded, hoping to placate any misplaced drunken anger.

"I really—really—really tried," she said with a sleepy slur.

He thought she was about to laugh again.

Instead, tears began falling. "I'm sorry."

He caressed her hair.

"What am I going to do?" she whimpered. "I'm as screwed-up as you, Karns."

"Why, thank you."

She tried to smile.

"You'll be fine, Deb," he assured her. "Now go to sleep. I've got an important job for you tomorrow."

"Really?" she asked, sniffing.

He nodded *yes*.

"What're ya' wantin' me to do?" she asked, her voice slurred with exhaustion and alcohol.

"The first thing is to deliver a message to the Chancellor."

"Good 'ol Mr. Sad Secrets," she mumbled with a yawn.

"Yeah," Gray said quietly, "sad secrets."

Her smile faded and her eyes fluttered shut. She drifted off into sleep.

56

It was mid-morning of the following day when the Chancellor found Karns Gray facing the Vietnam War Memorial—head bowed. While he looked younger than other veterans lingering nearby, his shoulders carried the same weary weight: he had survived while comrades had not. For some, surviving was a blessing. For others, many of whom journeyed here in search of answers, it was an unrelenting burden. For Gray, the Chancellor knew, it was something in between those extremes.

The Chancellor silently came to a stop beside Gray. As both men were wearing their, "work," clothes of suits, they were probably the best dressed "tourists" at the memorial.

"I'm here," the Chancellor said unnecessarily, which was volumes for him.

"Security?" Gray queried, without turning,

The Chancellor nodded *no*, indicating he had followed Gray's instructions. "Against my better judgment."

"Your, 'judgment,'" Gray echoed. "My first reaction to your judgment, was to beat the living shit out of you, Robert."

"Your second reaction?"

"Why?" Gray said, ignoring the Chancellor's remark and turning to look at him for the first time that morning. "Why didn't you tell me about Gail?"

"Because you would have screwed everything up."

The Chancellor could see the answer didn't sit very well with Gray.

"I haven't the time or inclination to play Cupid," the Chancellor added. "I didn't need you blowing everything out of the water."

"What about *me?*" Gray came back angrily. "What about the way *I* feel?"

"What about the teenage addicts to whom Ŝulok sells crack?" the Chancellor came back, watching Gray turn and move a few feet away.

"Or the countless terrorists and third world countries to whom we suspect he's sold nuclear weapons? God only knows if he's expanded into biological weaponry."

Gray remained silent.

"Let me tell you something," the Chancellor continued calmly. "You're one of the best—maybe *the* best. But you've got an Achilles heel—"

"I'm not here to talk about me," Gray interrupted.

"Yes you are. This isn't really about Gail. It's about how you've been wronged or handed a raw deal. It should be about lives—other people's lives. But you've got tunnel vision because you screwed yourself up—you. Not me. You broke the rules, Karns. A civilian can't conceive the pressure out there. A civilian can't think clearly when faced with decisions they're unequipped to make. Did you think about that 20 some-odd years ago? No! You went right ahead and balled a country girl who barely knew her ass from first base!"

"I swear," Gray took a step forward.

"That would solve everything wouldn't it?" the Chancellor asked, stopping Gray's advance. "You wouldn't have to stand here listening to the truth."

"You had no right—"

"I had every right," the Chancellor cut in. "I can't hold your hand out there, Karns. Make a bad decision, get involved with someone who has no concept of who and what you are—that's a fool's choice. You messed up, and I picked up the pieces."

The two men stood facing each other, one calm and the other angry.

"I have a daughter that's in her 20s—a daughter that you knew about. The fact is you should have told me."

"I wanted to," the Chancellor admitted.

Surprised, Gray looked at the other man.

"It was just easier and safer not too."

"And that gave you the right?" Gray snapped back.

"I would have liked to have handled it differently, Karns," the Chancellor said. Had their roles been reversed, the Chancellor was certain Gray would have handled it differently. In his heart of hearts, the

Chancellor admired Gray for usually doing the right thing regardless of the consequences. *A man responsible in the small things*, Gray had once told him, *is responsible in the large things*.

"Look, Karns," the Chancellor said, "you shuffled the deck, and I played my hand the best way I knew how. It was right for Gail to help us, and it was wrong for me to keep you out of the loop. But the fact of the matter is, had I not done the wrong thing, she wouldn't have done the right thing."

"You did it because of the creed?" Gray asked rhetorically, already knowing the answer.

"That's what we're all about," the Chancellor responded.

Gray wanted to shout at the man. He wanted to grab his coat lapels and scream in his face—to call him an idealistic pompous ass for using some damn sworn oath as an excuse to keep everyone in the dark. The Chancellor had, after all, said that it was the easier choice. But Gray could only seethe because he too believed in the creed. And as much as he wanted to place blame anywhere but on himself, he couldn't. He had —years ago—allowed personal interest to interfere and totally lost perspective during the Ŝulok assignment. The evil and damage Ŝulok had undoubtedly spread over the years was worthy of every effort to first prove he was actually responsible, and then destroy him.

Men like Ŝulok were the very reason for the existence of OCSTO, the Chancellor agents and the Chancellor Creed—their oath of office, as it were. Gray had taken it and meant it. No one worked for the Chancellor that didn't live by the creed. Even as he burned with the desire to visit vengeance on the man before him, Gray could not help but admire the Chancellor's steadfastness to that oath:

> *The spirit of the law is justice. The letter of the law is a tool of defense for the innocent or clemency for the guilty. Let us concern ourselves with those forsaking the law, those for whom the spirit of the law is a nemesis. We stand aside for those within the law, and to all others we pledge this creed. Leniency within the law: Truth and Justice beyond the Law.*

Truth and Justice beyond the Law. It was usually a euphemism for all sorts of retribution meted out to those beyond the reach of the legal system. Some of those people were thought of as outstanding citizens while others were just as likely to be serial killers and thieves. All of them, however, had severely injured others or compromised issues of national security.

All of this having passed through his mind, Gray could only say he had managed to intellectualize the Chancellor's secret. Gray felt no better—he was still angry. Only now, he had to accept the blame. After all, he could have hardly expected Gail to comprehend the full impact of his indiscretion. In the final analysis, Gray did what he always had—he internalized the pain and moved on.

"I guess you know," Gray finally said, "that after this, I'm through."

The Chancellor nodded. If he had trepidation regarding Gray's anger or relief at its apparent dissipation, it remained hidden beneath a veneer of flat affect.

Gray guided the Chancellor by the elbow and they moved down the sidewalk.

"Debbie says you can tie everything up in a nice little package," the Chancellor noted.

"Just about," Gray answered.

"Let's hear it."

"First," Gray said, "I assume you didn't connect Seth Ŝulok to the satellite failures because Gail told you his drug export activities increased after the failures, right?"

"Yeah," the Chancellor confirmed. "I didn't have anything else connecting him with the CIS and he still had enough government contacts to have been aware of the satellite problem."

Gray nodded. "Considering their history, why didn't you associate Trenton with Ŝulok?"

"I had nothing to indicate they had any ongoing relationship," the Chancellor answered. "The discovery of the Nova bugs in Austiff's house even made me completely dismiss Ŝulok—of course, at the time we didn't even think to run an ownership check on them. I figured Trenton was up to some sort of industrial espionage. The *TG-3* is something Nova would try to develop—my thinking was along those lines."

"Have you uncovered bills of sale for the Nova Blacktooths and the bugs?"

The Chancellor nodded *yes*. "And after you wade through the corporate records, they end-up being owned by Ŝulok. The same is true for the Nova bugs."

"That's why it's a bit fuzzy," Gray said. "In every instance in this case, Trenton's pretty clean. Maybe he shouldn't have sold the equipment to Ŝulok, but you can hardly hang 'em out to dry for that. Not considering their long-standing association."

"We should hang *something* on him," the Chancellor asserted. "He certainly was out for blood when you broke into Nova."

Gray smirked. "Just try to hang that on him and you'll be laughed right out of a courtroom. I was the one breaking in."

"I just can't believe he's not involved somehow." The Chancellor didn't bother pointing out what they both knew: that the courtroom wasn't their battlefield. High profile criminals—even those as well-connected as Trenton—were candidates for truth and justice beyond the law.

"He's involved only by association," Gray pointed out. "He may know what Ŝulok's up to, but there again, you can't nail 'em for that, either."

The Chancellor nodded acceptance.

"Was there anything else of value on the tape I supplied?"

"There seems to be quite a bit regarding some sort of historical research—nothing of which we've made heads or tails."

"What about the blackout areas?"

"They're wide open, now," the Chancellor answered. "As soon as surveillance of Mexico was restored, Drug Enforcement moved in and curtailed several drug operations that had been doing a booming business. But there wasn't much else going on. In fact, we've got global surveillance again and it all looks pretty quiet."

Gray nodded. "Discounting the drug traffic, you've found nothing to indicate why the jamming began in the first place, right?"

If the Chancellor was surprised, he failed to show it: "Correct."

"That means one of two things. Either the jamming was a ruse of some sort, or they got what they wanted."

"They?"

"Ŝulok and whoever's helping him. And whoever that is, it includes a spy in the Office—OCSTO."

"Could you be more specific?"

"Someone with knowledge or access to the Einstein project—"

"Project Hacksaw?"

"Yeah."

"Because of the Power Converter?" the Chancellor asked, not one to lag in the, "keeping up," department.

Gray nodded. He said: "The mole had access to the Office truth serum; knew Austiff's lunch plans on July 10th; knew I was breaking into Nova and warned them; knew the security plans for Gail and Alex on my yacht and has made a killing in the stock market."

The Chancellor furrowed his brow: "I was with you up until, 'the stock market.' How did you figure that?"

"I checked."

"The income of all of Austiff's people are monitored closely by two independent accounting offices," The Chancellor objected. "Whoever you have in mind couldn't have been paid directly."

"You're sort of right," Gray agreed. "But a private stock deal some years ago—something that allowed the purchaser to buy at about 20 cents a share, wouldn't raise any questions, would it?"

"No. I'd hardly call that proof of a payoff, either."

"Even if the value of the stock had been artificially deflated by the owner of the corporation, and then after the buy, the stock bounced up to its actual value of $400 dollars a share?"

The Chancellor whistled. "That's slick."

"I'll say. Our spy spent $10,000 buying 50,000 shares of World Pleasure Cruises stock at 20 cents per share. The stock split, becoming 100,000 shares at 10 cents each. Then, within two or three months, the price went back up to $400 per share."

"My God that's—that's—"

"That's turning $10,000 into $40,000,000 within about two months."

The Chancellor's mouth dropped slightly and then he recovered.

"Shortly after that, our spy transferred the stock, spreading it over a number of investments overseas. Just the returns on the $40,000,000 alone, are unbelievable. Meanwhile, back at the ranch, World Pleasure Cruises went belly-up and no one was the wiser."

"There was no SEC investigation?" the Chancellor asked, referring to the Securities and Exchange Commission, the regulatory body overseeing the operations of the stock market.

"Oh yeah," Gray came back, "but everyone came out smelling like roses. Neither our spy nor our spy's money came under scrutiny. Now, wouldn't you call that the perfect payoff?"

"Yes, I would," the Chancellor admitted frankly. "World Pleasure Cruises? Sounds familiar."

"It was owned by Consolidated Investments—a corporation in which Charlton Trenton was a board member."

"Trenton again?"

"I know what you're thinking," Gray said. "But the entire thing was handled legally—more or less. We'll never know how Trenton manipulated the deal and there's certainly no paper trail left to follow. So yes, Trenton knows what's up. But unlike Vietnam, Trenton's just the deep pockets for Ŝulok's show. Ŝulok's the driving force this time. I think Ŝulok hatched the plan to buy the spy and Trenton arranged for the funds through stock manipulation—insider trading—whatever you want to call it."

"Well, Trenton's not exactly lily-white."

"No, he's not," Gray agreed. "But he's just not the one we're after, this time. As for the World Pleasure Cruises deal, the SEC cleared him.

"The only thing I can't really understand is why the mole didn't split. Forty million isn't shabby. The interest hasn't been too shabby, either."

The Chancellor waited.

"It has practically quadrupled."

The Chancellor nodded. "For that kind of money, Trenton had to believe Ŝulok was getting his money's worth."

"For that kind of money I'm sure *everyone* got their money's worth," Gray came back.

"Anything else?" the Chancellor asked.

"The spy we're after didn't know Arch, or the CIS mission he undertook. They may have had some input on the *TG-3* flight path, but I suspect that was skillfully manipulated by the choice of satellite blackout areas."

"Hmm," the Chancellor thought out loud. "I hadn't thought about it that way."

"Don't you think it was terribly convenient to have the *TG-3* in nearly the perfect place to launch a Mexico recon flight? And isn't it odd that the blackout area, the *TG-3* launch site and the *TG-3* flight path all contributed to practically passing right over the FORBS Power Converter?"

"Someone—Ŝulok and this inside spy—pulled the strings and we danced, huh?"

"That's the way I see it."

"That means it was all to power-up FORBS, then."

"That's as good a guess as any," Gray admitted.

"So if FORBS is still out there, how'd it end-up in Ŝulok's hands?"

"I'd be wildly speculating. The only safe deduction is he got hold of some NASA telemetry indicating some of it fell in our backyard. Not hard to believe when you realize *Skylab's* lab and living quarters was an empty third stage Saturn V rocket—that's as big as a three-bedroom house. There must have been chucks of it scattered halfway across the planet. It would have taken a bundle to find, but he has the resources. After finding and recovering it, though, it's just a matter of putting the blackouts in the right places, killing a few people and then sitting back to wait for us to deliver a nuclear battery in the form of the *TG-3*."

"That's a delicate line of reasoning," the Chancellor said. "Why go to so much effort?"

"It wasn't all that much effort," Gray pointed out. "Think about it. All he had to do—after salvaging FORBS—was send up orbital helicopters, jam a few satellites every day and kill a few agents. That's it. Everything else was just smoke and mirrors. We delivered the *TG-3* and all he had to do was hit a few keys on a computer. It's all a question of a few numbers and having a power source."

The Chancellor nodded, impressed with the simplicity of the plan.

"You know," Gray added, "the smartest thing you did was to drop those depth charges on that Converter."

"Yeah, well I didn't want a repeat of what happened with you. I guess it's safe to assume that Ŝulok was completely unsuccessful?"

"It seems that way."

"So who's the spy, Karns?"

"One of the very few who knows nearly every ongoing OCSTO operation," Gray answered. "And we're going to handle it this way..."

57

The last of the nine-to-five employees had clocked out. A skeleton nightshift security team and the occasional handful of projects people in Engineering Inc. remained. Blake Clines was one, although he wasn't working. Instead, he nervously paced the floor of his private office, occasionally looking out toward the street. For about the fifth time in as many minutes he looked at the two-way radio in his hand. Actually it might more accurately be described as a *four-way* radio, as it permitted many different users to access its particular band. It wasn't the most secure type of communication device, but it served the purpose when absolute secrecy wasn't an issue.

"Mr. Clines," the radio suddenly called out, startling him even though he was looking right at it. It was the voice of one of his assistants. The man was seated at the guard desk on the first floor of the building. The usual guard, who became ill just moments before leaving for work, was at home in bed with what would prove to be a less-than-twelve hour stomach virus.

"Go ahead," Clines said into the radio.

"The suspect is now en route."

"Roger that. Am I clear?"

"You are now."

"I'm on the move," Clines said and left the office.

The first floor guard—Clines' assistant—had looked to the floor monitors only moments before. On the fourth floor, Kate Kegley had managed to get to the elevators before he saw her. In her role of temporary acting Director, she had been staying past the usual 5:00 p.m.

Just as Kegley was stepping into the elevator, the owner of Corporate Investigations, Dana Masters, had locked the door to her first floor office, walked past the numerous work stations and into the hall. She did exactly the same thing at exactly the same time every evening. Like a Swiss timepiece, she would be at the elevator at 7:02 p.m.

A moment later, her approach was announced by the sound of her heels echoing through the empty halls. Carrying a briefcase, she waved to the guard as she moved across the rotunda and hit the elevator's down button. The doors opened and she disappeared into the lift.

She was surprised to see the OCSTO Deputy Director.

"Kate," Dana said, smiling. "Working late again?"

"Like I have time for anything else," Kegley responded. "I don't know how Jim managed it."

"I think he usually left on time in spite of the deadlines," Dana said. "Have there been any new leads?"

"No," Kegley said.

The elevator rang and the door opened, letting them out into a wide gray-carpeted corridor that smelled faintly musty. They started through an underground tunnel that connected with the parking garage.

"What about poor Tammy?" Dana inquired.

"She's really a mess," Kegley answered, pushing her hair behind her ear and shifting her briefcase to the other hand. "She's been seeing a psychotherapist to deal with the abuse she suffered."

"Is she still in that house?"

"Oh no, she's been in a psychiatric care facility since it happened."

"That poor child—does she know about Jim, yet?"

"No."

Dana looked at her. "If he's dead that could really mess her up."

"Not preparing her for that eventuality is a big gamble, I admit."

They had walked through the tunnel and opened the glass doors leading into the parking area.

"Did the doctor recommend *not* telling her?"

"No, I did."

Dana looked at her reproachfully. "*You did?*"

Kegley nodded and the two women came to a stop.

"What *are* you thinking? You know he's probably dead. No ransom note, no anything."

"Actually, it was Jack Graham's idea."

Dana eyed the Deputy Director cautiously. "Kate—"

"Please don't ask who he is," Kegley interrupted.

"Actually, I was going to be sarcastic and ask if he's a doctor."

"He's not," she said, and started walking again.

"It doesn't take a frequent flyer to figure that out," Dana responded, referring to the mathematics required to determine the free miles the airlines offered for her patronage.

"He thinks Jim is still alive."

"Does he know something?"

Kegley shrugged. "I don't know, but I trust him."

"You can use that as an excuse when poor Tammy learns her father is dead and they lock her away for good. Honestly, Kate, you've been in this business too long."

"*Me?*" Kegley retorted. "*You* were here when *I* got here."

"Yeah, but I don't sound like Jim Austiff."

"He's a good man," Kegley said in defense of her boss.

"*Was* a good man," Dana corrected. "And good or not, he was still the typical cloak and dagger sort."

They stopped at Kegley's car, a black European sports sedan. There were only about four cars scattered across this level of the dim parking garage, the nearest of which was Dana's. Farther away, nearer to the corridor from which they had walked, was a black 1960 Studebaker Lark Convertible belonging to Blake Clines' girlfriend Zelda Jacobs. Dana realized she had never met the girl.

"Believe me, Dana," Kegley was saying, "it wasn't an easy decision. You can't tell me you've not made a few of those yourself."

"A few," Dana conceded, checking her watch.

"Well, I won't hold you up," Kegley said, unlocking her door.

"See ya' later," Dana called and started for her car. It was parked about 50 feet away.

"Have a safe trip," Kegley called.

"What?" Dana asked, her voice only a slight pitch different. She had stopped.

"Have a safe trip home," Kegley called back.

"You too," Dana said, watching Kegley get into her car.

Dana had covered half the distance to her car when the overhead lamps flickered out. The deserted garage was bathed in the dim glow of an inadequate system of backup lights. Three steps later the backup system failed, submerging her in total darkness. She stood indecisive for a moment, unsure of which way she had come or in which direction her car was parked. She heard the opening and closing of a car door.

"Kate?" she called, her heart starting to race.

"Thought you might need some light," Kegley's voice came back, followed by a splash of light flooding the garage away from Dana. Dana looked back to see Kegley halfway in her car, her headlights the source of the sudden illumination.

"Thanks," Dana said, genuinely grateful. She made it to her car and stooped to enter the door code.

Just as she opened the door, Kegley killed her headlamps and the area was bathed in black again.

It was an odd thing to do, Dana thought, but she was too hurriedly getting into her car to question it. She also failed to realize that the car door she had heard in the dark, had opened *and* closed. Kegley's car door had only been opened when she last saw it.

Inside her car Dana realized the overhead dome light was out. She put her briefcase on the next seat and then turned the light switch several times, but to no avail. She clicked on the dashboard lights in order to find the ignition key. Stabbing the key in the ignition she cranked the car.

She breathed a sigh of relief and reached up to retrieve an airline ticket from the point where the headliner met the plastic molding.

It was gone!

"What the hell...?"

She looked down into the dark floorboard.

"Back seat's smaller than my gun," came a voice from behind.

Startled, Dana gasped for air while reaching for the gun she kept hidden under the seat. It too, was gone. She was reaching for the derringer she had fastened to the holster on her thigh when she felt a pistol barrel on the back of her skull. She could see the dark form of a man in her rear view mirror.

"I'll take the, 'lady's gun,' you wear on the inside of those evil creamy thighs," the familiar voice said. "Be *very* slow about it and with two fingers only."

She did as ordered and his hand appeared out of the gloom, taking the gun.

"Boy, Dana, you were loaded for bear," he said, apparently enjoying the moment. "Well, no guns now and no ticket, Ms. Smith. That's the name you made the reservations under, I believe. You should have skedaddled this morning."

"Who are you?" Dana snapped, more angered than frightened.

"Just an electrician," Archer Commons joked, tossing the dome lightbulb into the front passenger seat.

"John Wilson?" she questioned, finally recognizing his voice.

"Give the dog a bone," Commons replied.

"What da' you want?"

"I'll say it simply and only once," he came back in a methodical voice. "I want you to take me to your boss."

"The Director—"

"Suit yourself," Commons interrupted and pulled back the pistol hammer.

"Okay," she said with a rush, "You made your point."

"Good. Now tell me everything I already know."

"His name is Ŝulok."

"I didn't really mean to tell me *everything* I already know," he came back almost jovial. "Keep talking."

"He's on an island in the Pacific."

"Wow, that really narrows it down."

"It's called Aysien."

"And who else might be there?"

"Austiff, if he's not dead. Gail and Alex Ŝulok."

"And?"

"I don't know anyone else."

Commons came across the back of her head with the gun, knocking her into the side window.

"Shit!" she cussed, seeing blood dripping from her mouth. She didn't need to touch the wound on her head to know she was bleeding there also.

"Now obviously I want you alive right now," Commons calmly said. "But I can keep you that way even while I pistol whip the shit out of you. Now who else is on that island?"

"Kalvin Reedy most likely," she responded, looking at the blood dripping on her cream-colored skirt. "I'm sure there's some Arabians—Ŝulok has some working for him—I don't know how many."

"That all?"

"All that I know about," she replied, expecting another swipe across the head.

Instead, she heard Commons and a tiny click—the sound of a transmit button.

"Everyone get all that?" Commons said into a hand-held radio.

"Roger," came Clines' voice. "We'll have the helicopter waiting for you at the field."

"I copy," came the voice of Clines' assistant. "Do you want the lights now?"

"Yes," Commons replied. They heard a car engine turn over.

The garage was suddenly lit again and Zelda's Studebaker sped past, driven by Clines.

There was a tap on the widow, and Dana looked through the blood-coated glass to see Kegley standing beside the car.

"Don't keep the lady waiting," Commons commented.

Dana pressed a button and the window opened.

"You fucking bitch," Kegley all but snarled. In her hand was a small radio transmitter. "How could you do this?"

"Fuck you," Dana snapped back. A second later she received the gun butt across the head that she had expected earlier. Although it hurt just as much—maybe more—she was too dazed to say anything this time.

"That's no way to talk to a lady," Commons said.

Dana's eyes watered-up with tears brought on by the pain.

"Forty million dollars," Kegley said. "And it still wasn't enough?"

"Actually, it's around 160 million now," Commons cheerfully put in.

Dana didn't respond.

"Get this whore out of my sight," Kegley said to Commons and then to Dana she added: "If Jim is dead, you're going to wish *you* were."

She turned and walked back to her car.

"I think she's mad at you," Commons commented, then pressed the gun into her neck again. "Well, you heard the lady, Ms. Whore, let's go."

Dana had literally forgotten that the engine was still running. She reached down and shifted into drive.

"Don't forget," Commons added, "the hammer is cocked. I don't want you alive so bad I'd risk you doing something stupid."

She only nodded, and slowly accelerated the car.

Forty minutes later, the repaired Nova Blacktooth flew from the OCSTO hangar in a blur of speed. Rusty Griggs, the new OCSTO security Director, was leaning over the shoulder of an air traffic controller at the nearby airport.

"There they are," the air traffic controller said, pointing to a blip on the screen. The blip was courtesy of an enabled setting on the Blacktooth transponder. "They'll be out of our range any time now."

The Chancellor—who had been talking on a cellular phone—offered it to Griggs. Having been briefed on his new role by Kegley, Griggs took the phone and into the open line, read off the Blacktooth's altitude, speed and heading. He listened a moment, nodded his head once and looked over at the man in the black trench coat standing nearby.

"They said they have them on satellite now," Griggs reported. "They'll probably pass through at least two more areas of coverage."

The Chancellor nodded.

Griggs offered the phone back.

"Keep it," the Chancellor said. "After you radio Blake and tell him his transponder modification works, check in with the CIA periodically to get updates on the satellite tracking."

"The CIA?"

"Well who do you think you were talking to, young man?"

Griggs didn't respond.

"They're the second programmed number. Just ask for Fisher."

"Yes, Sir."

"I'm the first programmed number."

"Yes, Sir."

The Chancellor turned and headed for the door. He stopped and looked back.

"Oh, and Griggs?"

"Yes, Sir?"

"You can hang it up now."

"Yes, Sir."

As the Chancellor left, Griggs did just that.

58

As was his endless habit, Gray unnecessarily looked at the luminous face of his Rolex, even though he knew the time. Seven minutes had elapsed since the throbbing Blacktooth engine went silent. Inside the dark womb of the Blacktooth's cramped cargo bay, he strained his ears to detect any noises. Satisfied that Dana Masters had led Commons and Debbie away, he decided it was time to follow. He felt along the smooth bulkhead of the confined space until he found the safety release button and struck it. The deck gave way beneath and he tumbled from the chopper onto the sandy beach.

Regaining the freedom of his cramped legs, he wobbled from underneath the helicopter, his black clothing speckled with white sand. Looking up, he could see that the star formations indicated he was somewhere in the area of the southern latitude of 2° and a longitude of about 168° or so. He was right smack in the middle of the Pacific Ocean.

Dusting the sand off his clothes, he surveyed the beach.

Farther inland, two Blacktooth helicopters sat dwarfed by the island growth. Unlike the Blacktooth from which Gray had tumbled, they were undamaged: one of them hosted a single cable that protruded from the power plant located just beneath the tail. The cable disappeared into the trees and merged with a wide path leading into the heart of the island.

Off to Gray's sides, the shore faded into jagged angles, looking like a white crayon line separating the dark sea from the thick island vegetation.

He slipped across the sand and into the foliage, choosing to travel parallel to the well-worn path. The most obvious and easiest path, he had learned long ago, was rarely the safest.

Thirty minutes of struggling later, he found the arrangement of old buildings at the island's center. The cable extending from the Blacktooth on the beach led out from the path and into the center building.

According to Dana Masters, that was the most probable place to find trouble. Double trouble if he didn't first secure the surrounding buildings.

He pulled out the dart pistol Clines had given him for the Nova mission. Although he was still carrying the .38 and his old Wafffnfabriken Simson, he preferred to keep the body count down—as well as the noise level. Having moved the .22 to a shoulder holster, a loaded pistol under each arm wasn't a bad confidence booster either, he thought.

He moved toward the nearest building. The dilapidated structure belied the door's condition as it opened noiselessly on well-oiled hinges.

A dark four-foot-wide hall stretched out for 45 feet, ending at another door. There were four doors spaced along the left side of the hall, and five on the right. Judging from their placement, the left side doors opened into equal sized rooms, while the right side had one room larger than the other four.

He pushed the dank smell in his nostrils to the back of his mind and aimed the gun outward while concentrating on sound. To either side, the chambers were empty.

Halfway through the building, he heard the steady sound of breathing—faint breathing coming from a chamber to his right.

He moved to the door and slipped an iron rod from the snug place where it had barred the door. This door also easily opened on well-oiled hinges. Inside, the furnishings consisted of a bed of wood slats and a man in tattered clothes—what had been a suit at one time.

Gray moved to him and stood only a moment before the other man sensed another presence. A gaunt face, splotched with bruises and cuts, looked up. Even in the faint starlight from the bar-covered window, Gray could easily make out the vacant expression and puffy eyes: both indicative of physical beatings and mental hardship.

"Jim," Gray said, hoping the Director still had his wits about him.

Austiff only stared.

"Jim, it's me, Karns Gray."

"Karns?"

Gray waited.

"Thank God," Austiff mumbled, sitting up.

"Listen, Jim," Gray said, kneeling down. "I need to know what I'm up against—how many?"

"I don't know, maybe three or four. Listen, you can't stay here—you've got to leave."

"Why?"

"He has FORBS," Austiff said with a scratchy voice.

"You mean Ŝulok, right?"

"Yeah, yeah—he's had it for months. You've got to go."

"He's got Gail and Alex."

Austiff pulled Gray close. "It don't matter—you can't stay."

"I'm not planning to," Gray responded. Austiff seemed okay, but his warnings seemed like uncharacteristic ramblings.

"He'll power it up—it'll kill us all—you've got to get out of here!"

"How's he powering it up?

"The helicopter and you."

"What?"

"Just get the hell out of here, man!"

Gray handed his .38 pistol to Austiff. "Stay here. Shoot anything that comes through that door. I'll be back for you."

"Oh no you don't," Austiff said. "You've got to go, and I'm going with you."

Austiff went to stand, but his leg gave way and he tumbled to the cement floor.

"I hate to tell you this," Gray said, retrieving the gun the Director had dropped and pressing it into the older man's hand, "but you're in a shit-load of a mess—I'll be back."

"Yeah, right," Austiff called, watching Gray move from the room.

Gray slipped into the hall and to the exit. He crossed an open space of ground and entered a second building identical to the last. As the musty smell was absent, he assumed the sleeping quarters were here.

A sudden guttural whine broke the silence. It escalated into a high pitched cry—something between a plea and a scream. Gray moved down the hall, finding the room from where the desperate voice was coming. He could also hear a very faint buzzing sound.

The door was locked from inside. He leaped up by one leg and snapped a kick. The door flew open, banging against the cement wall.

Even before the door came to a rest, Gray entered with the gun aiming. Strewn about the floor were clothes and sheets. Princess Fonna was on her elbows and knees in the bed. Still handcuffed to the headboard of the bed and wearing nothing but a tan, her buttocks were in the air for all to see. She was the one screaming. There was something else strange about her anatomy, but Gray had other immediate concerns and swept his eyes around to see a nude Kalvin Reedy who had sprung from the bed and flattened against the wall. In his hand was a knife.

Gray merely twitched the gun at the knife and Reedy obediently dropped it.

"Pull it-it-ttttt-outtt!" Fonna cried with a jolting voice.

Keeping the gun trained at Reedy, Gray looked back to the bed. He spied the anatomical aberration he had skipped on first examination, and found the source of the buzzing noise he had heard from outside the room. A handle grip of sorts protruded from the Princess' body and she seemed to be held up by the invisible force of electricity.

Gray motioned at the device: "Take it out."

Reedy carefully moved to the bed and withdrew the vibrator. With a flip of a switch, it stopped humming.

"Kill him," Fonna panted. She had dropped flat, gasping and making a noise which Gray realized was "dry heaving." She had obviously cried her tear ducts dry. Soaked in perspiration, her wrists were bloody from straining against the handcuffs with which she had imprisoned herself. The room faintly smelled of urine and feces.

"Aren't you guys on the same team?" Gray asked.

"Kill him," she gasped. "He was going to kill me."

"Is that what you used on Sarah Austiff?" Gray asked Reedy.

Reedy smiled. "You know about that, huh?"

"Get the key to those cuffs," Gray ordered, ignoring Reedy's question.

Reedy moved to the dresser and opened a drawer.

"I know you're thinking something stupid," Gray commented. "Just don't do it."

Reedy withdrew the key.

"Now cuff yourself to her and the headboard."

"You can't do this," Fonna protested as Reedy followed Gray's instructions. She had never expected help, and now that it had arrived, she had not expected her savior to become her tormentor.

"Watch me," Gray calmly said.

When Reedy was finished, Fonna was laying on her back and he was kneeling over the edge of the bed.

Gray pocketed the key and tightened down the cuffs.

"What about me?" Fonna asked, watching Gray move around the bed, checking for additional weapons and finding none.

"What about you?" Gray asked rhetorically, scooping up the hunting knife Reedy had dropped. It went into his back pocket.

"You've got to get me out of here. This sicko will kill me."

"Really?" Gray said, moving to the opened dresser drawer and rifling through it.

"Yes," Fonna was saying, "he's crazy!"

With a shake of his head, Gray pulled a pistol from beneath some folded clothes.

"At least you weren't stupid this time," he said to Reedy, stuffing the gun into his waistband and finishing his search.

"Well?" came Fonna's frightened voice.

"Well what?"

"You're not leaving me, right?"

Gray paused, as if considering her dilemma. "Maybe you can help me with something?"

"What?"

"Well, you are Princess Fonna—one of the most wealthy and powerful women in the world, right?"

"Yes," she said, with relief. If he knew who she was—

"Then explain to me how is it that you're butt-naked, in bed with a psychopathic sexed-craved killer, in the middle of the Pacific Ocean—not to mention having one dandy of a sex toy to play with?"

"I—uh—he kidnapped me!" she replied, realizing the precariousness of her situation and trying to explain it with an obviously unconvincing lie.

"Hm, was that before or after you were on board that bogus news yacht while keeping an eye on the bait for Ŝulok?"

"I—I—"

"You see my problem, don't you?" he asked. "There's no way in hell you could be an innocent bystander."

"But—"

"And you either wear a white hat or you don't."

"You can't leave me like this," Fonna cried, realizing her fate.

"I also seem to recall reading about you thumbing your nose at some of our citizenship laws some years back."

Even in her dire predicament, this was completely unexpected and it showed on her face.

"Yeah," Gray said with almost a laugh, "I bet you never thought that'd come back to bite you in the butt."

"You can't be serious," she said, panic in her voice.

"Dead serious," Gray responded. "You conveniently danced around the law then, and you've outright made a mockery of it in this instance. There's no telling what you're guilty of."

"You can't prove anything," she came back, switching from victim to royal dignitary.

Gray just looked at her.

"I will not be treated...this..." Her voice trailed away as she saw the expression on his face.

"That's exactly what I'm talking about," Gray summed-up.

Reedy laughed.

"But—but—the law—I mean you can't just leave me like this!"

"I guess you're right," Gray said.

She visibly relaxed.

Gray looked at Reedy. "Get on top of her."

"What?!" Fonna gasped. "My God, no!"

Reedy did as ordered, but tried forcing himself onto her even as she fought him. Weakened from her short captivity, it was a losing battle.

Gray moved across the few feet and whipped his pistol through the air, completely knocking Reedy off the other side of the bed.

"Now, back on top."

Reedy meekly did as ordered, his mouth streaming blood.

"Tell me something, Jack," Reedy said, his blood oozing onto Fonna's breasts, "why aren't you dead."

"Same reason you aren't. Dumb luck."

Reedy laughed again, amused even in his deranged hatred of Gray.

"Please don't do this," Fonna cried, back in the role of victim, "you can't leave me this way!"

"But you two make such a lovely couple."

"I'll do anything," she pleaded.

Gray smiled, backing to the door. "You already have."

He disappeared down the hall, Fonna's voice fading behind.

Once outside, Gray scouted the other buildings.

He was halfway down the dim hall of the fourth building when the exit ahead opened to admit a large Arabian man.

The man went for the gun in his waistband.

Gray fired once, and the silent dart dropped the Arabian on contact. The door to Gray's right swung open.

"Don't move," said a heavily accented voice, freezing Gray in mid-turn. The man remained halfway behind the door for protection. "Drop the gun."

Gray let the dart pistol clatter to the floor.

"And the rest of the arsenal, too."

Gray reached for the .44 he had stuck in his waistband.

"Easy."

Gray pulled it out and dropped it. He followed that with dropping his own pistols.

"You're a regular one man army," the man commented. "Now, slowly walk to the door."

Gray moved his leg to walk, but kicked to the side instead. The door protecting the Arabian slammed against him, knocking him into the door frame. Gray whipped Reedy's knife from his pocket.

The Arabian screamed as the knife sliced into his eye socket. Dropping to his knee, Gray scooped up the first available weapon—the Magnum—and fired.

Even with the knife in his face the Arabian had been bringing his machine gun up to fire. He never made it. The bullet tore into his face and blew out the back of his head as it exited. He was dead without another thought occurring to him. The body fell to the floor.

Gray removed the knife from the dead man's eye socket and wiped it clean on the shirt of the corpse. He re-pocketed the blade and returned his guns to their places.

Leaving the building, he moved to the center and largest building. At the last moment, he exchanged the dart gun for Reedy's Magnum. Flattening his back to the wall, he inched to the door where the fiber-optic cable from the beach snaked in. He slowly took a breath, and then moved.

He swung around through the door—coming face-to-face, gun barrel-to-gun barrel with Seth Ŝulok.

59

Three seconds.

Five seconds.

Ten seconds.

Each man stood as if transfixed in time—their arms extended with guns silently aiming.

A blast never came. Slowly, as if instructed by an unseen referee, Ŝulok lowered his weapon. It wasn't submission—or even acceptance. The problem was Gray didn't know why the man lowered his gun while smiling the whole time. Gray could neither deduce what Ŝulok found amusing, nor looked forward to finding out. He immediately shifted to the left of the door, ensuring his back was against a solid wall.

"I can see it in your eyes, Jack," Ŝulok said with a wave of a finger, as if he were talking to a school child. "You're thinking, 'I can just blow the old fool's head off, and still take the other two.' Hey, you might—you're pretty good."

Ŝulok turned his back giving Gray the chance to more calmly consider the situation. It was a packed house. Debbie, Commons, Gail and Alex were all kneeling on the floor, in the classic execution position. Dana Masters, with Commons' pistols stuffed in her waistband and her mouth black and blue from the collision with her window, had a pistol trained on the backs of Commons and Debbie. An Arabian held a pistol on the head of Gail. Standing off to the side was a man Gray didn't recognized but correctly guessed to be Steve Andrews. Beside Andrews was the thing Gray had hoped never to again encounter: FORBS.

"Let's just say, for the sake of argument," Ŝulok was saying, as he turned back around, "you decide to take out Mike here."

Ŝulok waved his gun in the direction of the man holding a gun on Gail.

"Well," Ŝulok went on, "I'd then take out Gail. Or if you take out me, Mike takes out Gail—I'm sure you get the picture."

"What—" Gray began.

"—do I want," Ŝulok finished for him. He hefted himself upon a wide table covered in papers and computer disks.

As Gray grew accustomed to the situation, he realized that the building's interior had been completely replaced. The building had become, in essence, an 18x30 foot metallic vault—even the floor and ceiling were metallic. There were two doors: one behind Dana and Commons and the other through which Gray had just walked.

"That's what I like about you," Ŝulok went on. "Straight to the point. You know, I was a little concerned you weren't going to make our little get-together here. Dana says you didn't come in with them. But I bet you hid in the cargo bay—looking for that little edge of surprise. Am I right?

"Ŝulok—"

"Oh, all right," Ŝulok said, knowing Gray wasn't playing along. "What I want...? Actually, I want you. The immortal Jack Graham—or Karns Gray, if you prefer—I just can't get used to it. I mean really, Jack, 'Karns Gray?' Is that for real? It's kind of like going into an arts and crafts store and saying, 'Yes, I'd like a tube of Rubens' madder, raw Sienna and hey, while you're about it, throw in a tube of that Karns Gray.'"

"You're trying my patience, Seth."

"But you can afford it," Ŝulok came back. "You have all the time in the world."

"What the hell are you talking about?"

"You see, Mike," Ŝulok said to the Arabian, "that's the problem with people these days. They just don't want to be friendly."

Ŝulok looked to Gray. "Let me tell you a story—it won't take long, okay—"

"Look, Ŝulok—"

"Now, Jack, I can't very well help you if you won't let me."

Gray didn't respond.

"That's better. Now as I was about to say, once upon a time, somewhere in the mid-1800s, there was a Russian alchemist who was intent on finding an elixir of youth. But this guy wasn't just any ol' crackpot. No, sir. He took cadavers and studied them. And whenever there was a catastrophic injury, he sometimes opened up the dying person just for a peek around. I don't know the whole story—it's not all that important now that I have you—but suffice it to say this guy perfected his youth elixir. Fearful it would fall into the wrong hands, he divided the handful of samples he had made—along with his notes—and gave one-half of everything to his assistant. Agreeing to meet-up at some future destination, they separated and went two different routes.

"I'm not boring you, am I?"

"Ŝulok—"

"Just a moment more, Jack," Ŝulok rushed on. "As I was saying, they intended to meet-up. But it never happened. And even this much of the story is known only because of a book unearthed in Alaska. Alaska, of all places. Somehow or another, one of them—probably the assistant—hooked-up with a venture called the America-Russian Fur Trading company—"

The data from one of the Nova Fiche suddenly made sense to Gray.

"Ah," Ŝulok exclaimed, catching the recognition on Gray's face. "You've heard of it?"

"I've heard of it," was Gray's response.

"Well that's the only surviving record of the elixir that I've found. And it makes for fascinating reading, I must say. Especially the parts about the production of a very unusual chemical in the brain—an enzyme, actually—I think. It's described in minute detail and in chemical notes that are, frankly, baffling. And that's where you come in."

"Oh boy," Gray said dryly.

"Aren't your arms getting tired?"

They were in fact. But Gray had yet to find a solution to the standoff. He had been in worse situations, though, and a little muscle strain was a small price to pay.

"You sound like you're headed somewhere," Gray said. "Maybe it's something that we can discuss without anyone dying."

"You just never know," Ŝulok said, then continued with his narration. "Anyway, some years ago I managed to bribe Ms. Masters after she started with OCSTO. She was the one who first alerted me to the shelved Project Hacksaw. But it wasn't the wide reaching power of FORBS that intrigued me; it was your medical records, Jack."

"My medical records?" Gray echoed.

"Now don't be coy, Jack," Ŝulok said, slipping off the table with a computer CD in his hand. "Here they are, Jack, the complete and unabridged medical records of the Hacksaw test subject—you. Of course, I didn't know it was you until recently—sorry about trying to have you offed so many times before. Anyway, the doctors were amazed, baffled, even shocked. And you know why, don't you?"

Gray understood. "Yes."

Ŝulok smiled.

"That's why you did all this?" Gray asked.

"What better reason?"

"Look," came Common's voice, "If I am gonna' be killed, I'd like to know why."

Ŝulok glanced to Commons then at Gray. "He doesn't know?"

Again Gray didn't respond.

A look of sudden enlightenment lit Ŝulok's face. "Neither does sweet Gail."

He moved to his wife. "Dear sweet Gail—who thought I was so stupid as to believe this was my daughter here."

Gail looked surprised.

"I'm not a moron, you know," Ŝulok remarked, then addressed Alex. "Hell, you've hated me since the first day I looked into those unmistakably Jack Graham eyes of yours. After all I did for you. You bitch."

To her credit, Alex remained silent.

"Where was I?" Ŝulok said, and then: "Oh yes. I realize most of you think I'm a complete lunatic. I mean why would a man with more money than he could ever spend, go to such great lengths to obtain a possibly dangerous device like FORBS? Hmm, why indeed? Well, ladies and gentlemen, there is your answer."

Everyone except Gray, Dana and Debbie looked confused by Ŝulok's pointing at Gray.

"Think about it people," Ŝulok went on. "What could possibly prompt such outlandish behavior in someone like me—or even Ms. Masters—who has over 160 million bucks to her name. Hmm? What could we possibly want that we couldn't buy?"

No one answered.

"Well look at *Jack*, will ya'? What do you see? A young man in his prime—maybe *30 years old?*

"People, Jack Graham—Karns Gray—is as old as *me!* He's looking at 60 just around the corner—if he hadn't already passed it. When I called him the *immortal* Jack Graham, I was not speaking figuratively or being facetious. FORBS did that—made him *forever young*."

He now had the rapt attention of his audience.

Ŝulok moved to the Plexiglas bubble housing the lifeless FORBS unit.

"When I saw the report regarding the chemical activity in your brain," Ŝulok said, looking at Gray, "I can't describe the joy I felt. And then the blood work—I mean, everything almost perfectly matching the Russian alchemist's notes—absolutely miraculous.

"Well that was the good news. The bad news was, we couldn't figure out who you were. And the information we had seemed to indicate you died in a coma. Looking back, I realized that was just one of the ways OCSTO kept their secrets. A little misinformation here and there and you can track who leaked what. Well, anyway, we settled on searching for FORBS—never really believing it survived re-entry. And the rest, as they say, is history. We were doing pretty darned good until the Chancellor blew-up my Converter."

"And now you can't use FORBS," Gray concluded.

Ŝulok smiled. "Tell 'em what he's won, Steve."

"Actually, we believe we can," the electrical whiz said. "The Converter powers-up FORBS by transmitting a kind of, 'boot-up signal.' After that, it's simply a matter of transmitting power."

"Yeah?" Gray asked suspiciously.

"The problem is the access code—that boot-up signal. It's a one of a kind, not to be imitated type of thing. When the Converter was destroyed, that left only one copy of the access code available—at least in theory."

"A copy?" Commons couldn't help but ask. "I thought it was a one of a kind code."

"Perhaps I should have said, 'replicated.' I could never sit down and replicate that code. But that doesn't mean the code—the signal—couldn't be, or hasn't been, stored in another location."

No one said anything, thinking Andrews or Ŝulok would pick-up the thread of thought.

"Yeah—so?" Commons finally prompted.

"You see," Andrews explained politely, "FORBS actually accesses something after sending that signal. The signal's not just a boot-up signal per se—it records or maps the computer it's sent to and then tells FORBS, 'hey, this is an IBM computer, or this is an Old Macintosh or this is a human brain.' The signal leaves a signature in the accessed system for future use—kind of like a temp file just sits in your computer's temp directory doing nothing. It's just there."

Andrews turned to Gray. "You, Mr. Graham were connected to FORBS—it was in your head—your brain. You are the only system FORBS ever had the chance to access. You, Mr. Graham, have the access code, just waiting to be activated—theoretically."

Gray looked at the man as if he were daft.

"Oh it's true, all right," Ŝulok chimed in. "I need FORBS to get that chemical and I need you to get FORBS."

Gray looked from one man to the other.

"That's right Jackie," Ŝulok said. "You may not know it, but you be da' man!"

They were all staring at Gray. Gray looked at Debbie, the only person he thought might have a clue as to the validity of what he had just heard.

"I don't know," she said to him.

"So here's the deal," Ŝulok said. "We hook you up, you activate FORBS and I'll let you walk—with that whore of a wife of mine. In fact, I'll let all of you go."

"Not this one," Dana said, indicating Commons.

Gray looked over, noticing Dana had extracted her pound of flesh by a fair sized bruise on the side of Commons face.

"Okay," Ŝulok conceded. "Everyone but him."

"Seth," Debbie called.

Ŝulok looked around.

"Karns was nearly killed by that machine. It killed everyone in the experiment chamber."

"Thought of that already," Ŝulok chirped. "That's why I designed this room based upon Bio-Chem's design for their own experiment chamber."

"What's to stop it from doing the same thing as it did last time?" Gray asked, not that he was in any way considering the prospect.

"Well, FORBS was up to full speed that time," Andrews answered. "We're going to supply it with only enough juice to bring it online. Without access to more power, it shouldn't be a problem."

"You're nuttier than I thought if you expect me to just lie down and chance that," Gray said to Ŝulok.

"Not really," Ŝulok came back, all flippancy gone from his voice. His entire demeanor had changed. "I've got a room full of reasons why you will—two of them alone are enough, I should think."

Mike pressed his pistol into the back of Gail's head.

She nervously gasped.

"You don't have to do this," Gray told Ŝulok.

"Mike" Ŝulok said, "do the daughter first."

Mike moved the pistol to Alex.

"Wait!" Gray said, moving forward a few steps.

Ŝulok could see the struggle going on beneath Gray's apparently calm facade. Gail had always been his weakness. It was only natural that would extend to Alex, now.

"Hey look," Ŝulok said with less aloofness than before, "People have undoubtedly died because of things I've done, but very rarely at my hands. I'm not really a blood-thirsty murderer—that'd be Kalvin, he enjoys it—but not me. I don't really want to waste anyone.

"But we are talking about the culmination of my life's work here. The chance to create virtual immortality. The elimination of illness as we know it. You of all people should understand this—I mean you haven't even had a sick day since your little accident, have you?"

"No, I haven't."

"That's right. And you owe it to the very thing I'm trying to duplicate. Surely you can understand that."

Gray didn't respond. He might have sympathized with Ŝulok's position had he not been desperately searching for an edge—a way out of the standoff. He was uncertain if he could shoot more than one of them before the other killed his daughter or Gail.

"Just hand over the guns, butt first—it's the only way."

He considered the ruse of handing the guns over, but using them in the process—but again, he just couldn't be sure of Gail and Alex's safety. Backed into a corner from which he still didn't have to fight his way out, he had little choice.

"It's your move," Ŝulok said.

Gray pulled the Wafffnfabriken Simson out with his right hand and held it out along with the Magnum, handles first.

"No," came yet another voice from the doorway through which Gray had entered. "It's my move."

Kalvin Reedy slithered in, grinning with his face dripping blood. He held out another .44 Magnum, drawing a bead on Gray.

Those who could freeze in place any more than they already had, did.

"How—" Gray began.

"I chewed the slut's hand off," Reedy interrupted with a cackle for a laugh and dangled the bloody handcuff still locked on his wrist.

"Kalvin," Ŝulok said, trying to maintain an element of control. "I need him alive."

"Bullshit," Reedy barked. "I just keep missing and missing. Not this time, Jack-o. Good bye, you Bastard!"

The gunshot sounded, echoing as if the sound of two shots—which there actually were. Reedy stood teetering momentarily. His eyes went from the mass of blood blotting his T-shirt to Dana Masters, who he had hit instead of Gray.

Confusion and surprise were still on Reedy's face as he fell to a useless heap on the floor. At the same time, Dana collapsed backward. Behind Dana, avoiding her falling body by doing a side-shuffle on a machine gun improvised as a crutch, was the source of the first gunshot: Jim Austiff. He had slipped in and shot Reedy. That was the cause of Reedy's aim going wild and Dana's death. It had happened so suddenly, Austiff had yet to lower the pistol Gray had given him earlier.

"Shoot," Ŝulok ordered, bringing up his own gun—too late.

Having anticipated the problem, Gray was completing the, "Border Roll"—flipping his pistols around and firing off the Magnum in his left hand and jamming the .25 caliber into Ŝulok's eye.

"Don't," was all Gray told him, even while firing the Magnum.

While Mike was being blown back by the shot to the head, Ŝulok had the good sense to freeze in place.

Several seconds of silence went by. The only movement was Gray taking the pistol from Ŝulok.

"I'll be damned," Commons said at last. "We're all still alive!"

Gail and Alex actually laughed.

Commons climbed to his feet, and recovered his guns from Dana's body as well as the radio transmitter she had taken from him. While he was doing this, Debbie moved over to Gray.

Smiling, Gray's attention was on the scraggly OCSTO Director.

"I got tired of waitn'," Austiff barked.

"I was pretty tired of waiting myself," Gray came back.

"You're a lucky son-of-a-bitch," Ŝulok mumbled.

"Maybe you're just unlucky," Gray responded.

Commons appeared, taking possession of Ŝulok's gun from Gray. He then bent down to check on Reedy's vital signs.

"Well?" Gray inquired.

"This bastard's still alive," Commons said in disbelief.

Reedy's eyes fluttered open. "Am I going to...die...?"

"I hope so," Commons replied.

Reedy started to say something, but his eyes rolled back and he fell unconscious again.

"What about him?" Debbie asked, pointing to a petrified Steve Andrews.

"Here Debbie," Gray said, producing the key to Reedy's handcuffs. "Cuff Ŝulok and Andrews together. We'll drag Reedy."

Pistol in hand, Debbie took Ŝulok by the arm, leading him to the pale-faced Andrews.

Gray rubbed one of his aching arms and then returned his pistols to their holsters. Austiff hobbled over.

"So," Gray said to Austiff, "how are you doing, Jim."

"I'll live, I guess. Why the hell didn't you get out of here like I told you?"

"I thought you were just ranting and raving."

"I was ranting and raving," Austiff replied. "But I knew what I was ranting and raving about."

Gray smiled "I guess so."

He turned and walked over to FORBS. Austiff followed.

FORBS sat upon a metal base that Andrews had built to host the power supply from the Blacktooth. Beneath the Plexiglas bubble was the synthetic intelligence that Gray felt he knew intimately, but couldn't recall actually having seen. The gelatin-like mass that had at one time pulsed with light, now looked like a misshapen blob of melted plastic. The gelatinous substance, through which artificial synaptic pathways were formed, was sunken inward, exposing the more recognizable computer components. The maze of hair-like fiber optics still crisscrossed its dead surface, but were now a mass of dull gray elements. It looked less like an artificial brain and more like a melted wax statue. Even the Plexiglas bubble had become misshapen, scratched, pitted and in some places scorched.

"So this is FORBS," Gray mumbled.

"'Fraid so," Austiff responded.

Debbie walked up, looking down at FORBS.

"Kind of sends a shiver up the spine," Gray commented.

"Mr. Andrews," Debbie called.

"Yes ma'am?" he asked, looking up from the handcuffs anchoring him to Ŝulok.

"I think you should disconnect the cable to FORBS."

"It'd take a good 15 to 20 minutes," he responded.

"Just the same—"

"Takes two seconds at the Blacktooth."

"Oh, okay."

"We're ready to ride," came Common's voice.

"Fine," Gray mumbled, mesmerized by the thing in front of him. "Check on housekeeping's ETA."

Commons pulled out his radio transmitter and switched it on. The Housekeeping unit was a team of Chancellor agents sent in for any number of reasons ranging from completely erasing any trace of someone's presence to the documentation of a crime scene all the way down to the microscopic level.

"This is Alpha 1 to Wingman, over," Commons said into the mic. He had plugged in an ear phone and nodded his head. "The LZ is secure, what's your ETA, over?"

He listened a moment and then said, "Roger that, Wingman. We'll be waiting. Out."

Gray looked over at Commons.

"They're still 75 minutes out," Commons reported.

Gray nodded, returning his attention to FORBS.

"Ladies," Commons said to Gail and Alex, indicating the door.

"We're waiting for Karns," Gail said steadfastly.

"Nothing wrong with that," he remarked and moved over to the group by FORBS.

"Let's go," Commons said.

FORBS, Gray thought, leaning lightly against the bubble. *What a nightmare*.

"Karns," Commons said lightly.

"What?" he said, looking up. "Oh, yeah, let's go."

They started toward the door.

"You bastard," Gail quietly said to Ŝulok, shouldering past him.

"Bastard?" he questioned with surprise. "I didn't lie about my daughter for over 20 years."

She ignored him.

Debbie pushed Ŝulok and Andrews to the door while Commons was lifting Reedy's limp body.

That's when Gray heard it—in his head.

Karns? the voice said, smoothly.

Gray stopped, recognizing the voice. "Debbie, Arch, get everyone out."

Debbie looked at him. "What—"

"I am FORBS," came the smooth voice, now audible to all of them.

The voice was new to everybody but Austiff, Debbie and Gray. But Gray remembered the voice in a very different and more personal way. He remembered being unable to move, unable to communicate—unable to warn the doctors. He had listened to the calm voice as it reassured everyone that everything was fine—every word of it a lie. Gray had never forgotten the voice and the words that only he heard that day. The voice that he was now hearing again.

Slowly, an unseen fear spread through the room—like the tension of something stretched beyond its endurance. Realizing the new danger, they focused their attention on the large bubble in the center of the room—its mass of gray beginning to glow as its fiber optics began surging with power.

"How'd that happen?" Commons asked.

Gray closed his eyes, realizing what he had done. "I did it."

"What?"

"I don't know, I just thought it, I guess."

"Well, unthink it."

"It's online," Ŝulok mumbled in amazement. "I did it. I powered it up.

"Andrews," Gray said, "can you shut it off."

"Uh, yeah,"

Gray had his pistol out. "Do it."

"Sure I—"

"Wait a second," Gray said, looking at the gun in his hand. He turned and fired at the bubble.

To everyone's amazement, the bullet literally exploded inches from the bubble.

"What the hell?" Gray said.

"Oh no," Debbie said.

"What?"

"You can't shut it off."

"Sure you can," Andrews came back.

"Didn't you see that?" she asked. "It's already drawing in power from the room. "

"You mean like the heat or the friction of the bullet was—was—"

"Used by FORBS," Debbie finished. "We've got to go. Come on, we've got to get out of here."

Ŝulok broke loose, dragging Andrews with him. Together, they fell against the door. But it didn't shut all the way because of the cable.

"Don't you understand," Ŝulok said to them, "It has the secret to immortality."

Debbie pushed Ŝulok and Andrews out of the way.

"Come on," she ordered the other women. They filed out, followed by Austiff and Commons, the latter having hefted the unconscious Reedy over his shoulder. Debbie grabbed Ŝulok by the collar and pushed him out of the building. Andrews was only too happy to go along.

Only Debbie and Gray remained in the building.

Debbie looked up at him. "We've got to get this cable out of the doorway in order to seal the room—I just hope it's really as secure as Ŝulok thinks."

"An ax would be nice," Gray said, looking around.

Debbie pulled out her pistol and aimed with the intention of severing the cable.

A burst of electricity arced from the bubble, striking her in the chest. Debbie was jolted into the wall. She slid to the floor with tears in her eyes.

A second arc lanced out, passing through the empty airspace where Gray had just been standing. Having avoided FORBS' first salvo, he grabbed the moaning Debbie and hauled her out of the building.

Gray eased her to the ground, against the side of the building.

"Oh, shit," she cussed, holding her side in pain while leaning against the wall.

"You okay?" Gray asked.

"Do I look it?" she snapped, irritated by his question and the pain.

"Well actually," he said with a lop-sided grin, "this is about your usual temperament."

Even though she was hurting, she couldn't help but love the man.

"Look," she said, "FORBS is just going to get more powerful unless we seal the building."

"Let's sever the cable out here," Austiff recommended. "Then toss it in and shut the door."

"No, that won't do," Gray came back thoughtfully. "The only access to power FORBS has is to the Blacktooth and that opened door. Sever that cable without shutting off FORBS and there's no telling what it might do."

"There's also the problem of not having an interconnecting chamber," Debbie pointed out, looking straight at Ŝulok.

"What's that got to do with anything?" Ŝulok asked.

"You can't seal the room safely, dumbass," Debbie answered. "Even if we could cut the cable and seal the building, somebody has to open the door at some point in the future."

"Instant power," Gray concluded. "And that's the best case scenario. I don't even want to consider what'll happen when FORBS realizes it's in a building held together by termites holding hands.

Debbie nodded while Commons couldn't help but grin at the visual imagery.

"We've got to do something," Austiff pointed out.

The others looked on helplessly.

After a moment, Gray looked at Ŝulok. "You really want immortality?"

"What?"

"You heard me."

"Yeah," he answered with a nod of his head.

"Then today's your lucky day, Seth," Gray said reaching to remove the handcuff's key from Debbie's pocket.

"Don't mind me getting in your pants, do you?" Gray said with a playful grin.

"Ha," she grunted, still hurting from the jolt of electricity. "Like you would."

He retrieved the key and removed the handcuffs from Ŝulok. "Go to it, boy."

Ŝulok looked at him. "What's the catch?'

"No catch, exactly," Gray said. "You'll end-up dead probably—save the taxpayers some dough."

Ŝulok gave a salute and disappeared through the door.

"What the hell are you doing?" Debbie asked.

"We've got to stop it, right?"

"Yeah."

"Only one way to do that—and that's to give everybody what they want."

"What's that mean?"

"It means Ŝulok just went in there for immortality. FORBS, on the other hand, wants to survive and become human, as it were. Two birds with one stone."

Gray looked to Commons. "Give me a couple minutes and then sever the cable with a machine gun or something."

"Right."

"If I'm not back in 15 minutes, take a Blacktooth and turn this building into rubble."

"Provided that thing doesn't do with missiles what it did with your bullet."

"Why do you think I'm trying this first?" Gray came back rhetorically.

"Be careful," Debbie said.

"Karns," Gail said.

"Don't worry," Gray assured her.

He turned toward the door.

60

Gray re-entered the building.

In the center of the room, both Ŝulok and the FORBS unit were bathed in a brilliant glowing light radiating outward from the bubble.

Ŝulok suddenly collapsed to the floor.

You have returned, Gray heard inside his head, or at least he thought it was.

"Yeah," he answered aloud.

"We must complete the transfer," came the audible voice of FORBS.

"I don't think so," Gray said, moving to Ŝulok and checking his pulse. Ŝulok was alive.

An arc of electricity whipped out from the bubble and Gray leaped to the side only to be struck by a second arc. He was knocked into the wall.

Contributing to the effect of having hit a wall, there was a sudden and familiar stabbing pain in his head—it was FORBS, just as it had been so many years ago.

The lights began flickering.

Gray heard a machine gun outside and he started crawling for the cable that was holding the door open. He heard the sizzle of the next arc of electricity and leaped forward to avoid it—knowing that he would receive a second jolt. At approximately the same time, the air seemed to grow thinner.

Even though the next jolt knocked him into another wall, he grabbed the cable and yanked. It cleared the threshold and the door shut.

Outside, Debbie stood in shock just as the door slammed. "Oh God."

"What?" Gail asked.

"FORBS is pulling all the power it can get again—it's trying to transfer."

"What?"

"It means one of them isn't coming out alive," Austiff supplied, "and I don't even want to think about the other one."

"We've got to do something," Gail pleaded.

"It's better if the building stays sealed," Debbie responded, bending over and holding her side. "I think I broke something."

"Like hell," Gail snapped, and swiped the machine gun from the unsteady OCSTO Director. She then kicked the door and rushed in.

Austiff started after her, but his injured knee gave way and he stumbled into the grass. Although in pain, Debbie was already in pursuit.

Gail entered the building just as Ŝulok was rising to his feet in the center of the room. Debbie had been right behind Gail, but was now literally doubled-over in pain. Ŝulok, his eyes unaccountably bloodshot, his chest peppered with four of Gray's chemical nerve darts, rushed toward Gray, pell-mell.

Lying near the center of the room were Gray's pistols and the dart gun that had suddenly proved useless. At the other side of the room, a groggy Karns Gray was trying to get up from the floor. What Gail didn't realize, was that each of Gray's movements constituted the T'ai-chi ch'uan martial arts position of *Snake Creeps Down*. Approximating a wide crouching position, with one leg completely extended, and the other supporting his weight, Gray dropped his left hand in front of his chest and swept his right hand up into the legs of Ŝulok, who was now upon him.

The effect for Ŝulok was the same as having taken a running dive. Ŝulok's momentum, assisted with the lightest of support from Gray's right hand, carried him over the top of Gray. Helplessly flailing, Ŝulok crashed into the wall with a bone-chilling crunch.

Without delay, Gray gracefully came to his feet.

With blood gushing from his cracked skull, Ŝulok still came blundering back. Gray performed a simple T'ai-chi *Single Whip* movement, which again utilized Ŝulok's momentum and propelled him away in another direction.

As Ŝulok stumbled to the floor, Gray glanced over to Gail, who was just now realizing that Gray had a bleeding gash on one leg. It was the reason he had chosen to fight standing in one place: Master Yen Hwúi would have been proud.

Gray saw the machine gun in Gail's hand and yelled: "Shoot 'em!"

She raised the gun, aimed and...*click*.

The magazine was empty.

For a second, Ŝulok had expected the bullets and stopped.

It wasn't much, but Gray figured it was the only break he could expect and dove for the pistols lying in the floor.

Rolling, he managed to grab both weapons and came up with all his weight on the uninjured leg. One gun he fired into the Plexiglas bubble, which shattered, spewing coolant liquids into the air amid an array of sparks. Gray's other pistol was, for the second time that evening, pointed at Ŝulok's face. That face, however, was the blank expression of another entity.

Gray fired.

Ŝulok dropped in a pool of blood—FORBS dying with him.

Ghost white and holding her side, Debbie was leaning against the door frame. "Karns?"

"I'm okay," he said, sitting down—really falling down.

Gail rushed to him and he hugged her.

"I didn't know the gun—"

"Oh hush," he interrupted with a smile and then added; "I hope you're better in the kitchen."

"Oh Baby," she whispered, then looked to his leg.

"It looks worse than it is," he assured her.

She started to look around at Ŝulok.

"Don't," he said gently and then wearily rose to his feet. He re-holstered the pistols.

"What happened?" Debbie asked when they reached her.

"With the room sealed, FORBS didn't have the power to transfer to me—just like the first time."

"But how were you able to shoot the FORBS unit," Debbie questioned, looking over at the shattered bubble. The remains of the computer hissed and sparked.

"FORBS transferred to Ŝulok," Gray explained. "After that it was simply a matter of two bullets."

"But if it couldn't transfer to you...?" This from Gail.

"Because I didn't want it to," Gray explained. "Ŝulok, on the other hand, did. That's what I was counting on when I sent him in here."

Gail nodded her understanding. She said: "Pretty smart, Baby."

"I try."

"Your leg?" she asked.

"Reedy's knife," he answered. "Ŝulok was pretty good with a blade."

Debbie grinned.

"What about you?" Gray asked Debbie.

"Well it still hurts, if that's what you mean."

Gail and Gray helped her stand.

"Gail," Debbie said, turning to the other woman. "About everything I said to you that last night..."

Gail waited.

"I really wish I... Well, I'm sorry."

Gail nodded.

"Did I miss something?" Gray asked, hobbling along behind them.

"Like I'd tell you anything, Mr. Temperament," Debbie retorted.

The three of them moved out into the night air.

The others greeted them just outside the door.

"Well?" Austiff asked.

"We can close the book on this one," Debbie responded.

Gray pointed to the unconscious form of Reedy. "He is still alive?"

"Just," Commons said. "He's a candidate for Truth and Justice, if you like."

Gray looked at the other agent, knowing exactly what he meant.

"Wouldn't take a second," Commons added.

Gray glanced at Alex, wondering what she would think if she realized her father could justify an execution style murder just like that. Reedy certainly deserved it.

"Ah, bring 'em along—maybe he won't make it and Truth and Justice will be served anyway."

"It's your show," Commons said, then looked at Andrews who was still handcuffed and sitting idly by. "Let's go, pal."

"Aren't you supposed to be dead?" Austiff asked with a grin.

"Not today," Gray came back with a smirk while ripping out his left shirtsleeve. He tied it around his leg wound while watching Alex embrace her mother.

"So what happened in there?" Commons pressed.

Debbie explained it to everyone's satisfaction.

"Are we going home now?" Alex asked, more to get them moving than anything else.

Commons laughed hoarsely: "Hell yeah, let's go."

"Is there anyone we've missed," Gray cut in. "Those are the guys that do you in."

"You mean besides the guy with a dart in his gullet?" Austiff asked.

"Yeah, besides that guy."

"Not any more," Austiff said, patting Gray's .38. "And I damned well enjoyed it, too."

"What about that other woman?" Alex asked, referring to Fonna.

They were all silent, thinking of Reedy having actually gnawed through Fonna's wrist.

"To quote Scarlet," Gray finally said, "'I'll think about that tomorrow.'"

Gail handed Austiff the machine gun he had been using for a crutch. She said: "It's empty."

"Of course it is," Austiff came back. "I tried to tell you that when you ran off a while ago."

"Oh."

"Do you think I wanted to shoot my foot off?" He added grumpily.

"Sorry."

Commons heaved the blood-soaked Reedy over his shoulder none to gently and lightly moved down the path to the beach. The rest of the group straggled along behind him. Taking into account their exhaustion and injuries, the trek to the beach took about 45 minutes—and they made good time at that.

Just ahead Gray could see the starlight breaking through the overhanging tropical growth and brightening the white sand of the beach. Gail reached out, restraining him by the arm. The others continued loudly on, leaving the two lovers behind.

A cool breeze drifted in from the Pacific, caressing the palm trees into subdued swaying motions. Looking down at Gail, Gray could see a sliver of moonlight highlighting her eyes.

"I knew you'd make it," she said in a soft voice.

He leaned over, kissing her deeply. "I love you."

"And I love you, too." she said sweetly.

They embraced tightly.

"I never want to lose you," she said quietly, then in a more admonishing tone added: "You are through with this kind of work, right?"

"Yes, ma'am," he said, smiling. He kissed her again, running his hands through her shining black hair.

"Come on guys," Commons called, his voice faintly filtering up from the beach.

They glanced down the path to see Commons' silhouette against the white sand—still totting Reedy.

Gail looked up at Gray, his features barely visible in the vague light. "Voices are calling."

He smiled, putting his arm around her shoulders.

They strolled out onto the beach, halting to look at the ominous black helicopters.

"They frighten me," Gail whispered.

"The helicopters?"

She nodded, "They're so...evil looking."

He chuckled.

"I'm not being funny," she came back, affecting a pout.

The tide had turned, and the Blacktooth was now sitting in the surf. They waded out to it.

"It's going to be a tight fit," Commons commented, shifting the weight of Reedy's body on his shoulder.

"I can sit on mom's lap," Alex offered.

"Or we could steal another helicopter," Gray suggested.

"1109 would just love that," Commons rebutted.

"Just a thought."

Commons propped Reedy against the helicopter and held him in place with one hand while releasing the front hatch for Debbie: "Open the side hatch, will you?"

Reedy began slipping and Commons reached to catch him under the arms. When he did, Reedy grabbed the 9mm pistol in Commons' shoulder holster.

"Don't...move," Reedy wheezed, moving a couple of steps back.

The others turned to see Reedy holding a gun. His T-shirt was so soaked with blood that Gray felt as though he could count each falling red drop.

Swaying slightly, Reedy coughed-up blood and grinned through a mixture of pain and pleasure.

"You can't kill all of us," Gray said.

"Just...you," he spat. "You bastard—"

Reedy pulled the trigger.

The gun fired.

61

For the first time in his life, Gray panicked in terror. Helplessly, he listened to the explosion of weapon fire—completely unable to stop Gail from stepping between him and Reedy. A mixture of various weapons resounded as Austiff, Commons and Debbie brought their guns into play. Reedy was thrown back, his face and chest disappearing in an obliterating mass of blood.

The gunfire resounded in Gray's ears, fading to a memory he would forever hear.

Oblivious to the world, his universe consisted of Gail. Her eyes had locked with his momentarily and then she was propelled sideways into his arms—the bullet's impact sprawling them into the waves.

Regaining balance, Gray felt the warmth of her blood spreading across her back and through his hands while he cradled her in the dark, cool water.

She calmly gazed up, as if saying, *It's okay.*

"Gail," he whispered, his face etched in frightened shock—sickening fear. "Baby..."

"Mom!" Alex screamed hysterically, trying to stand up in the rushing water. "Oh—God! Momma!"

Training kicked in and Gray lifted her. With Commons' help they eased her into the chopper. Alex clawed her way into the helicopter.

"Gail," Gray was saying over and over, moving in beside her.

Crying, Alex crawled up to the other side of Gail: "Momma...?"

Gail only stared back at Gray, trying to smile. She wanted to tell them she was fine—just a little tired. But she felt too exhausted and sleepy to say even that much.

"Can you fly this thing," Commons asked Debbie, finally shoving his back-up pistol into his waistband.

"I can," Austiff said, climbing into the cockpit.

"I'll keep Andrews here and wait for housekeeping," Commons told them, and stepped back.

The rotor blades began swishing before the hatch was closed. The black machine rose into the sky and turned toward the states.

Commons moved through the water, grabbing Reedy's near headless body and pulled it to shore. Andrews meekly followed.

Commons found his transmitter and switched it on without using the earplug. "This is Alpha 1, over."

"Roger, Alpha 1. This is Wingman," Clines' voice came back. "Go ahead."

"What's your ETA, over?"

"Ten minutes tops, over."

"Take your time," Commons added. "No one's going anywhere fast."

He shut the transmitter off, noticing the blood on his hands for the first time. He exhaled a deep sigh and sat down, a little ways off from Reedy's body.

"What's uh, what's going to happen to me," Andrews asked.

"Well," Commons said matter of fact, "if shitheadless here hadn't lost my gun in the surf a moment ago, I probably would have shot your ass already. As is, I'm out of ammo and just too damned tired to kill you."

Steve Andrews didn't make another sound.

Sitting in silence Commons listened to the lapping waves. Glancing at the body again, he realized he wasn't all that far from the bloody Nicaraguan jungle.

It always ends in death and blood, he thought.

A dark helicopter swept in low over the water and landed.

Several men with stretchers appeared.

"I thought we'd never get here," Clines said, approaching Commons.

"All the bodies and live ones, except for these two, are in the buildings," Commons said to the other men and tilted his head inland. The men trotted off in the direction he indicated.

"Where is everyone?" Clines asked.

"Well, Ŝulok, Reedy and Dana are dead," he answered in a tired voice. "Oh yeah, the Princess is probably dead too."

"Princess?"

"Princess Fonna," he clarified.

"Shit, anybody left alive?" Clines asked jokingly.

"Gail was hit."

Clines grabbed Commons by the arm. "What happened?"

Commons motioned at the body of Reedy. "He took my gun. They left only a few minutes ago."

"Will she be all right?"

"It didn't look good," Commons admitted in a tired voice and brushed past Clines to go sit in the helicopter. He climbed into the back and sat down, resting his head in his bloodstained hands.

A single gunshot brought him back to full alert. Instinctively he reached for his missing pistol, then his empty backup. He glanced out to see Clines walk up, re-holstering his own pistol.

"Just wanted to be sure," Clines said, explaining his having shot Reedy's corpse.

Commons nodded, watching the body of Ŝulok being loaded.

"You want to shoot him too?"

Clines looked as though he was seriously considering it.

Austiff radioed ahead to the Chancellor who arranged for a special medical team and security task force that arrived at the San Diego Hospital by 4 a.m. The hospital's emergency exit was cleared of all vehicles. The on-duty doctors and nurses were politely and firmly instructed out of the way.

A scant six minutes later the sleek Nova chopper howled over the city and dropped within feet of the emergency entrance.

The hatch was opened and Gail was removed as the landing gear touched the pavement.

62

Debbie Allinder and the Chancellor met Dr. Baker and Dr. Richard Tave at the door of the Operating Room. It had been two hours since Gail had been rushed into surgery.

"Well?" Debbie asked.

"It's not good," Tave replied. He was a young man of 32 whose dark brown eyes emoted compassion with as little effort as it took for him to blink them. Oddly it was his eyes—and not the blood on his surgical gown—that Debbie saw first.

"There isn't much time left," Baker said solemnly. "Get Karns and Alex."

Debbie was shocked and it showed. Richard Tave was, after all, the best money could buy. In fact, he was better than money could buy.

"We're fighting too many obstacles here," Tave explained, seeing the disbelief in Debbie's face. He had seen the look many times before, and each time he hoped it was the last.

Debbie unconsciously smoothed her hand over the bandages beneath her blouse. The pain she had experienced on Aysien Island had been the result of three separate hairline cracks in as many ribs.

"I can only do so much, Dr. Allinder," Tave said, looking at the tired face of the woman in front of him. "The loss of blood, the fragmented bone and bullet—taken individually, wouldn't poise an insurmountable problem. But all three on top of the severely damaged heart..."

Tave shook his head.

Debbie nodded numbly and went out to the waiting area. She returned a few seconds later with Gray and Alex at her side. Debbie stayed behind as the other two walked over to the three men in front of the door to the O.R.

"Karns," Baker said, putting his hand on Gray's arm. "We've done all we can do, son."

The eyes of the two men met—both reflecting the pain of the moment.

Alex began weeping.

"It's just too much damage, honey," Baker told the young woman.

"I'm sorry," Tave put in.

"You two best go right on in," Baker said gently.

Gray nodded and led the tearful Alex through the doors.

Tave exhaled a deep breath and looked at the Chancellor.

"No need to apologize," The Chancellor said. "You did what you could."

"If anybody wants me," Tave said, removing his surgical cap, "I'll be nursing a whisky in the Doctors' Lounge."

The surgeon moved off down the hall.

Baker shook his head, watching Tave. "He's the best. How'd you get 'em here so fast?"

"We landed in his front yard and took 'em," the Chancellor answered.

Baker looked surprised.

"We go back a-ways—he owes me a few."

Baker nodded, then: "Did his wife see it that way?"

The Chancellor shook his head *no*. "About Gail...?"

Baker glanced down the hall, making sure no one was within earshot.

"The memory copy?" the Chancellor prompted.

"We got it," Baker assured him. "No problems."

The Chancellor looked relieved.

"But I don't recommend telling him," Baker added, jerking his thumb back at the O.R.

"I hadn't planned on it," the Chancellor replied, then turned toward the direction Tave had taken. "If anyone asks, I've left already."

"The exit is the other direction, Robert."

"The Whiskey's not," the Chancellor said, and walked down the hall.

Inside the O.R., the emergency team moved away from the operating table and discretely left the room: their jobs were finished and they knew they had lost this battle.

Alex moved to the left side of the operating table and Gray to the right.

Gently, Gray took Gail's hand.

She opened her eyes, looking first at Gray, then at Alex.

"Oh Momma," Alex cried, tears gushing.

"Baby," she said weakly, lifting only her hand and closing her eyes for a moment.

Alex gripped her mother's hand and nervously, but ever-so-carefully, caressed her mother's cheek.

"Please, Momma, please..." Her voice was carried away in a flood of tears.

"It's okay, Baby," Gail mumbled, opening her eyes again. "It's okay... You take care of Karns, darlin'."

Alex could hardly see for the tears. "Okay, Momma... I love you."

"I love you, too...sweetheart..." Gail came back weakly. She looked over at Gray.

His face was set as if in stone.

"I'm sorry," she said to him, closing her eyes longer this time.

"Oh, Baby," he said at last, his voice broken. He eased down next to her face.

"I don't want to leave you," she cried, her eyes fluttering open and a trail of tears cascading down the side of her face. She squeezed his hand.

"I love you," he cried, "I love you so much..."

"I love you, too. I love both of you..." Gail whispered weakly, her voice ebbing away.

She turned her head slightly to kiss Gray, brushed her lips with his and closed her eyes again—for a much longer time.

∞∞∞

In the South Pacific, a United States aircraft carrier launched a sunrise military exercise. By mid-morning, FORBS and Aysien Island had vanished.

EPILOGUE

HUDSON CEMETERY

October 14, The Present
Kennedale, Texas

63

On the outskirts of Fort Worth, one-mile southeast of Kennedale, Hudson Cemetery Road discretely crossed the two-lane Mansfield Highway and snaked off westward into seldom seen countryside. For the most part, local residents were forgetful of its existence.

Hidden from the highway, a reservoir constructed alongside the small road enhanced its isolation—oddly insuring solitude.

Having weathered 112 years, Hudson Cemetery quietly faced the reservoir like an icicle in the cold white of winter—frightfully sharp and shrouded in alarming silence. Overseen by just under 500 varying sized headstones, many awkwardly askew from settling, Hudson Cemetery was the last of an era. Appropriately, it was but a remnant of a time dead in history.

The burial service, attended by only a handful of family members, was long over. In a faint mist of rain the workmen had raced the weather in order to seal the underground vault and fill in the dirt. They finished the task just before dusk.

After all the others had left, Karns Gray knelt by the red rose-covered grave and freely shed tears over the death of a part of himself. Huddled next to the ground, he cried as a child, drowning in his soul's pain—foundering in anguish.

Just beyond the grave, outside the chain link fence surrounding the cemetery, Alex and Debbie waited under umbrellas by a black Sedan. Alex tightened the belt of her coat and moved across the grass. Opening the gate, she walked to her father.

"Karns," she said in a small voice, shattering the stillness. "Dad."

He stood, facing away. His raincoat was beaded over with water and his hair was soaked. As he turned to face Alex, her tears welled-up and they melted into an embrace.

"Come on," she implored through streaming tears. "We should go."

"I—I just don't want to leave her again," he whispered, his voice deep from having hardly spoken since Gail's death.

"She's—not here, dad," Alex managed to say before her body was racked by sobbing.

"I know," he came back, whispering in her ear. "But—I—can't let go..."

"I don't want to either," she admitted. "But I need you, dad—please..."

He nodded, not wanting to leave, but knowing it was time.

"We'll come back another day," Alex said, "Okay?"

"Yeah," he mumbled. "Another day."

They walked to the fence, meeting Debbie at the entrance.

"Karns..." Debbie said, her voice loud in the silence. She really didn't know what to say. After all, what was left to say?

He shook his head, saying volumes—and saying nothing. Debbie fell in beside them and the three walked to the car. Gray disengaged his arm from Alex and opened the front passenger door for her.

She looked into his eyes for a moment, her lips trembling, and then sank into the car. He shut her door and opened the rear door. Debbie watched him for a moment then slipped beneath the steering wheel and waited.

Pausing, Gray looked to the gravesite. Even in the dying light the white marble marker stood out in contrast against the surrounding evergreen trees.

He took in a breath of air, surprised at how refreshing it was. He looked around for a moment—he hadn't done that. His attention was drawn back to the grave.

Alex was right. They would have to come back on another day.

But, he decided, not tomorrow.

He disappeared into the car.

The sedan turned in the road and slowly began the meandering trek back.

In the cemetery, the hazel gray twilight darkened to cool shadows. The mist fell to rain, cleansing tears from the grave's solitary white rose.

A Note From The Author

While the gestation of this novel covered a number of years, I attempted to include the most up-to-date information. However, there are instances where I intentionally or unintentionally, missed the boat—the USS *Lexington* in particularly. At the time the Blue Ghost (the *Lexington's* nickname) was first written into the story, she was indeed primarily used for qualifying flight students. Her decommissioning in 1991 eventually relegated her to a floating Museum on the bay in Corpus Christi, Texas. I just didn't have the heart to replace her in the final draft. The ONR's saucer-like one-man fighter of 1955 is (or was) the Real McCoy and the *XND-1* is loosely based upon drawing board plans. I conjured the USS *Boston* out of thin air, and it is not to be confused with the USS *Boston* (CAG-1) or the USS *Boston* (SSN703). My apologies to the former crews of these excellent naval vessels if I've completely botched everything.

The "Russian" political and socioeconomic changes of the last decade have been so wide-sweeping and numerous that fictional representations can be outdated while going to press. As such, the conditions portrayed in this novel are one part historical and the other part conjecture. However, I confess to taking liberties with the portrayal of Arabic mores and throw myself upon the leniency of the reader in that regard.

Special thanks to my friend, Jim Kavanagh. Any errors in data regarding diving depths and pressures are the sole result of my misinterpreting what he—a Dive Master—explained at length.

A word of thanks to Pat Guinn, Carol Bott and Gerri Dye: these R.L. Paschal high school teachers offered encouragement of substance.

For encouragement above and beyond the call of duty, I am forever thankful to Ms. Helen Wallace, one of my high school English teachers. After stomaching the hand-written first draft so many years ago, she not only wrote, "This shows great promise," but also voiced faith whenever our paths have since crossed.

I am also thankful for having been in the classroom of Mr. Robert Reed, also of Paschal. If ever there was a man of high literary caliber and insight, it is Mr. Reed.

A heartfelt, "thank you," to Diana Turner. A Tarrant County College instructor and newspaper adviser extraordinaire, she is a person of "uncommon common sense" and strength. Her tutelage and support are cornerstones of my accomplishments.

"Thanks," also to my sister, Judy, for laboring over a draft that was doomed despite her efforts and Margaret Mullen for proofing yet another doomed draft while enduring my daily inquiries.

"Thanks," also to Alexandra Tzoumas for her work prior to the initial publication of this novel. Of course, a tip of the old fedora to Curtis Farrar for "insuring" (play on words there) I found publication in the first place.

And finally, 749 "thank yous" to Robin Ladd and Stephanie Anne McKee—both of whom unselfishly labored over problems subsequent to the initial publication of this novel. While the three of us may not have perfected post-publication editing, Robin certainly gave her copy machine a workout and Stephanō's proofreading via e-mail was an art form second only to her generosity.

—DL Tolleson

2016 UPDATE: According to the publisher's planned news release, this novel was unavailable for years because, "...stock exhaustion, coincided with a major logistical problem associated with relocating from Florida to Alabama."

It is true that when the publisher settled in Alabama, every *Stopgap* copy—be it in electronic or physical form—was gone. Also true: they contacted me for a manuscript copy. This was when I realized that my own electronic copy was corrupted. Scattered with gibberish. Practically worthless. Re-creating the manuscript was a daunting task that took time —lots of it. And that is the ultimate reason for the novel's long absence.

When I finally reconstructed the entire manuscript, I utilized both the corrupted file and The Lighthouse Press printed edition. My effort included correcting issues found in both sources.

It is my hope that I have corrected those things which slipped past the editors of previous editions as well as problems that such editing introduced (measurements, minor narrative sequencing, etc.). Whatever errors that may now exist, their presence here is entirely my fault for having made or missed them over the course of three revised printings.

Minor details aside, I have not altered the story or the way in which it was originally written—both of which were for specific purposes and effect (see the *Author's Introduction*).

And finally, I want to share this... The book industry (bookstores, book reviewers, many authors, etc.) associates legitimacy with publishers putting their money where their authors' mouths are. Conventional publishers assume the burden and expense of vetting, polishing and publishing books borne out of well-written manuscripts. These traditional, conventional publishers have given birth to a presumption of quality. Fair or not, for all others there is an expectation to the contrary.

That expectation arose out of what technology now offers: self-publication. While this provides occasional successes (mostly for celebrities and folks during their 15 minutes of fame) it is usually the road to ostracization. Why? Because the book industry has seen a virtual landfill of unvetted, sub-standard work from self-published, print-on-demand and vanity publishers. As a result, books published at the expense of writers are rarely reviewed or stocked and nearly always shunned. The unexpected consequence of this history is that it is now more difficult for lesser-known, small and independent publishers to garner book industry recognition. By extension, that difficulty extends to their authors.

In fact, from the perspective of writers, the only thing of similar difficulty and value is acceptance by a discerning publisher. And for that, as well as a reasonable accommodation for my creative differences, I am humbly and unbelievably grateful to The Lighthouse Press.

—DL Tolleson

About The Auhtor

Receiving one of the Texas Intercollegiate Press Association's highest awards for Journalistic Excellence, DL Tolleson also garnered awards for Feature Writing and News Photography from the Texas Community College Press Association. He was a one-time Fine Arts Consultant/ Instructor under a state grant program to ARC of Texas. He taught Creative Photography in the College for Kids program at Tarrant County College and writing at the elementary level in an after school program under a federal grant to the Fort Worth Independent School District.

A former member of the Texas State Bar's Legal Assistant's Division he spent over 14 years in litigation support. As a Paralegal Specialist in the U.S. Small Business Administration's Office of Disaster Assistance he was awarded recognition for creating a method to merge Disaster Credit Management System data with loan modification documents. For six years he was one of the four-member team overseeing compliance of Dealer Franchise cellular contracts at the RadioShack Corporation headquarters in Fort Worth, Texas.

As a photographer/videographer, Tolleson's portfolio of work covers a wide spectrum; news, litigation, depositions, surveillance, evidentiary documentation, accident/incidence scenes, personal injury, property damage, postmortem evidence, modeling, portraits, events and weddings. He now primarily photographs wildlife and nature for pleasure, predominantly focusing on the Big Bend region of Texas.

In addition to authoring the atypical espionage thriller, *The Gray Stopgap*, Tolleson's novella, *Socials*, is planned for publication. A sequel to *The Gray Stopgap* is also planned for publication.

He holds a Bachelor of Applied Arts and Sciences from the University of North Texas. He also holds an Associate in Arts and an Associate in Applied Sciences, both from Tarrant County College. A freelance writer/ photographer, DL Tolleson resides in the north central region of Texas referred to by locals as the Dallas/Fort Worth Metroplex.

www.ingramcontent.com/pod-product-compliance
Lightning Source LLC
Chambersburg PA
CBHW020603310726
48979CB00008B/1326/J
* 9 7 8 1 9 3 2 2 1 1 2 3 8 *